STREET DREAMS

ALSO BY FAYE KELLERMAN

Ritual Bath

Sacred and Profane

The Quality of Mercy

Milk and Honey

Day of Atonement

False Prophet

Grievous Sin

Sanctuary

Justice

Prayers for the Dead

Serpent's Tooth

Moon Music

Jupiter's Bones

Stalker

The Forgotten

Stone Kiss

FAYE KELLERMAN

DREAMS

DOUBLEDAY LARGE PRINT HOME LIBRARY EDITION

WARNER BOOKS

An AOL Time Warner Company

This Large Print Edition, prepared especially for Doubleday Large Print Home Library, contains the complete, unabridged text of the original Publisher's Edition.

Copyright © 2003 by Faye Kellerman
All rights reserved.
Warner Books, Inc., 1271 Avenue of the Americas, New York, NY 10020

 An AOL Time Warner Company

Printed in the United States of America

ISBN 0-7394-3704-6

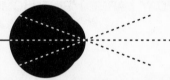

This Large Print Book carries the Seal of Approval of N.A.V.H.

For Jonathan

STREET DREAMS

Prologue

Because the murder had been kept "secret" for so long, it had taken on mythological proportions. Yet here was the proof, the tangible evidence that it really had happened. In the dead of night, in the privacy of her own home, Rina gingerly slit open the manila envelope postmarked from Munich and, with shaking hands, pulled out the papers within, photocopies of documents dated from the late 1920s. Mama had always said she was ten when it happened, but now it appeared that she'd been even younger. The faded writing would be almost indecipherable even if it had been in English. It was going to take more than her knowledge of Yiddish to make out the text.

The envelope had arrived in the late-afternoon mail. This was her first opportunity to view the pages without the kids or Peter as distractions.

Peter.

She hadn't told him. It had happened so spontaneously, during one of Rina's solo strolls through the Bavarian capital, getting some air while he had been sleeping off jet lag. She had taken the walk to shake off that niggling restlessness plaguing her since the plane had touched down on German soil.

To think that she had chosen Munich for leisure. Then again, she'd had only one week to plan something, so her options had been limited. Mainly, she had given in to laziness. She had been so tired after New York's ordeal that she was more than willing to leave it up to a third party. And it wasn't as if she and Peter had any choice. Peter was on the verge of total shutdown. They *needed* to get away.

Things were better now—or so she told herself—but were still far from normal. Rina had been privy only to the superficial facts, to what Peter had told his superiors and the press about the murders and his being shot. But there was much more lurking in his gray matter. Incidents that he didn't choose to share with her, though thankfully, he had done some talking to his cop brother, Randy.

God bless Randy. He had demanded that they go, and go alone, assuring them that he'd watch over Hannah so that Peter's parents wouldn't have to shoulder the entire burden alone. It had been desperation that led them to Europe, to a week in Munich with everything set up by Rina's friend Ellen Nussburger.

I can't believe I'm actually agreeing to this, Rina had told her.

You won't be sorry, Ellie had responded. *It won't be anything like you think.*

But it had been like she'd thought, her gut constricting as soon as she'd heard German as a living language. She had purposely declined going to Dachau. What Peter didn't need was more destruction in his life, or in her life—come to think about it. But there remained a certain heaviness throughout the week, because it was impossible to walk the cobblestones of Kaufingerstrasse in the Marienplatz without thinking about all the Jewish blood that had been spilled on German soil. Every time they passed the Hofbrauhaus beer hall, it was as if ghosts were belting out the "Horst Wessel Song."

The saving grace was Ellie's work. Here was a woman who was trying to build up a religious Jewish community, not toss it into the furnace. The fact that Ellie and her husband, Larry, chose Germany was a testament to their nonconformity, but that was Ellie to a T. Rina remembered their years together in school, in kindergarten when both of them had been five years old and it had been Purim. All the other girls had dressed up as Queen Esther or some other unnamed princess. There were also a few ballerinas, several clowns, and a couple of butterflies. Ellie had come to school wearing a homemade costume that wasn't much more than a sack. It was designed in sandwich-board style with two sides. The front was imprinted with a blue sky and white fluffy clouds with a big felt sun stuck in the center. The back fabric was black and glitter-studded with a crescent moon in the corner.

What are you? Amy Swartzberg had demanded to know of Ellie.

Ellie had retorted in her most adult voice:

I am Bereshit—*the creation of the sun and the moon. It's a* conceptual *costume!*

Rina had no idea what conceptual meant, but by the way Ellie had stated the word, conceptual had to be pretty darn important.

From the moment they had arrived overseas, Ellie greeted them with such warmth that soon Rina's misgiving melted and it was old times again. Ellie's enthusiasm was infectious.

This is Hitler's worst nightmare, Rina, a resurgence of Jewish life where the Nazi party was born.

Not a particularly *big* resurgence, Rina thought, but everything had to start somewhere. Munich had several synagogues, a small kosher shop owned by a Moroccan French Jew in the main Viktualienmarkt, a kosher bakery in Schwabing, and a kosher restaurant in the old Isarvorstadt area. The Bavarians were a particularly unique lot. When they thought she and Peter were Americans of possible German descent because of their surname Decker, they were outgoing and friendly, boastful and proud. But the minute she spoke to them in Yiddish, a clear indication that she was Jewish, most probably with relatives from "that other period," they'd remain polite but the conversation turned stilted, their words carefully chosen.

Still, it had been a different adventure, more soul-searching if not rip-roaring fun. And there had been some breathtaking scenery, the two of them exploring the countryside and the foothills of the Alps, holding hands and sipping tea from a thermos while hiking through the wet foliage, with spring just around the corner. The rushing streams and the incredible vistas seemed to be a balm to Peter's troubled mind.

And yet the more relaxed he became, the more she tensed internally. Germany was not only the land of her national destruction, but was also the soil of a personal catastrophe—an unexcised cancer on her mother's soul. What mystical forces had led her into that police station some two months ago, asking the Munich desk sergeant where could she find information about a seventy-five-year-old crime? At the time, all Rina had wanted to do was provide her aged mother with some peace of mind. Now she wondered if she wasn't stepping into a hornet's nest.

There was no reason to pursue what

had become a cruel distant memory in an old woman's mind. But as she scanned the pages of the crime report, reading her grandmother's name Regina—Rina's English name—followed by the word "*totschlag*"—homicide—she knew with surety that she had to see this through.

1

I saw him frantically waving the white flag, a man admitting defeat. As I pulled the cruiser into one of the alley's parking spaces, blocking a silver Mercedes S500, I realized that the banner was, in fact, a napkin. He wore a solid wall of white, the hem of a long, stained apron brushing his white jeans midshin. Though it was night, I could see a face covered with moisture. Not a surprise because the air was a chilly mist: typical May-gloom weather in L.A. I radioed my whereabouts to the dispatcher and got out, my right hand on my baton, the other swinging freely at my side. The alley stank of garbage, the odor emanating from the trash bins behind the restaurant. The flies, normally shy in the dark, were having a field day.

The rear area of The Tango was illuminated by a strong yellow spotlight above the back door. The man in white was short, five-seven at the most, with a rough, tawny complexion, a black mustache, and hands flapping randomly. He was agitated, talking bullet-speed Spanish. I picked up a few words, but didn't ask him to stop and translate, because I heard the noise myself—the high-pitched wails of a baby.

"Where?" I yelled over his words. *"Dónde?"*

"Aquí, aquí!" He was pointing to an army-green Dumpster filled to the brim with blue plastic refuse bags.

"Call 911." I ran to the site and pulled out several bags, tearing one open and exposing myself to a slop of wilted salad greens, mushy vegetables, and golf balls of gray meat and congealed fat. As I sifted through the trash, my clean, pressed uniform and I became performance art, the deep blue cloth soaking up the oils and stains of previously pricey edibles. "I need help! *Necesito ayuda! Ahorita."*

"Sí, sí!" He dashed back inside.

The crying was getting louder and that was good, but there was still no sign of the wail's origin. My heart was slamming against my chest as I sorted through the top layer of bags. The bin was deep. I needed to jump inside to remove all the bags, but I didn't want to step on anything until I had checked it out. Three men came running out of the back door.

"Escalera!"—a ladder—I barked. *"Yo necisito una escalera."*

One went back inside, the other two began pulling out bags.

"Careful, careful!" I screamed. "I don't know where it is!" I used the word "it" because it could have been a thrown-away kitten. When agitated, felines sound like babies. But all of us knew it wasn't a cat.

Finally, the ladder appeared and I scurried up the steps, gingerly removing enough bags until I could see the bottom, a disc of dirty metal under the beam of my flashlight. I went over legs first and, holding the rim with my hands, lowered myself to the bottom. I picked a bag at random, checked inside, then hoisted it over the top when I satisfied myself that it didn't contain the source of the noise.

Slow, Cindy, I told myself. *Don't want to mess this up.*

With each bag removed, I could hear myself getting closer to the sound's origin. Someone had taken the time to bury it. Fury welled inside me, but I held it at bay to do a job. At the bottom layer, I hit pay dirt—a newborn girl with the cord still attached to her navel, her face and body filthy, her eyes scrunched up, her cries strong and tearless. I yelled out for something to wrap her in, and they handed me a fresh, starched tablecloth. I wiped down the body, cleaned out the mouth and nose as best as I could, and bundled her up—umbilicus and all. I held her up so someone could take her from me. Then I hoisted myself up and out.

The man who had flagged me down offered me a wet towel. I wiped down my hands and face. I asked him his name.

"Martino Delacruz."

"Good job, Señor Delacruz!" I smiled at him. *"Buen trabajo."*

The man's eyes were wet.

Moments later, the bundle was passed back to me. I felt grubby holding her, but obviously since I was the only *woman* in the crowd, I was supposed to know about *these* kinds of things.

Actually, I did know a thing or two about infants, having a half sister eighteen years my junior. Her mother, Rina—my step-mother—had become very ill after childbirth and guess who stepped up to the plate when my father was in a near state of collapse? (Who could have blamed him? Rina almost died.)

The positive side was the sisterly bonding, at least on my part. Hannah Rosie Decker was my only blood sibling, and they didn't come any cuter or better than she. I adored her. Matter of fact, I liked my father's family very much. Rina's sons were great kids and I loved them and respected them as much as anyone could love and respect step-relatives. Rina took wonderful care of my father, a feat worth noting because Dad was not the easiest person to get along with. I knew this from firsthand experience.

"Did anyone call 911?"

"Yo hable." Delacruz handed me another clean rag to wipe my dirty face.

"Thank you, *señor.*" I had put a clean napkin over my shoulder and was rocking the baby against my chest. "If you can, get some warm sugar water and dunk a clean napkin into it. Then bring it to me."

The man was off in a flash. The baby's cries had quieted to soft sobs. I suddenly noticed that my own cheeks were warm and wet, thrilled that this incident had resolved positively. Delacruz was back with the sugar water–soaked napkin. I took it and put the tip of a corner into her mouth. Immediately, she sucked greedily. In the distance I heard a wail of sirens.

"We've got to get you to the hospital, little one. You're one heck of a strong pup, aren't you?"

I smelled as overripe as rotten fruit. I placed the infant back into Delacruz's arms. "*Por favor,* give her to the ambulance people. I need to wash my hands."

He took the bundle and began to walk with her. It was one of those Kodak moments, this macho man cooing in Spanish to this tiny, displaced infant. The job had its heartbreak, but it also had its rewards.

After rotating my shoulders to release the tension, I went through the back door of The Tango and asked one of the dishwashers where I could clean up. I heard a gasp and turned around. A man wearing a toque was shooing me away with dismissive hands. "Zis is a food establishment! You cannot come in here like zat!"

"Someone dumped a baby in the trash outside." My stare was fierce and piercing. "I just rescued her by opening up fifteen bags of garbage. I need to *wash* my hands!"

Toque was confused. "Here? A *bébé?*"

"Yes, sir! Here! A *bébé!*" I spotted a cloud of suds that had filled up a sink. Wordlessly, I walked over and plunged my hands inside very warm water. What the heck! All the china went into a dishwasher anyway, right? After ridding my hands of the grime, I ran the cold water full blast and washed my face. One of the kitchen workers was nice enough to offer me a clean towel. I dried myself off and looked up.

The ambulance had arrived, red strobe lights pulsing through the windows. I pointed to Mr. Toque and gave him my steely-eyed look. "Like heartburn, I'll be back. Don't go anywhere."

The EMTs had already cut the cord and were cleaning her up. I regarded the medics as they did their job. A sturdy black woman was holding the baby in her arms while a thin white kid with a consumptive complexion was carefully wiping down the infant's face. Both were gloved.

"How's she doing?" I asked.

They looked up. The thin kid smiled when he saw me. "Whew, you musta been hungry."

The kid's name tag said B. HANOVER. I gave him a hard stare and he recoiled. "Jeez. Just trying out a little levity, Officer. It breaks the tension."

"How's she doing?" I repeated.

The woman answered. Her name was Y. Crumack. "Fine, so far . . . a success story."

"That's always nice."

The infant's placenta had been bagged and was resting on the ground a couple of feet away. It would be taken to a pathology lab, the tissue examined for disease and genetic material that might identify her. For no good reason, I picked up the bag.

Crumack said, "We'll need that. It has to be biopsied."

"Yeah, I know. Where are you taking her?"

"Mid-City Pediatric Hospital."

"The one on Vermont," I said.

"Only one I know," Hanover said. "Any ideas about the mom?"

"Not a clue."

"You should find her," Hanover informed me. "It would help everyone out."

"Wow, I hadn't thought about that," I snapped. "Thanks for sharing."

"No need to get testy," Hanover sneered.

Crumack opened the back door, strapping the baby in an infant seat. The wailing had returned. I assumed that to be a positive sign. I gave her the bagged placenta and she placed it in the ambulance.

"She sounds hungry," I said.

"Starved," Crumack answered. "Her abdomen is empty."

"Her head looks . . . I don't know . . . elongated, maybe? What's that all about?"

"Probably from being pushed out of the birth canal. Main thing is, it isn't crushed. She was real lucky, considering all the things that could have gone wrong. She could've swallowed something and choked; she could've suffocated; she could've been crushed. This is an A-one outcome." She patted my shoulder. "And you're part of it."

I felt my eyes water. "Hey, don't look at me, thank Señor Delacruz," I told her. "He's got good ears."

The man knew enough English to recognize a compliment. His smile was broad.

"Any idea how many hours she's been alive?" I asked the techs.

Hanover said, "Her body temperature hasn't dropped that much. Of course, she was insulated in all that garbage. I'd say a fairly recent dump."

"So what are we talking about?" I asked. "Two hours? Four hours?"

"Maybe," Crumack said. "Six hours, max."

I checked my watch. It was ten-thirty. "So she was dumped around four or five in the afternoon?"

"Sounds about right." Crumack turned to his partner. "Let's go."

I called out, "Mid-City Pediatric!"

Hanover reconfirmed it, slid behind the wheel, and shut the door, moving on out with sirens blaring and lights blazing. My arms felt incredibly empty. Although I rarely thought about my biological clock—I was only twenty-eight—I was suddenly pricked by maternal pangs. It felt good to give comfort. Long ago, that was my primary reason for becoming a cop.

The clincher was my father, of course.

He had discouraged me from entering the profession. Being the ridiculously stubborn daughter I was, his caveats had the opposite effect. There were taut moments between us, but most of that had been resolved. I truly loved being a cop and not because I had unresolved Freudian needs. Still, if I had been sired by a "psychologist dad" instead of a "lieutenant dad," I probably would have become a therapist.

I unhooked my radio from my belt and called the dispatcher, requesting a detective to the scene.

2

"When was the trash last emptied? . . . Before Mr. Delacruz?"

I was addressing Andre Racine, the sous-chef at The Tango. He was taller than I by about three inches, making him around five-eleven, with broad shoulders and the beginnings of a beer belly hanging over the crossed strings of his apron. His toque was slightly askew, looking like a vanilla soufflé. We were talking right near the back door so I could keep an eye on what was going on outside.

"Ze trash is emptied at night. Sometimes eet is two days, not longer."

"The back door was open at the time. You didn't hear anyone crying or rummaging around back here?"

The man shook his head. "Eet is a racket in a keetchen with all zee equipment and appliances running. Eet is good if I can hear myself think!"

I had spoken to several other kitchen employees and they had said the same thing. I could confirm the noise myself. There were the usual rumbles and beeps of the appliances, plus one of the guys had turned on a boom box to a Spanish station specializing in salsa music. To add to the cacophony, the restaurant featured a live band—a jazz combo that included electric guitar, bass, piano, and drums. The din would have driven me crazy, but I supposed that these men felt lucky to have steady jobs in this climate.

Though the back door was open, the screen door was closed to prevent infestations of rodents or pesky, winged critters. It was hard to see through the mesh. Nothing seemed suspicious to my eyes, no one was giving off bad vibes. Quite the contrary: All these good people had come out to help. They were exhausted by the incident and so was I. Looking up from my notepad, I thanked the stunned chef, then walked outside to catch my breath and organize my notes. My watch was almost up and a gold shield was on the way to take over the investigation. I began to write the names of my interviewees in alphabetical order. After each name, I listed the person's position and telephone number. I wanted to present the primary detective with something organized . . . something that would impress.

A few minutes later, a cruiser pulled up and parked in the alley, perpendicular to the spaces behind The Tango, blocking all the cars including mine. Greg Van Horn got out, his gait a bowlegged strut that buckled under the weight of his girth. He wasn't fat, just a solid hunk of meat. Greg was in his early sixties, passing time until retirement. He'd been married twice, divorced twice. Rumor still had him as a pussy hound, and a bitter one at that. But he was nice enough to me. I think he had worked with my father way back when, and there had been some mutual admiration.

Greg was of medium height, with a thick top of coarse gray hair. His face was round with fleshy features including a drinker's nose. His blue suit was boxy on him. Anything he wore would have been boxy. I gave him a thirty-second recap, then showed him my notepad. I pointed out Martino Delacruz. "He lives on Western. He's worked at The Tango for six years."

"Green card?" Van Horn asked.

"Yes, he has one. After things calmed down, he showed it to me without my asking." I paused. "Not that it's relevant. It's not as if he's going to trial as a witness or anything."

"Never can tell, Decker." He moved a sausage-size finger across the bridge of his nose. Not wiping it, more like scratching an itch inside his flaring nostrils.

"He went outside to take out the trash and heard the baby crying," I continued. "He was going to call for help, but then he spotted my cruiser. You want me to bring him over to you, sir?"

Van Horn's eyes swept over my face, then walked downward, stopping short of my chest. His eyes narrowed. "I think you need to change your uniform."

"I know that. I'm going off duty in twenty minutes, unless you need me to stick around."

"I might need another pair of hands. Sooner we find the mother, the better."

I gave a quick glance over my shoulder.

"Not much here in the way of a residential area."

"Not on Hollywood, no. But if you go south, between Hollywood and Sunset, there are lots of houses and apartments."

"Do you want me to go door-to-door now, sir?"

A glance at his watch. "It'll take time. Is that a problem for you, Decker?"

"No, not at all, Detective. Where would you like me to start?"

Van Horn's nose wrinkled. "You really need to put on something clean, Decker."

"Want me to go change and then come back?" I spoke without rancor. Being polite meant being cautious. As far as I was concerned, the less my personality stood out, the happier I was.

"I take it you have no plans tonight, Decker?"

"Just a hot date with my shower."

He smiled, then took another peek at his watch. "It's late . . . probably too late to canvass thoroughly."

"I'll come back tomorrow and help you search if you want."

"I doubt if your sergeant will want to pull you out of circulation just for that."

"I'll do it in the morning, on my own time."

"You're ambitious."

"And knowing my stock, that surprises you?"

A grin this time. "You're gonna do just fine, Decker."

High praise coming from Greg.

"While I talk to the people on your list, you cordon off the area and look around for anything that might give us a clue as to who the mother is. I suppose at this late hour, our best bet could be a request for public help on the eleven o'clock news."

A news van pulled up just as the words left his mouth. "You're prescient, Detective. Here's your chance."

"ABC, eh?" A flicker of hesitancy shot through his eyes. "Is that the one with the anchorwoman who has the white streak in her black hair, like a skunk?"

"I don't know. . . . There's NBC. The others can't be far behind." I patted his shoulder. "It's show time."

"How's your Q, Decker?"

"Me?" I pointed to my chest. "You've got the gold shield, Greg."

"But you found the baby."

"Yeah, but I stink and you're in a suit." I

waved him off. "I'll go yellow-tape the area and look around."

"You sure?" But he was already straightening his tie and smoothing his hair. "Yeah, tape off the area. Don't sweat it too much, Decker. I can pretty much take it from here. And hey, I'll take you up on your offer . . . to canvass the area tomorrow."

"That'll work for me."

"Good. We'll coordinate in a moment. Just let me get these clowns off my back."

"Of course."

"Show 'em what a real detective looks like, huh?"

"You tell 'em, Greg."

Van Horn made tracks toward a grouping of handheld Minicams, lurching like a cowboy ready for the showdown.

In Hollywood, everybody's a star.

▼

A half block from the restaurant was a pool of something that didn't smell like water and shone ruby red under the beam of the flashlight. There were also intermittent drips from the puddle to the Dumpster behind The Tango. Because of the location, I thought of a homeless woman or a runaway teen, someone scared and unstable. She would have to be on the skids, pushing out a baby in a back alley, all alone amid a host of bugs and rats.

The blood of childbirth—if we were lucky.

If the mother was someone local, it would narrow the search. Maybe knocking on doors wouldn't be the answer. Maybe my best bet would be to hunt down the throw-aways, to crawl through the underbelly of Hollywood, a city that offered so much but rarely made good on its promises.

I showed the spot to Greg Van Horn after he did his dog-and-pony show for the nightly news. He regarded the blood while scratching his abundant nose.

"Homicide?" I asked him.

"Can't be ruled out." His jaws were bulging as if chewing on something hard. "My instincts tell me no. The configuration doesn't look like a murder."

"The concentration of blood in one spot as well as the absence of spatter."

Van Horn nodded. "Yeah, exactly."

"I was thinking about someone homeless. Who else would squat in a back alley?"

"I'll buy that." Eyes still on the pond of blood, he took out his cellular phone. "Time to call in the techs."

"Want me to walk around the area, sir? See if I can find some street people?"

"Did you finish roping the area?"

"Yes, sir."

"Sure. Go pretend you're a gold shield, Decker."

Low blow, Greg. I said with a smile, "Just testing out my mettle."

"I thought you already passed that test."

This time the smile was genuine. "That was nice. Thank you."

"Get out of here."

I skipped over the yellow tape, walking about a hundred yards north through the alley and onto Hollywood Boulevard. The sidewalks weren't paved with gold, but they were filled with lots of black-stoned stars set into red granite. Each star represented a different icon of the entertainment media—TV, film, radio, or the recording industry. The good news was that recent gentrification and climbing real estate prices had preserved some of the older architecture and had cleaned up lots of the seedier aspects of the area.

The western part of the boulevard was breaking through, probably like Times Square had done a dozen or so years ago.

The city planners were smart enough to face-lift its known quantities, like the famous movie houses—Mann's Chinese Theatre, Egyptian, and El Capitan—as well as the sideshow carnival attractions like Ripley's Believe It or Not and the Hollywood Wax Museum. In addition, the renovated sector now boasted several eye-catching shopping galleries and a spanking-new gold-and-black-granite live theater built by Kodak. These landmarks drew lots of tourists, those hoping to be touched by magic or, at the very least, bask in its afterglow.

It was the night that brought out the predators, individuals who thrived on marginal life. The eastern portion of Hollywood was the domain of tattoo parlors and bail bondsmen, of cheap retail shops, several no-tell motels and fast-food joints.

The Tango sat on the border between the bright lights of old glamour and the slums of decay. As economic revival crept eastward, some of the neon spilled over, but not nearly enough to illuminate the hidden cracks and crevices. I didn't have to walk too far before I found someone. She sat on the sidewalk, her back against the painted glass window advertising 50 percent off bargain-basement clothing. Her knees were pressed against her chest, and a thin blanket was thrown over her body and tucked under her chin. Her age was indeterminate—anywhere from twenty to fifty. Her hair was matted and dirty, her complexion so pancaked with grime that it could have held membership to any race. Black pupils peered out through vacant red-rimmed orbs, her mouth a slash mark with skin stretched tightly over a bony framework. By her side were a coin cup, several paper bags, and a tattered backpack.

I dropped a dollar in the cup. She nodded but didn't make eye contact. I sat beside her and she stiffened. She stank of sweat and misery, but right now I didn't smell too wonderful myself.

"What happened to you?" she pronounced in a raspy voice.

I raised my eyebrow. "What do you mean?"

"Your clothes need a cleanin', Officer."

"Oh . . . that. I went rooting through the garbage tonight."

"Then we's got somethin' in common."

I smiled. "I don't think we've ever met."

She looked down at her covered knees. "You're Officer Cindy."

I let out a laugh. "Beg your pardon. The mistake is mine."

"It was raining. You gave me a ride. . . . Brang me to a shelter."

I squinted, taking in her face. *"Alice Anne?"*

A hint of a smile appeared on her lips.

I made a face. "You promised me you'd stop hitting the sauce."

"I kept my promise."

"For how long? Twenty-four hours?"

"A little longer."

"Tsk, tsk, girl."

This time, she took in my face. "What happened to you?"

"Funny you should ask. I found a baby at the bottom of a Dumpster."

"Ugh!" Alice Anne exclaimed. "That be terrible! Is it okay?"

"The baby is fine."

"Hard enough bein' an a-dult out here." She spat. "Ain't no place for a baby."

"Any ideas, Alice Anne?"

"Me?" She sounded surprised. "It ain't mine, sister."

"I'm not pointing a finger. But do you have any clue who it *might* belong to?"

She was quiet.

"Come on, Alice Anne. We need to find her."

"Don't know nothin'."

Maybe yes, maybe no. "Could be you've seen someone out here who was pregnant—"

"Maybe like a hunnerd out here is pregnant. That's why they's out here. 'Cause they's pregnant and got nowhere else to go."

"Where would I find these hundred girls?"

She threw me a disgusted look. "How long you work here?"

"Alice—"

"It ain't that hard, sister. You just be looking on the wrong street."

"Sunset?"

Alice Anne nodded.

Sunset was the next major street south. It was where the female prostitutes did their business. The boy toys were out on Santa Monica Boulevard, the next major street over from Sunset. Most of the men bartered in West Hollywood Sheriff area, but sometimes they strayed into LAPD territory—my territory. All these discarded lives. It could make a girl blue sometimes. Of course, Alice Anne was right. What else could an underage, pregnant runaway do to keep her stomach filled?

I checked my watch. "I'll drive by tonight. You wouldn't have any names, would you?"

"Names, *pshhh . . .*" She bundled up. "Can't be gettin' close to people. Here today, gone tomorrow."

I went inside my wallet and took out another buck. "Buy yourself some hot chocolate. And if you hear about anyone dumping a baby, you'll give me a ring."

This time, I offered her my card. To my surprise, she took it.

"Pass the word," I told her. "If the girl goes to the police within three days, nothing will happen to her."

"Yeah, right."

"It's true, Alice Anne. It's the law."

"Yeah, I know what the law's worth." Again she spat.

"Well, if you hear about anyth—"

"Yeah, yeah."

I forced her to make eye contact with me. "You wouldn't be holding back on me now, would you?"

Alice Anne appeared to be horrified. "Lookie here, Officer Cindy. I may be a crazy, ole bag lady. I may have fallen on some hard times. And I may take too many sips of rotgut 'cause I gots lots of pain in this ole body. But I ain't no raging alcoholic, and I don't like baby killers."

Elegantly stated. I sighed, then said, "Do you want me to arrest you?"

Alice Anne stared at my face.

"Three squares and a hot shower," I told her.

"No." She drew herself tighter under her cover. "No, but thanks. You can give me mo' money if you be feeling charitylike."

I took out a five and showed it to her. "Don't spend it all in one liquor store."

She laughed, then closed her eyes.

Having nothing more to say, I got up and left her to what were hopefully more pleasant thoughts.

By twelve-thirty, I had showered and was in civilian clothes en route to home. The U-turn happened by remote control, because I didn't even realize I had changed directions until I was headed the opposite way.

To the hospital, naturally. Haunted by the image of that frail bundle left behind for Monday-morning garbage pickup, I knew I had to see her in a different environment: safe and blanketed, warm and fed.

Mid-City Pediatric was about two miles east of where the infant had been discarded. It was a Medicaid hospital, meaning that most of the patients were poor. Despite its location, it had a world-renowned reputation. When my baby sister, Hannah, needed some minor surgery, Rina insisted that she be taken to Mid-City instead of one of the bigger, more moneyed behemoth hospitals on the affluent west side of town.

It was a five-story building, modern and functional. The interior made stabs at being bright and cheerful—a mural of painted balloons, a gigantic stuffed teddy bear holding an armful of candy canes—but it couldn't rid itself of that antiseptic smell. One whiff and I knew where I was.

It was relatively quiet—the lateness of the hour and the luck of the draw. The uniformed guard at the door looked bored. There were about a dozen people milling around the lobby, mostly Hispanic mothers with small children. There was one Asian family—a mother and three little girls—sitting on orange plastic chairs, no one talking, hands folded in their laps.

I went up to a glass-partitioned counter. A middle-aged intake secretary smiled at me, her eyes enlarged behind magnifying corrective lenses. I pointed to the family. "Have they been helped?"

"The Parks?"

"I guess."

"Yes, they've been helped. They're waiting for the father to bring over the Medicaid card. He works alone in an all-night liquor store, so he had to lock it up before coming over here."

"Is one of the kids sick?"

Her eyes narrowed. "Why are you asking so many questions?"

I got out my billfold and showed her my badge. "Just wanted to make sure they were taken care of. Sometimes people are reticent to ask for help when they need it."

"That's true. What can I do for you, Officer?"

She was suspicious and I didn't blame her.

"Two EMTs—Crumack and Hanover—brought in a newborn a little over two hours ago. I was the police officer who found her. I'd like to see her, if possible. Just to see that she's safe."

"Can I see that ID again?"

Again I pulled out the badge. Even after I showed it to her, she was leery. She told me to wait.

I waited.

Finally, a twenty-something pixie named

Marnie Sears, R.N., M.N., took over. She asked me to follow her and smiled when she spoke to me. Perhaps she liked me because we both had flaming red hair. But that was where the similarity ended. She was small and slight and cute—everything that I wasn't. What did I expect having been sired by a six-four, 220-pound-plus father. I had lost weight the past year—a lot of it, and not because I was dieting. The appetite suppressant came in the form of recurring nightmares of renegade cops chasing me off a cliff. My therapist kept telling me that it takes time for the psyche to knit the holes. I was still waiting, but I didn't expect much.

If I were honest, I'd say things were looking up. Certainly, my appetite had returned. Not in full force, but I didn't look gaunt anymore. Frankly, I didn't mind the underfed model look—pronounced cheekbones, full lips, white teeth, and tight chin—but it bothered my parents something fierce. The couple extra pounds I now carried had softened my face. The main thing was I could digest a cheese sandwich without the sour stomach.

Marnie and I rode the elevator up to the

neonatal unit. She told me that the baby was doing well, that her temperature was back up to normal.

"That's very good."

"You just want to see her, huh?"

I nodded. The elevator stopped and the doors opened. We walked the hushed halls of the hospital. The lighting was bright, bordering on harsh.

"She's over here."

Marnie had stopped in front of a picture window. As I stared through the glass, my heart stopped. Fifteen tiny creatures poked and prodded with tubes and needles. I had eaten steaks that weighed more than the smallest of them. The teeniest looked just over a pound. I could have held her in my palm.

"She's third from the right."

Sandwiched between two little blips of life hooked up to oxygen masks and IVs, my little girl looked enormous and hearty. No tubes, no oxygen mask, just a lump of pink blanket with a hood on her head. "My goodness, she looks so big."

"She's probably full term."

I wanted to pick her up. To rock her and

kiss that little forehead. I turned to Marnie. "Is it possible for me to hold her?"

"The baby?"

"Yes."

Marnie sighed. "I shouldn't let you . . . but human contact is very good for her right now. You'll have to suit up."

"That's fine."

Marnie took me into an office and gave me disposable blue scrubs. By the time I had finished, I was covered head to toe— suit, mask, head cap, gloves, even paper casings over my shoes. Finally, she led me into the nursery and picked up Baby Girl Doe—weight six pounds seven ounces, length nineteen inches. She had me sit down and then placed the sleeping infant in my arms.

Her face looked like a ball of brown butter—tiny lips, onionskin eyelids, and a nose no bigger than a button. My eyes got moist, but I couldn't wipe the tears because my hands were housed in latex. I just let them run down my cheek. Marnie stared at me. I shrugged.

"It's camp, but it's true. What a miracle."

The redheaded pixie smiled. "Why, Officer, you're an old softy."

"Don't tell anyone, all right?"

The symphony of cries was music at its most primal. My eyes swept over all the tiny preemies. All the little lives hanging in the balance . . . all those worried parents out there. I wondered how people like Marnie worked in a pediatric hospital and kept their sanity.

Over the high-pitched wails, a disembodied voice announced a name over the PA system. I turned to the nurse. "You're wanted?"

"Yes, I am. I can't leave you up here unsupervised. I'm sure you understand that."

"Absolutely. A few more minutes?"

"Sorry. Duty calls."

I sighed, about to place the baby back in the bassinet. Her lips pursed and suckled air, then went slack. I stroked her cheek with a rubber finger. "Good night, little one."

"You can hold her if you like."

The voice that spoke was deep. I looked up . . . then up some more.

He was tall, lean, and high-waisted, with smooth cinnamon skin that stretched over high cheekbones. His face appeared to be long, although it was hard to tell under the mask. The cover-up did serve to showcase magnificent eyes: big and round and pale whiskey in color, set under arched black eyebrows and topped with an awning of *long,* dark lashes.

Why did guys have the best lashes?

He wore blue scrubs, his hair hidden under a paper cap. He was holding a tray of vials, tubes, needles, and slides. Some of the tubes were filled with blood, others empty. I had been so focused on the baby, I hadn't heard him come in.

Marnie said, "I just got paged to Four West. She can't be left unsupervised."

"Why not? Is she a felon?"

"I'm not kidding, Koby. You *cannot* leave her alone with the baby. When you leave, she leaves."

"I will watch her like a marine."

Marnie was already walking away. "Your charm's going to fail you one day, Koby. Then what will you have?"

"I think I will have my job," he retorted. "From you it is shown that charm is not necessary for the position."

"Ha, ha, ha!" She scurried out of the room, and through the glass window, I saw her racing down the hallway.

He set the tray down on a metal table and directed his jeweled eyes down to my face. "So you are the one who found treasure in the snake pit?"

"I'm the one who pulled her out of the Dumpster. How did you know?"

"The paramedics told me the story." He checked the clock, then signed a clipboard attached to my baby's bassinet. "I need to take her blood."

"She's sleeping so soundly."

"I have a light touch. Perhaps she will sleep through the entire procedure. If you continue to hold and rock her, it will make it easier."

I made a face. "Where do you take the blood from?"

"From the heel."

My eyes crawled upward to his badge. Though Marnie had called him Koby, his name tag revealed him to be YAAKOV KUTIEL— R.N., M.N., M.P.H. CRITICAL CARE NEONATOLOGY. Yaakov was my stepbrother's legal name, although my dad usually called him Jake or Jacob. Yaakov was a name associated with Jews or Russians. The man didn't appear to be of either stock. "How is she doing?"

"Very well, although she did have some drop in temperature from exposure." He took several slides out from their protective wrappers, marking each one with a number on its label. "Not too much of a drop because, the EMT tells me, she was covered up with the garbage bags."

"Yes."

"She was crying when you found her, no?"

He enunciated his words in the clipped cadence of those from Africa.

I told him yes, she was crying.

"So she had plenty of oxygen in her little lungs." Out came a blue-capped needle. "She was fresh from the womb, you know."

"I know. The cord was still attached."

"The EMTs tell me that someone didn't bother to wipe off the amniotic fluid, just pushed her out and dumped her."

"Now that's not entirely true," I balked. "I wiped her face with a sterile napkin."

"Perhaps they were referring to her body." He unwrapped a small glass tube. "It is good you found her so soon. Always babies lose weight after birth."

"Miracles happen."

He let out a soft laugh. "Sometimes they

happen to you." He stood close to me, peeling back her little pink blanket and exposing a tiny foot. "Has someone found her mother?"

"Not yet, but we will . . . hopefully."

The nurse furrowed his brow. "We?"

"Yes, we . . . I'm a police officer."

A slight raise of his eyebrow, though he said nothing.

"I see they didn't tell you the complete story."

"No, that is true."

"I was riding solo last night. A busboy flagged down my cruiser when he heard the crying," I said. "I was thinking about doing a door-to-door search for her mother tomorrow morning before I go back on duty."

"A dedicated cop."

I said, "It's the way I was made."

"Dedication is good." He examined the heel, swiped it down with some yellow cleansing liquid, then gave it a quick stick, squeezing it with gloved hands to extract droplets of blood. The infant wrinkled her nose and pouted, but after some gentle rocking, she decided that her best option was to stay asleep.

Silence as the man worked, gathering the

blood into a pipette and smearing it onto the slides. When he was done, he placed a bandage on the infant's heel, then gently tickled the sole of her tiny foot with a gloved hand. She retracted her leg in her sleep, then let it fall loose.

He chuckled. "Good reflexes."

I smiled. "Well, she didn't wake up." I finally screwed up the nerve to make eye contact. "You must indeed have a light touch."

"I should have been a surgeon."

"Why didn't you?"

I winced as soon as the words came out. His topaz eyes went from the infant to me. There was motion behind the mask. I could tell he was smiling.

He said, "I speak in metaphors."

"Oh . . ." I felt my face go hot. "That was nosy as well as tactless. Sorry." I should have kept my mouth shut. Should have known better by now.

He laughed as I got hotter and hotter. "Are you disappointed in me?"

"Disapp— I . . ." *Stupid, stupid, stupid.* I kept my voice even. "Just making random conversation."

His eyes crinkled upward at the corners. "I must take these slides to the lab. You have to put her back now."

I looked at the package in my arms and sighed, again stroking her cheek with my gloved hand. I could have held her forever. "Good night, pumpkin." So soft. "Don't let the bedbugs bite."

Reluctantly, I stood up and placed her back in her bassinet. He picked up his tray and walked me to the nurses' station next to the baby nursery so I could remove my protective shell. Off came the face mask, then the cap. I unpinned my hair, shaking it out with a little more drama than necessary. Then I began to peel off my paper suit. First the shoe coverings, then I rolled down the pants, pulling them off, leg by leg, feeling rather clumsy because I was standing instead of sitting. It also felt a little peculiar, this pseudo-disrobing in front of a stranger. As I attempted to lift the shirt over my head, I realized it was tied in back. I reached around to undo the strings but was having trouble with the knots.

I glanced at my chaperon and caught heat from his staring eyes. The intensity caught me off guard and I felt myself go warm. Immediately, he looked away, his complexion darkening a shade. He had undone the top ties of his mask, exposing the rest of his face—an aquiline nose, a generous mouth, and a strong jawline ending in a square chin.

His gaze fell over the top of my head. "Need help?"

"If you could."

He fumbled under my long tresses, his fingertips brushing my back as he undid the knotted strings. I felt an electrical surge. I think I might have shuddered, but he didn't comment if I did.

"Thanks."

"You're welcome."

I slipped off the shirt, snapped off the gloves from my hands, and picked up the discarded suit. He pressed the pedal of a trash can and I threw the disposable clothes away.

"Much obliged," I said.

His eyes engaged me for a moment. "I will walk you to the elevator."

Again I knew I was blushing. "No need."

He broke into a slow smile, exposing big

white teeth. "But I must escort you. If I don't, Marnie will disapprove."

"Something tells me you can handle Marnie."

"You think so?"

"I have a sixth sense about these things."

"How does that work?"

"It's an intangible."

"Like a woman's intuition?"

"More like a cop's intuition."

"Being as you are a woman and a cop, does the intuition level double?"

"On good days, it probably quadruples." By golly, we were flirting. Silence . . . but we maintained eye contact for much longer than was socially acceptable. I finally broke it. "It's late. I should be going."

To get to the door, I had to reach around him. I waited a moment, but he made no effort to move.

"May I ask your name?"

"My name?"

"Please."

"Cindy."

"I am pleased to meet you, Cindy." Again he smiled. This time, I noticed how his big, straight white teeth contrasted with his dark skin. "I am Yaakov."

"I know. I read your badge." Then I realized how *that* sounded. I wanted to crawl into a hole. It had been eons since I had allowed myself to be alone with a man. I had forgotten what sparks felt like and how to handle them. "I noticed your name because it's the same name as my stepbrother."

His smile gained wattage. "So you are Jewish?"

"Yes, I am Jewish."

He pointed to himself. "Already we have something in common."

It was my turn to laugh. "You're *Jewish?*"

"I keep forgetting that Americans find this unusual. In Israel, it is nothing because there are many of us. I'm an Ethiopian Jew. As a matter of fact, I am not only Jewish, but also a *qes*. That is Kohen in English. Do you know what that is?"

"Yes. It's a Jewish priest. My stepfamily is very religious."

"Stepfamily?"

"My father's family. I don't want to keep you from your duties. We really should go."

"Yes, we should. Do you have a boyfriend?"

"You're very forward."

"I say curious. Still, you don't have to answer."

I didn't. He gave me a closed-mouth smile. "I am taking a break as soon as I drop off the tray. Would you like to join me in some hospital cafeteria coffee?"

It was an innocent enough request. Much easier than an actual date.

And then I realized how long it had been since I actually had a real date. Trust was a problem for me in general. Trusting men was the impossible dream, but who could blame me after such a horrendous experience. Ironically, because Yaakov was black, it made things easier. All the dudes that I loathed and feared had been white. I said, "Depends on how long a break you have."

"Usually five to ten minutes."

How much trouble could I get into in ten minutes? I shrugged. "Okay."

The man's grin was abundant. Since he was carrying a tray, I opened the door for him. But he used his shoulder to keep it open for me. Standing next to him, he appeared a half foot taller than I was, about six-one or -two.

"After you," he insisted.

I walked out first. "Just being polite or don't you trust me out of your sight?"

"I work on my manners." He let the door close behind us. "Israelis have a reputation of being rude. It is not unfounded, but only because we are too honest." He smiled. "More like blunt." He spoke as we ambled down the hallway. "You can call me Koby, by the way . . . as in Kobe Bryant. Although I spell it with a *y* and not an *e.*"

"You know, you look a little like Kobe Bryant." I frowned. *Jeez, what is wrong with me?* I felt as stupid as a schoolgirl. "You've probably heard that before."

"Yes. But it is strange. People tell me, but only after I mention my name. Especially in L.A., they hear the name Koby, see a tall black man, and automatically make this weird connection. Really, I don't look like him."

His words gave me an opportunity to regard him in earnest. I said, "I think it's the cheekbones . . . maybe the nose."

"The famous Haile Selassie nose."

"You're both tall, thin, and black. But that's it. It is bizarre how people make an association to what's familiar." I smiled.

"Besides, you don't have that little tuft of chin hair."

He laughed. "It is funny you say that. Last year, I got it in my head to grow facial hair. I get about three weeks' worth of beard, then change my mind and shave it off—too hot under the face mask. But I shave it off in stages and I wind up with a half beard . . . some chin hair. So one afternoon I get off shift and meet a friend who works in Hem-Onc—oncology is cancer. I usually don't rotate through that wing, so the kids don't know my face so good. Plus, I was in my regular clothes and wearing boots with big heels, so especially to the children, I must have appeared very tall. I think I have on sunglasses, too."

"Big diamond earring?"

"No, no diamond earring." His smile was soft. "They wear on one ear a down payment for apartment in Israel."

"No justice in this world."

"That is true. But at least they entertain." He looked at me. "Where was I?"

"You're tall and have sunglasses on."

"Ah, yes." He broke into a grin. "So I hear my name, Koby, and I turn around. It is this boy, maybe twelve—bald from chemotherapy. He has an eye patch, probably lost an eye from his disease, so maybe he doesn't see so good. And this is when the Lakers were doing their three champions . . . third champion . . ." He made a face. "What is the noun?"

"Championship."

"Yes, third championship, so everyone is thinking basketball." He led me to the bank of elevators. "You want the basement."

I punched the down button.

"So I hear my name, look at the little boy, and smile." He chuckled. "In thirty seconds, I have twenty children wanting my autograph. My one time with fame."

"Were the kids disappointed when they found out you were the wrong Koby?"

He let out a soft laugh. "No one say a word! Everybody on staff—doctors, nurses, orderlies, techs—they all know *exactly* what is going on. Plus, Oncology often get celebrities visiting the kids." He raised his eyebrows. "This little boy . . . he just saw what he wanted, and the rest of the kids are also willing to believe. I sign a bad handwriting starting with a *K* and they were happy. Absolutely thrilled."

The elevator dinged.

Abruptly, his expression turned pensive. "Such sick children, Cindy. So weak . . . knocked out. It's all so unfair."

The doors opened.

He shrugged himself out of it. "If I can bring a bit of joy to them, I say, why not?"

4

Koby carried the coffee as we walked to an orange plastic table sided by four blue molded chairs. Because of the late hour, the kitchen was closed, but there were still some prepackaged cold sandwiches—slices of something pink covered by wilted green stuff—for the truly famished. Drinks were also available. We sat across from one another. He had taken off his head covering, exposing a close cut of tight black curls.

"When I came to America from Israel, I was lucky because I came with a skill." Large, thin fingers wrapped around a paper cup. "Otherwise I end up taking parking tickets at the booths at LAX."

I nodded.

He sipped black coffee, then said, "You

see, many of the ticket takers at the airport are Ethiopian."

"Oh."

"So I was making a joke." A pause with a raise of an eyebrow. "Not so good one."

I felt myself smiling and quashed it by drinking my coffee. It was very acrid. "So how long have you lived here . . . in the U.S.?"

"Eight years. First I moved from Ethiopia to Israel in 1983 before Operation Moses. I was eleven. Things were very bad for my people after Haile Selassie was deposed. Ethiopia became Marxist country and not friendly to Beta Yisrael. They outlaw our practices. Sometimes they torture our elders. Then came the drought. My mother died shortly after childbirth with my sister. Then we begin our trek through the Sudan. By then, we were all sick with starvation. I lost another younger sister, but four of us siblings survived—my two older brothers, Yaphet and Yoseph, my younger sister, Naomi, and me. In Ethiopia, my father was very respected *qes*—a priest. He knew *Orit,* of course, which is our Torah, but that is in Geez or Amharic. But my father also knew Hebrew *Chumash,* and this is very, very unusual. He only knew because his grand-father was Yemenite Jew who came to Ethiopia in 1900 and brought with him He-brew books including *Chumash.* So I have a little *Mizrachi* in my blood. My father tells me it is from my great-grandfather where I get my light eyes."

"I noticed." Under the fluorescent bulbs, they were sauterne. "They're lovely."

"Thanks." His smile was shy. "I trade you my eyes for your gorgeous red hair."

I smiled back. "Thank you. Just be care-ful what you ask for."

"Indeed." He took another sip from his cup. "Bitter tonight. Must be dregs. Anyway, my great-grandfather's last name was Yeku-tieli. It became Kutiel."

"So you have family in Yemen?"

"No. They all move to Israel in 1950s in Magic Carpet when Israel takes Yemenite Jews. My brothers and I actually know some Hebrew when we go to the Holy Land. Most Beta Yisrael have to learn. As sons of a *qes,* we were started on *Orit* at two, be-cause in our culture it is the *qes* who reads *Orit.* I pick up languages very quick. By bar mitzvah—which was new custom to us, by the way—I had most of *Orit* and *Chumash* memorized, although I forget much of what I learned. My brothers too."

"That's amazing," I said. "What about your sister?"

"The girls learn *nothing.* They obey their husbands, keep house, and have babies. Maybe make a little pottery to sell in the marketplace. But, of course, they give the money to their husbands."

"Now you're baiting me," I told him.

His smile was playful. "It all changed when we settle in Israel. My little sister embraced liberation very well. Still, she must thank my father. Now there are about seventy thousand of us in Israel."

My eyes widened. "Seventy *thousand?* I had no idea."

"Have you ever been?"

"No." I felt my face go warm. As if by failing to visit the Holy Land, I betrayed my ancestral heritage. "One day, I'll go. My father went about ten years ago. My stepmother lived there for a while with her first husband."

"Your stepbrother's father."

"How'd you . . . Oh, yeah. The one who's also named Yaakov. We call him Jake or Yonkie."

"And he is your only sibling?"

"No, I have a half sister named Hannah and another stepbrother, Sam. The boys are much younger than I am. They go to college back east. Hannah is ten—the baby."

He nodded. "My entire family lives in Israel now. My brothers are officers in *Zahal*—the Israeli army. My sister is also a nurse and lives in Tel Aviv with her family. My father re-married an Ashkenazi woman whose husband had been killed in Lebanon. Batya had four children with her first husband. So for a while we were ten in a very small apartment. Then she became pregnant by my father and they had twin girls. But by that time my brothers and my three stepbrothers had moved out, so there was more room. A year later, I move out at seventeen to do *Meluim* for three years."

"'*Meluim*'?"

"Army service. After that, I decided to be a nurse. From the army, I already knew the skill. I just needed the book learning. I did an accelerated course and was out in two and a half years with a B.S. in nursing, and a job."

"So you kind of paved the way for your sister."

He thought a moment. "Yes, I think so, although in Israel many Ethiopians learn nursing. She is the nurse with a nice, clean office job. My father was very mad at me for becoming a nurse. As a Kohen, I am not supposed to be near dead bodies. My stepmother said if I don't respect the *Kahuna*—the priesthood—at least be a doctor."

"That sounds like a Jewish mother."

"Yes, Batya is a very Jewish mother. In the end, I follow my heart and my parents make peace with me. I am the youngest son in the family . . . very spoiled. They don't stay mad. It is good that I am aware of death. If a baby codes on my shift, I do *everything* to revive that infant. Of course, the best way not to get a code is to be very watchful. I am very, very watchful."

"Dedication is good," I said, throwing back his own words. He smiled at the recognition. "You have a master's in public health."

He regarded his badge. "That was four years ago. First the hospital sent me to get a master's in nursing for one year. They get more federal money if their staff has degrees. I come back and do exactly the same things, except now I have more letters after my name. And I got a bump in salary, so that part was good. Then I think I want even more money, so I do the M.P.H. at state university for another year during the day and work at night. The M.P.H. is for hospital policy, so I get an administration job. And the work does pay better, but it is so *boring.*"

I smiled.

"Oh my goodness, Cindy, it is one meeting after another. I go out of my mind. I last six months; then I say forget it and go back to nursing."

I inwardly smiled, flashing to my own parents. My mother had expected more from my father than just a cop's salary. Dutiful man that he was, he went to law school, passed the bar, then set up shop with my maternal grandfather, doing wills and estate trusts. He also lasted about six months. "You had no trouble getting your old job back?"

"Yes, I have problem because now Marnie has been promoted to my old position. I let her be in charge as long as they don't cut my money. They say okay because with nurses, there is always a shortage, especially if you have degrees and specialties. I am a critical-care nurse. I specialize in pediatrics because I like to help the children. In Ethiopia, they do nothing for the children and the babies. We were the last to be given food. We were the first to die."

"That's horrible," I exclaimed.

"It is cruel, but it has to be that way." His eyes darkened as they intensified. "If the parents starve, who will take care of the children? Who will work? If the mother goes hungry, how can she nurse? You need working adults to keep the family going."

"I don't know, Koby. It goes against everything I was taught. But I've never lived in a subsistence economy."

"Baruch Hashem," Koby stated.

I couldn't help myself. I laughed. *Baruch Hashem* was an expression that Rina used all the time. It meant "thank God" in Hebrew. To hear those words uttered by a black man was simply incongruous.

Koby smiled. "You know what that means?"

"Yes. I'm not a total Jewish ignoramus." I sipped coffee, then made a face. I had forgotten it was so bad. "Do you like working here?"

"At Mid-City Peds, you mean?"

"Yes."

"Yes, it is a very, very good hospital. And the doctors care so much. Why else would they work in an inner-city hospital? As for me, I love the little babies because they represent life. I love life. It is easy to love life after seeing so much death."

"I can certainly understand that. It must be nice being around something so pure, especially after seeing the worst in human beings." I thought a moment. "But I've also seen lots of heroics, too. In my job, you see both extremes, and often side by side. Like tonight. Someone abandons an infant in a garbage dump, leaving her for dead. Then, by accident, a man hears a cry, and the next thing we know, she's alive and well."

"God had different plans for her. I hope you find her mother. Postnatal women need care."

"I hope so. It's such a shame because she had options. If she had dropped the infant off in front of a police station or at a hospital, she wouldn't have committed any kind of crime. And even now, if she gives herself up within seventy-two hours, she'll escape prosecution. We have laws that protect desperate women."

"I'm sure she does not know the law. Or maybe she was too scared." His pager buzzed. He looked down at the number, then back up at my face. "I must go back to work. I would like to see you again, Cindy. Would that be possible?"

I looked at him, making the quick mental calculations about his age based on what he had just told me. He looked younger than thirty-two, but then again, people say I look younger than twenty-eight. "What did you have in mind?"

"Dinner is always nice."

"When?"

"You tell me."

I flipped through my mental calendar. "Friday night?"

He winced. "I am not *shomer Shabbat*. I do drive much to my father's disapproval, but I don't usually go out Friday, except maybe a *Shabbat* dinner."

"I understand. Look, I work evening watch. Nights are hard. How about lunch?"

"Lunch would be fine. How about Wednesday? I don't start here until six in the evening."

I didn't start work until three. I told him that Wednesday would be fine. "Let's meet at the restaurant. That way I can go straight to work afterward."

And it avoided giving him my phone number or e-mail address.

He seemed tickled. "Perfect! Have you ever had Ethiopian food?"

"Never had the pleasure, but I'm adventurous."

"Meet me on the corner of Fairfax and Olympic—southeast corner—at twelve, maybe?"

Little Addis Ababa. It was only a block or two in length, but it was in striking contrast to the Jewish area around it. "Twelve it is. Any vegetarian dishes in your cuisine?"

"Many. You are vegetarian?"

"Not strictly, but most of the time."

"I am kosher and the restaurants are not. So I will eat vegetarian, too."

His pager went off again. I stood and so did he. "It was really nice meeting you, Koby."

He laughed. "You sound shocked."

"Not shocked." I shrugged. "It was just . . . unexpected."

"That's when it is the nicest," he said, beaming. "It was lovely meeting you, Cindy. I look forward to Wednesday."

He turned and walked hurriedly out of the cafeteria. He moved with grace and confidence, a man clearly comfortable in his own skin.

▼

The streets held scant traffic and I made good time, catching all green lights down Sunset Boulevard. This was my district, and out of habit, I slowed at the hot spots—the pay phones used by the hookers at the pimp motels. Still some foot soldiers out at two in the morning, but nothing too heavy. Poor girls were shivering, wearing micro-miniskirts and tank tops with only thin shawls to warm their bare shoulders. They teetered as if drunk, but it could have been the ultrahigh platform shoes.

I thought about my upcoming date. There were three immediate things in Koby's favor: He didn't appear to be a psycho, he was employed, and he seemed genuinely nice—more interested in *me* than in my *profession.*

Civilian guys usually split into two camps—those intimidated by female cops, and those obsessed with the fact that I carried a gun. The only men who truly didn't care were those involved with the Job—

other cops, DAs, PDs, probation officers, private detectives, and bail bondsmen. Those dates usually dulled very quickly because after we talked shop, there was nothing else. It wasn't anyone's fault. The Job was consuming, and those of us immersed in it often forgot that there was a whole other world out there.

Scanning the streets, I recognized one of the working ladies and immediately slowed. She had on fishnet stockings whose tops came below the hemline of her sleeveless red minidress. Smooth brown arms swayed as she walked. Her lemon-colored hair, marred by dark roots, had been pulled into a ponytail.

I rolled down the window. "I hope you're on your way home, Magenta."

She squinted. She was nearsighted but never wore glasses while working. I found this out after she claimed to have witnessed an assault on a bag lady. The detectives had a specific perp in mind and put him in a lineup. After peering at the men, Magenta had picked out Detective Elgen Halkhower from GTA detail. Now she said, "Who's there?"

"It's Officer Decker."

"Officer Decker? You still on duty?"

"An officer's work is never done."

"Same here."

"Except I don't give my money to a pimp."

"Just the U.S. government—biggest-ass pimp in the whole wide world."

She had a point. "C'mon, honey. Tell Burton if I find your ass out here again, I'm gonna haul you in. The money you'll make will just about square with bail."

She sighed. "All right, all right. I'm goin', I'm goin'."

She'd turn back around as soon as I was gone.

"How's your son?" I asked her.

Her smile was genuine. "Gettin' bigger and bigger. Like his dad."

Her pimp, Burton, had fathered her child along with six other children by four other women. In some regard, the extended family made it easier for the girls. While they peddled their asses, someone was home watching the kids. "Hon, you need to get off the street."

"I said I'm goin'."

I pulled away and hit the pedal until I was going around forty. At the corner of La

Cienega Boulevard and Sunset, I turned left, my car tobogganing down the steep hillside as I headed toward home.

Home was Culver City, a small throwback just south of L.A. The hamlet still contained free parking and one-of-a-kind shops. I could walk the streets and pick up just about anything—from discounted clothing at designer outlets to exotic spices from the Indian markets. The area held a salad of ethnicities and maybe that's why I felt comfortable with Koby. There was safety in diversity, with no one race thinking that it owned the world. Maybe it was naive, but to me, that was what America was all about.

5

Darkness surrounded him, yet it was emptiness that he sensed, that caused his body to break into a cold sweat.

Four A.M. and he was alone. Where'd she go?

Clad only in pajama bottoms, Decker bolted from the bed, too panicked to bother with his robe and slippers. He found Rina at the kitchen table. "Are you all right?"

"I'm fine."

"When did you get up?"

"Actually, I never went to sleep."

She hunched over dozens of Xeroxed papers and duplicates of black-and-white photographs. The initial burst of artificial light had caused him to squint. When he realized what his wife was looking at, he felt his eyes go wide.

"Good Lord, what in the *world!*"

Rina stood up, pulling her terry-cloth robe tightly around her body. "You're shivering. Go put a robe on."

Ignoring her, Decker picked up a picture. It was a head shot. The eyes were closed, the mouth slightly agape, the hair pulled off the face. The woman appeared to be around forty. Even without benefit of color, he had seen enough postmortem photos to know what he was studying. "Rina, what's going on!"

She took the picture from him and set it back down on the table. "My grandmother." She slipped her arms around her husband, biting his mustache gently. "In case you didn't hear me the first time, you're shivering. Go put on a robe." She kissed his nose. "Or better yet, go back to sleep."

Sleep was definitely *not* on the agenda. He regarded his wife, with her pale skin and her intense eyes that shone sapphire in the dim light. Her raven hair was mussed and flyaway, brushing against her shoulders. It was longer than he had remembered. He rarely saw her tresses loose. As a religious woman, Rina kept her hair pinned or in a braid with the top of her head covered by a tam or kerchief. He tried out a suggestive look. "I'll go back to bed if *you* go back to bed."

Her smile was tired. "That'll work for me. Just let me clean up."

His eyes went back to the table. Among the array of handwritten pages and photographs was a German-English dictionary. His brain started to fire. "Okay, I'm awake now. You snagged me. I am now curious. What is this all about?"

"You want the lowdown on this before or after?"

It wasn't even close. "After. You got my hopes up, woman."

"I have no intention of dashing them. Go on. I'll be there in a minute."

"I'm going to brush my teeth."

"Hygiene is a turn-on." She swatted his rear. "Go."

"Should I shave?"

"It might wake up Hannah."

Nix the shaving. He went back into the bedroom, with his expectations and the free-floating anxiety that was now his ever-present companion. He'd become accustomed to the knots in his stomach, gauging his agitation by the constriction of his gut. It was as if an invisible belt encircled his belly. Sometimes it was tight, sometimes it went slack, but it was always there.

Under the covers, his body turned warm, but his feet were still cold. He was careful not to rest them against Rina's smooth legs when she joined him. To Decker, sex was a beautiful thing. For twenty-plus minutes, he traveled a different universe, a man free of a cerebral cortex. The lack of conscious thought during the act was so incredibly liberating, not to mention the ultimate act of release. Afterward came the intimacy. As Rina nestled in his arms, her head resting against his chest, he stroked her hair, his thoughts flashing on images he didn't want to think about.

"Okay. Now you can tell me. What's with the photographs?"

"It happened one day while you were sleeping off jet lag. I passed a police station. I got curious."

"About your grandmother."

"Yes, my grandmother."

"Does your mother know?"

Rina raised her head. "Absolutely not.

You can't tell her, Peter. Not until I get more information."

"I have no intention of telling her anything. The less I talk to your mother, the better."

Rina hit him softly.

Decker said, "What brought this on? Being in Munich?"

"I suppose so. The city is haunted with all my ancestral souls. They spoke from the grave, Peter. Does that make sense?"

"Some of my unsolved cases . . . they still talk to me."

"So you understand."

"Unfortunately, I do."

"It was a very weird trip," Rina confided.

Who remembers? Decker thought. The fatigue had been overwhelming. Most of the time, he was sleeping. Even when he had been awake, trudging through the wet detritus that covered the mountainous region, his thoughts had been elsewhere. Admittedly, the bitter cold had been invigorating. He wished he were there now—anywhere but back home pretending that things were normal.

Rina snuggled closer. "As I passed a police station, I thought . . . well, if not now, when?"

"Are you sure you want to know?"

"No. I'm not sure of anything," Rina told him. "I lost lots of relatives in the war. There was no closure. No bodies to bury, no way of knowing exactly when it happened. Their deaths were the product of unimaginable evil. But with my grandmother . . . maybe there's a story behind it. I can't ask my mother about it. God forbid I do anything that would cause her pain. She's had enough suffering in her life. But I'm a generation removed. My grandmother is my heritage, too. I feel I have a right to know."

"And what have you found out?"

There was a pause. Then came the sigh. "Nothing. That's the problem. I can read the words, and even understand a few sentences. But my German isn't good enough to comprehend the full text, let alone the nuances. And even if I understood every word in the file, I'm still not a detective. I can't interpret what it all might mean." She ran her fingers across his chest. "I can get someone to translate the notes. But I need a well-seasoned homicide professional to give meaning to the results—"

"Rina—"

"But only if you're interested."

No one spoke.

Then Decker said, "I know what you're doing."

"What am I doing?"

"You're trying to engage me in your business to keep my mind off my failures."

"You didn't fail!"

"I most certainly *did* fail!"

She felt his body tighten. It had been months since the New York ordeal. It was time to come clean, even though it was bound to cause discord. She chose her words carefully, speaking in a whisper. "Peter, I don't know what happened in the warehouse—"

"I know that. And I'm not ready to talk about it."

"I'm not asking you to talk about it, Peter. All I want to say is . . ." A sigh. "I know you weren't alone."

"What does that mean?"

"It means I know who you were with."

Abruptly, Decker sat up, knocking her head off his chest. He encircled his knees with his arms and stared straight ahead. "I was with Jonathan."

"But we both know there was someone else—"

"Have you been talking to my brother?"

Anger in his voice. Rina said, "Do you honestly think Randy would betray a confidence?"

Decker continued to direct his gaze at nothing. He didn't speak.

"I saw Donatti in New York, Peter. He was following me—"

"What!"

"Can you lower your voice?"

"He was *what?*"

"It wasn't like it sounds."

"That *motherfuc*—"

"Peter, *shhhh!*"

"That is it!" He sprang out of bed, threw on his robe, and began to pace. "I'm going to *kill* him—which is what I should have done in the first place."

"Are you going to rant or do you want to hear what I have to say?"

He suddenly turned against her. "And *now* you're telling me." His voice was rife with hostility. "Any particular reason for keeping *me* in the dark?"

"Yes, I had my reasons. And I will tell them to you if you'd like to listen."

Decker glared at her. He was glad that it was dark so she couldn't see how furious he was. "What'd the bastard do? Come on to you?"

"Yes, he tried to intimidate me—"

"That *motherfucking son-of-a-bitch bastard!* I will strangle him with my own—"

"Peter, he took a bullet for me."

He barely heard her above his own tirade, but he did hear her. In the sudden stillness, he realized he was panting heavily. Sweat was pouring off his forehead. The image materialized in his brain—a shadow lifting up his shirt . . . the bandage around his ribs.

Now we're twins.

"*What* did you say?" His voice was softer now.

"I said, I think he took a bullet for me."

He sat down beside her, his hands shaking. "You *think?*"

"It happened so fast. He'd been following me, although I hadn't noticed it. The next thing I knew, I was pressed against the hood of a car and he was on top of me, bleeding from a gunshot wound. I know you hate him. And I'm sure you have every right to hate him. I hate him, too. But even reprehensible people can do noble acts."

Decker was still breathing hard. "How do

you know the bullet was for you? It could have been meant for him, you know."

"Perfectly true. I'm sure he has scores of enemies. But at the time, you had enemies, too. He acted quickly, Peter. It was strictly by instinct. And now it's over . . . all of it. So I guess we'll never find out."

Again the room fell silent.

Rina said, "Come back to bed. It's only five. You can still catch a couple of hours of sleep."

He let out an absurd laugh. Sleep was elusive under optimal conditions. Under these circumstances, it was damn nigh impossible. He longed to be next to his wife, to feel her body against his clammy skin. Still, he resisted, trembling like a leaf in the wind.

She held out the covers. "C'mon, soldier. Life is short. Don't be mad."

"I'm not mad." He hesitated, then quickly slipped under the welcoming duvet, trying to calm his nerves as adrenaline shot through his body. "I'm just . . . shocked. I can't believe you didn't tell me." He turned to her. "Why *didn't* you tell me?"

"Because a family was in distress. I thought it would have been a distraction. It was a judgment call. If I made the wrong decision, sue me."

Decker slumped against the pillow. "Now here's a sobering thought. I compromised your life by dragging you along. And that bastard saves you." His laugh was bitter. "God almighty, I actually owe the son of a bitch!"

"I'm sure he evened the score in the warehouse. So consider the slate cleaned."

Again he laughed—hard and angry. Suddenly tears welled up in Decker's eyes. Before he could blink, they were running down his cheeks. "If anything had happened to you . . ."

"But nothing did happen to me." She leaned into his body and threw her arm around his chest. "I love you, Peter."

"I love you, too." His body was quivering with what might have been, his nerves raw and tender. He was still angry, of course, but not *quite* as angry. The bastard had been good for something other than plugging him with holes.

God had His reasons.

"I love you," he whispered. "I love you, love you, love you."

"Thank you. It's nice to be appreciated."

Decker burst into laughter, hugging her fiercely. He remained entwined with her, neither of them talking, allowing the contact of skin against skin to speak volumes. Holding her . . . feeling the rhythm of her heart until he heard her breathing slow and lengthen as she drifted into sleep. Gently, he disentangled himself and rose from the bed.

"Where're you going?" she said sleepily.

"I'm getting dressed."

"It's not light yet."

"I'm meeting Cindy for breakfast." He stretched lethargy from his aching bones. "I might as well get an early jump. I'll take Hannah to school."

"Are you sure . . ." Her voice was already in dreamland.

"I'm sure."

"And later on, you'll help me with Omah?"

"What?"

"My grandmother?"

Oh, *that*. "Yes, of course," he said. "Anything you want."

"I didn't die. Stop being so nice."

He felt himself chuckle. It was a legitimate expression of joy. Though still burdened by his abject failure—that wasn't going to disappear overnight—he felt lighter than he had in months. In an instant, a searing holocaust of hatred was reduced to . . . well, maybe a bonfire, burning hot and bright, but controllable. Her confession had opened a pressure valve, and for the first time in weeks, he could see again with impartial eyes.

He took a bullet for me.

Potent words. They gave him a whole new perspective on things. Now, maybe, *maybe,* he could concentrate enough to do his friggin' job.

6

I was running late, going over the canyon and into the Valley: poor form because Dad had made a special effort to meet me. By the time I got to the deli, it was past nine, and Dad was already sitting in a booth, sipping coffee, reading the Calendar section of the *Times.* My father was a handsome guy with a full head of hair, although there was lots of white where once it had been orange. His mustache still had color. It was full and bushy and made him look like the macho guy he was. His cheeks were smooth and without shadow as in a recent shave. He had on a white shirt and a dark blue tie. His brown eyes went from his watch, then over the top of the newspaper. When he saw me, he put down the paper and smiled. But there was irritation in his expression.

I slid in on the opposite side, gasping for breath. "Sorry I'm late."

Dad took off his glasses. "No problem. Bad traffic?"

"Not really. Just a late start."

At least, I was honest. I picked up a menu and buried myself in the process of selection. "How're you doing, Lieutenant?"

"Fine. I heard you had quite a night."

"What do you mean?"

Dad looked at me with skeptical eyes. "The baby?"

"Who tells you these things?" I snapped. "Do you have spies planted in each station house?"

He checked his watch. "We've been together eighty-three seconds and already you're sniping at me."

I felt my face go hot and covered it with a laugh. He was right. "I'm sorry. Let's start again." I leaned over and pecked a kiss on his forehead. "Thanks for taking time to meet me. You're very busy and I appreciate it. And I'm sorry I'm late. How are you?"

This time, Dad's smile was genuine. "I'm fine, thank you very much. You look nice."

"This old thing?" I was wearing a dark blue blouse over blue trousers and a camel jacket.

"Well, you put it together with panache."

"Thank you, Daddy. I'm sorry I grumped at you."

"S'right. I only found out about the baby because I went into work early today. The police grapevine was in full force because babies in Dumpsters are always big news. How's she doing?"

"As of one last night, very well. Now all we have to do is find the mother."

"We?" Lieutenant Decker's eyes twinkled. "You don't trust the gold shields?"

"Last night, I talked to the detective in charge—Greg Van Horn. You know him, right?"

"Greg's a good guy."

"A bit past his prime," I said. "His words, not mine."

"He must be close to retirement."

"I think he dreams of golf clubs. Anyway, he said he didn't mind if I did a little door-to-door searching on my off-hours."

"I'm sure he doesn't mind at all. But even if you find out something, he'll take the credit. What are you getting out of it?"

"Goodwill from a seasoned detective who admires you, and satisfaction of a job well done. Also I care about the baby. I'm the reverse mallard duck. I've imprinted on the kid."

Dad gave me the courtesy of a laugh.

"I really hope we find the mother soon. She's probably not in a wonderful state herself."

"You mean medically?"

"Medically, emotionally. Any ideas, Decker?"

I always called him Decker when we spoke the trade. Still, he smiled at the address.

"First tell me what you know."

"We think it's someone local without a car because we found a pool of blood where we think she gave birth."

"How much blood?"

"I didn't quantify it, but Greg didn't think it was enough to be a homicide, if that's what you're thinking."

Decker shrugged.

"I agree with him, Loo. I mean, why kill the mother but not the baby?"

"Sadistic killer? A botched abortion? A bleed-out like Rina had with Hannah? She almost died on the operating table. A girl in an alley wouldn't stand a chance. It all depends on how much blood you found."

"It didn't look like *that* much blood. Like a little puddle."

"Splatter marks around the puddle?"

"No . . . just an amoebic blob."

"Drip marks to the Dumpster?"

Eureka. I had an answer for that one. "Yes, I noticed them. I showed them to Detective Van Horn."

"Good job."

I bit my lower lip, holding back a smile. "Still have a ways to go, but I'm trying to keep up with the experts."

"Good Lord, I hope you don't mean me," Decker retorted. "Saving a baby's life is quite an impressive feat. I'm just throwing out a few observations because you like when I do that."

"You're right. I do like it. Your questions hone my brain, when they're not driving me crazy."

"Too bad. I'm a complete package. You can't pick and choose."

I chuckled. A twenty-something waitress came to our table. Judging from the shadows under her washed-out eyes, she, like me, didn't get much sleep. Neither Dad nor I was particularly hungry. The Loo ordered a half cantaloupe and asked for a refill of his coffee. I settled on coffee, a large orange juice, and rye toast *with butter and jam,* if you please. I may like the underfed look, but dieting was for chumps.

Decker said, "I bet you could tell if the blood was from a birthing mother. Because the puddle might contain some of the baby's blood as well. The hospital lab could help you out with that one. Now tell me your line of reasoning . . . why you think it was someone local."

Anticipating this discussion, I had organized my thinking. "Why would someone choose to have a baby in that *particular* back alley? So this tells me a couple of things. One, she was scared and wanted to get rid of the kid ASAP without anyone seeing. Second, if she had any kind of resources—like a car—she wouldn't have delivered in an alley. So maybe the girl is below driving age, or doesn't have a car. So she walked to the spot. Meaning I'm looking for a postpartum girl who lives within walking distance to the alley."

"Or . . . ," Decker prompted.

"Or possibly a homeless person."

"There you go," Decker answered. "What's the skin tone of the baby?"

"Medium brown. From the looks of her, she could be just about any race except for maybe Nordic. My district is a real polyglot of races."

The sullen waitress with the baggy eyes brought over our meager order. Her disposition would improve when the meal was over. Today was my treat and I was a big tipper.

After she left, Decker said, "The blood work might help you out with the baby's race, too. If I were on the case, I'd call up the hospital lab."

"Don't I need some kind of court order to do that?"

"Probably. But sometimes, if you just go down and make an appearance, you can persuade the technicians to talk to you."

Koby came to mind. I wondered if he was working today. "Right. Good idea." I warmed my fingers on my coffee mug. "Things okay with you, Dad?"

"Things are coming along."

I looked at my father in earnest. Over the past couple of months, he had traversed some rough roads, things he refused to talk about. He kept up a stoic appearance—big worries rarely registered on his face—but I knew better. There was always a telltale sign. The twitch of his mouth, the shift in his gaze. I switched the discussion to neutral ground. "How's the family?"

"Great." He sounded like he meant it.

"How's my Hannah Banana?"

"Your sister's scary."

"At ten, her vocabulary is probably bigger than mine."

"Well, it's definitely bigger than mine."

"Is Jacob adjusting to college all right?"

"Yes, very well, thanks." Dad looked at me. "It's nice of you to ask, Cindy."

"And Sammy? Didn't you say something about a girlfriend?" Surprise in Dad's eyes. "See? I listen when you talk."

"Sammy and Rachel are still an item as far as I know." Decker took my hand. "How are *you* doing, Princess?"

"I'm all right, Dad. Waiting patiently for my turn in the Detectives squad room. In the meantime, I'm studying for the Sergeant's exam. It's been a long time since I've been in school, but it's going well."

"Brains was never your problem." He

dropped my hand, then fiddled with his coffee cup. "Getting out at all?"

He was staring somewhere over my shoulder, trying to hide his concern. The truth was that both of us had experienced terrible ordeals, events that had almost cost us our lives. And neither of us was eager to talk about them.

"I'm still in the bowling league." I scrunched up my eyes and made a moue. "Don't worry. I'm fine. If you want to help me, give me some tips on finding this mother. Even if the mom never sees her child again, the kid deserves to know something about her genetics, don't you think?"

"Sure."

"Any advice other than the lab?"

"Visit the local schools—Mid-City High or even the local junior highs because you're looking for a girl without a car. Ask the teachers who has been missing, who was pregnant, who may look like they're pregnant but is not saying anything."

"That's a good idea." I felt suddenly dispirited. Why hadn't I thought of those things? Of course, Decker picked up on it.

"Cynthia, I *should* know more than you at this stage." His smile was tender and a bit sad. "Although sometimes I wonder. I'm certainly not immune to failure."

I waited for him to say more. Of course, he didn't. So I told him I thought he was terrific.

Decker smiled. "Likewise. I'm your biggest fan."

"I know you are, Daddy."

"Anything else?"

"No, not . . . well, how about this? Suppose . . . suppose, I find the mother. Let's say she's fifteen and *her* mother won't let me talk to her or see her. What do I do?"

"You use psychology to convince the mother that it's in her best interest for you to interview her daughter."

"How do I do that?"

Decker smiled. "Charm."

I busied myself with my toast, eating quickly and without talking. The meal was essentially over in ten minutes. When I saw Decker sneaking a look at his watch, I knew I should let him go. He had taken time off from work. It would be rude of me to keep him longer.

I left a ten on the table. When he balked, I insisted. Decker walked me to my car, opening the driver's door like the true gentleman he was. I hesitated before getting inside.

"I don't know if I can be charming, Decker."

"It depends on how badly you want that gold shield," he responded.

I didn't answer.

Decker said, "Practice smiling in front of a mirror, Princess. It'll help to wipe the sneer from your face."

7

Located smack in the center of Hollywood just east of the famous Sunset Strip,
Mid-City High connoted glamour to the
uninitiated, but in fact, it was a dispirited
school in a depressed area. It compensated
for its age by being big—blocks long with
intermittent patches of green lawn. The
flesh-colored pink stucco building was constructed with lots of curved walls and glass-
block windows—fashionable architecture in
the '40s and '50s. Some of the exterior was
painted with patriotic or ethnic murals, other
parts held smudges of unwanted graffiti. A
couple of smog-tolerant palm trees and
clumps of banana plants rounded out the
picture of old Los Angeles. I jogged up the
twenty-plus steps leading to the front en-

trance and pulled open the brick-colored doors.

I was no stranger there, having been sent before by the Department to deliver the "earnest" drug talks with the students. Last year, I also manned the LAPD booth with George Losario on Career Day. We were deluged with working-class teenage boys interested in excitement and power. The biggest problem for most of them was the high school diploma required by the Police Academy. The dropout rate at Mid-City was substantial. George and I used the opportunity to encourage them to stay in school.

Quite a few of my colleagues had more than the requisite high school education. Some had A.A. degrees from community college; others had B.A.'s. I had a master's from Columbia. It made me an oddball with the other uniforms as well as an object of suspicion. I was working really hard to overcome prejudice and had met with some success. I wasn't complaining, and it wouldn't help if I did.

The hallways were crowded and sweaty with adolescent hormones and nonstop activity; school was now year-round in the L.A.

unified district. Noisy, old, tired, Mid-City was only several miles away from the cultured Hollywood Bowl Amphitheater, but light-years away from the West L.A. area, where the privileged often eschewed the neglected public institutions in favor of posh private schools. I had to hand it to my stepmother. Though Hannah was an outstanding standardized-test taker, Rina wouldn't ever dream of sending my half sister to a private *secular* school. Instead, she elected to send her to a private *religious* school—a seat-of-the-pants Jewish day school. She prized religious studies above all, and in return for her faith in God, she was rewarded by not having to worry about entrance exams and interviews for my ten-year-old sister.

Jaylene Taylor held the title of Girls Vice-Principal. She was tall and big-boned with a broad forehead, long equine teeth, and dark eyes. She wore a beige blouse that sat over navy slacks and sensible flats. When I told her why I was there, the dark eyes narrowed and her mouth screwed up into a distasteful look.

"I can't just hand out names of our students. Everyone has rights, even minors."

Not technically true, but now was not the time to get legal.

"Besides," Jaylene continued, "you don't want pregnant students, you want girls who were formerly pregnant. You know the dropout rate we have with pregnant girls?"

"I bet it's high."

"Skyscraper high. We've got all these state-mandated testing-program requirements. *Our* main problem is getting the students to show up and put in the hours to graduate. Academics?" She stuck out her tongue. "What's that?"

"I went to public school."

She threw me a sour expression that screamed: *Look where it got you!*

"All I want to do is talk to them, Ms. Taylor."

"They're scattered, Officer Decker." She was regarding me with contempt. Or maybe that was contempt at life in general. "We don't run a school for wayward teen girls who can't say no." Under her breath: "Although sometimes it feels that way."

"Don't these girls have special classes?"

Her laugh was mirthless. "They have an entire major. It's called Household Arts, although you don't have to be pregnant to declare it as your area of study." She rolled her eyes. "Diaper changing 101." A sigh. "It's not that bad. And I suppose it's a lot more relevant to the girls than Shakespeare."

"I would think *Romeo and Juliet* would be very relevant to a teenage girl. Relevant as well as romantic."

"Your assumptions are predicated on their being able to read."

I stopped being adversarial and resorted to pleading. "Ms. Taylor, the mother dropped her infant in a Dumpster like garbage. Maybe if we can *impress* upon these girls that there's no reason to *ever* hurt their babies, that there are ways to give up infants that are legal and anonymous, then maybe we can save a life in the future."

"You don't think we *tell* them?"

"Of course you do. But there's nothing like a real-life case to illustrate it. You know, kinda bring it home anecdotally."

She twisted her mouth and glared at me. Then, abruptly, her face softened and I knew she relented. "We offer a fourth-period prenatal class for pregnant girls who are excused from regular gym. I suppose hearing it from an officer won't hurt." She eyed me with suspicion. "It would have helped if you had come in your uniform."

"I'm doing this on my own time. If it's a big success, I'll go through official channels next time."

"All right. Let's go. Don't get your hopes up. And don't believe everything they tell you. These ladies are notoriously good bull-shitters."

▼

There were twenty-three girls, none of them married, and in most cases, the boyfriends were peripheral. Most were from broken homes, and none had any money. What kind of future did these girls have? How were they going to support their children and themselves without becoming a statistic on the slippery slope downward?

I tried to speak to them without conde-scension, lecturing with passion and honesty. But after the first couple of minutes, I had lost 90 percent of the attention in the room. Their restless eyes went to the wall clock and skipped around space. They regarded their long, polished nails; a couple of them refreshed their mouths with generous lipstick applications; several girls pulled out copies of *Teen* magazine and thumbed through the pages as I spoke. So I concentrated on those who still deigned to make eye contact with me.

I started off with the laws concerning infant abandonment. If the child is dropped off in front of a police station or at a hospital, the mother will not be prosecuted if she has given birth within twenty-four hours. And even if the child is abandoned, the mother can still escape prosecution if she makes herself known within seventy-two hours. There was no reason *ever* to discard an infant.

When I brought up last night's case, I detected a whiff of interest from some of the girls. Just a whiff, though. Mostly, the girls continued to shuffle their feet, clear their throats, and watch the clock. Ten minutes before class was up, I asked if anyone knew of a desperate pregnant girl who might be the mother. I told them that the mother needed psychological help and medical attention. Surely they could understand her emotional position. I directed my pleas to a girl sitting in the second row, left-hand side. She wore a sleeveless rus-set tent dress, the hemline resting against smooth thighs. She had round brown eyes and long, straight blond hair that reached her shoulders. A pretty little thing, even with the butterfly encased in a heart tat-tooed on her left shoulder. Her right shoul-der held the name CARISSE done in florid script.

Her eyes took me in, although as soon as the bell rang, she was out of her seat, her books pressed against her ample bosom and oversize belly. I called out the name etched in blue on her skin. She turned around.

"Can I talk to you for a moment?"

Carisse waited.

I said, "You seemed to be paying atten-tion . . . focusing on what I was saying—"

"I'm gonna be late for class."

"I'll write you a note."

A swish of the hair.

"C'mon," I prodded. "Help me out. You know who I'm talking about?"

"No." A shake of her head. "It's not like I know every knocked-up girl in the city."

"Okay, so you don't know her personally.

But maybe you've *seen* a girl who fits the picture?"

Carisse shifted the books in her arms. "Not too far from here . . . maybe . . . a couple of blocks east . . . maybe more."

"Yeah?"

"At a bus stop at night. It's not far from where I live. I seen this girl sittin' on the bench. She never goes on the bus, and I never seen her comin' off the bus, either. She just sits there. Like, I'm not saying she's homeless. And I'm not saying she's preggers. But she is fat and dressed weird. Just sittin' on the bus bench, readin' the same book. I haven't seen her for a couple of weeks . . . maybe longer. I was wonderin' if like . . . you know, something happened to her."

"Like what?"

"Hey, you're a cop. This far east . . . it ain't Beverly Hills, you know. Lots of hustlers and lots of poor slobs."

"Hey, Carisse, I know who you mean."

I turned to the sound of the voice. This one had short black hair, white foundation, and black lipstick and eyeliner. She wore a black dress that fell past her knees. Her boots disappeared under the ragged hem-line. I thought the Goth look was long gone, but I guess I was wrong. She stuck out her hand. "Rhiannon . . . like the witch in a Fleet-wood Mac song."

Carisse rolled her eyes. "It's really Roseanne—"

"It's whatever I want it to be, *be-ach.*"

"Hold on!" I broke in. "Let's keep it friendly."

"Fine!" Rhiannon clutched her books to her chest and regarded me with wounded eyes. "I think I seen her, too. That homeless girl. She carries a purse made outta shells."

Carisse nodded. "Yeah, that's the one."

"I didn't know she was pregnant."

"I'm not saying she *was* pregnant, only that she was fat and was readin' this book."

I said, "Do you remember the title of the book?"

Carisse shook her head. "You know, she didn't look like she was really readin' it. Just like . . . looking at the pictures."

"Why don't you think she was reading the text?"

"'Cause she was moving her lips as she went through the book . . . like turnin' the pages *way* too fast. And mumblin' as she turned the pages. Like talkin' to herself."

"Can you describe her?"

"She had a pink face and she was fat," Carisse told me.

"She was Caucasian, then?"

"Yeah, she was real white . . . like pink."

"Something's wrong with her." Rhiannon twirled an index finger next to her temple.

"And she talked to herself?" I repeated.

"I dunno," Rhiannon said. "Never got that close."

"Like I said, she mumbled," Carisse told me. "She dressed weird, bundled up in layers of clothing. You could tell she was hot. She was sweating. Her face was covered in sweat . . . kinda piggish looking . . . real pink, you know."

I nodded encouragement. "Eye color, hair color?"

"Blondish hair," Rhiannon volunteered.

Blondish hair. For Rhiannon to have noticed blond hair at nighttime, it must have meant that the woman was very blond. Also, it meant something else to me: that the woman's hair was relatively clean. Even blond hair gets dark when it's dirty and greasy. Neither girl mentioned anything about her smell, usually the first thing people noticed when dealing with the homeless.

"And you haven't seen her for a while?"

"I haven't looked for her," Carisse said. "You asked me for ideas, I gave you some."

"Thank you. You've both been very helpful." I gave each of them my business card. "If you see her again, you'll give me a call."

Rhiannon squinted at the card. "'Cynthi-a Decker.'" She looked at me. "That's you?"

"That's me."

"How long have you been a cop?"

"Two years."

"So you're still, like, new at it?"

"I've been around," I told her.

"You like it?"

"Very much."

"So, like, what does it take to be a cop?"

There was the long answer. Being a cop for me meant a passionate desire to help people and a fierce determination to seek justice. It meant courage, fortitude, physical stamina, and a tolerance for long, lonely nights. It meant having a clearly defined sense of self, a scrupulous honesty, and comfort with alienation. It meant wrestling with demons in nightmares that sometimes come true. It meant all those things to me, and a lot more.

But I gave her the short answer. It takes a high school diploma and a warm body. Oh, and if you have a clean record that always helps, although it's not *mandatory.*

What's a misdemeanor drug possession between friends?

8

"I didn't get a chance to check up on the blood work."

"Okay." Dad didn't say more. He was expecting my next request.

I shifted my cell from one ear to the other. "I don't suppose you'd like to make a phone call to the hospital?"

"Cindy, it's not my place. Also, maybe Van Horn placed a call. Did you check?"

I knew Greg was twelve hours away from vacation time . . . not a chance. "I don't think so. I just thought it would sound more official coming from a lieutenant. But you're right. I'll make my own call. Get my own feet wet, right?"

"Why don't you coordinate with Detective Van Horn?"

"I will in two weeks, when he comes back from vacation." Silence over the phone. The Loo wasn't rescuing me. "It was nice seeing you this morning, Daddy."

A long sigh breathed over the line. "What did you do after breakfast?"

"I went to Mid-City High School per your suggestion. It was a good one." I related the conversation I had with Carisse and Rhiannon. Decker picked up on the blond hair as well.

"If Rhiannon could tell she had blond hair, it means to me that the woman probably has access to a shower or bath. Any idea of the age?"

"No."

Decker said, "If there's something off about her, maybe instead of homeless shelters, you should try looking into vocational schools for the developmentally disabled. Maybe the girl was well cared for, but retarded."

"That would be so sad," I said. "A retarded girl giving birth in the back alley of Hollywood. She must be so frightened. And what kind of chance does the kid have?"

"Some people are remarkable survivors." A pause. "I'm talking to one of them."

I felt myself smiling. "Funny, Decker. I was going to say the same thing."

▼

After such an extraordinary night, I was glad that my shift contained the usual suspects: drunks, hookers, hustlers, and other various and sundry miscreants. I rode with my sometimes partner—Graham Beaudry—who wavered between hours on the Day and Evening watch. He was one of the few men in the department whom I didn't absolutely distrust.

Tonight was made up of banal traffic tickets and motorist warnings sandwiched in between other "hot" incidents. On the plate were a couple of alcohol-related domestics, a hysterical wife who had blown up her stove, a bad fender bender that sent a couple of people to Adventist (they would be okay), and a missing teen who turned out to be sniffing glue in her boyfriend's garage apartment.

I finished my shift at eleven, and because the station house was so close to Mid-City Pediatric, I figured I'd take a chance and try to find out something about the baby's blood work. I knew that Koby was my best bet for information, but I didn't want to give the guy the impression that I was stalking him. But if I saw him, well, what could I do? And if I couldn't get any information on the abandoned infant, perhaps I could just hold her in my arms again. Like Marnie the elfin nurse had said, babies thrive on human contact.

After checking in at the front desk, I was allowed to go up to the neonatal ward. Marnie wasn't on shift, but Koby was. He was wearing a white coat over a denim shirt and jeans. He saw me through tired eyes and his face lit up.

"You are here. I hope it's me and not hospital coffee."

I smiled. "Have you gone home since last night?"

"Why? I look that tired?"

"You look fine."

"I'm sure I don't. Two people called in sick. I do a double shift, working with five hours of sleep."

"That's rough."

"I can manage. You look lovely."

"Thank you. I like the white coat. Very eminent."

He smiled. "Almost like a real doctor, no?"

I felt myself getting warm. "I didn't mean it that way at all."

"I am teasing you because you blush so easily. I find it charming."

"To me, it's just annoying."

"You are forced to wear your emotions. I can hide behind my dark complexion. I wear the white coat because I just finished up a teaching seminar with a group of nursing students from one of the colleges. USC, I think." He checked his watch. "I finish maybe fifteen minutes ago."

"This late?"

"Night classes . . . it's part of the curriculum. I take them on rounds . . . the hands-on approach. Of course, all it does is scare them." He rolled his eyes. "The hospital likes us to wear white coats instead of scrubs when we lecture. It's ridiculous—first the scrubs, then the coat, then back to the scrubs. I change so much, I should be on a catwalk."

I laughed.

"Your smile is so nice. And what are your plans?"

"I just got off work. After my stop here, I'm going home."

"A pity. I won't be off until six in the morning. Two camels passing through the night."

"Are you going to be up for tomorrow's lunch?"

"Yes, most certainly. *Please* don't cancel on me."

"No problem." I lowered my voice. "I have a favor to ask you."

He chuckled. "What can I help you with, Cindy?"

I patted his shoulder. "You're very nice. They've done lab work on the infant I brought in, right?"

"You were there when I draw the blood. What's on your mind?"

"Is there any marker in her blood that would suggest that she is of one race or another? I'm trying to search for the mother, and the only lead I have so far is a blond white woman. The baby doesn't look Caucasian to me."

"That is because she isn't, and I don't need a lab to tell you that. She is of mixed blood—black and white."

"Why not Hispanic?"

"The skin tone is different, and the features don't suggest it. Hispanic infants just don't look like she does. The thicker lips, the flaring nostrils, the broad forehead—suggestive of African blood, but it's not as pronounced. My own siblings are mixed race. It's not so hard for me to spot."

"So if the mother is white . . ."

"Yes, it means the father is black."

"Thanks, Koby. You've been a big help."

He smiled, but it was tinged with uneasiness. He appeared to be wrestling with something.

"What?" I said. "You're not supposed to be talking to me? Don't worry. I won't say anything."

He looked around, then beckoned me into an empty hospital room. He closed the door. We were alone, but no sexual electricity this time. He was all business. "The baby. She has pronounced spatulate thumbs. I notice it as soon as she came in."

"What does that mean?"

"It means her thumbs are short and look like spoons. Also, her eyes. It's hard to tell because she's a newborn, but I thought I detect epicanthic folds. I pointed it out to the resident. She agrees with my observations."

"Okay. And they are significant because . . ."

"They may not be significant. We'll know when the chromosomes are looked at."

"Chromosomes?"

"Possibly the baby has Down's syndrome."

My heart dropped. "Down's syndrome?"

"Possibly." He smiled sadly. "I'm not sure, Cindy. I could be wrong."

"Why don't I expect that to be the case?"

"You're saddened, I understand. But I see it differently. The child is different, this is true, but basically she's healthy." He laid a large hand on my shoulder. "So much sickness here. Life has thrown all these families curveballs. She still needs love. Hopefully, we'll find a home that will take care of her special needs. I'm only telling you this because you are looking for the parents. If I am right—and maybe I am not—you might want to keep this private information in mind when you do your search."

Of course, that was why he was bending the rules. Not to sadden me, but to help in my quest. The parents might be normal looking, but maybe one of them was Down's as well. I was more determined than ever to find my little baby's parents.

"When will the results come in?"

"Maybe tomorrow. I'll tell you when I know something definite."

Mixed race and one of the parents *might* be Down's. I knew a lot more going out than I did coming in. And wasn't that the purpose of this visit?

"Can I hold her, Koby?"

"It's a very busy night, Cindy."

I stood my ground. He exhaled. "I give you five minutes. And that includes the time it takes to suit up."

"I'm a very fast dresser."

"Come." He led me into the office that adjoined the nursery. He watched me with intensity as I donned the paper suit, observing my every move, but this time his eyes were not at all hungry. They held an expression of wariness. I asked him what was wrong.

He said, "You are getting attached to her, Cindy. Watch yourself or you'll be in for a broken heart."

"The question is, how do you *not* get attached to them?"

His smile was a plaintive memory. "After many broken hearts, you learn."

9

Breakfast was a quick affair—coffee, juice, and a bowl of granola with skim milk. In working mode, I dressed for efficiency: gray slacks, black ribbed crewneck sweater—merino wool because it and cashmere were the only kinds of wool I could wear against my skin—and black flats. Because I was meeting Koby for lunch, I brought along a pair of pumps and a colorful scarf to offset the look of a funeral director. Scarves were wonderful. Throw them around your neck and people thought you took great pride in your appearance.

There was just one vocational school that looked promising. Fordham Communal Center for the Developmentally Disabled sat just east of Hollywood in the Silver Lake district—yes, there really was a reservoir lake. The neighborhood was predominantly Latino, but it held smatterings of other nationalities who had gone through the portals of INS. The school's address was a half block from Sunset Boulevard, that handy crosstown thoroughfare that began at the Pacific Ocean and died east of Dodger stadium.

I found a parking space on the side street and got out of the car, armed with a badge and medical information. The building was a renovated two-story Arts and Crafts hunter green bungalow surrounded by a porch and topped by a peaked roof. Buttermilk-colored wood trim framed the front door and encased two multipaned side windows. Leading up to the door was a lovely stone walkway. After giving the knocker a few judicious raps, I was buzzed in.

I was surprised that the house appeared to have maintained its original floor plan. There was a tiny vestibule that led into a sun-drenched living room replete with desks and other office paraphernalia. Natural light was made possible by windows and French doors in the back wall through which I could see a panoply of color—an array of flower gardens fit for any Impressionist painting. I could make out figures tilling and tending the soil.

The woman who manned the desk closest to the entry was already on her feet. She was blond and thin and appeared perpetually nervous. "Can I help you?"

I showed my badge and ID. Lapis eyes widened as she read the pertinent information. "Officer Decker, is it?"

"Indeed it is. I'm trying to find out information on someone. Who would I talk to for that?"

"What kind of information?"

"It might be personal. Are you in charge?"

"No, that would be Mr. Klinghoffner."

"Could I speak to him, please?"

"I think he's upstairs."

I didn't say anything and neither did she. After a few seconds passed, I smiled and said, "When do you think he might come downstairs?"

"Oh, I can go get him if you want."

"Yes, I would like that, thank you."

"Okay." She didn't move, her eyes nervously scanning around the room. "You can sit down if you want."

"Thank you."

"Okay." I decided she wanted me to sit before she fetched the boss. There was a cozy arrangement in the center of the room—a floral upholstered sofa and two matching overstuffed chairs. I elected to park myself on the couch and sank down into the cushions. She stared at me for a moment, then bounded up to the second story.

The house still had much of its old-world charm—arched entryways, hardwood floors, casement windows, a wood-beamed ceiling, and lots of built-in oak bookshelves and cabinets. The room was square and at each corner was a work area—a desk and chair, a file cabinet, and a computer station. With the nervous woman upstairs in search of Mr. Klinghoffner, the only other person on the floor was a beanpole man in the right corner. He appeared to be in his late twenties with a short haircut and a mottled complexion. Buried in his paperwork, he didn't bother to look at me. But that didn't stop me from staring at him. When he did look up, he colored red and went back to his piles of pulp.

It was time for me to interject some novelty into his life. "What are you working on?"

"Pardon?" His eyes jumped to my face, his cheeks still pink. "Are you talking to me?"

"Yes, sir, I am. You seem to be working on something very important."

"Not important, just vast." His eyes went back to his desktop. "All this paperwork: rules, regulations, statutes, ordinances. Whoever the government doesn't tax to death, it drowns in paperwork. Either way, it's going to kill us all. You, me, my dog, your cat—"

"I don't own a cat."

"I wasn't talking literally!" he replied, bristling. "Forget it!"

"You seem stressed," I remarked.

"Oh please! If I hear that word one more time, I really will upchuck! Anyone who works with bureaucracy is stressed! Obviously, you don't."

"I work for LAPD. They don't come any more bureaucratic than that institution."

"Or any more corrupt, if you don't mind my impudence. What are you working on?"

"Talk about impudence."

"Top secret?" he asked in a bored voice.

"Nothing important. I'm Cindy Decker, by

the way." Silence. "I suppose your mother christened you with a name?"

"She did."

More silence. The guy was a first-class tool. His desk was set against a window, and abruptly a female face pressed itself against the glass. She had short dark hair, hooded eyes, and a gaping mouth with triangular-shaped teeth. She seemed short and was holding a hoe, almost a takeoff on *American Gothic.* She bore a worrisome expression. With deliberation, she raised her fist and tapped on the windowpane. The beanpole looked up and gave her a half smile that almost humanized him.

"Back to work, young 'un!" he shouted through the glass. "Rest is for old folk."

The lines on her forehead deepened. She started to complain about something. I could tell by her tone of voice, although I couldn't understand her. Her speech wasn't clear and she spoke through a glass barrier. "Skinny Man" rolled his eyes, then got up and opened the door. They talked for a moment and then she left. He sat down and resumed his paperwork.

"Is she okay?" I asked.

He stared at me. "Of course, she's *okay.* Why wouldn't she be *okay?*"

"She just seemed . . . I don't know . . . a little lost."

"I hope you're a better cop than you are a psychologist." A derisive sneer. "She wants to know how long until lunch. Then after lunch, they want to know how long before dinner. Their lives revolve around meals. Life would be simpler if we had bells, like in school. You'll have to excuse me. Some of us have deadlines to meet."

As in: *Shut up.* But it didn't matter because "Nervous Girl" had reappeared with whom I assumed was Mr. Klinghoffner—a man who looked to be in his mid-fifties. He had a shock of thick gray hair, was fat across the middle, and had chubby cheeks to match. All he needed was the suit and the white beard and I was looking at Santa Claus. I got up and extended my hand. He took it politely with a limp-fish shake.

"Jamie tells me you're from the police?"

Jamie must be the nervous girl. "That's right, Mr. Klinghoffner. I was wondering if I could talk to you for a moment. Privacy would be preferred."

"Don't bother, I'm not listening, I couldn't care less," Skinny Man chimed out.

Klinghoffner laughed. "Don't mind Buck."

Buck? I had the good sense to keep my smile in check.

"It's evaluation time for the Center for funds." Klinghoffner kneaded doughy hands. "Lots of paperwork. He's a bit tense. Let's go into my office. This way."

He led me through a kitchen that still had its original cabinets and fixtures. The counters were tiled in sunny yellow, and a diamond pattern of midnight blue and yellow made up the backsplash. Klinghoffner's office was off to the right—a tiny room that was probably once a pantry. When he closed the door, it was pretty tight inside, but it did have a nice-size picture window and a skylight giving a blue clue to a world beyond.

"How can I help you, Officer?"

"If you read the papers on Tuesday morning, you'll know that LAPD found an abandoned baby in Hollywood."

"Yes, yes, of course. Terrible."

"The baby is doing well. We have reason to believe that the mother is Caucasian and possibly developmentally disabled."

"I see."

"Any ideas?"

Klinghoffner appeared to be thinking about it. "I'm not . . . aware of any of our women being pregnant."

"Was pregnant."

"Or was pregnant. But I don't know everything."

Covering his rather commodious butt. "Okay. Maybe we could talk in theoretical terms."

"I'm not being cagey, Officer Decker, I just don't know. We try to teach our students about the birds and the bees, but most of their guardians—the parents, the siblings, the aunts—they don't like to leave things to chance. Many of our women are sterilized coming in. The last thing anyone needs is another special child to deal with."

I thought about my poor little baby. Maybe she'd be okay. Maybe Koby was wrong. "You said many of your women are sterilized."

"Yes. But it's *not* a back-alley thing. There is full consent—from the families, from the women themselves. They request it, Officer. They know that they are in no position to raise a child, should they have sex."

"You allow them to have sex?"

"No, not here. But drives are drives. We are realistic. And the women who aren't sterilized, we give them the pill every day along with their vitamins. We make sure they take it."

"Are the women aware that by doing this, they can't get pregnant?"

"We explain it to them. Some comprehend more than others."

"But you don't require them to take birth control, do you?"

He heaved a great sigh. "We don't strap them down, if that's what you're implying."

"I'm sorry. I know you have a difficult task. I'm not passing judgment."

"That's good," the director said. "It's hard enough teaching our students about hygiene, let alone sex. We just try to make sure that if sex happens, the women are not left coping with something they're not equipped to cope with."

"Do the women know what they're doing when they have sex?"

Klinghoffner pursed his lips. "I'm not sure what you mean."

"Is it consensual as opposed to forced on them?"

"Good Lord, I hope it's consensual, although I suspect I know what you're saying. The young women here . . . They're not used to having control over their bodies. They've been told what to do all their lives. We have counselors here to help them integrate sex and health education."

He looked away.

"We do not allow sex within these walls. But the few times I've actually caught a pair in the act, I've looked the other way in terms of punishment. I did take the parties involved aside and insist they get some couples counseling. For precisely the reason you stated. To make sure that nothing was forced."

"And?"

"The parties were all right with the sexual relationship. But their guardians were not. A few times, I've had students pulled out of the programs because of it."

I tried being charming. "And might you know any woman pulled out of the program because of having sex, say . . . within the last nine months? Maybe one with Down's?"

"Not Down's, although we do have students here with Down's."

"So you're thinking of someone specific."

Klinghoffner stalled. "I shouldn't be telling you this."

"The girl needs medical attention."

"Yes, of course." Klinghoffner drummed his fingers on the table. "We have a girl here. She's been sick on and off for the last year. I haven't seen her in a month. She lives with her sister."

"Heavyset and very blond?"

He thought for a moment. Then he nodded.

"But not Down's," I said.

"No, she's not Down's. She has cerebral palsy, although that doesn't tell you anything. It's a garbage-can term. Her gross motor coordination is very, very poor. Her fine motor coordination is not as bad as you'd think by looking at her. She's mentally disabled, no doubt about that, but she has skills. She can take care of herself—bathe, dress, go to the bathroom, even cook a little. And she can work a computer. She does some data entry for us. Quite good at it."

I was quiet.

"A very sweet girl. Maybe a bit more subdued the last couple of months. I probably should have said something, but there are so many kids here." Now he was upset.

"They're like children. They upset easily. Sometimes I miss things."

"We all do."

"Let me walk you back to reception. I'll get you the address."

"Thank you, Mr. Klinghoffner. You're doing the right thing."

"I hope so."

I sat back on the couch and waited. I hoped I didn't have to tarry too long, because "Beanpole Buck" had taken a real dislike to me. He glared at me over his piles of paper. I guess if I looked like him and was named Buck, I wouldn't be too happy, either.

At last Buck spoke. "Find what you're looking for?"

"Maybe."

"If you tell me what you need, maybe I could help you out."

A legitimate offer for help? I couldn't believe it. Nor did I trust him.

"Thanks, but I'm okay."

He stiffened. "Only trying to help."

"I know. I appreciate it."

Klinghoffner returned, ending the awkward moment. "Let me walk you out."

He handed me the paper once we were

outside and away from prying eyes. I thanked him again, and he left me at the curb. The name was Sarah Sanders. Her guardian was Louise Sanders, her sister.

They lived in the foothills of Hollywood.

I turned the address over and over in my hand. I really, *really* wanted to go to the house, but it wasn't my place to be the primary interviewer. I was just too low on the food chain. At this point, all I could do was collect the data and give it to someone else to interpret.

Still, I didn't call Greg Van Horn right away. I had a lunch date to keep. No sense in making decisions on an empty stomach.

10

Little Addis Ababa sat on the corner of Fairfax and Olympic—an incongruent disk of Ethiopian culture encircled by predominantly Jewish areas and establishments. On my way home from work, I must have driven by there dozens of times, but I never paid much attention. Now I observed with virgin eyes. I found metered parking on the street a few yards away from the ubiquitous Star$s. Catercorner to where I was standing was a block-long Jewish school called Shal-hevet—grades six through twelve.

Standing directly across from me, Koby was dressed in black jeans and a long-sleeved coffee-colored shirt two shades darker than his skin tone. Several gold chains rested around a bare neck. He waved and so did I. After I traversed the heavily trafficked street, he greeted me with a peck on the cheek and a wide smile. He was carrying a large blue paper bag from The Gap.

"You look lovely," he said. "Nice outfit. I like the scarf. It adds flair."

"You look rather fetching yourself. I like the jewelry."

"Sort of retro disco, no?"

"All you need is a gold razor blade to complete the image."

"Yeah, then I really give the cops an excuse to pull . . ." He looked away and clenched a fist. "I don't believe I say that!"

I laughed. "That's all right. I would have pulled you over. Feel better now?"

"I am very stupid!"

"You are very honest." I quickly switched gears, pointing to the school across the way, specifically to a lit candle painted on the wall. "Does 'shalhevet' mean fire in Hebrew?"

"Fire is 'aish,'" he told me. "'Shalhevet' is flame."

"My stepmother would love you. You should come to the house for Shabbat dinner sometime."

"That would be great. I am free this Friday."

My mouth opened and I shut it quickly. My foot was so far down my throat, it was in my stomach. "Uh, I'll ask her. I don't know her plans. . . ."

His laugh was good-natured, but tinged with embarrassment. Even through the dark complexion, I detected a rosy glow. "Again I speak without thinking. I am too anxious. Sorry. Whenever is fine, Cindy. You barely know me."

If I reneged now, I'd be a chump. "No, really, it's fine. I'll ask her."

"If you ask and she says yes, I'll come. So I give you an excuse. You can always say that she said no."

"I don't need excuses, Koby, I have an open invitation." Now it was a matter of pride. "You're invited. I'll tell my dad to tell my stepmother, all right?"

"If you still feel that way after lunch, I'd be happy to come." He handed me the sack. "This is for you. I didn't have a chance to wrap anything."

I knew how late he had worked, and was touched by his thoughtfulness. "Thank you. How do you know my size?"

"I don't. Look inside."

I did, pulling out a pound of coffee and a round, spongy brown disk packaged in plastic. He took the coffee from me and opened it. "Special blend. Smell."

"Hmmm. Cinnamon."

"Better than the hospital cafeteria's brew, no?"

"Much better." I held up the plastic package. "What's with the Frisbee?"

"It's *injera*—Ethiopian spongy flat bread. It is made from teff—our special grain." He placed the items back into the bag. "I give you food. For an Ethiopian, that's a most precious gift."

"I'll bet."

"I didn't make a reservation. How about we walk around and see what looks good?"

I told him that sounded fine. We started down the busy street accompanied by vehicular noise pollution and the blare of rhythmic music coming from the Lion of Judah travel agency and CD emporium. The block was a mishmash of retail outlets— Jewish thrift shops, a junkyard, discount stores, a cake shop, and, of course, the Ethiopian contingent. Within seconds, I cleverly surmised that the state colors were green, yellow, and red because at least five storefronts were emblazoned with stripes in those hues. Even the distant Shell station fit right in.

There were three restaurants, all of them having marquees in English as well as squiggles I assumed to be Amharic. There was a store that specialized in *injera* and exotic spices. Even through the closed door, I could smell the tantalizing aromas. There was a dress shop boasting organic fabrics with a white cotton smock in the window festooned with red, green, and yellow ribbons around the neck. The shelves around the clothes offered a variety of silver rings and crosses, lots of shell jewelry, and a whole host of primitive-looking dolls. Koby saw me staring.

"Do you want to go in?"

"No, it's all right. Maybe later."

"Here is Gursha. Would you like to try it?"

"Great."

He opened the door for me and we walked in.

The place was small and homey with a chockablock decor. The wallpaper was a pattern of various animal footprints and served as a backdrop for posters of

Ethiopia, a map of the world, and dozens of photographs of smiling patrons. The tables and chairs were constructed of hay-colored cane painted with red geometric shapes, the ensemble topped by large, fringed cloth umbrellas. A couple of men ate in a pseudostraw hut next to the window, dining *a mano*: eating with their hands. The hostess was thin and delicate, with a long nose and round eyes typical of other Ethiopians I'd seen. She glanced at me, then spoke to Koby in her native language. They carried on a short conversation. Then she seated us at a table and distributed menus.

"I told her we were vegetarians," Koby said. "She assured me that they have lots of vegetarian specialties."

"Here we go," I said. "There's a vegetarian delight for two. It includes *yater alitcha—*"

"Peas with spices."

"Yatakilt alitcha—"

"Mixed vegetables with spices."

"Yemiser wot—"

"Lentils with red-pepper sauce."

"Collard greens—"

"Collard greens."

I laughed. "Very funny. There's baklava.

Aha, something familiar. Let's split that. Does that sound all right?"

"Yes."

"Do you eat with your fingers like you do in Moroccan restaurants?"

"Very similar. The meal is served on *injera.*"

"The Frisbee bread."

"Yes, exactly. You use the *injera* as your utensil and plate. You eat it as you go. Very little dishwashing."

Again I laughed. The waitress came, looking askance at me and focusing on Koby. He ordered the food for both of us, but I ordered my own drink. After she left, I said, "I don't think she likes me."

"Could be because she's shy and doesn't speak English too good. Or it could be because you are with me and you are not one of us. In reality, I am not really one of them because I am Jewish."

"A black Jew. Don't make life too hard for yourself, Koby."

"It is good to move in many worlds. Besides, I am what God made me. Just like the baby you found. Speaking of which . . ." He leaned over and spoke barely above a whisper. "I have good news." His eyes were animated. "The baby . . . A preliminary genetic profile came back."

I grew excited. "She isn't Down's—"

"Shhhh. I shouldn't be talking to you about patients. Even babies."

I nodded, then whispered, "So she's normal?"

"Not exactly. She is what we call mosaic. That means she has some regular cells and some that are trisomy 21."

"How does that happen?"

"Down's is the result of the egg having an extra chromosome. Mosaic, the accident, happens in the second pass when the nucleus splits incorrectly."

I nodded, but my face must have spelled confusion.

He said, "The union produces one zygote, yes. It splits into two normal cells. Then one of the normal cells splits incorrectly, making the body have half normal cells and half with trisomy 21—an extra twenty-first chromosome. What it means is the prognosis for her intellectual capacity is greater. She could be anywhere from retarded to normal."

"That's a long range."

"True, but it's still good news. This was unexpected, Cindy. Mosaic is very rare."

My grin was real. "That's wonderful." My expression turned sober. "What does it say about her parents?"

"One of them could be Down's, maybe not. We don't know. The only thing I can tell you is that she has both white and black blood in her." Our drinks came. "Enough of business. You know very much about me, but I know little about you. Tell me about your father and your religious stepmother and the rest of your family."

I was momentarily taken aback. I had expected him to ask about me. Not to do so would have been rude. But I thought he'd start out with the usual: Why did I decide to become a cop? To ask about my family meant he was curious about *me,* not my profession. So I answered his question. I spoke about Rina and my father, about her influence in my father's religious development. I segued to my mother and her current husband, Alan. Then I spoke about how I had grown up without any religious guidance, so it was a big shock when my father married my stepmother.

The service was slow. Normally, I'd be impatient, but I was yapping so much, I barely noticed. When the food finally came, I hadn't even thought about the waiting time. The cuisine was piquant, not unlike Indian and Middle Eastern cuisine, but unique because of a sour taste from the *injera.* I couldn't say it was love at first taste, but my tongue wasn't complaining.

"What do you think?" Koby asked after a few moments.

"It's good." I tore off some *injera* and used it to eat the lentils. "Something really primal about eating with your fingers. Like when you were five and playing in the sandbox, getting your hands all dirty."

"Enjoy."

"Thank you. You've hardly said a word," I remarked. "You're a very good listener."

"You're very interesting."

"Now that is bald flattery." I hid my face behind my water glass. "I think it's because you're a nurse. You're used to listening to people."

"Of course. And you too, no?"

"Yes, that's true. Ninety percent of what I do is listening to people."

"I as well."

"Even with kids?"

He thought about that. "With the small children . . . The small ones don't talk much. You make games to get them through the procedures. We have on staff several psychologists who do this. When they are too busy, the nurses do it. The little girls play with dolls, the boys . . . They like to hit and punch. Boys always like to hit and punch. When they are sick and angry, they really like to hit and punch. I spend a lot of time dodging punches from very angry boys."

"It must be hard being around sick children all the time."

He shrugged. "Sometimes. But it is rewarding. Like your job?"

"Yes." I nodded. "Like my job."

Koby said, "I change the subject now. The word *'gursha'* means mouthful, but it's also a tradition that we Ethiopians do."

"What's that?"

"We share our food. That is why everything is served on one plate. If we have *very* good time, we feed each other."

"What?"

He placed some spiced peas atop the *in-*

jera and made a minisandwich. *"Minhag Hamakom.* That is Hebrew for the custom of the house. You must eat from my hands. Otherwise they think you don't like me."

"This is for real?"

"Look around."

I did. There was a twenty-something Ethiopian couple across from us. He wore a T-shirt and jeans and had Rastafarian curls; she had on a hot pink silk blouse and black stretch pants, and had her hair tied in a ponytail. She was indeed feeding her lunch companion with her hands.

"Okay," I said warily. "As long as I get to feed you."

"Of course. That is the point."

As soon as his hands touched my mouth, I started laughing and instinctively backed away. But then I ate the proffered morsel, my tongue grazing his fingertips. I returned the gesture by feeding him *injera* wrapped around collard greens. He had the grace to take the food without being sleazy about it. But it didn't matter. Feeling his lips against my skin set off my juices. Apparently, he felt something, too.

We locked eyes. Then I looked down. I

knew I was red-faced. "It's an icebreaker, I'll say that much."

His eyes were still focused on me. "I have good reasons for suggesting Ethiopian."

I wagged a finger at him.

He scooped up some cabbage. "Here. We do it again. Second time is easier."

He could have been talking about other things.

I took the food without protest, enjoying his fingers on my mouth. Then I fed him a chunk of pumpkin. He chewed, the tip of his tongue giving a brief swipe at the corner of his mouth, his topaz eyes having dilated so they looked nearly black.

I gave him a half smile. "Is it extra to rent a room in back?"

He burst into laughter. "Eating should be stimulating."

"Stimulating, yes, not X-rated."

Again he laughed. We ate a few minutes in silence, letting the air around us cool off. Finally, I sat up in my chair and let out a whoosh of breath. "I think I've had it."

"It was okay?"

"It was terrific. It was more than lunch, it was fun. Thank you."

"You're very welcome. For me too. Coffee?"

"Sure." I paused. "You drink your own coffee, right?"

He smiled. "Yes, you drink your own coffee . . . unless you make your own new tradition."

"Thank you, I think I've had enough adventure for one day."

Koby signaled the waitress and ordered for us in Amharic.

"You come here often?" I asked him.

"More in the beginning when I feel a little homesick. If I miss anything now, I think I miss *Shabbat.*"

I said, "So Friday night is still on, if you want."

"No, no, no. I didn't mean it to be a hint."

"It's fine, Koby." A pause. "I insist you come."

He regarded my face with intensity. "I can be pushy. You feel okay about it?"

"Of course." I was aiming for low-key confidence. "Since I know the way, I'll pick you up."

The waitress brought over the coffee in a small clay pot and poured it into two demitasse cups. It was stronger than espresso, but not as strong as Turkish coffee. We exchanged smiles as we drank. Awkwardness stood between us because electricity had gotten in the way of simple platonic conversation. Absently, I glanced at my watch. My eyes widened. "Oh gosh! I'm late." I slapped my forehead. "The meter!"

He stood first and helped me with my chair. "You check the meter. I'll pay—"

"We'll split it."

"No, no, I asked you out."

I didn't insist. "So I'll see you on Friday, then." I pulled out my business card, thought about giving him my phone number, but gave him my e-mail instead. As attractive as he was, I still had my reservations. I hadn't Googled him yet or run him through the network to see if he had a sheet. "This is the best way to reach me. I'll need your address. You do have e-mail, right?"

"Absolutely." He took my card without disappointment, then handed me his. "My home phone, my work phone, my cell phone, and, at last, my e-mail. You can contact me however you want with the details and I'll explain how to get to my place. It's in the hills. I enjoyed your company very much, Cindy. Go."

I gave him a slight wave and took off, feeling featherlight, despite a heavy gun weighing down my purse.

11

Just before roll call, I caught up with Greg Van Horn as he was signing out for his two-week vacation, the field roster marked in green highlighter. His face was filled with good cheer, and he had a spring in his step. Already, he had loosened his tie. I cornered him while he was waving his last good-byes. He frowned when he saw me, but too bad. Out there was a girl who needed medical attention. I gave him the slip of paper and explained myself.

"You did this by yourself?"

"All by my little lonesome."

"On your own time?"

"Yes, sir, on my own time."

He was still staring at me.

"Golly, that woman does have a brain in her head—"

"Decker!"

"Sorry, sir." I stifled a smile.

He tapped his foot. "You're putting me in conflict, Decker, and right before my vacation. I'm not thrilled about this."

"Next time, I'll try to be less effective."

He glowered at me, but it lacked feeling. "The case belongs to Russ, but he don't deserve the credit. You do."

"It may not be anything, sir."

He handed me back the slip of paper. "So why don't you check it out first?"

"Then what if it is something?"

"Follow it up."

"Should I contact Russ?"

"Play it by ear."

Giving me leeway. He was being very gentlemanly. I thanked him and stowed the slip of paper in my pocket. He noticed the uncertainty that I felt.

"What?"

"This is a little different from what I'm used to. Talking to a retarded girl about babies and sex." That sounded fearful. "I can do it. No problem. Just . . . any suggestions? I don't want to blow your case."

"More like *your* case." He held out his hands helplessly. "I'm on vacation, Decker. You got contacts in the Department. Use 'em."

▼

Home had always been Decker's refuge, but of late, it was his office as well. At the station, there were issues and problems and details. There were meetings with superiors, meetings with the detectives, meetings with county supervisors or reps from the city council or congressional districts. There was PR that amounted to a lot of BS. Smiling through all of it gave him one giant headache. Once he'd been able to handle it, fielding calls as smoothly as a Vegas dealer. Now he constantly felt distracted, and the sudden images of blood and death didn't help.

He took off his glasses and set them on the desktop, rubbing his eyes without relief. Rina had set up a comfortable home office in the guest room/den. In the daytime, the back windows showed a view of the mature fruit trees. At the current hour, the vista was dark. But because the room was situated next to a pittosporum tree in full bloom, sweet jasmine scents wafted through the open louver slats.

In the peace and quiet of his own sanctuary, he could go through some of the more puzzling case files, often breathing life into stagnating investigations.

He was able to keep his job and his equilibrium because he was working twice as hard as he should have been. He'd get through it—he had no choice, his family needed the money—but it would take a while. Rina's confession had helped, but Decker knew she wasn't being completely honest with him. By and by, it would all come out.

"How much longer?"

Decker jerked his head up. Rina was dressed in black sweats. With no makeup and her hair down, she could have passed for her twenties.

"What time is it?" he asked.

"Eleven-thirty."

"Did I say something about coming in at eleven?"

"You did."

"Sorry."

"S'right." Rina stood behind him and began to massage his neck. "You look tense. Maybe this will help."

"Oh man, that feels good. What's the catch?"

"I've got another file for you to look at."

"Now?"

"It'll take you five minutes."

"Nothing ever takes five minutes anymore."

Rina gave his back a slap. "Thank goodness for that. Now I'm going to make some tea while you clear the desk."

"Yes, ma'am. Do I get tea, too?"

"You do."

He smiled, watching her sway as she went. By the time she returned from the kitchen, the desktop was visible. She was carrying a tray with a pot of tea, two mugs, and a Pendaflex folder. She set the tray down and pulled up a chair.

"How about you pour and I explain what I've done?"

"Are you ever *not* organized, Rina?"

"It's part of my job description. I don't see you pouring."

Decker took up the steaming teapot dressed in a quilted cozy, held the lid, and poured two cups of steaming, brewed tea. "One lump or two? Or three if you count me."

She kissed his cheek. "You are far from a lump. And you know I take my tea plain." She pulled out three neat stacks of typewritten pages. "Maybe you'd like to take notes?"

Decker laughed and held up a pen. "I'm ready, Professor."

"Very funny. This sheet has the names of all the people in the file."

"Who translated the file for you?"

"Laurie Manheim's mother-in-law. But we didn't get through all of it. Do you know Laurie? She's Rabbi Manheim's wife."

"I know neither Laurie nor Rabbi Manheim."

"He teaches at the high school. Yonkie had him for tenth-grade Gemara. I got to know him very well because Yonkie wasn't doing well in his class."

"Well, he's doing well now. The child has hit his stride."

"Yeshiva life agrees with him."

"More like college, Rina. But we digress."

"Indeed." Rina smiled. "Anyway, as far as Laurie's mother-in-law could tell, I think this guy at the top of the list—Rudolf Kalmer—was the lead investigator in the case. But this other guy—Heinreich Messersmit—was also involved."

"Partners?"

"I don't know. It almost seems that both of them were working on it, but independently. Different handwriting."

"Who's this number three guy—Axel Berg?"

"He came in a little later. Berg had been working on two other unsolved homicides, and we think that Kalmer and Messersmit asked him for a consult on my grandmother's death. Berg later took over."

"What other homicides?"

"Here . . . wait." Rina flipped through the pages of her translated text. "It's hard to tell, Peter, because they, like you guys here, use abbreviations. Mrs. Manheim thought that this page"—Rina sifted through the faxed copies of the original documents—"here, this over here. They brought in Berg for a consult on the MAK of two women—Anna Gross and Marlena Durer." Rina read to herself. "Okay . . . this word—'*tötungsdelikt*'—that's premeditated homicide. '*Totschlag*' could be like regular homicide."

"Regular homicide?"

Rina was exasperated as she groped for words. "You know . . . like defensible homicide."

"Self-defense?"

"Yeah, yeah. It could mean killing in self-defense." She hit her head. "'*Tötungsdelikt*' implies lying in wait."

"Okay. So these two women, Durer and Gross, were premeditated murder victims."

"Yes, we think so."

"What does 'MAK' mean?"

"We're not sure. Mrs. Manheim thinks it *might* be an abbreviation for '*mordakten*,' which would be a homicide file. '*Mord*' is murder. '*Akte*' is any file. See? They have it in front of my grandmother's name—MAK Regina Gottlieb."

Decker regarded his wife's blue eyes. "Regina? So you're named after her?"

Rina nodded.

"Ah."

"I think that Kalmer and Messersmit wanted to know if my grandmother's murder was related to the murders of Durer and Gross."

"What? Like a serial killing?"

Rina shrugged. "Beats me. That's your domain."

Decker scanned through Rina's translated notes as he sipped tea. "You translated the autopsy report."

"Yes, we did. It was gruesome."

Again he regarded his wife. "Your grandfather allowed the body to be autopsied."

"He didn't have a choice because her death was unnatural."

Reading over the specifics: *a white Jewess, well developed, well nourished, 155 centimeters in height, with a weight of 45 kilograms.* "They specified her religion?"

"There's a shock." She rolled her eyes. "I'm surprised they didn't write her up as 'Jewess dog.'"

"But 1928 was pre-Hitler."

"In Germany, yes. He didn't come into official power until 1933. But Munich was a different story. In the late '20s, Hitler was a very strong force. Munich was where his family had originally settled from Austria. That's where he led the famous Beer Hall Putsch in the early '20s."

"Sorry. I slept through world history. What's a 'putsch'?"

"A 'putsch' is like a . . . It's like a coup . . . an insurrection. The Nazis tried to take over Munich. It was unsuccessful. They threw

Hitler into jail. That's where he wrote *Mein Kampf.* Any of this sound familiar?"

"I knew Hitler was from Austria. I also know he was a failed artist. You might have to give me a crash course in prewar Germany."

"Doesn't matter."

"No, Rina, it might be important. Maybe the murder was an act of anti-Semitism." Decker skimmed through the sheets for several minutes.

Rina let him read, then said, "Anything in there to verify your theory?"

"Nothing so far. I have to study this in detail." He backtracked several pages. "Yeah, definitely this guy Berg was working on several female homicide cases. And they considered your grandmother to be a possibility. Except in these two cases—Durer and Gross—they were strangled . . . and your grandmother was bludgeoned on the back of the head." He closed the file and connected with Rina's eyes. "Do you really want to find out about this?"

"I know it's weird, but yes."

"It's not weird, Rina. But you're getting into some very strong material."

"It can't be worse than the camps."

"You have a point, but things that are less than horrendous can still affect you deeply." Decker tapped the ends of the sheets to even them up. "I'm a little tired now. But I'll read it over carefully tomorrow night and let you know what I come up with."

"Thank you."

Decker thought a moment. "Don't under-play the historical context, Rina. I think the anti-Semitism is going to be very relevant somewhere down the line."

"I'm sure you're right." Rina sighed. "And that's really sad."

▼

It was after midnight by the time I crawled into bed, but Dad was a night owl. I phoned his business number and he picked up after two rings.

"Decker."

"It's me. Did I wake you?"

"No, you caught me just in time. Why are you calling my work line?"

"I thought if I called the private line, I'd scare you."

"You would have. Good thinking. Thank you. What's up?"

"A couple of things. First off, can I come over Friday night for dinner?"

"Of course. You don't even have to ask. The boys are home, you know."

"No, I didn't know. What's the occasion?"

"Summer vacation."

"It's only mid-May."

"Both got their finals over with very early. Lucky me."

I smiled. "Poor Dad. So beleaguered."

"Nah, I'm just joking. It'll be wonderful to see my entire family in one sitting. Any particular reason why you're coming?"

"Not really." An out-and-out lie. "But I was thinking about bringing a friend. But if it's too much work for Rina, we can make it another time."

A momentary pause. "Of course, you can bring a friend. Is it a he or a she?"

"It's nobody serious, Daddy. I just met him a few days ago."

"And already you're bringing him to your parents' house for *Shabbat* dinner?"

"My father's house. Mom doesn't know about him because it's not relevant. I'm *only* bringing him because he's traditional. His family lives in Israel and I thought it would be nice for him to have a real *Shabbat*."

"An Israeli?"

There was excitement in his voice. I could

picture the smile on his face. I wondered how wide it would stay once he saw Koby's complexion. I should have said more, if nothing else than to prepare him, but then I figured why should I? My parents had raised me without prejudice. Now was the time to test their theoretical tolerance.

"He's lived here for eight years. This is stupid, Dad. He's just a friend, *all right*?"

"I hear you, Princess. Sure. Bring him over."

"I have another reason for calling."

"Uh-oh, this sounds more serious."

"It has to do with business. I *might* have tracked down a good candidate for the baby's mother." I told him everything I had found out. "What do you think?"

"I think you're terrific."

He was still thinking about my "friend." I could hear it in his voice.

"I gave the information to Greg Van Horn, but he's going on vacation. He told me to check the lead and see if it goes anywhere. If it does, he told me to play it by ear."

"He's giving you opportunity to flex your muscles. He's being nice, Cin."

"I know that. I thanked him. He's giving me a chance and I don't want to mess it up.

You wouldn't happen to have a spare morning, would you?"

His laughter was immediate. "Now, what good would it do if I tagged along?"

"You could poke me in the ribs if I get off track?"

"Go get a pencil."

"Okay." I pulled out a pencil and a pad of paper from my nightstand. I always kept them there in case I thought of something inspirational. "I'm armed and ready."

"Listen up! You want to find out about this girl, but you have to go through the sister. What you don't want to do is alienate the sister. First you introduce yourself. You ask if you can come in and say that you won't take very long. That's important. If they think you're going to take a long time, it makes them even more nervous. You act casual. You tell them you've been doing a little searching that led to the Fordham home. The girl . . . What's her name?"

"Sarah."

"Sarah hasn't been in school for a while. Is everything okay? The sister may not answer the question. She may ask, 'What is this all about?' You say, you're coming to that. How is Sarah? Now the sister will probably say something about her health. 'Yes, she's fine,' or 'No, she hasn't been fine. What's going on?'"

"Wait, wait, wait." I was writing so fast that my hand was cramping. "Okay. Continue."

"When she asks about your business the second time, you get to the point. It should go something like this.

"You say: 'A couple of days ago, LAPD found an abandoned baby in a Dumpster. Maybe you read about it in the paper?'

"She says: 'Yes, that was terrible, but I still don't understand why you're here.'

"You say: 'Mrs. So and so—'"

"I don't think she's married," I interjected. "The name is Sanders, by the way."

"Okay. So say something like . . . 'Ms. Sanders, I think you might like to know that we're actively looking for the mother of this child. It's very important that we find her, not to *punish* her, but to *help* her.' By now, if she has any brain in her head, she knows what you're getting at."

I wrote furiously, then put the pencil down for a break. "Well, then, let's hope she has a brain." I laced my fingers together, flipped them around, and stretched out my arms until my knuckles cracked.

Dad continued. "Cindy, it's very important that you talk to Ms. Sanders and get her on your side before she brings in Sarah. She's probably used to treating Sarah like a child, so her first reaction might be to yell at her or confront her. . . . Don't let her do this. Calm Ms. Sanders down first and then interview Sarah. It's very important that no one feels threatened—the sister or the girl. When people are defensive, they don't talk.

"There's another possibility—that the sister will be completely protective and not let you get within ten feet of Sarah. If this happens, you calm the sister down and assure her that you have Sarah's medical and psychological interest at heart."

"I do. It's the truth."

"I know, honey. Look, Cindy, it's late. I've got to get some sleep. But I'll be reachable all morning. If you have a problem, don't hesitate to call me on my cell. But honestly, I don't think you'll need to, because I know you'll handle it perfectly. After what you've gone through, this should be easy."

"Thanks for the confidence. I love you, Daddy."

"I love you, too." A pause. "So how'd you meet this guy?"

"We're not having this conversation, Dad."

"Just use me and discard me."

"What else are parents for?"

12

It was a one-story Spanish house sitting in a block of Arts and Crafts bungalows, the stucco so white it sparkled like snowdrift. Nestled among large-leaf banana plants and cocoa palms, the home had the requisite red-tiled roof and the little gated courtyard. Full of curb appeal: That was real estate lingo for something that looked good on the outside. I had tried to dress soothingly—a sage blazer over cream-colored blouse and slacks—but I suspected that Ms. Sanders wouldn't be focusing on my sartorial splendor.

It was just past eight in the morning, early enough to catch her before she went to work, and I chose not to phone beforehand because I didn't want to scare anyone off. I rang the bell. The peephole door opened.

"Yes?"

"Good morning. I'm Officer Cynthia Decker. I'm looking for Louise Sanders."

"Who are you?"

"Officer Cynthia Decker of Los Angeles Police—Hollywood."

She opened the door a fraction of an inch. The chain was still attached. "Can I see some ID, please?"

Billfold already in hand, I slipped it through the crack. She took it and, after a few moments, passed it back. The door opened all the way.

She was much older than I expected—in her late forties or early fifties. I was led to believe that Sarah was in her twenties. That meant there was quite an age gap between them. Louise had short, blunt-cut gray hair that framed an oval face and gray-green eyes. Her features were regular, and once, she had been pretty. Now, she was handsome in her black skirt suit and crisp white blouse.

"Yes?"

"May I come in for a few minutes?"

"What's this all about?"

"I'll be happy to explain everything, but it's better if we talk inside."

Reluctantly, she allowed me to cross the threshold. The living room was small but restored beautifully—dark beamed ceilings, Saltillo tiled floor, textured beige stucco walls, and lots of molding and niches. There was a brown leather couch with matching chairs; the accent tables were made of heavy dark wood. An upright piano stood in the corner; a sheet of music rested on the stand. I asked her who played.

"My sister. What's going on?"

"Thank you for your patience. Can I sit down?"

"Yes, of course."

I settled into one of the leather chairs. She sat on the couch. "A case I'm working on led me to your sister's school—the Fordham Communal Center. . . ."

"Yes, yes. What about it?"

"I understand Sarah hasn't been feeling well. How's she doing?"

The woman was taken aback. "That's why you're here?"

"Is Sarah all right?"

"As a matter of fact, she's not well. She

has some health issues. I was thinking of taking her to the doctor's this morning."

"I think that might be a good idea."

"Why?" She became startled. "What's wrong with her?"

"I honestly don't know if anything's wrong with her. Let me tell you why I'm here and then you decide. Several days ago, LAPD found a newborn infant in a Dumpster behind a nearby restaurant. Perhaps you read about it in the paper?"

"I saw it on the news."

"I pulled her out. It was pretty scary, but I'm happy to report that the baby's doing well and is in very good health."

"That's nice." A glance at the watch. "Can we get to the point?"

"I was just wondering if . . . well, maybe Sarah's lost a little weight recently?"

The woman's eyes widened as shock swept across her face. "What!" She stood up and screamed, "Sarah! Get here—"

"Wait, wait, wait!" I gently touched her arm. "Before we get her involved, how about if we talk about this calmly."

She broke away and started pacing. "I don't believe this! It's one thing after another! All I want is a little peace and quiet, and then . . ." She plopped back down on the sofa and slapped her hands over her face. Her voice cracked as she spoke. "I'm just so . . . *tired!*"

"It may be nothing."

"It *isn't* nothing. It's *never* nothing! It's always something! She's been bleeding hard. I just thought it was a rough period. I didn't even *think* about pregnancy." Again she started to pace. "Is she in trouble with the law?"

"Obviously, there are circumstances here."

"It's going to be hell! I just know it! I'm going to need a lawyer. I'm going to have to make a court appearance! And I'm going to look like a total idiot! How could I have not known!"

"She's a heavy girl. It's completely understandable. The main thing is to get her medical attention. That's the reason I'm here. To help her, not to hurt her."

She stopped racing about, covered her mouth with her hand, then let it drop to her side. "Of course. You're being very understanding."

"Both of you will be okay."

She looked at my face. "The baby's okay?"

"She's absolutely adorable."

A smile spread over her distraught face. "Thank God!"

"Ms. Sanders . . . did you know that Sarah—"

"No idea! She never mentioned any boy . . . any special boy. She mentioned lots of boys. She was *supposed* to be on the pill."

"Birth control isn't perfect."

"Especially if she didn't take it. It wouldn't be the first time. She has a bad gag reflex. It's hard for her to swallow little things like pills. And liquid medicine makes her gag because it tastes so awful. I should have sterilized—" She cut herself off and looked away.

"I know that lots of the girls in Fordham are sterilized. I am not judging you, ma'am. It is extremely arrogant for anyone to judge you."

"Thank you." She wiped tears from her face. "Please call me Louise."

"All right. How about we both sit down, Louise?"

A nod and we reclaimed our respective places.

I said, "So you don't know if Sarah was having sex or not."

"Obviously, she was having sex!"

I tried to put this as delicately as I could. "Consensual sex, I mean."

"Oh my God!" She leaped to her feet. "She was *raped?*"

"Louise, let's not assume anything. It was just a question. That's why I need to talk to her. That's why she needs medical attention."

She sighed and tried to calm herself. "Do you want to talk to her now?"

"Yes, but not for too long." As long as she was standing, I figured I should get to my feet. "Our first concern is getting her to a hospital. I'll take you there, if you want."

"You are being so *nice,* Officer Decker." Again the tears started. "That's all right. I have a car. What are they going to do to her?"

"I imagine that after checking her out, they'll take a blood test and verify that she's the baby's mother. You know, first things first." I hesitated. "Louise, the baby's bi-racial."

She blinked several times. "She's *black?*"

"Part black."

Silence.

"Thank you for telling me." She choked on her words. "I'll go get her. Please be gentle. Despite how it may appear, I love her very much."

"Louise, I don't doubt it for a second."

She clasped her hands together. "You know, it doesn't matter to me what the baby is as long as she's healthy."

"She's healthy."

"That's all that counts." A moment's hesitation. "I'll go get Sarah."

▼

By the way the young girl carried herself, it appeared as if her chin were attached to her chest. Though her eyes were squeezed shut as tightly as humanly possible, tears managed to leak through. Limp strands of blond hair covered her cheeks. Her hands were white-knuckled, balled up into fists. Her brown smock pulled against her generous breasts. Louise placed a hand on her shoulder.

"It's going to be all right, Sarah. You just have to talk to the nice police officer. And you have to be honest."

No response from Sarah. I said, "Does your tummy hurt, honey?"

A slight nod of the head.

"We're going to take you to a doctor to fix that, okay?"

Silence.

"Do you know why your tummy hurts?" I pressed on.

She didn't answer, but I noticed that she had turned her knees inward. Her pink cheeks had become damp with tears. I said, "The baby is fine, Sarah. It's a beautiful, healthy girl. And maybe one day, your sister, Louise, will take you to see her."

She raised her head and glanced at me. Then she dropped her chin to her chest.

Louise broke in. "Sarah, who *did* this to you?"

I squeezed Louise's arm. She exhaled with a *whoosh,* shook me off, and stomped off to the other side of the room. Though I really wanted to ask Sarah about her sexual experience, I knew my limitations. This little girl required a specialist. As a police officer, I was concerned with only one thing: if the sex was forced or not. But right now, there were more pressing issues at stake—her health, confirmation that she was the mother, legal ramifications of her act of child endangerment. I decided to forgo the questioning until I had notified the proper channels.

And until I talked to Dad.

"I think we should take her to the hospital now. I'll call up my sergeant and have someone meet us down there. We should probably get in touch with someone from Mental Health. Does she have a psychologist?"

"She has every single specialist in the world. She's been well taken care of."

"I don't doubt that."

"Will I need a lawyer?" Louise bit hard on a thumbnail.

"If you have one, it would be a good idea to call him up."

Another heavy sigh.

I said, "She'll be okay."

"I know, I know. She's always okay. She's al-ways o-kay!"

"You'll be okay, too, Louise."

"Me?" Louise's laugh was hard and bitter. "Sister, my welfare is another story altogether!"

13

There were pats on the back from my colleagues and smiles from the brass. There was a time when my accomplishments would have been viewed with suspicion. But last year, I had played the game, drinking with the guys and girls after hours and attending more backyard barbecues than I'd care to recount. I kept my mouth shut, bowled in the Hollywood Women's League, and did my job. The "incident"—as I refer to it to my therapist—had kicked a lot of life out of me. Bad for the creative spirit, but great for blending in with the masses.

Sarah was out of my hands now, kicked upstairs to the gold shields and the professionals who made their living by helping people talk. I was left with the satisfaction of a job well done, and a curiosity about who had fathered this baby girl. I knew more than Russ MacGregor—the detective who had taken over for Greg—because I had inside information from Koby. If Russ was decent enough, I'd share the facts.

I was off all Friday and had the day to relax. I Googled Yaakov Kutiel, and thankfully he came out honest. Koby's public claim to fame was being part of the hospital's outreach program for unwed mothers and fatherless children who lived in Central L.A. For this evening's *Shabbat* dinner, I kept my look simple: a Kelly green sweater over a black midiskirt and knee-high black boots. Around my neck was a gold chain; my earlobes sported a set of round pearls. I topped off the outfit with a gray pashmina draped over my shoulders.

Koby lived in the hills of Silver Lake, his street on an incline of around thirty degrees. The address corresponded with a tiny, square stucco box that peeked out from the boughs of eucalyptus gone wild. I parked in the driveway behind a ten-year-old Toyota compact, making sure the emergency brake was on. I made the climb up to the front door and knocked, noticing the large ceramic mezuzah attached to the door frame. I'm not sure what I expected when I came in, but I didn't expect what I saw.

There was pride inside—a mélange of Art Deco and African decor. Highly polished, rich rosewood tables were mixed with a zebra-print plush sofa and leopard-print club chair, both pieces embellished with primary-colored throw pillows. Multicolored textiles with geometric shapes and primitive designs hung on the walls; a bright, bold carpet covered the hardwood floor. Actually, there were several carpets, because as I looked more carefully, I noticed that they were overlapping. The room was teeny—I could almost span the walls with outstretched arms—so it was amazing how much stuff he had crammed in there. More amazing was how well it was put together.

"Wow!" I told him.

He was all smiles. "You like it?"

"Yeah . . . yeah, I do."

"Had to think about it?"

"Not at all. It was just . . ." I shook my head. "Most single guys don't bother."

"I like color."

"I'll say. But it works. Do you rent?"

He pointed to his chest. "All mine. I have the mortgage to prove it."

"I'm impressed!" I really was. Home ownership was out of my reach. Despite my supposed austerity, I just couldn't seem to save very much. That's what happens when one has parents as backups.

"It didn't look like this when I bought it," he explained. "But the price reflected the condition."

"You fixed it up yourself?"

"Of course. After the purchase, I was completely broke. I had no choice."

"You did a wonderful job."

"As long as you don't look under all the covering. Why do you think I hang so much cloth all over?" He checked his watch. "*Shabbat* is in an hour. We should go, no?"

"Yeah, we've got a ways to travel."

He picked up a bouquet of flowers and a bottle of wine. "These are for your stepmother." He gave me a paper bag. "This is for you for extended . . . extending the invitation."

It was a hand-painted doll from the Ethiopian gift shop. I smiled and thanked him. He told me I looked nice and I returned the compliment. He was dressed conservatively—dark green suit, white shirt, red-and-green paisley tie—but his yarmulke was more like a rimless cap that burst with colors.

The first half of the ride was taken up by my success story with Sarah. The next topic was the baby and how well she was doing. After we had exhausted work, things got real quiet. I turned on the radio to provide audio filler.

Koby got the ball rolling. "Did your father ask about me?"

"Yes, of course. He's a father."

"What did you tell him?"

"I told him that I had just met you a couple of days ago, so I didn't know much about you."

"That was a good answer."

"I thought so. Of course, it didn't stop him from prodding me about you."

He waited for me to continue.

"I did tell him that you were somewhat observant and your family lives in Israel. That you'd appreciate a traditional *Shabbat*."

"That's true." He looked out the window. "Did you tell him anything else?"

"Not really. I figured you could talk about yourself better than I could."

He was quiet.

"What?" I said. "That's not true?"

"Yes, that is very true. But I think you left something out."

"What difference does it make?"

"None to me. But to your father, I cannot say."

"If he's that way, then he's not the man I think he is."

"It's just better to prepare him, I think."

"Prepare for *what,* Koby? Being black is not a defect. Why should I have to prep my father?"

"To make him feel more comfortable when he meets me."

"If I say you're my friend, he should automatically feel comfortable."

"To make *me* feel more comfortable, maybe?" He fingered the flowers. "I'm not fond of surprises."

I glanced at him. He shrugged. I felt my stomach drop. "Okay. So maybe that wasn't so smart. Sorry."

"It's all right, Cindy. No problem."

"You've had bad experiences before?"

"Not really," he said. "I never meet parents . . . never any reason. Last time was maybe fifteen years ago when I take Aliza

Goldberg to the movies. Her father was a colonel in *Zahal*." He laughed. "Old feelings. So maybe I overreact."

We rode for several minutes, one-way chatter coming from the radio.

"He's a great guy, Koby. I'm sure it'll be fine."

"I'm sure you're right."

But neither of us was sure of anything.

▼

Dad had a very powerful poker face; it was a necessary component of being a great detective. But knowing him well, I detected the minuscule rise of an eyebrow. Still, he masked it with aplomb, his smile never wavering. He shook Koby's hand while inviting us inside. My father was slightly taller than my date, but must have outweighed him by a good fifty pounds. Daddy looked handsome in a dark blue suit.

I spoke quickly, doing the introductions. Everyone was nice and polite. It was a stiff moment, but not unbearable. Koby had good social skills—way better than mine.

"*Shabbat Shalom.* Thank you for having me." He presented Dad with the wine bottle and held the flowers aloft. "This is for your wife."

"I'll go get her. That way you can give them to her. Would either of you like something to drink?"

"I'm fine," I answered. "Koby?"

"No, I'm fine."

"Great." An odd pause. "I'll get Rina."

Dad was about to escape behind the kitchen door, but Rina came out before he could go in. She was wiping her hands on her apron, her hair tucked into a beret. Again I made introductions. Her smile was wide and welcoming.

"Ah, Koby. Yaakov. *Yesh lee Yaakov gam ken. Ma nishma?*"

"*Beseder gamur.*"

"That good, huh? You're doing better than I am, but I'm always frazzled before *Shabbat.*"

"That is the same for women worldwide." Koby extended the flowers to her. "Thank you for your hospitality."

"You're welcome." She took the bouquet. "I hope you're hungry."

"I'm from Ethiopia. I'm always hungry."

Rina smiled. "When did you emigrate to Israel?"

"It was 1983."

"Where did they settle you? Near Kiryat Arba?"

"Exactly."

"I knew that because I used to live in Kiryat Arba. I remember when you all came over. The government recruited us for help. I ran an *ulpan* for the Ethiopians that summer."

"You're kidding!"

"No, I'm not. For all I know, you could have been one of my students."

"I don't think so. I would remember."

"You would have definitely remembered. I was out to here." Rina made a pregnant stomach by extending her hands forward. "They gave me the four- to eight-year-olds."

"I was twelve. Do you remember names?"

"I've got to think." She furrowed her brow. "I remember a little boy named Elias Tespay."

"I know the Tespays."

"And someone named Welda."

"Yoseph Welda?"

"No, it wasn't Yoseph . . . Eliahu maybe."

"Probably one of his younger brothers or a cousin. There were lots of Weldas. I think about sixty of them came."

"Yeah, you guys were crammed into the

housing like sardines. Where did you finally settle?"

"Petach Tikvah. My father remarried, so the housing didn't improve much. There were ten of us in a three-room apartment. But at least it was our own apartment."

"That's not exclusive to Ethiopians, you know. Everybody's cramped in Israel. You learn to be a good team player."

"Or you leave," Koby stated.

"Gotcha." Rina held up the flowers. "I should put these in water and check on dinner. I'm actually planning to go to shul." She looked at Koby. "Did you want to go to shul? It's Ashkenaz *davening.*"

"No problem. The *beit knesset* I go to—when I go—is Ashkenaz."

"Which one is that?"

"It is in Los Feliz, near my house. It is Conservative service, but the rabbi has Orthodox background, I think. He's Hungarian."

"I'm Hungarian," Rina said. "What's his name?"

"Robert Farkas."

Rina shrugged ignorance. "Lots of Hungarians in this city." Another shrug. "I should check on dinner."

"Anything I can help you with, Rina?" I piped in.

"Yes, you can help your sister get dressed. The child is a turtle." Rina looked at my father. "Are you ready?"

"Yes, I am. Need help in the kitchen?"

"If you're offering, I won't say no." She smiled at Koby, then at me. "See you in a minute." She took Dad's hand. It might have been my imagination, but it looked as though she was trying to calm him down.

▼

"Don't say a word," Rina whispered.

"I'm not saying anything!" Decker whispered back. "And you don't have to tell me how to behave. I am not a racist!"

"I know that."

"Well, I don't think you *do* know that. Otherwise you wouldn't look so damned worried."

"I'm not worried."

"Yeah, you are." He clutched the wine as he spoke. "I'm going to have a wonderful meal with my family, all right? So stop giving me those looks! And don't tell me you wouldn't have had some feelings if it had been Sammy or Jacob bringing home an Ethiopian girl."

"As long as she was Jewish, I wouldn't care."

"Well, aren't you the liberal one!"

"Peter, why don't you make yourself useful?" She handed him the bouquet of flowers. "Put these in a vase and set them on the *Shabbat* table. Then open the wine before you break the bottle." She stirred a pot of lentil soup. "We'll let it breathe while we're in shul."

Decker regarded his wife, then looked at the objects in his hands. He set them on the kitchen counter, realizing that his jaw was clenched. He took a deep breath in, then let it out. Reaching his long arms to the top cabinet, he opened the door and took down a cut-crystal vase. He placed it under the sink and began to fill it with water.

"Flowers . . . wine . . . the man has manners." He growled out, "More than . . ."

He left it at that. Rina filled in the blank. "More than Cindy?"

"He's probably too good for her."

"She's a good girl, Peter. She's gone through hell—"

"I know that, Rina. Stop giving me perspective, okay? I'm not angry. I just don't know why she didn't . . . Forget it!"

Rina checked the meat thermometer in the lamb roast, then turned down the temperature. She opened the refrigerator and took out green beans. "I'll put these on the hot tray. That way they won't overcook. Nothing worse than limp green beans."

"It smells good," Decker said quietly.

"What does?"

"Everything." He turned off the water and planted a kiss on his wife's forehead. "Thank you for making this delicious meal. I'm snapping at you. I apologize."

"I know you're not a racist, Peter. And I'm not trying to one-up you, okay? It would have been nice if she had leveled with you. Just to prepare you."

"*Exactly!*" Decker plunked the flowers into the vase. "That's *exactly* what I meant!" Rummaging through the drawers, he found a corkscrew. "She tells me he's a traditional Jew from Israel; I get a certain picture in my mind, that's all." He plunged the bit into the cork. "I'm too involved, that's the problem. It's her life."

"He seems lovely," Rina said.

"How can you tell that in thirty seconds?"

"He's got beautiful eyes. They're windows to the soul. I can just tell."

"Nonsense, you're being irrationally optimistic."

"Peter, he's Jewish, around her age, and gainfully employed."

Decker stopped a moment, then shrugged. "True." He went to work on the cork. "Well, if I say I'm not prejudiced, I guess I shouldn't prejudge."

A moment later, Cindy came in. Decker took in her face, then popped open the cork. He smelled the wine. "Not bad. It'll be better after it breathes a little."

"You like Cabernet," Cindy said.

"Yes, I do." Decker smiled but didn't continue the conversation. Rina tried out a nervous smile. She was so tired of playing referee, but that seemed to be her lot in life. "Everything okay?" she asked her stepdaughter.

"Just fine. Hannah's dressed and ready to go."

"Thank you."

"No problem." Cindy was trying to make eye contact with her father, but he had busied himself with flower arranging. "Koby needs candles."

"Of course," Rina said. "Do you want to light, Cindy?"

"Yes, thanks."

Rina went into the pantry and brought out four tea lights. Decker was looking at his daughter with deadpan eyes.

Cindy said, "I found the baby's mother, you know."

"Congratulations," Decker said. "I should have told you that right away."

No one spoke for a few moments.

"I'd like to talk to you about it," Cindy said. "I have some concerns."

Curiosity flickered in Decker's eyes, but he kept his equilibrium. "Sure. Go ahead."

"I don't think this is the right time. It may take more than a few minutes."

"Okay. Why don't you give me a call to-morrow night?"

Cindy knew her father was giving her the brush-off. But she proceeded as if she didn't know better. "Actually, if you have time, I'd like to meet with you on Sunday. Could you come out to my place?" She tried a sheepish smile. "I'll even cook you breakfast."

Decker remained expressionless. "I told Hannah I'd take her to the movies."

Rina said, "There's a two o'clock show. You could probably make it back in time."

Decker raised a disapproving eyebrow at his wife. But she was right. If he didn't back off, he'd deserve what he'd get. "It's important to you, Cynthia?"

"Kind of, yeah. I'd really appreciate your help."

He gave a forced smile. "Sure, honey. Around nine, then?"

"That would be perfect."

"Here you go." Rina handed her the tea lights. Cindy thanked her and they all left it at that.

14

When I came back into the living room, Hannah was seated next to Koby, the two of them turning the pages of an oversize art book entitled *Solomon's People.* The tome was almost as big as she was. She looked splendid in a lime green dress and matching jacket that magnificently offset her red hair. She was learning the tricks of being a carrottop at a very early age. "What's that?"

Koby said, "A book of Ethiopian Jews. I know several of the people."

"Who?" Hannah asked.

"This lady here," Koby said. "She was a very good friend of my older brother Yaphet. She married a rabbi and lives somewhere in the Negev."

"She's beautiful."

"Oh yes, very, very beautiful. I had a terrible crush on her. Alas, my affections were not returned."

"Then she's stupid," Hannah said.

"No, but I thank you for the support. It was more like she was seventeen and I was thirteen, though I was as tall as she. For an Ethiopian, I am very tall."

Hannah stared at him. "I thought all Africans were tall."

"Hannah!" I scolded.

"It's fine." Koby smiled. "No, not all Africans are tall, especially North Africans. Most Ethiopians are Coptic Christians . . . more like Egyptians than anything else. I just happen to be tall because my parents are tall." He looked up at me. "Would you like a hand with the candles?"

I had forgotten I was holding them. "I'll just set them next to Rina's candles. That's where I usually light."

Koby stood up. "I think you'd better put on your shoes, Hannah."

"Should I wear my boots or my high heels?" she asked me.

"What's more comfortable to walk in?" I said.

"The same." She shrugged and turned to Koby. "What do you think?"

"With that dress and jacket, heels, definitely."

"I'll be right back!" She rushed off to her room.

"She likes you," I told him. "You have a way with kids."

"I work with kids."

I hit my forehead. "Uh, yeah . . . duh!"

Koby caught my eye. "How'd it go in there?"

I shrugged, trying to act indifferent. "He's still talking to me."

"A good sign. I like your stepmother. She seems . . . genuine."

"She is genuine." Just then my two stepbrothers appeared. Sammy had reached the benchmark age of twenty. Jacob had attained the majority of eighteen. They were tall, good-looking guys, both of them in suits with their hair still wet from recent showering. They came out chattering about something, and when they saw me, they stopped talking. First they looked at me, then at each other; then their eyes went to the floor and back up again.

Sammy was trying to stifle a grin. He

extended his hand to Koby. *"Shabbat Shalom."*

Koby took it, then shook hands with Jacob. *"Shabbat Shalom."*

Sammy said, "My father said you were Israeli."

"Yes, but before I was Israeli, I was Ethiopian."

"I see that," Sammy answered. "Jewish Ethiopian."

"Yes, Jewish Ethiopian." A pause. Koby said, "If you have doubts, you can check my *millah.*"

The boys burst into laughter and so did Koby. I didn't get the joke, but I smiled anyway.

Sammy said, "I think I speak for my brother when I say, we'll pass. Since Cindy's not bothering to introduce us, I'm Sammy. He's Jacob."

"You didn't give me a chance," I told him. "This is Koby."

"Also a Yaakov," Jake said. "Where did you live in Israel?"

"My family still lives in Petach Tikvah."

"That's near Kfar Saba, right?"

"Yes, it's the next town over."

"I have a ton of friends from yeshiva who live there and in Ranana."

"Yes, both those places are very American."

Sammy said, "You want something to drink before we go to shul?"

"No, I'm fine." He checked his watch. "It's time to light the *nerot.* I need a match, please."

"In the breakfront," I said.

Koby and I lit our respective candles, both of us saying the blessing, although he understood the words that I mouthed. When we were done, we wished each other *Shabbat Shalom.* Rina lit candles for her household. Within a few minutes, we were on our way to synagogue.

One good thing about my stepbrother Sammy. No one could talk as much as he could. When we reached the tiny storefront that acted as the neighborhood Orthodox temple, I knew we wouldn't be sitting together. Right before we parted ways—men on one side of the wall, women on the other—I asked him what the word *"millah"* meant. Straight-faced, he told me it meant circumcision.

I waited until I was on my side of the fence, then I broke out into laughter.

▼

Orthodox Judaism was a religion of routine, and at the dinner table, the first order of business was always welcoming the metaphorical Sabbath Bride in a song called *"Shalom Aleichem."* This ode was followed by a tribute to the real woman of the house—a poem from Proverbs called *"Eshet Chayil,"* or "Woman of Valor." I've read the English a couple of times, and the gist of it centered around a woman slaving away without complaint to support her husband and family, words that seemed quaint and a bit shallow in the postmodern feminist world. I've had many a Sabbath dinner with my father's family and when it came to this part, Dad, who hadn't been blessed with a natural singing voice, always mumbled his way through the stanzas.

Tonight was a different story, however. My father sang, of course. But this time, the Loo was joined by my stepbrothers, who were fluent with the Hebrew text and sang with grace and meaning, their voices ringing clear as they smiled at Rina. But it was Koby who gave me pause, his voice deep and crystal, singing along note perfect with my stepbrothers in crisp, beautiful Hebrew. Here was a black man from Africa sitting with my white family from Los Angeles, people he had known less than two hours, and he was more integrated than I was. It brought it all home, that a traditional Sabbath cut through cultural lines. When the chorus came and the men broke into spontaneous harmony, an involuntary lump formed in my throat.

Within a short period of time, everyone at the Friday-night table appeared relaxed, eating great food and swapping stories of the week. My father's family was a noisy bunch and with my stepbrothers' swiftness of speech and Hannah's relentless interruptions, it was sometimes hard to keep up with the conversation. If anything, I was the least comfortable person there. Though I was family, there were times when I was the odd person out with all the Hebrew, Israeli, and religious references flying around. Koby, however, appeared totally at ease. He was a good storyteller because his life had given him lots of raw material to work with.

"I was twelve when I had my first actual outing in civilization," he said. "We had been in Israel, oh, maybe six months. We had gone through *ulpan,* and we spoke Hebrew in school, of course. But the refugee camp was exclusively Ethiopian and we spoke Amharic to the elders, who were not as fast as the kids in learning Hebrew."

"I can relate to that." Dad had just polished off his second glass of wine. Nothing like alcohol to take the edge off. Koby refilled his glass, then his own.

"It's pretty good, no?"

"Very good," my father agreed. "You're a red-wine drinker?"

"Primarily, yes."

"So what was your first outing?" Sammy asked.

Koby laughed. "My friend Reuven and I were given over to two eighteen-year-old yeshiva boys from Itri or Hakotel, someplace in Jerusalem. It was supposed to be a morning of learning *Chumash* and an afternoon of fun and adventure. The morning was a bust. Their Hebrew was poorer than ours was. Perhaps it was the Long Island accent. We kept asking, *'Mah atem omrim?'* 'What are you saying?' We couldn't understand a word! Besides, someone had set up a hoop in our refugee camp and all we want to do was shoot baskets. Finally, after lunch, they take us to the bus stop for our first day in the city. Reuven and I have never been on a real bus before."

"I can see where this is leading," Rina said.

"Up and down the aisle, people were screaming at us. We didn't care. Then the boys take us to *Kanyonit*." He turned to me. "A minimall. Only it's brand new and there are no shops inside. Just this one little store that sells *goofiot*—T-shirts. That's it. All this empty space and nothing but T-shirts. The rest of the bottom floor of the mall was empty except for the escalators . . . which we had never seen before. To us, it was Disneyland. Up the down, and down the up, and over and over and over. Drove those poor boys crazy because, let me tell you, we were fast little bugs. I ran competitive track in Maccabee competition."

"That's really cool," Jacob said.

"How'd you do?" Sammy asked.

"Good enough for my coach to say, think about the Olympics for Israel. But that would have meant devoting hours to running. I lacked the drive to work that hard.

Without drive, forget it. Still, I could move, as the yeshiva boys found out."

"Those poor white boys never had a chance," Sammy remarked.

"Such is life." Koby turned to Rina. "The lamb is delicious."

"Then you'll have more," Rina said.

"Please." Koby took another small piece, then started laughing. "Okay. So after the escalator rides, they get the bright idea to take us bowling. That is upstairs—a bowling alley and a snack bar. We're running across the lanes. The manager screams at the boys in Hebrew, the boys scream at us in English, which, of course, we don't understand. And the few Israelis there . . . they're smoking away, shaking their heads in very much disapproval, saying *'Ayzeh chayot'*—'those animals.' The boys finally hold us by our shirts—literally. Then we start begging them to buy us something to eat."

He turned to me.

"The snack bar has no *teudat kashrut*—a certificate that states a place as kosher—and these two religious boys do not want to buy us anything from an uncertified place. We beg and beg and beg. They cave in and buy us a Coke. We beg some more. They cave in and buy us potato chips in a bag with a kosher symbol. Then I see this boy blowing up the bag and punching it until it makes a pop."

Sammy started laughing. "I used to do that."

"I know you did," Rina said.

Koby said, "It is no problem if the bag is empty. Only I don't know this. I do it with the potato chips still inside."

Dad smiled. "So what happened after they arrested you?"

"The boys get us out in time, otherwise I'm sure I have a record. It was an unmitigated disaster. But I tell you this. Those boys . . . they had patience. They came back the next week and tried again . . . and again. They make a deal with us. If we learn our *Chumash,* they'd play basketball with us in the afternoon."

"Were they any good at basketball?" Sammy asked. "It's a yeshiva sport, you know."

"Yes, I know. They teach us the game, Sammy. What do we know about organized sports in Ethiopia? I come from a small village near Lake Tana, not Addis Ababa."

"Do you still play?" Sammy said.

"Basketball? I used to play all the time. Point guard, of course. Speed was never my problem. And I can shoot, hit layups in a game of HORSE and do swish shots from the perimeter. But I have problems when I play with people." He laughed. "They get in my way."

"A perfect metaphor for my life," Dad said wryly.

Rina thumped his shoulder.

Koby said, "Especially here in L.A., they play rough. They block you and push, and slam and hit and shove. And then you push and shove and slam and hit. It gets very physical. In three months, I saw one guy twist an ankle, another break a wrist falling on it the wrong way, a third fall on his face and crack his two front teeth. The final thing was a very good friend of mine was guarding against a layup. The guy with the ball did a one-eighty spin with a raised elbow and caught my friend's nose, snapping the septum. I had just turned thirty; I say, that's it. God gave me one body. I keep it in shape by running four times a week, but no more weekend basketball."

"One day, I'd like to play a game of one-on-one with you," Sammy said.

"Sure, that I don't mind. It is safe."

"Now Dad here . . . he'd have to play center, don't you think?" Sammy said.

"That's because I'm too heavy and slow to move across the court." Dad looked around the table, then at Rina. "Where's Hannah?"

"She was reading on the couch. Maybe she fell asleep."

It could have been my imagination but Dad looked envious. What he did was smile at Rina. "The meal was superb."

"Thank you."

Decker sipped wine. "Notice she doesn't offer me another helping."

"Take whatever you want, dear."

"Actually, I'm full . . . more like stuffed."

"Me too," Jacob concurred.

"You hardly ate," Rina said.

"Not true. I'm just leaving room for dessert."

Dad said, "I need to take a walk."

"I'll come with you," Jacob said. "God forbid you should have any solitude."

My father smiled at my stepbrother with loving eyes, an expression he had yet to grace me with this evening. "I would love for you to come with me."

"Wanna come, Shmuli?" Jacob asked.

"I'll help Eema clear."

"I'll help her clear, Sammy," I told him. "Go ahead."

"Then let's make this a true male-chauvinist outing," Sammy announced. "Koby, you can come with us."

He shook his head. "I thank you, but I shall pass."

"Go," I told him.

"No, no," he insisted. "I'm fine."

For the first time, I noticed the fatigue in his eyes. "Did you work a double shift again last night?"

"I'm fine, Cindy."

"You're falling off your feet."

He shrugged. "Could be the wine. Perhaps we should say *Birkat Hamazon.*"

"Absolutely." Rina passed out prayer booklets for Grace after Meals.

My dad gave Koby the honors of leading the family in the singing of the prayers, not only because he was a guest but also because he was a Kohen. Five minutes later, Rina stood to gather up the dishes.

"I'll help you clear," I told her.

"No way," Rina said. "I'll make you a care package and then you both go home."

"Oh please, don't bother," I said. "I've eaten enough for a week."

Koby echoed my sentiments. He shook Rina's hand. "Thank you so much, Mrs. Decker. This was a real treat for me."

"Anytime . . . with or without her," Rina answered.

"She means it," I told him.

"You're very gracious." Koby turned to my father. "It is a pleasure meeting you, sir."

"Same." Dad gripped his hand and shook it with spirit. Then he patted Koby on the back, walking him to the door with his arm looped over his shoulder. I think at final count, Dad had polished off half the bottle of wine. "Drive carefully."

"She's driving," Koby told him.

My father looked at me and rolled his eyes. "All the more reason for the caveat."

15

I left Decker's house, knowing that the Loo was peeved, but what could I do? He had played his part, had been gracious after the initial stiffness, even downright funny. I was thankful that however miffed he was with me, he had had the decency to keep it under wraps.

It was late by the time I pulled into Koby's driveway. He offered a nightcap, but I declined, feeling drained and not very sexy. Plus, I still had some miles to travel before I got home. I think Koby was relieved not to play host, having worked so much overtime. We settled on a dinner date for Sunday.

I slept in Saturday morning, then met Mom for lunch. My luck was holding because she was in a great mood, and the hours passed as smoothly as oiled gliders. When I got home, I took a long bike ride west down Venice Boulevard, hitting the ocean and back in a little over an hour. After showering off the sweat and salt, I checked my phone messages and my e-mail. Koby had my phone number but hadn't called. Instead he had e-mailed me, telling me how much he had enjoyed last night. I answered him back, then turned off the computer, along with the rest of the outside world.

Dinner was a tuna fish sandwich and a good book in bed. I turned in at midnight, determined to sleep eight hours without nightmares. Partial success. But even after being jolted awake with the usual shakes and a rapid heartbeat, I was able to calm down enough to fall back asleep.

I got up early on Sunday to prepare something warm and fuzzy for Dad, deciding on a breakfast of French toast and vegetarian breakfast links, with fresh orange juice and Ethiopian coffee. Even if no one ate anything, at the very least my place would smell good. Unlike Koby's house, my interior decor was generic—basic furniture and a serviceable kitchen. The best part of my tiny apartment was the fireplace mantel that had once been filled with glass figurines and family photos representing better times in my life. Now it lay bare. I had meant to fix it up with homey touches, but after a maniac had trashed and violated my personal space, the energy was lacking. I needed an infusion of something.

Dad was on time, as usual, casual yet handsome in a black leather bomber jacket, a dark green polo shirt, and black jeans. He greeted me with a kiss on the cheek and a controlled smile.

"What's cookin', good-lookin'?" I said to him.

"Something smells good." He unzipped his jacket and took it off.

"I'll take that." I opened the guest closet and hung it up. It was incredibly heavy and made the wire hanger sag. "Thanks again for Friday."

"Our pleasure."

I hesitated a fraction just to make sure he had nothing else to add. He didn't. "I hope you're hungry."

"I am now."

"Then . . . let's eat." I had set my small dinette table for two, complete with cloth napkins. I poured him some coffee and orange juice as he speared a piece of French toast onto his plate.

"I should wash," he told me.

"Lucky for you, I have running water."

He smiled and washed his hands, saying the ritual prayers before he bit into his breakfast. I drowned my French toast in maple syrup and dug in. "Not bad, if I say so myself."

"Delicious." Dad cut the bread into neat little bites. "So . . . you found the baby's mother. I'm very proud of you."

"Thank you."

"Your interviews must have gone well."

"You gave me some good advice."

"Still, you must have executed it with aplomb."

"I do listen when you talk to me."

He stopped eating for a fraction of a second. "I know that."

"You're irritated at me."

"Not at all."

"Yes at all. Would you like to say what's on your mind?"

"No, I'd like to enjoy this delicious French toast and help you with whatever you need help with."

"I can't concentrate if you're mad."

"That's fine, because I'm not mad."

"Did you like him?"

"Very much."

"But . . ."

The Loo put down his fork and knife, then looked me squarely in the eye. "No buts, Cynthia. He's a good guy. End of story."

We ate in silence for a few moments. I suppose there was no purpose in pressing him until I found out how viable my relationship with Koby was. "I really did ask you here for a purpose other then getting on your nerves."

He leaned over and kissed my forehead. "What do you need?"

"Spoken like a true parent. The baby's mother, Sarah Sanders, I never really got a chance to interview her. Even if it had been my job, I didn't feel capable of questioning her."

"That's okay, Cin. After you get your gold shield, you'll feel much more comfortable with interviewing."

"I talked to Russ MacGregor about it. He's taking the case over for Greg Van Horn, who's on vacation. I don't know, Dad. I just want to make sure that certain questions are asked."

"Like what?"

"Questions about the father of the baby. I think it's important to know."

"Russ didn't ask about it?"

"Russ interviewed her for about fifteen minutes, mostly details of her abandonment. Where did you give birth? Why did you throw the baby away? Why didn't you tell your sister? Like she was the felon . . . I mean, she is a felon, but there are circumstances, you know."

"I'm sure a judge will take her mental capacity into consideration." Decker sipped coffee. "Why are you concerned? Did the sister call you up with a complaint?"

I shook my head.

"It'll be okay, Cindy. You can't mother the world."

"I still think someone should ask about the father."

"Talk to Russ."

"I did. I spoke to him on Friday before I picked up Koby for dinner. He said he danced around the topic, but she wasn't talking. He didn't know if she was protecting someone or didn't understand the questions. He said he'd deal with it on Monday when he came back from Mammoth. Then I asked him if *I* could talk to her over the weekend."

"And . . ."

"He was reluctant, Lieutenant. Didn't say yes right away, but I played dumb and waited him out. In the end, he said to go ahead, but just don't screw anything up."

"Meaning don't screw up the case, and don't screw him by showing him up. He doesn't want you to make him look bad. That's understandable."

"I understand about seniority. I'll give him all the credit: I don't care about that." I leaned over the table. "I just want to make sure that the girl wasn't raped—"

"Whoa! Hold on." Decker put down his coffee cup. "The girl was raped?"

"I don't know."

"So why do you think she was raped? Retarded adults have sexual drives, too."

"I know that. It's just she didn't have lots of opportunity. They're watched pretty closely in the center."

"All it takes is one time."

"Shouldn't it be considered as a possibility?"

Dad gave my question some thought. "If it were my case . . . I would consider it a possibility." He rubbed his hands together. "Go interview her."

"I'd like you to come with me."

"For an independent woman, Cynthia, you are full of contradictions. Why do you want to bring *Daddy* into this?"

"Because I don't want to screw anything up."

"Somewhere along the line, you're going to have to learn to trust yourself."

"How about if you do the interviewing and I watch and take notes?"

"Not a good idea."

"Loo, I know this makes me look wussy. I don't care. I want this done right."

Decker shook his head. "Cin, I don't work on cases out of my jurisdiction. That's stepping on toes and I don't know when and where I might need these guys."

"All right." I gave him a charitable smile. "More coffee?"

"Yes, it's very good."

"It's Ethiopian."

Dad caught my eyes. "I'm sure there's more where that came from."

"I've got a source."

Decker chuckled. "Okay, Officer, this is what I'll do. I'll *accompany* you."

Better than I thought he'd do.

"You'll nudge me in the ribs if I'm doing something wrong?"

"If I nudged you in the ribs every time you did something wrong, you'd have a hole in your side."

"Aha! I knew you were mad!"

"I'm not mad—"

"Yes, you are. Just say it so we can move on."

Decker locked eyes with me. I felt my face go warm.

"What? *What?*"

"This has nothing to do with Koby. I meant it when I said he seems like a good guy."

He gave me one of those scolding-parent looks. At twenty-eight, I don't know why I had to deal with it, but that's the nature of being a daughter.

"Go on."

"You should have told me, Cynthia. That would have been common courtesy."

"Why? I wouldn't have made a point of telling you if he had been white."

Decker rolled his eyes. "I think you like to see me squirm."

"That's ridiculous."

"Well, I don't think so." He stood up and cleared his plate. "I wash and you dry?"

"I can handle two plates." I brought my own plate in. Together we cleared the table. "So that's all you want to say about it?"

He lifted a strand of hair out of my eyes. "Yes. That is all I want to say. Now get a paper and pencil. Tell me what questions you want to ask this girl and why."

I went to fetch my notepad, not happy about the dialogue between us. But at least it was a dialogue. By the time we were done refining our inquiries, it was almost eleven. I wrapped up the cold leftovers and stuck them in the fridge. I faced my father and made eye contact. "I like him, Daddy."

"It's important to like the person you're dating."

I tapped my toe. "Well, we'll see what happens. It's probably premature to talk about it."

"For what it's worth, I liked him, too, Cin."

"It's worth a lot to me."

"A definite step up from your last fling."

I hit my father's shoulder. "I'm ready if you are."

"Then let's do it." He threw his arm

around my shoulder. "You tell your mother about him yet?"

"Like I said, it's premature."

Dad didn't respond. He knew bullshit when he heard it.

16

Earlier in the weekend, Sarah had been discharged from the hospital. She was facing a court hearing on Wednesday, but for now she was out on a five-thousand-dollar bail bond and placed in her sister's charge. Dad was pleased that Sarah was home: It was much easier to interview someone in the comfort of familiar surroundings. By the time we made it to Louise Sanders's house, it was after twelve. She answered the door wrapped in a terry-cloth housecoat, a steaming mug of something in her left hand. She wasn't overjoyed about our visit, but she did invite us in.

"It's nothing personal, Officer Decker," she told me. "You were very nice to us. I'm just tired of answering questions."

"I can understand that."

"I should get dressed."

"You don't have to bother, Louise. This is my father, Lieutenant Decker. We were in the neighborhood and thought we'd drop by to see how Sarah was doing."

Dad and Louise exchanged smiles. He said, "How's she dealing with everything?"

Louise laughed. "Honestly? I think she's delighted by all the attention."

"And how are you coping?"

Nice choice of words, Dad. Louise's exasperation oozed out. "You *don't* want to know. Would either of you like some coffee?"

We both accepted coffee. She told us to sit while she fetched our drinks. It took longer than it should have. When she came back, she had changed into a loose set of black sweats. We sipped java for a moment; then I broke the silence.

"If Sarah has a moment, we'd like to talk to her."

Louise said, "Officer Decker, we already went over everything with Detective Mac-Gregor."

"I spoke to Detective MacGregor, Louise, and that's why I'm here. He told me that

Sarah didn't say much about the baby's father. There is someone else responsible for what happened."

"I know. I hadn't wanted to go there." Louise threw up her hands. "She was supposed to be on the pill."

"Why was she on the pill? Did Fordham know that she was sexually active?"

"She was under a doctor's care," Louise said. "Her gynecologist put her on as a precaution as well as a way to even out her periods. The decision wasn't haphazard."

"Of course not," I concurred. "Listen, Louise, if her sexual activity was voluntary, then the baby's father is her own business . . . or at least not police business. But like I said last week, if the activity was forced, that's another matter."

She stood up and began to pace. "I'm *not* going to put her through a rape trial. That's out of the question!"

"I understand your reluctance. But shouldn't we at least find out?"

"No, we shouldn't! Some stones are better left unturned."

"Maybe she needs therapy—"

"She *has* a therapist. If the topic comes up in therapy, let her deal with it then."

"Louise, *if* there's a person out there raping disabled girls like Sarah, I want him behind bars. At least, let her tell me *yes* or *no.*"

Louise tried to stare me down. But her eyes told me she had relented. "Give me a few minutes."

"Take your time."

She disappeared into the back room.

Dad said, "Good job. You don't need me."

"Daddy, I always need you."

Decker patted my knee. We exchanged shrugs and finished our coffees. When Louise came back, Sarah was holding on to her arm. The girl was dressed in blue pajamas with lambs on them. Louise settled her into a chair. "Do you remember Officer Decker, Sarah?"

The girl nodded. She was round and pink and her yellow hair was tied into a ponytail. I glanced at her hands. Her thumbs were short and stubby. She was looking at her lap.

"Sarah, can I . . ." I stopped myself, hearing my father's words of warning. Don't request to do something if you're going to do it anyway. "Sarah, I'm going to ask you a few questions. It shouldn't take long."

Silence.

Louise said, "Go ahead."

"Do you know how the baby got in your tummy?"

A nod.

"Can you explain it to me?"

She gave me a blank stare.

Dad broke in. "How do babies get in tummies, Sarah?"

Her eyes darted about the room. "They teached us in school. They showed us pictures." She spoke haltingly, as if the words came from her diaphragm instead of her throat. Suddenly she giggled and turned red. "They were real"—again she giggled—"real em*barrassing.*"

"They showed you pictures of boys and girls naked?" I asked her.

"Not real pictures. *Drawings.*"

"Oh." I smiled. "It's good that you know about it . . . about sex."

She giggled. "That's a *bad* word."

"No, it isn't," Louise assured her. "It's okay, Sarah. That's what making a baby is. It's called sex—"

The giggles smothered her words.

"Did you have sex to make your baby, Sarah?" I said.

She turned scarlet and broke into unre-
strained laughter. "Yeah, I think I did."

"Sarah, who did you have sex with?"

She shook her head. "I can't tell you. I
promised."

Louise said, "Sarah, you must answer
their questions—"

"No!" The girl's face became defiant. "It's
a secret!"

Decker held up his hand to Louise. His
demeanor was as casual as a handshake.
He smiled at the girl. "Do you have a
boyfriend, Sarah?"

Her face darkened. "No."

"A pretty girl like you—"

"I'm not pretty," Sarah told him.

"Sure you are," Decker said. "All that
beautiful blond hair. I bet you do have a
boyfriend."

She looked away. Her eyes were downcast.

"What's wrong, Sarah? *Did* you have a
boyfriend?"

She nodded slowly.

"What happened? Did he move away or
something like that?"

Again with the nod.

Dad gave me the go-ahead to continue

the questioning. I tried to follow his line of reasoning. "Was he someone from your school?"

"Yes."

"Do you know why he moved away?"

"Maybe." She looked down. "But I can't tell you. It's a secret. I can't tell a secret."

Louise exhaled loudly, but Decker broke in before she had a chance to reprimand her sister. "Sarah, I'm going to tell you something. Because I think that you're very smart—"

Her face drew tight. "I'm not smart. I'm *retarded.*"

"Well, you can be retarded and smart at the same time. So listen carefully, all right?"

Sarah didn't answer.

Decker said, "In this world, there are good secrets and there are bad secrets. The good secrets are things like . . . well, when your sister buys you a Christmas present and doesn't tell you about it even when you ask. Does that ever happen to you?"

She smiled. "Yeah, that's happened."

"That's what you call a good secret. Your sister, Louise, wants you to be surprised, so she doesn't tell you. A good secret. Do you understand?"

"A little."

"See? I told you, you are smart."

Her smile widened.

"Sarah, bad secrets are when people do bad things to you . . . then tell you not to tell anyone. Those bad secrets . . . those secrets you can tell. Those secrets you *should* tell. Especially to me or to Officer Decker because we're the police. You can tell a police officer those secrets."

"They said not to tell the police."

"*They* told you not to tell?"

Both the Loo and I were doing some quick reassessments.

I said, "There was more than one boy who told you not to tell?"

Sarah said yes.

Decker said, "Those boys . . . Sarah, look at me."

She lifted her face and glanced at my father. He said, "Those boys are very bad boys. I don't like those boys."

"I don't like them, too," Sarah said. "They hurt me."

"I'll bet they did," Decker said. "Where on your body did they hurt you?"

Louise looked away, but I could see the tears in her eyes. But Sarah talked calmly about it. "On my bottom . . . They hurt me on my bottom."

Dad looked at me to continue, but I gave him a slight shake of the head. This was too important for me to ruin. He said, "Did they put things in your bottom?"

Tears rolled down her cheek as she whispered yes.

"I told you they were bad boys," Decker said. "They were very bad to do that to you. What kind of things did they put in your bottom?"

She didn't answer, her eyes squeezed tightly.

"Was it sex? Like the drawings that they showed you in school?" he asked her. "Did they put the boy's thing in you? You know what I mean . . . the thing that makes a boy a boy?"

She turned away.

"It's okay, sweetheart," Decker said. "You don't have to talk. Just nod."

She nodded.

"Where in your bottom did they put it?" Dad paused. "Did they put it where you poop or where you pee?"

Sarah said, "Where I pee."

"Those boys . . . ," I said. "They did sex with you."

"I didn't like it at all. It hurt!"

"I'm sure it did."

"It hurt like when the baby came out."

"I understand."

"Not like with David." She covered her mouth and abruptly giggled behind her fingers. "Oops."

Decker and I exchanged glances. I said, "David was your boyfriend, right?"

She sighed. "He went away."

"But he went to your school before he went away?"

"Yes."

"I don't know any David," Louise told us. "What's his last name, Sarah?"

She shrugged.

"We'll find out," my father whispered to her. "So . . . you had sex with David. But it was good sex, right?"

"Well, I didn't like that sex, either. But David was my boyfriend. It's okay with your boyfriend."

I was trying to organize my thoughts. Two things appeared to be going on—consensual sex with David and then maybe an incident that could have been a gang rape. "Do you know why David went away?"

She nodded. "Because they put him in the trash can."

Again I exchanged looks with my father.

Decker scratched his head. "Tell me about that. When they put David in the trash can."

"They told me not to tell anyone. They said that if I told a policeman, they would kill me."

I said, "The bad boys are *not* going to hurt you!"

"You can't be sure of that!" Louise spoke up.

Decker said, "Ms. Sanders, why don't we try to figure out what happened first. Then you can decide how you want Sarah to help."

Giving her the choice, empowering her. My father's skills were amazing. Louise told him to go ahead.

He said, "Sarah, I want you to tell me what happened. Because that's what you have to do." He tried to make eye contact with her. "You're a big girl now, Sarah. You had a big, strong baby because you're a big, strong girl. So you can do this. You can tell me what happened. How did David get into the trash can?"

She started shaking her knee—up and down, and up and down. "We were in the park."

"Who was in the park?"

"David and me."

"When?"

"Long time ago. Before David went away."

"Like . . . last year?"

A shrug. "Maybe six months."

"Okay. You were in the park with David," I said. "Which park? MacFerren Park?"

She nodded.

Decker said, "Good. Now tell me what happened in the park."

"I was supposed to go home right after school. But I didn't."

"I know. You didn't go home. You didn't listen to your sister." Decker looked at Louise. "But Louise isn't mad at you . . . right?"

In fact, Louise was furious. But she toed the line, even though she spoke through clenched teeth. "No, Sarah, I'm *not* mad."

Dad's smile was endearing. "See? She's not mad. Tell me about the park."

"They came over."

Dad looked at me, signaling with his eyes for me to continue. I said, "Who came over?"

"The bad boys."

"Sarah, do you remember how many bad boys there were?"

"Three or four."

"Three or four," I repeated. "So they came over to you and David?"

"Yes."

"And where were you in MacFerren Park when the bad boys came over to you?" Empty eyes regarded my face. "Were you by a tree, or sitting on a bench, or—"

"In the bathroom."

"Oh, okay. You and David were in the bathroom together?"

She blushed.

"Were you having sex with David in the bathroom?" I asked.

"No . . . just . . . you know . . ." She smiled and made chirps with pursed lips.

"You two were kissing?" I asked.

"Yeah . . . we were kissing."

"Then what happened?"

"The bad boys came in."

"Did the bad boys say anything to you?"

"Bad words."

"What kind of bad words?"

She looked down. "The F-word."

"I see." My brain was scrambling for the right order to ask my questions. "And after they said the words, what happened?"

"They hit David hard. His nose was bleeding—"

"My God!" exhaled Louise. She turned away and put her fingers over her mouth. "This is . . ."

"Am I doing something bad, Louise?"

"No." She smiled and wiped her eyes. "No, you're doing something good. You're doing the right thing. Go on, Sarah. Tell them what happened."

Sarah dropped her head. "They put him in the trash can. He didn't like it. He was yelling. But then they turned the can upside down"—she closed her eyes—"and one of them sat on it, so David was stuck inside. And every time he yelled, the boy would kick the trash can hard and tell him to shut up."

She was flinching as she related the incident. I said, "And after David was put in the trash can, what happened next?"

Her voice was as soft as new snow. "They pushed me down and tore my underpants.

Then . . . the first one did it . . . the sex. It hurt real bad. I wanted to yell for him not to do it, but I didn't want to make him mad . . . because when David yelled, it made them all mad. I didn't want my nose to bleed. So I closed my eyes and didn't say anything."

"That was very smart," Decker said. "See, I told you, you were smart."

Her chin was pressed against her chest, her eyes still shut.

Decker said, "Do you remember how many boys had sex with you?"

Slowly, she held up two fingers.

"Two boys had sex with you."

She held up three fingers.

Louise blanched. I took her hand and squeezed it. Dad said, "Three boys?"

She nodded.

"Okay, Sarah. Now this is very important. What happened after they were done with the sex?"

"That's when they made me promise not to tell. They said if I told the police, they would kill me. I believed them!"

"Yes, of course. And then did the bad boys leave the bathroom first or did you?"

"The bad boys did."

"And what did you do?"

"I pushed the trash can over to help David. It was real heavy and I hurt from the bad boys and I was crying. . . ."

"You must have been very scared," I said.

"I was!"

"But you don't have to be scared now because you're safe," Decker said. "Sarah, I want you to tell me this. When you pushed the trash can over, was David all right?"

She shook her head no.

Decker rubbed his face. "Was he moving?"

"His face had lots of blood on it." She started to cry in earnest. "I wanted to help him. But I promised I'd keep it a secret. I didn't know what to do!"

"You did the right thing," my dad said soothingly. "What did you do after you saw David's face?"

Her crying got stronger. Louise put her arms around her sister and let her cry on her shoulder. "It's all over, Sarah. Don't worry, it's all over."

But everyone in the room, including Sarah, knew it wasn't over.

Decker kept his voice even. "Sarah, did you leave David in the trash can?"

She sobbed loudly. "I ran home. I washed myself. I was real scared."

"Of course, you were."

We waited until she had cried it out. It took quite a while. Finally, she looked at me. "I went to school the next day. He wasn't there. He doesn't come to school anymore. I want to ask Mr. Klinghoffner about it, but I'm too scared."

"Then how about if I ask him for you?" I said.

"Thank you." She smiled with wet eyes. "I don't see him anymore. Maybe he didn't like that the other boys had sex with me."

"I'm sure that's not the reason," I told her.

"I didn't want to do it. They made me."

I told her I understood. "What did these boys look like?"

She closed her eyes. She was conjuring up something. "Maybe two were Mexicans."

"Mexicans?" I repeated.

"Yes. Like the janitor in the school. His name is José. He's Mexican. But he's a nice Mexican. Sometimes he gives us candy and treats. The bad-boy Mexicans were mean."

"Did they speak Spanish?" I asked.

She shrugged. "I don't know."

"So you think that two might be Mexicans," Decker said. "You said there were other bad boys. What about them? Can you tell me what they looked like?"

Again she closed her eyes. "One was bald. He was the meanest one. He hit David first."

"Was he white-skinned or black-skinned or brown-skinned?"

She made a face. "Not brown like José, but not pink like me. The not-bald one had lots of pimples. The bald one was the meanest. He didn't have pimples."

"And the other two were Mexican?" I asked.

"Yes. They had black hair and dark skin and looked like José, the janitor at our school."

"Anything else?" Decker said.

"No."

Decker said, "Sarah, do you think if I showed you pictures that maybe you could pick out the bad boys to me?"

"Maybe."

"Ms. Sanders, we'd like to bring Sarah in and show her some mug books. See if she could pick out anyone."

"Perhaps a little later, Lieutenant Decker.

We have a court case on Wednesday. I need to settle things before I have her go through another ordeal. I hope you can understand that."

"Okay. Later then."

It was my turn to get some information. "Sarah, was David a black person?"

Sarah glanced at her sister. Louise said, "It's okay, Sarah. You can answer the question."

"Yes." She bit her lip. "I'm sorry, Louise."

"What are you sorry for?" Louise asked her.

"'Cause I liked David. You said to stay away from black people. That they do lots of bad things. But David was nice. He wasn't mean . . . except he did the sex. But he was nice about it."

By this time, Louise was bright red. After all she'd gone through, I decided to give her a little solace. "Everyone makes judgment calls, Louise."

"I'm just trying to keep her safe. . . ." She let out a mirthless chuckle. "I haven't done a very good job."

"Walk a mile in my shoes," I said.

She laughed loudly. "You should have been a therapist."

Sarah said, "Is my baby okay?"

"The baby is fine," I told her.

"Can I see her?"

Louise said, "We're working on it, Sarah."

I said, "Louise, is it possible for you to bring Sarah down to the Hollywood Station tomorrow just to make a statement? That way we could get something going."

Louise said, "I don't think so, Officer Decker."

"No mug books," I told her. "Just let her repeat her story to Detective MacGregor, because he's in charge. We'll worry about identifying the perpetrators later on."

Her sigh was heavy. "Lunchtime—twelve-thirty. I'll give you twenty minutes. Then I have to get back to work."

"Thank you so much," I said. "I'll clear it with Detective MacGregor and call you if there's a change in plans."

"Your cooperation will be favorably looked upon by the judge," Decker told her. "This is not for pressure, Ms. Sanders, just to let you know."

"Right."

The sarcasm was evident. We all stood except Sarah. Dad extended his hand to the girl. "Thank you for talking with us, young lady. Tomorrow, Louise is going to bring you to the police station to talk with Detective MacGregor. Do you remember him?"

Sarah nodded.

"You'll need to tell him exactly what you told us."

"Okay . . ." Sarah was tentative.

"Don't worry," Decker said. "It will be easier the next time you talk. I promise. You're a very good girl, Sarah."

"Mr. Man?"

We all smiled. Louise said, "His name is Lieutenant Decker."

"I thought her name was Decker."

"We both are Decker," I told her.

"Oh . . . you're married."

"Father and daughter," Dad explained. "Was there something you wanted to tell me?"

She nodded.

"What, honey? Tell me anything you want."

"Are you sure it's okay to tell bad secrets?"

"Positive." My father regarded her face. "Do you have another bad secret you want to tell me?"

"No." But Sarah responded way too quickly.

"It's okay," Decker soothed. "If you want, you can whisper it in my ear."

"Is David dead?" she asked.

"I don't know, Sarah," I told her. "I'm going to find out."

"Will I get into trouble?"

"No, sweetie. It's okay. You did the right thing by talking to us." Decker gave her his card. "Anytime you have a bad secret, you can call me, okay?"

She nodded. I followed the Loo's example and gave her my card as well. We exchanged good-byes and walked back to the car.

I strapped myself in and turned on the ignition. "Is Sarah sitting on something?"

"Definitely."

"So what do we do about it?"

"Nothing."

17

Staring out the window of his daughter's apartment, Decker organized his thoughts. His gaze shifted onto Cindy's face. "This is the deal. It would be a good idea to type up your notes for when you talk to MacGregor. That way, you not only have something organized to look at, so you don't have to grope for words, but also you have something concrete to hand him after you're done. You don't want to overwhelm him with detail. It'll make you look like a hot dog and it'll irritate—" Abruptly, Decker stopped talking. "Are you listening?"

Cindy's eyes went from her lap to his face. "Yes, Dad, I'm listening."

"Then can you stop playing with the

fringes of your couch pillow and look like you're paying attention?"

"I *am* paying attention. Why are you chastising me like I'm five years old?" She jumped up. "I'm going to make some fresh coffee. Would you like some?"

Decker rubbed his aching temples. After a pause, he told her yes he would like coffee. As his eyes skipped over the place, he noticed how stark her apartment had become. Once the decor had been homey, almost girlish, as if her room as a teenager had been moved in toto. Now it bore the scars of its rape. He stood up and walked into her small kitchenette. It could barely contain both their bodies. "You can't have it both ways. I can't be a father and a lieutenant at the same time. So take your pick."

She poured water into the machine. "I'm going to ask you this one more time, and I expect you to be totally honest. Are you pissed because Koby is black?"

"No."

She turned to face him. "So *why* are you still pissed that I didn't mention it to you?"

"*Mention* it to me?" Decker regarded her

dubiously. "Cindy, you deliberately withheld it from me!"

"What *difference* does it make?"

"It's descriptive. You went out of your way to tell me he was Israeli—"

"He *is* Israeli."

"No, Cindy, he lived in Israel. He is a self-described Ethiopian. All you had to do was tell me that. Instead, you caught me off guard." A pause. "I probably acted like an idiot."

"You were *fine.*"

"Well, I didn't feel *fine,* I felt uncomfortable. That's *my* problem, not yours. But you could have helped me along. What were you afraid of? Do I make you that nervous?"

"Yes."

Decker sighed. "Well . . . then I'm sorry. That's never my intention."

"I know. It's all right."

Shoving his hands in his jeans pockets, he stared at her blank walls. Just once he'd like to end their time together by congratulating himself for a parenting job well done, instead of walking to the car feeling like a failure.

"I'll try to do better, Cin."

"You don't have to do better. You're great, Daddy. I love you."

"I love you, too." He threw up his hands. "I don't know. I keep thinking I should be mellowing with age. Instead, I'm more on edge . . . more frantic."

"That means you're vital, Dad." Cindy took her father's hand. "That's a good thing. And I wasn't being fair. Most of the time, you don't make me nervous, just when you bark orders at me. I know it's not personal, especially because I dragged you into this. When you chide me, it sets off something primal. But that's *my* hang-up."

Decker rolled his tongue in his cheeks. "He'd better treat you right or I'll kill him."

"Don't commit homicide on my behalf. I barely know him."

"He likes you—a lot. Make sure you're moving at the same rate."

"That's my business, Dad."

"Fair enough. Shall we go on with *our* business?"

"You were saying I should type up my notes."

"Why don't you do this—after you've organized your thoughts on paper, e-mail or fax them to me and I'll go over them."

"That would be great. Thank you very much."

"You're welcome, Princess. Keep your sentences simple, Cin. The average detective has maybe a few years of college."

"I know."

"Any questions?"

"No, not really." She looked at her nails, bitten almost to the quick. "So you don't think I should ask around about gangs in my area? The fact that these bad boys were a mixture of Hispanic and non-Hispanic narrows it down."

Decker waited a beat. "Cindy, you are not a detective yet. You have to wait for Russ MacGregor to call the shots. Tell him what you told me and see what he says."

"It'll be junked in the circular file. What would be wrong with asking my street contacts a couple of questions?"

"You're goading me."

"I'm trying to give an old rape case some CPR."

"Cynthia, listen to me." A pause. "Are you listening?"

"Yes, Dad, I am listening."

"Okay. Here goes. Every day you put your butt on the line. That means you need backup on occasion. And that means you have to be a team player. Besides, you don't know who these punks are, so you don't know what you're dealing with. You ask the wrong people the wrong questions, your body winds up with homemade air-conditioning."

"Very funny."

"I'm not laughing, Cynthia."

She looked at her watch. "You'd better go. Otherwise, you're not going to make a two o'clock movie with Hannah Banana."

"I'll go. But you have to promise me not to get involved unless asked to do so."

"I promise I won't do a thing without Russ MacGregor's explicit permission."

"That was even better than I expected. Thank you."

Just then, a chime dinged. Cindy said, "Coffee's ready. How about one for the road? I have a travel cup."

"Why not?"

She went into her kitchenette and poured the steaming liquid into a thermal cup. She closed the lid tightly and handed the cup to him while formulating her thoughts. "I like him, too, Daddy."

"Great."

"I think that despite all the superficial differences, we have a lot in common."

Decker waited.

"Our jobs, for instance. We both love our jobs. And our jobs have lots in common."

"A nurse and a cop?"

"Yeah, when you think about it. Most of the time, our jobs deal with routine. Lots and lots of routine. But when it *isn't* routine . . . man, that's when the adrenaline starts pumping . . . flowing full throttle. Boy oh boy, that's what separates wheat from chaff. And if we're good . . . really good . . . it's in the clutch when we shine."

▼

He awoke with a crick in his neck, his nostrils piqued by the smell of barbecue, his ears hearing the whir of a kitchen fan. Rina was grilling indoors, and despite his drowsiness, his stomach rumbled as the aroma translated its signals to his brain. He lowered his feet from the ottoman, then got up, stretching his too-tall frame until he was steady enough to walk. His mouth was dry and parched. He went into the kitchen, spotting a hunk of roast with grid marks, bathed in onions and mushrooms, sizzling in the skillet.

"Have a good nap?" Rina asked him.

"Very good. Hannah is a great kid, but she's exhausting."

"The feeling must be mutual. She's been a zombie since she's been home."

"Well, that makes me feel a little better." He took a bottle of water from the refrigerator and gulped it down greedily. Rina was wearing an apron over a black knee-length knit skirt and black sweater. She had socks and sneakers on her feet and her hair was tied back in a high ponytail. She looked like a bobby-soxer. "Man, that smells good. What is it?"

"Flanken."

"Beef on Sunday? What's the occasion?"

"The boys are home. We're healthy. Hannah's not grumpy. Take your pick."

"Where are the boys?"

"They'll be back in fifteen minutes or so." She took the cast-iron grill pan from the stovetop and slid it into the oven. "Dinner will be ready in about twenty minutes."

"Medium rare?"

"Absolutely. We all dislike shoe leather."

"You're incapable of serving shoe leather."

"Thank you very much." She wiped her

hands on a napkin and turned to face him. "If you have a few minutes, I'd like you to scan my grandmother's file."

"Goody."

"Don't get cranky. The papers are on the dining-room table. I've done homework for you."

"Like what?"

"I got you a map."

"It's a start." He washed his hands in the kitchen sink and splashed water on his face. He glanced at the coffeepot. "I'll need forti- fication."

"I will make coffee." She stood on her tip- toes and kissed his forehead. "First you have to deal with Cindy. Then Hannah. Now me. And this is supposed to be your day off. I'm not without sympathy."

Decker slipped his hands around her waist, her hair smelling of garlic powder and soy sauce. "All I want is a little appreciation. Having gotten it, I will be happy to help you out."

"Thank you."

He kissed her soft lips, then sat down at the dining-room table. Rina had laid it all out for him—a neat little stack of papers in a folder, an empty notepad, a pen, a pencil, and a good street map of Munich. In all honesty, he was happy to be occupied. His mind abhorred a vacuum because that meant that sooner or later it would fill with images he'd rather forget.

He picked up the folder and opened it.

Regina Gottlieb's body was found in a tangle of foliage inside the Englischer Garten—a long stretch of parkland that ran parallel to the Isar River but was separated from it by several city streets. From the map, it looked like the two areas intersected in the northern neighborhood of Schwabing. But then the garden ended and the Isar broke away.

Decker sat back, visualizing his morning jog through the parklands that abutted the Isar—a hint of the indigenous Bavarian wilderness—the area so long that it went under city streets. The cement pillars that supported the roadways above had been stamped with graffiti that was—not surprisingly—written in German, the same crude epithets as in America no doubt. He recalled his body washed with numbness as his face hit the frigid air at six in the morning. Jet lag had been playing games with his diurnal clock, and at that hour it was still black outside, dawn at least an hour away. It was dangerous for him to be out so early, but he took a perverse pleasure in flirting with peril, daring anyone to try to mug him. The leafless trees had dripped gelid moisture, the ground wet and muddy in spots, filled with detritus from the nighttime Munich rains. The air reeked of moss, mold, and rotting flora. The Isar was roiling after the storm, bubbling over with water and spray, boisterously shouting as it rolled over rocks and boulders that lined the riverbed.

Toward the end of his jog, a gray light shrouded the city. Decker's mind flashed back to the upscale neighborhoods on either side of the river. All around had been imposing stone buildings constructed with perfect proportions and mindful of detail.

He wished he had paid more attention to his surroundings. The trip was lacking the sharp, defined angles of clear retrospection, like reading the paper in bad light. Although he had passed many landmarks, he had no idea where they were in relation to one another. Then again, how was he to know that his sight-seeing might be crucial in solving this long-buried, unsolved case?

Looking at the city as a whole entity—not

just a road map to chart where the hell they were in relationship to the hotel—Decker discovered that the Englischer Garten was located in Munich's northeast corner. He and Rina had stayed at a hotel on Maximilianstrasse, a thoroughfare that housed great restaurants, five-star hotels, and most of the designer boutiques. When he was there, the distance between the hotel and the garden didn't seem very far at all. On the map, it looked much more distant.

Rina had also provided him with a detailed map of the garden, vast with long stretches of lawn and lakes and lots of walking paths. The rebuilt Chinese Tower lay in the center, a bronze-colored, spire-shaped piece of architecture that approximated a pagoda. Next door was one of the many Munich *biergartens,* a summer gathering spot filled with tables and chairs, where people sat around, drank beer, and enjoyed the open space. The concession stands were closed in the wintertime, naturally.

The garden also contained Munich's Cricket Grounds, and along the northern perimeter, there was an area called Aumeister, which featured an early-nineteenth-century hunting lodge. Those landmarks failed to jar loose any recollections. What he viscerally remembered was empty copses of trees in steel-cold air, wetness, and the smell of decay.

It was probably his mood.

Rina came in with a cup of coffee and set the mug in front of him. "Anything?"

He glanced at his watch. "I've been here for four minutes."

"I expect miracles."

"Wait in line." He sipped coffee. "Wow, this is good. Thanks."

Rina sat down and placed her hand over his. "Take your time. Seriously."

"I'm trying to picture the geography. The Englischer Garten is big. Your grandmother was dumped in the northern end. So that brings several questions to mind."

He picked up a pencil and wrote on the notepad. "First, what was she doing there? From the guide books and my own pitiful memories, that area is and was very ritzy. Your omah wasn't aristocracy. She wasn't even petite bourgeoisie. She didn't go on daily strolls through the park, twirling her parasol in a silk-embroidered gown. Your grandmother was a poor Jewish woman. She probably worked from the moment she woke up until she went to sleep. What was she doing in the area?"

"Maybe she wasn't in the area. Maybe she was just dumped there because the park was big and a good place to hide bodies."

"So then the murder wasn't a random killing. Someone *brought* her over there with the specific purpose of killing her or at the very least, dumping her there. Now these other two women—Marlena Durer and Anna Gross—they're different stories. They lived near the garden, so they could have been random rapes and homicides—in the wrong place at the wrong time."

"So why did the other guy include Omah with Gross and Durer?"

"What other guy?"

"This one. Kriminalpolizeiinspektor Axel Berg." She smiled. "That's a tongue twister. I think all the homicides might be related. Did you read all of Inspektor Kalmer's notes?"

"No. Why?"

Rina flipped through to his interview notes. "Read this. You'll find it interesting."

Decker's eyes scanned over the writing until he came to the sentence in question.

He backtracked and read it carefully: *An interview with Julia Schoennacht was conducted. The victim, Regina Gottlieb, was in Frau Schoennacht's employ for three months, with Frau Gottlieb's employment ending after her services were no longer required.* He looked at Rina. "Your grandmother worked outside the home?"

"The first I've heard of it."

"What do you think she did? A maid?"

Rina tried out a winsome smile. "I've got a confession to make."

Decker sneered. "Do tell."

"I screwed up my courage and called my mother this morning after you left."

"I *knew* this was going to happen! Did you get into a fight with her? Rina, the woman is in her eighties!"

"No, I did not fight with her. To my surprise, she was actually receptive to talking about her past. I was shocked."

"Did you happen to tell her what you were doing?"

"Not exactly."

"Here we go again." Decker was used to his wife's little white lies. "What yarn did you spin?"

"I told her Hannah was doing a family

tree. I just needed to know what her mother and father did. I told her that I knew that Opah was a tailor. Then I said I assumed that Omah was a housewife. I asked if she had anything to add. . . ."

"And?"

"There was this pause. Then, in a voice bursting with pride, Mama told me that Omah was also a very fine seamstress. She used to make Mama and her sister beautiful party dresses. They were the best-dressed girls in the neighborhood, and the most beautiful girls as well."

"Your mother's words? I've never known her to brag."

"Old age . . . I guess her inhibitions are lowered. Then she told me that Omah used to sew dresses for some of the richest people in Munich. Then . . . almost conspiratorial, as if my grandfather could hear from the grave, she said that Omah was a better seamstress than Opah was a tailor. Then"— Rina's face took on a slight blush—"Then she said if Hannah needs more information, she'd be happy to talk with her."

"Have you informed Hannah about your deception?"

"Hannah was happy to help me out. I

think she likes playing detective. Truly her father's daughter. So putting two and two together, it stands to reason that Omah worked for this woman Julia Schoennacht as a seamstress."

"Where did Julia Schoennacht live?"

She pointed to her address. "Near Ludwig-Maximilian-University in Schwabing . . . not so far from the Englischer Garten. So maybe Omah *was* a random murder. Maybe she was walking through the park on her way home when someone grabbed her."

"I don't know where your grandmother lived. Would she have walked through the park to go home?"

"My grandmother lived around here." Rina located the area on the map. "Near the Gartnerplatz off Reichenbachstrasse."

"These names are going to kill me," Decker said.

"You've got to add imaginary slash marks."

"Your grandparents' house was nowhere near the park," Decker pointed out. "And to get to Julia Schoennacht's house near . . . what's this street . . . Ludwigstrasse or is it Leopoldstrasse . . . they look like they run into one another. . . . Anyway, there wouldn't be any reason for your grandmother to walk through the Englischer Garten. It's out of the way."

"It's not that much out of the way and it is more scenic. And look here"—Rina flipped through several pages—"Look at this, Peter. My grandmother was—quote unquote—relieved of her services about two weeks before she was murdered. Do you want to hear my theory?"

"Lay it on me."

"Maybe she went back to the house for some unfinished business. Maybe there was a pay dispute or something. Maybe a fight broke out and a tragedy occurred. The house was near the garden, so that was the easiest place to hide the body. And of course, Julia Schoennacht wouldn't tell the police any of this."

"So already you have decided that your grandmother's killer was her former employer. It's as good a theory as any." Decker closed the file. "So why don't we leave it at that. Besides, there're too many *strasses* on the map."

Rina said, "I want to know the truth—or as close as I can come to the truth. Besides, I can't picture a wealthy, aristocratic woman dragging my grandmother into a park and bludgeoning her to death."

"She hired a servant to do it. You said it yourself, Rina. What would be the big deal? Another dead Jew? Good riddance to bad rubbish. When was Kristallnacht?"

"In 1938."

"So this was before."

"About ten years before. But Hitler was already a dominant force." Rina rubbed her hands together. "Since everything was going so well with Mama, I accepted an invitation for dinner at her house on Tuesday night—if that's okay with you."

"If you want to be a masochist."

Rina hit him. "Don't be like that."

"I like your parents. I don't fight with them. You do."

Silence.

"Okay, you have a point," Rina admitted. "Look. I promise I won't fight. Besides, they want to see the boys. So maybe we can continue the family-tree ruse?"

"And you don't think Mama will catch on when I start to take notes?"

"Could you be a little more subtle?"

"Subtlety is not my strong suit," Decker

remarked. "However, if I should think up the questions and you should ask them . . ."

"Better still, let Hannah ask them."

"What kind of a mother would use her own daughter as a shill?"

"Not a shill—a cohort." Rina patted his shoulder. "Detection as a family affair. I see a screenplay in the making."

"Funny. All I see is trouble in the making."

18

The urge to comb the streets for information was overwhelming. But I had made a promise to my father, and that was that. Even so, I devised a mental list of how I'd proceed if I were a gold shield. First I'd talk to Klinghoffner, and find out all I could about David—who he was and where he might have gone. Then I'd ask him if there had been any trouble between his students and street gangs. There were also the girls I had talked with at the high school. If anyone would know about street gangs, it would be those who lived where the hoodlums operated. I also knew street people: Alice Anne, Magenta and others of her ilk, and even her pimp, Burton. There were times I could have busted him, but I chose not to because, after some strong prodding, he had closed shop for the night. I had come by my "ears" honestly.

I also thought about how to approach Russ MacGregor. Would he want my help? Would he care about a six-month-old crime? Would he bother with a case that had never been reported to the police, where there was no physical evidence, *and* where the primary witness was a mentally disabled girl who had just abandoned her baby? I sorted through all these what-ifs because the morning's conversation with Sarah and Louise Sanders had piqued my curiosity.

Then I remembered the last time I stuck my nose where it didn't belong. A year of therapy and I could almost get through a session without breaking down. Progress was slow, and I didn't need another trauma. I kept telling myself to play by the rules, but the old rebellious urges kept surfacing like bottles bobbing in the ocean. I guess that meant I was getting better.

At loose ends, I wanted to be anywhere but home. Once, I had loved my place, but now it was just a pit stop. I should have moved, but I didn't want yet another upheaval in my life. So I slept and I ate and I pretended I was doing fine. With Dad gone, I felt very much alone. I put on a bright blue blouse, black wool crepe trousers, and four-inch-high black boots that adjusted my height to almost six feet. I made up my face and hit the road in my five-year-old black Lexus, courtesy of Dad and Mom. They had thought a big car would increase my sense of well-being. All it did was increase my gas allowance. I wasn't complaining, though. My wheels had a drop-dead stereo and cushy seats with lumbar support, which helped my sore back as well as my bruised ego.

As I looked in the mirror, I struck a pose that said I hadn't a care in the world. I was always an accomplished fibber.

From my apartment, I drove north on Beverly Drive, passing the green lawns and flower beds of suburban Beverlywood, through the shopping district of Beverly Hills—lots of foot traffic out today—into the astronomically expensive and bloated estates of Beverly Hills. From there, I continued north until I hooked a right onto Sunset. I cruised through West Hollywood in slow-moving traffic, passing all the hot clubs, one of them sporting long lines even though opening time was hours away. I drove by a half-dozen edgy clothing boutiques, a couple of live theaters, and a block filled with kissy-kissy restaurants offering sidewalk dining, overpriced grub, and lots of lost souls.

When I turned onto Hollywood Boulevard, I purposely avoided looking for any of my sources, figuring why screw if you can't come. I opened the moon roof and enjoyed the heat and sunlight on my skin, the red downy hair of my arms bleached strawberry blond in the bright rays. Here, in the heart of old Tinseltown, pedestrians abounded. There were the tourists who gaped at the street show and snapped picture after picture of weirdo after weirdo. Joining the fray were scores of pierced and spike-haired kids, snacking on junk food, just hanging around. I even spotted some families out for the afternoon, reading the names on the famous star-studded sidewalks. I passed the Kodak Theatre, Mann's Chinese Theatre, the El Capitan, the newly constructed shopping malls, the old kiosk gift shops, the tattoo parlors, the tacky lingerie boutiques, the sex shops, and other various and sundry scamsters including budget lawyers advertising special rates for bail bonds. Mixed into the scene were the ubiquitous high-rise office buildings. I turned left onto Western, riding the boulevard until it dead-ended at Griffith Park. More people and more traffic, but I didn't care. I had a destination in mind, but I wasn't in any hurry to get there.

The route to Koby's place was circuitous, requiring me to snake through unfamiliar areas of Los Feliz. We had arranged to meet for dinner at a small Italian restaurant, a couple of miles from his house—good and fine, except I was four hours early. If he wasn't home, well, no big whoop. Maybe I'd drop in on my little sweetie still resting in the baby nursery at Mid-City Peds, pending the outcome of the court custody hearing. I sure hoped the infant wound up with Louise, who *really* wanted her. The woman was a saint and I hoped a judge was smart enough to see that.

I started the climb into the hills of Silver Lake. The day was bright and beautiful, and when the reservoir came into view, iridescent cobalt against the cityscape, my spirits lifted. There was a whole big world out there, my perspective reminded me. It was up to me to make the most of it.

Koby's ten-year-old Toyota was in the driveway. I parked curbside, got out, and skipped to the front door, where I rang the bell. It was one of those chimes that couldn't be heard from the outside. When there was no response, I knocked hard and waited.

After a minute of loitering, I figured he had probably taken a bike ride or a walk. The day was certainly gorgeous enough. I went around to the back metal gate that spanned the driveway. It was rectangular, about five feet tall, and easily scalable. Feeling a bit like a Peeping Thomasina, I gripped the iron top bar and hoisted myself up, peering down his driveway. Toward the back, I could make out an open door, from which I heard the clipped notes of reggae music. The gate latch was padlocked, but that didn't stop me. I flung myself over the top with minimum effort.

The music got louder as I approached the door, walking along the right side of his house. It was planted with espaliered citrus trees—vines of green weaving through white lattice. The leafy branches were frosted with perfumed white blossoms, and a gentle breeze blew through smogless skies. I was about to knock on the open door, but instead I elected to peer inside.

The room was devoid of conventional furniture, holding only a workbench with a circular saw. Koby was kneeling on all fours, hand-sanding the floor, dust flying every which way. He wore a yellow tank top and jeans, pads protecting his knees, and a surgical mask covering his nose and mouth. His well-defined muscles gleamed with sweat, as if sculpted and oiled. If I had a *real* vivid imagination, I could have added some jazz. Then the setting would have made a perfect backdrop for a blue movie.

I watched him for several moments, then rapped forcefully on the door. He looked up, turned to the source of the sound, then leaped to his feet, as graceful as a panther. He pulled his mask off his face and turned down the music. With Bob Marley in retreat, I heard the stream of fast patter/talk that could only come from a sports announcer. His face registered confusion.

"What time is it?" he said.

"I'm early," I told him. "Very early."

"Is everything all right?"

"Just fine." I walked inside the room. He was repairing the floorboards, replacing the rotted pieces with fresh strips of wood. The room was small but held a beautiful back-yard view: the red-tipped leaves of rose-bushes not far from bloom, beyond the bushes a glimpse of the lake. There was sawdust all over the place. It speckled his dark skin like freckles.

"You do your own gardening as well?"

His eyes followed mine out the back win-dow. "The yard is tiny—mostly the rose-bushes. I love the roses. In a week or two, it should fill with flowers."

"It must be beautiful."

"It is very beautiful."

I looked at the repairs he had done. The new strips fit perfectly into the running-board pattern. In the corner of the room was a small TV resting on the floor. The Lakers game was on. Conference play-offs.

I pointed to the TV. "What's the score?"

"Lakers are up by three, two minutes to go to the end of the second quarter. Lawrence Funderburke just scored off the bench for the Kings. They've been trading baskets. It's going to be close."

I tapped my foot. "I'm restless. Need any help?"

"If you give me about twenty minutes to clean up this mess, and another twenty minutes to clean up myself, we can do something together."

"You'll miss the game then."

"They will survive without my suggestions."

"Really, I don't mind helping out." I looked at the workbench. "I wouldn't trust myself with the circular saw, but I can sand with the best of them."

"You've done woodwork before?"

"I used to help my dad out when he did the add-ons. He's one of those handy guys." I regarded his repairs with admiration. "Probably not unlike yourself. Are you a perfectionist, too?"

Koby shrugged. "Is there any other way?"

"Now *that* sounds like my father." I continued to gaze outside. "I saw my father this morning. I asked him for help on a case, and he came through. It was productive. We got some good information. I would have loved to act on it right away, but I promised him that I'd wait until the lead detective got back from his weekend vacation."

"Why did you promise to wait?"

"Because technically, it's his case." I turned to face him. "There's this thing in LAPD. You've got to follow protocol. I have a little problem with that."

"It's a tightrope," Koby said. "To think independently—but not *too* independently."

"That sums it up."

"It is the same in my field. I am the one to spot the first signs of trouble, but I'm not supposed to act without consultation. I must talk to the doctor; I must talk to the psychologist. I consult with the physical therapist, the occupational therapist, the play therapist, and if the kids are older, the speech therapist, the educational therapist, and the reading therapist. In the end"—he smiled—"I use my own judgment. I was a medic in the army. If it's an emergency, I do what I have to do."

"Does it get you into trouble?"

"No, because most of the time, I do the consults. I even see the point of the consults. It slows me down. In medicine, to be too quick is often not good."

"Are you always this rational?"

"Most of the time, yes."

"That's also like my dad. Rational."

"Why do you sneer when you say that?"

I laughed. "I apologize. It is a compliment—even though I'm saying it like it was an insult. My dad is very rational. It makes him really good at what he does."

Koby caught my eye. "And how is he as a father?"

"He's . . . very caring. In general, I'd say we have a good relationship."

"I enjoyed meeting him."

Suave, I thought. The man was diplomatic. I said, "He was a bit miffed with me."

"Why?"

"Because I didn't tell him you were black."

"The color of my skin is important to him?"

"No. I think he was just taken aback. On the positive side, he thought that you were a good guy."

"That sounds promising. Unless you don't like good guys."

"No, I like good guys very much. I just haven't done a very good job of choosing them in the past."

Koby was quiet.

"You don't know me," I said.

"But isn't that what dating is for?"

I looked at the flowerless rosebushes. "True."

Koby studied his dust-coated hands. "So . . . this lack of good guys . . . Is there like an ex-husband in the picture?"

"No . . . thank God for that."

"So you . . . you've never been married or . . ."

I studied his quizzical face. "No, I've never been married. No kids, either. I'm a free agent. What about you? Have you ever been married?"

He shook his head, but his eyes seemed rife with relief. "Cindy, there's nothing wrong with experimenting, no? That is what youth is for. And it's good that both of us have never been married. One less piece of baggage."

"I've still got plenty to deal with."

"Don't we all."

Abruptly, he took my face in his hands and kissed me hard. When I didn't object, he kissed me again, this time long and slow, his teeth nibbling my lips, his tongue dancing against mine. It was a kiss filled with lust and desire, a kiss that was hot and vibrant. He wrapped his arms around my waist and pulled me into his body, his hands sweeping over my rear, his erection digging into my hip. I didn't mean to do it, but the next thing I knew, I was stoking the engine, so to speak.

Not that it mattered, but the man was more than proportional.

Who the hell was I kidding?

It mattered.

He closed his eyes and moaned. "I am sweaty."

"You smell like a man," I told him. "That's just fine with me."

▼

Eventually, he did shower. We both did . . . together . . . an act almost as intimate as the ones that preceded it. As he soaped my back, he kissed the nape of my neck, a sinewy arm snaking around me, his hand resting on my breast. I looked at his fingers, at his nutmeg-colored digits against my pale, freckled complexion, and for a moment, I fantasized about the progeny we'd produce—café au lait skin, with brown eyes and thick, thick hair. I always hated my complexion, and welcomed the thought of it changing in the next generation.

I got out first, toweling dry as I pulled off my shower cap, shaking out my hair. I shivered as water evaporated off my skin, then slipped under the crumpled sheets to get warm and catch my breath.

Several minutes later, he entered the room stark naked and eyed me in the bed.

"I'm just resting," I told him. "I'm spent. At least, for a couple of hours."

He picked up the watch on his nightstand, then slipped it on his wrist—still nude but now he could tell time. "Hungry?"

I sat up, letting the sheet fall from my breasts. "Actually, I am."

His topaz eyes were still on my body. But he said, "I'll get dressed then."

He was one of those lucky people who looked great in or out of clothing, and I enjoyed watching him move. He opened a door to a tiny closet, his shirts hanging neatly inside. He stared at the array for almost a minute—something a woman would do—then picked out two shirts to show me. One was lilac, the other was tomato red.

"What color pants?" I asked.

"Black."

I thought a moment. "The red."

He placed the lilac shirt back in the closet. "Red to match your hair."

"Then you'd need orange."

He slipped the shirt on. "Not orange. The shirt would be the color of a sunset—brilliant and fiery with copper—and even that wouldn't capture it."

I stared at him shocked. "That was beautiful."

He beamed. "Thank you. It took me twenty minutes to get the words right."

I threw a pillow at him. He blocked it with an elbow. "Isn't it the thought that counts?"

"Yes, that is worth something."

"Worth a lot. I used a thesaurus. English isn't my native language."

"Don't give me that. You're totally fluent."

He put on Jockeys, then slid into a pair of black jeans. "Now *that* is a very good compliment."

His face was dead serious. I had hit something important. "How'd you learn?"

"I learned at first in Ethiopia, more in Israel, but mostly from my stepmother." He buttoned his shirt. "She is English speaking . . . from Canada. I make her speak the language to me because I want to speak *real* English. I saw America as my ticket to freedom. I think my vocabulary is pretty good."

"It's *excellent,* Koby." I got up and started

to dress. "I have Ivy League friends who don't sound nearly as educated as you do."

"Thank you, that means very much to me because I work very hard on it. Now I must work on my spelling. Other than medical terms, my English spelling is absolutely atrocious."

"My spelling is atrocious and English is my native language."

He smiled. "That is nice for you to say. English is the third alphabet I learned. There is little in common between Amharic and Hebrew, although both are Semitic languages, and English is totally different. When I first get here, I could speak and understand quite well, but I couldn't read much except medical texts and that is only because the medical language in Hebrew is borrowed from English. There is an expression in Hebrew—to break your teeth, meaning to do a hard thing. I used to break my teeth reading the newspapers. Now I can read the words, but I still cannot spell them. That is the next hurdle."

I tucked my blouse into my pants and began putting on my boots. "You're very . . . driven, aren't you?"

"You are first discovering this?"

I laughed and shook my head.

"What?" he asked.

"I know I keep harping on this, but"—I laughed again—"you are so like my father—just thinner and darker."

"Don't they say that girls are attracted to their fathers, as boys are attracted to their mothers?" He sat down next to me. "Now, my mother died when I was young. She is not so clear in my mind. So I can create whatever fiction I want."

"What's your stepmother like?"

He thought a moment. "Tall . . . strong . . . brown eyes . . . pale skin."

"Sounds familiar," I said. "Red hair?"

He shook his head no. "Brown. Then after ten of us, it turned gray. Batya was tough as a mother, but fair-minded. No sense of humor, but I could make her laugh." He eyed me intently. "I like when you laugh. It's good music."

I looked down and patted his knee.

He raised my face and kissed me gently. Did it a second time, but with more passion. His hands stroked my arms, lust in those incredible jeweled eyes. "Still tired?"

"We're dressed."

"An easy thing to change if the spirit is willing."

I bit my lower lip. "If you're convincing, I could be persuaded."

He raised his eyebrows. "I like challenges. Especially this kind."

"Go for it, Yaakov."

He grinned and started by unbuttoning my blouse and unhooking my bra from the front. Then he unzipped my pants but kept them on. He laid me down on the mattress; then beginning at my forehead, he gently kissed a path downward, his lips traveling onto the tip of my nose, onto my mouth, between my breasts, and over my stomach and navel until he reached the top of my pubis. He lowered the waistband of my panties, his tongue dipping into my thatch of red hair. Softly, he bit the skin. "How do I do?"

My fingers dived into his kinky black hair as I moved his mouth lower. "Very convincing." I sucked in my breath when he hit the right spot. "Oh Lord, yes, I am *definitely* persuaded."

19

We eventually made it to dinner, then hit a ten o'clock movie. The cinema was followed by drinks at a small jazz club, talking and talking until the wee hours of the morning. We had been together for over twelve hours, and though I was zapped, I politely declined Koby's offer to bunk down at his place. I didn't have to work until the afternoon, but I wanted to wake up in my own bed, on my own time. He didn't look insulted. On the contrary, I felt he needed breathing room as well.

We were quiet on the way home, tapped out on ideas, and happy to let the stereo provide the background noise. We were sailing on Sunset back into Silver Lake, his car finally missing a light and gliding to a stop.

There were no other vehicles about us, no cross-traffic in sight.

But there was a lone pedestrian crossing the street. A woman—hunched and wrapped in a heavy black coat. She was clutching a purse to her chest.

I was suddenly alert. I looked at my watch: three in the morning.

"Poor thing," Koby whispered. "Can't we take her to a shelter?"

"I don't know if she's homeless," I told him. "No shopping cart, no bags . . . just a purse. She's also wearing sheer stockings, and in this light, her ankles look normal."

"Ankles?"

"Most of the homeless women have terrible ankles from walking in ill-fitting shoes. And also, the poor health."

"Hooker?"

"Not one that I recognize. To me, it looks like she had a fight with a boyfriend, and he kicked her out of the car. Look at the downcast gait."

"Then perhaps we can take her home. It's dangerous out here."

Before I could agree, the horrid scene played out in slo-mo. A Jeep Cherokee SUV, tearing *against* the light, smashed into her, five yards before the safety of the sidewalk. As the body flew upward, a Dodge Caravan minivan crossed the intersection, just in time for the Jeep to smack it broadside, flipping it over. As the woman fell back to earth, she was hit a second time by the minivan, spinning and bouncing on its roof, the van careening totally out of control until it crashed into a power pole. Electricity sparked. The noise was deafening. The woman had been propelled clear across the boulevard and had landed on the asphalt with a thud. The Jeep did a two-tire screeching turn, speeding off to freedom.

"Shit!" Koby screamed. He punched open a dashboard door, extracted a pair of latex gloves, and snapped them over his hands. He was out of the car before I could unbuckle my seat belt. *"Don't move, don't move, don't move!"* he yelled out to the passengers in the wrecked minivan. He was running over to the woman's inert body.

I raced out of the car, cell phone in my shaking hand.

"Go to the van and tell them not to move!" Koby ordered me. He was leaning over the pedestrian, checking her neck for a pulse. The face was unrecognizable pulp, her body as limp as a rag doll. I bit back bile and ran over to the van, calling 911 as my eyes gawked at the smoking hunk of sheared steel and tangled wires, the entire mess reeking of spilled gas and oil and the metallic stink of burned flesh. Inside, the air bags had deployed, but even so, there was so much blood, guts, and moaning that I nearly fainted at the grisly sight. But as soon as the operator came over my cell, I was surprised by my calm tone, telling him the precise location while requesting para- medics and the fire department stat.

After I hung up, with my mouth still agape, I stared at the carnage inside, unsure how to proceed. I just kept repeating over and over for the passengers not to move, hoping that the panic in my voice wasn't noticeable. When Koby finally appeared at my side, I ex- haled audible relief. Immediately, he went to work, his voice as soothing as lapping waves, as he told the passengers—two men, two women, a couple of kids, and a lifeless baby—not to move while he assessed the damage. Blood was spurting from the arm of one of the women. He tore off his shirt and tied up the artery. Though the night was cold, he was sweating and breathing hard. "You call 911?"

"Yes."

"I've got a first-aid kit and blanket in the back of my car."

"I'm on it." I rushed over to the car, my boot heels clacking against the street, then popped the trunk, taking out the kit as well as a flashlight and a blanket. He had another set of gloves in the kit, so I put them on, then brought the supplies to him and shone the light into the car.

"You brought the flashlight. Someone was thinking. Shine it here."

"What about the pedestri . . . ?"

"Gone. Ah, you're gloved. Press down here, okay? No, not there . . . here."

The wail of sirens in the background. At this hour, the noise could be heard blocks away. As I applied pressure to a leaking vessel with my left hand, I called 911 again with my right. Then I tucked the phone between my shoulder and cheek, so I could free up the other hand to direct light to where Koby was working. He was trying to liberate the infant—thankfully, he had found a pulse—but a web of razor-sharp metal was in his way.

"This is Officer Cynthia Decker from LAPD. I just reported a fatal hit-and-run traffic accident. I need to hook up with radio dispatch so I can give out pertinent information to all cruisers near the scene."

My neck was constricted, screwed up into a god-awful position to secure the phone, and the muscles began to throb. Adrenaline was shooting through my system, choking my breathing with pounding heartbeats. Still, when the police RTO came on the line, I had found my voice.

"Reporting a hit-and-run with fatalities. The vehicle was a late-model Jeep Cherokee, dark in color, last four digits of the license plate—Henry-five-two-three, again, Henry-five-two-three—last seen heading northbound on Terrazzo Avenue. All officers in the area respond immediately. Requesting additional units to the scene of the accident—Terrazzo and Sunset."

I waited until the operator repeated the information. When she did, I hung up, put the phone down, and rolled my neck. Koby was wrist deep in blood, dressing horrid gashes with gauze from the kit. It was like plugging up the proverbial dike with a finger.

The sirens grew louder. I could see flashing lights in the reflection of the shattered window glass. The EMTs arrived less than three minutes after my first call, though it had seemed much longer. When they pushed me out of the way, I wanted to say thank you. Koby spoke rapidly while continuing his work, informing them about the infant, then requesting to speak to the doctor on the ambulance phone. When my date started conversing in medical lingo, I walked away, trying to figure out how to be useful.

With great trepidation, I walked over to the thrown body and held my mouth. I regarded her—discarded, her limbs broken and distorted. Her skull had been cracked open and brain was oozing out. The urge to puke was almost as strong as the urge to pass out. I jerked my eyes away from the corpse just as an unmarked car pulled up. Two people got out, flashing their badges. They needn't have bothered, because I knew both of them by more than just name.

Hayley Marx was a fellow officer in Hollywood, the closest thing I had to a friend in the Department. We used to eat dinner together twice a month, but now our schedules conflicted. We kept meaning to make time, but never got around to it. She looked great, her tall frame svelte in a black pantsuit. She'd grown out her blond hair so that it now brushed her earlobes, softening her face.

The man she was with was the last guy on earth I wanted to see. Detective Scott Oliver worked Homicide under my father's leadership. Once, they had been colleagues, and there remained festering resentment over my father's promotion, further aggravated by my idiotic fling with Oliver. It was over almost before it started, but I was told by sources close to both of us that he wasn't thrilled. God only knew why. I wasn't a day at the beach.

Scott was a sharp dresser. He had on a black jacket, black T-shirt, and khaki pants. His face was handsome in that middle-aged-man rugged way, and his thick hair had silvered at the seams. Ordinarily, his penetrating stare would have put me under, but at the moment, I was preoccupied with other things.

"Decker!" he barked out.

"Oh my God!" Hayley gasped. "You all right, Cin?"

I started babbling. "We were sitting at the intersection when a Jeep just smashed into her." I realized I was sobbing. "I don't know if we should move her out of the way—"

"First just calm down!" Oliver told me.

"Okay, okay—"

"Because we can't move her until Traffic and Homicide get here. It was a hit-and-run, right?"

"Yes."

"We heard it go over the box; I'm sure others heard it, too. Just hang for a moment." Oliver turned to Hayley. "I've got some crime tape in the trunk of my car. Can you get it for me?"

"I'll go with you," I told her.

"No, you stay here and tell me *exactly* what happened."

Another cruiser had arrived: two more guys from my division—Bader and Guensweit. With others there, it made it easier to tell the story; the crowd mitigated the queasy feeling. Scott told the uniformed officers to rope off the body while he took me aside and pushed me for details.

"I told you, I only remember the last four digits of the license plate number, Scott. It happened so fast—"

"Just let me get a physical picture, okay?"

"Okay."

He sighed, making me feel like an errant child. Hayley said, "It'll be okay, Cin—"

"Can you not interrupt, Marx?" Oliver's eyes went to my face. "So you're heading eastbound, stopped at a light."

"Yes . . . exactly where the car is parked now. We haven't moved it."

"So where was the Jeep coming from?" Oliver asked.

"I told you I don't *know.* There were no cars on either side of us. The Jeep just came out of nowhere and ran the light."

"Then it came up from behind you?" Oliver asked.

"Maybe. Probably. I don't know, Scott, I wasn't driving. I wasn't checking the rearview mirror."

"Who was driving?"

"Koby." I turned toward the crash site. "My date. He's over there somewhere, helping out the paramedics."

"He's a doctor?" Hayley asked.

"A nurse."

"Oh." She sounded disappointed.

I exploded. "What the hell difference does it make?"

"Cin, I'm sorry—"

"She had a purse!" I suddenly recalled. "The woman . . . she was holding a purse. I remember pointing it out to Koby as we watched her cross the street. She looked so sad." I began to pace. "We've got to find the purse. It's bound to have her ID. I've got to find it—"

"No, you've got to sit down," Oliver told me.

"No, no, I'm okay. . . ."

Another cruiser pulled up. Oliver said, "Cindy, sit down! That's an order. I'll call it into Hollywood Homicide."

But I didn't listen. As Oliver left with Hayley to give instructions to the next set of units, I started hunting around for the handbag. There was blood all over the place. Piercing screams and sobs were coming from the pile of mangled metal. The group of EMTs working on the accident had grown. There were now two ambulances and two fire trucks with lots of firefighters in yellow slickers standing by. They were bringing out the Jaws of Life.

Koby emerged from the shadows, speaking to a paramedic, using his hands as he talked. I stared at him, in awe of how fast he had reacted. I jumped when Oliver tapped me on the shoulder.

"I told you to sit down."

"I'm okay."

"No, you're not."

Silence.

"Who's your date?" Oliver asked.

I pointed to Koby. "Him."

"Shirtless wonder?"

I jerked my head around and glared at him.

Oliver let out a bitter chuckle and shook his head. "Does Daddy know you're eating chocolate cake?"

Stunned didn't even remotely approximate the way those words hit me. Rage welled up so quickly, it made my eyes tear. The old Cindy would have slapped his face and berated him with a string of curse words. But if I had learned anything the past year, it was the value of saying as little as possible.

"Stay away from me, Oliver." My voice was feral. "Stay *far* away."

"Hey!" Hayley shouted as she tied up the last bit of crime tape. "Everything okay?"

The absolute fury must have showed on my face. "Just fine, Marx." I stalked off, snapping off my gloves, and continued searching for the purse. Oliver had the good sense not to follow. Hayley joined me a minute later with a flashlight. "What'd he say to you?"

"Nothing."

"Liar."

"Help me look for the handbag."

"That's what I'm doing." She swept the light across the dark ground. "Who's your date?"

I gave up on subtlety. "The black guy over there."

"Really." A pause. "Great body. Why's he shirtless?"

I couldn't keep the scorn out of my voice. *"Because* he ripped it off to tie up a gushing artery."

"Wow . . . that's cool."

"Hayley, shut up!"

She held my shoulders, and I started to cry. She hugged me tightly and I let her do it. "You're okay, Cin, you're okay."

"It was just so awful . . . that horrible noise!" I pulled away. "We've got to find the purse. We've got to find out who she is . . . was."

"I know he's a jerk, Decker. I know I'm a

jerk for going out with him, especially
'cause he still likes you—"

"Not the time for a psychodrama, Marx."
I stepped away from her and took in my surroundings. The body had landed around ten
feet from a stucco office building encircled
by a three-foot hedge of waxy privet. Maybe
the purse landed somewhere in the bushes.
I began separating branch from branch. It
was dark and I was looking into black holes.

"Maybe you'd do better if you could see."
Hayley offered me the flashlight. I took it
and shone the beam into the thick leaves.

"Thanks."

"How about I hold while you look?"

I nodded. "Thanks." A pause. "I know I'm
being a butt."

"You're fine, Decker, but you witnessed
something shocking. Oliver's right. You
should sit down."

Sharp twigs scratched the back of my
hands. "Oliver's not right about anything."

"How long have you been going with this
guy?"

"A week. It's nothing, okay? You know
you can shine the light and look at the same
time."

Hayley began a perfunctory search through the flora. "First date?"

"Third."

"Third . . . It's going well then."

"Can I get a little illumination over here?"

She shifted the angle of the beam. "You do anything yet?"

I didn't answer.

Excitement in her voice. "Is he good?"

Again I didn't answer.

More excitement. "Is it true what they say about black guys?"

It took herculean effort not to punch her out, but once more I didn't answer.

Hayley was staring into the bushes, bringing the light into focus on something. "What's this?"

"What?"

"That!" It was rectangular in shape and made from chrome or steel or silver. It winked in the dark. She squinted. "Maybe a pop-top?"

I went in for a closer inspection. "Too big. It could have come from her purse. We shouldn't touch it . . . although I don't know why."

"Just in case." Hayley reached in her own purse and pulled out a tissue. "Here."

I retrieved the metal and was surprised to find it attached to a chain. It was the type of dog tag usually worn by GIs. The surface was embossed with a name, a phone number, and a notice that the wearer was on Dilantin and phenobarbital, and was allergic to penicillin and all its derivatives as well as erythromycin and all its derivatives.

"This is one ill girl."

"'Belinda Syracuse.'" Hayley read the inscription in the beam of light. "Think it's her?"

I took out my cell phone, my heart thumping in my chest. "There's one way to find out." As I phoned the number, I had an eerie sense of déjà vu. Then I began to sweat, thinking about what I'd say to whoever answered the phone at three-thirty in the morning. After three rings, a machine kicked in. When the recorded voice told me who was on the other end of the line, I gasped and dropped the phone. It bounced several times but didn't break.

The wonders of modern technology.

20

I finally took Oliver's advice and sat down, because had I remained on my feet, I would have passed out. Hayley kept asking me questions. I could hear her voice but couldn't understand the words because my head was still spinning. Eventually, things began to register.

". . . you okay? Do you need water?"

"I'm fine!" I insisted.

The excitement in her voice attracted Oliver's attention. He jogged over.

"What's going on?"

"I don't know," Hayley said. "Decker called up the number on the dog tag. Then she dropped the phone."

"What dog tag?"

I showed Oliver the strip of metal that

Hayley and I had found in the bushes. "The phone number on the tag is for Fordham Communal Center for the Developmentally Disabled. If the hit-and-run victim is this woman Belinda Syracuse, then in the famous words of Yogi Berra, 'It's déjà vu all over again.'"

"What the hell does that mean?" Oliver barked.

"Can you give me a minute to catch my breath?" I snapped back.

The two of them waited, staring at me. Despite Oliver's incredible rudeness and brusque manner, there was concern in his eyes. He told me to take my time.

I said, "The baby that I plucked from the trash? The mother was a resident of the same center . . . the Fordham Center. . . ."

They continued to study my face. Oliver said, "And . . ."

"Well, don't you think it's a big coincidence?"

Oliver held out his hands as if he were balancing scales. "Yeah . . . I suppose."

I suddenly felt inane. What *was* the big deal?

"What?" Oliver asked. "You think they're related? Tell me. I'm listening."

"I don't know."

"So what are you getting all hysterical about?"

"I don't know, Oliver, maybe it's the shock of seeing a fellow human being batted around like a shuttlecock!"

I was talking louder than I thought. Koby shouted out, "Are you okay, Cindy?"

"I'm fine," I yelled back. "Just having a spirited debate!"

My voice was razor sharp. Koby gesticulated to one of the paramedics, then sprinted over. Someone had provided him with a blue short-sleeved scrub top. He took in my face, his eyes also concerned. "You look pale."

"I'm fine." I pointed to my companions, one at a time. "This is Officer Marx, also from Hollywood PD . . . Homicide Detective Scott Oliver."

"Yaakov Kutiel." He lifted up his bloodied gloves. "Forgive the lack of handshake."

Oliver nodded.

Koby directed his attention to me. "Do you need me to take you home right now?"

"I can take her home if you're busy," Oliver volunteered.

I cringed. If our past wasn't obvious before, it sure was now.

Koby spoke before I could. "No, that's fine."

"Just that you looked kinda busy," Oliver said.

I said, "What I really need to do is go over to the Fordham Communal Center and find out if Belinda Syracuse is sleeping in a bed or not." I showed Koby the dog tag. He read the information but didn't touch it. "I found this in the bushes. The number corresponds to the Fordham Center, the same school that Sarah Sanders went to."

"The abandoned baby's mother?"

I nodded.

"That's odd."

"I thought so. Probably one of those weird coincidences. Anyway, since I've already been to the place and dealt with some of the people there, I think I should go and find out about Belinda Syracuse. If she is the victim, it's only proper to give her an identity."

"You're not a Homicide detective, Cindy." Oliver found that necessary to point out.

"But you are. So come with me." I added, "Both you and Marx."

Koby said, "If you're going to work, then I will go to the hospital with the children. Since I've been with them from the start, I'm familiar with their medical conditions. I might have something useful to contribute."

"Koby's a—" I started again. "Yaakov's a critical-care nurse at Mid-City Peds."

"Very dedicated," Oliver said.

"You do your job, I do mine." Koby regarded me. "Are you sure you're all right?"

"I'm fine, Koby, honest." I stood up to prove the point. "Hayley will drive me to your place so I can pick up my car." I kissed him lightly on the mouth. "Go. We'll talk later."

"Maybe *I'll* talk to you later, too," Oliver told him. "Decker here is a little sketchy on the details."

Koby gave him the full force of his jeweled eyes. "I'm sure she remembers more than I do. But I will help you if I can." He turned and jogged back.

Moments passed. It was late and I was spent and impatient. "The officers can wait with the body for Hollywood Homicide. Are we going or not?"

Oliver shrugged. Hayley took my arm and together we walked to Oliver's Beemer.

▼

I sat in the backseat, giving out directions but otherwise mute. Hayley didn't push it, but Scott made some weak stab at chitchat, which mercifully died a natural death. I was livid at Scott, but I was trying very hard not to let the anger interfere with professionalism.

No traffic on the streets, just a misty fog that haloed road lights and turned Sunset into a blurred snapshot. We raced down the boulevard, the hour too late for even the dealers and hookers. Not a soul stirred, although we passed an occasional lump of covers on a bus bench. For all we knew, the body underneath could have been dead. The stillness was freaky, even to the most ardent of night owls, and time took on a surreal context. We made it to the Fordham Communal Center in less than fifteen minutes.

I rapped on the door, and it took several minutes to get a response. Once we did, I announced to the scared voice on the other side that we were the police. I'd never met the woman who answered. She was quite tall, swathed in a terry-cloth robe, her short dark hair sticking out at all angles, having been attacked by static electricity. She squinted when I showed her my badge, did the same when Hayley and Oliver showed theirs.

I started the ball rolling. "I'm very sorry to disturb you, ma'am. We have a couple of questions regarding Belinda Syracuse. We understand she lives here."

"Belinda?" The woman was confused. "Belinda's a good girl. What did she do?"

"Is she with you now?" I asked.

"No, she's out on a weekend pass to visit her brother. May I ask what this is all about?"

I showed her the dog tag. The woman gasped. "What happened to her?"

"We're not sure. That's why we're here." Oliver walked across the threshold, into the house. We followed, glad to be out of the chill. "Right now, we need the name and phone number of Belinda's brother."

"May I please see your badge again?" the woman asked.

Because the lights were so dim, Oliver held it up to her face. "I know this must be upsetting. The sooner you give us the information, the sooner we'll be able to tell you something."

"I've been to the center before," I added. "With the Sarah Sanders case."

"She found Sarah's baby," Hayley joined in.

"I spoke to Mr. Klinghoffner."

"He's not in," the woman told us. "He doesn't sleep here."

Hayley said, "And you are . . ."

"Myra Manigan."

Just then a voice came from above the stairs. "Ms. Manigan? Are you okay?"

"I'm fine," she shouted. "I'll be up in a moment, dear."

Oliver tossed her his most charming smile. "Please, Ms. Manigan. The number?"

"I'm sorry. It's just so . . . discombobulating." She turned on a few more lights. "Have a seat. What time is it?"

"Around four A.M.," Hayley said. "Do you need help?"

"No, I'm fine, but thank you. Wait a moment."

When she was out of earshot, Hayley said, "Poor girl. First being retarded, then dying so dreadfully. What kind of life is that?"

A few minutes later, Myra came down the steps. "I've phoned Mr. Klinghoffner."

"We still need the number," Oliver told her.

"Yes, of course. But if you find out—"

"I'll tell you what's going on, yes."

Still, she hesitated. Then, screwing up her courage, she handed me the name and number.

Terrance Syracuse.

The number was a West L.A. exchange.

I traded glances with Oliver. "You're the lead."

Oliver threw it back to me. "Help yourself, Decker."

I looked at Ms. Manigan. "Can I borrow your phone?"

"Of course."

I took a deep breath and phoned. The man who answered was groggy and pissed. I explained the dilemma as succinctly as possible but he was still at sea, although now he was agitated.

"She's not over there?" he asked me.

"No, sir, she's not. We were hoping she was with you."

"But she's supposed to be over there. What's going on? Who is this?"

"Hollywood Police," I told him again. "I'm at the Fordham Center right now. I think we could sort this out more efficiently if we spoke in person."

"First things first," Syracuse demanded. "Where is Belinda?"

"Sir, what's your address?"

"Something's happened to her, hasn't it?" His voice broke. "She told me she was going back early. She told me she had a ride."

"Did she tell you who her ride was?"

"Just someone from the center. What is it? What happened?"

"Sir, we really need to come down and see you."

"Oh my God." A heavy sigh. "Oh Jesus, just tell me what happened!"

"Your address, sir?"

He yielded to pressure. He lived in Mar Vista, not too far from my house. It didn't make sense to go to his place, only to go back to Koby's to pick up my car, but I couldn't keep the man waiting.

Another thirty minutes of riding with Oliver.

I gritted my teeth and pretended that we were one big, happy team.

▼

The brother was stocky, bordering on fat, with gray hair and lots of it. He was my height, but since I was wearing four-inch heels, I was looking over the top of his head. He had on black sweats, open-back slippers on his feet.

It went down like this. Terrance Syracuse was a self-employed personal-injury lawyer and sometimes his work intruded upon his weekends. This was one of those times. He had several cases pending, and really hadn't thought about hosting Belinda. But because his wife and two daughters were visiting his in-laws in Vermont, he decided to call her up. His wife was tolerant of his retarded sister, but lately his children were getting to that age where Belinda's presence embarrassed them. As much as he loved his sister, he had no problem choosing his daughters' needs over Belinda's because he had grown up with the stigma of a disabled sister. He could deal with it now, he was comfortable with the situation, but he knew that adaptation took time. He didn't want to force his kids into an artificial relationship that they weren't equipped to deal with.

"I suppose that won't be necessary now," he said, sobbing.

Before he left for the office, he had set Belinda up in front of the TV and told her he'd be back in time to take her out for dinner. He'd done it many times before. Belinda was a good girl, and she obeyed the rules. As far as he knew, she never opened the door for strangers. One time, his wife's sister had come to the house, but Belinda didn't know her. His sister-in-law was irate, yelling and screaming, but Belinda held fast and refused to let her in. She wasn't the type to go off on her own. She was retarded, yes, but she wasn't stupid. She knew that in the outside world, there were people who'd take advantage of her.

"And you don't know who took her back to the center?"

"No. But she insisted it was someone she knew. I had no reason to doubt her."

"We can check phone records," I told Scott.

"It had to have been someone familiar," Syracuse insisted. "Otherwise she wouldn't have gone." He gnawed on a raw thumbnail. "What in the world was she doing in that area at that time of night?"

I said, "I don't know, sir. She looked lost. I was about to pull over to help her when it happened."

"This car . . ."

"Actually, it was an SUV."

"Did it . . . Was it gunning for her?"

I refrained from sighing. "It's anyone's guess. It happened so fast, I didn't get all the details. Maybe later . . . if I think about it, something new will come to me." I bowed my head. "I'm so sorry."

He nodded, not daring to make eye contact.

Hayley said, "Did she know anyone else besides you who lived outside the Fordham Center?"

"She might have. My sister didn't talk to me about her private life. And when she did . . . I didn't listen too carefully. She was a typical teenage girl . . . only she was twenty-four. But she still had the teenybopper mentality—boy crazy, for one thing. Mostly movie stars. She talked about meeting them one day. She lived in a fantasy world and I zoned out half the time." He started pacing. "This is too awful. I'm grateful that my parents aren't alive to deal with this blow." He regarded Cindy. "When can I bury her? The thought of her lying on a slab in cold storage is sickening."

"We'll let you know as soon as the ME is done."

"What in the world is there to find out? She was massacred by some crazy or careless motorist. What will an autopsy tell you that you don't already know?"

"It's just procedure, sir," Oliver told him.

He drew his hands down his face. "I have to start making funeral arrangements." He checked his watch. "I don't suppose anyone's open at five in the morning."

"You might have to wait a few hours."

I said, "You won't mind if we check your phone records?"

"Of course. Anything that would help. She's been with the center over ten years. I can't imagine anyone wanting to hurt her."

"Has she been having any trouble with anyone there?"

"Not that I know about."

"Has she talked about anyone specifically?"

"Like a boy or a man? No. Or if she did, I'm sorry to say I didn't pay attention."

Again he checked his watch. "When can I make the identification?"

"How about if I take you down?" I offered. "See if we can speed up the process."

"I'll come with you," Hayley stated.

"We can all go," Oliver said.

"You have farther to travel to get home, sir," I told him. "We can handle it, Detective."

"We'll all go," Oliver insisted. "That way, it'll be done by the book."

I was in no position to argue.

Seniority had spoken.

21

By the time Terrance had identified his sister and we were finally done, it was half past six. Hayley offered to buy us breakfast, but I was too nauseous to even think about eating.

"Besides, I should see how Koby's doing."

Oliver's shoulders tensed. "I'll take you to his house after I drop off Marx."

Hayley said, "I'll take her, Scott. This is girl time, okay?"

That was Hayley to a T. It didn't surprise me. She'd been there for me before. Oliver didn't argue and the ride was wonderfully silent. We picked up Hayley's car and made it to Koby's by eight. My Lexus was right where I'd left it; his Toyota was nowhere in sight. I sighed. "I don't think he's home yet. He's probably still at the hospital."

"You aren't going there, right?" Before I could answer, she said, "Cin, you need to go home and sleep."

"You too."

"No problem. I'm going home. You do the same. That's an order." We hugged. She said, "Breakfast on Wednesday?"

"How about Thursday?" I countered for no good reason.

"Thursday is perfect."

I smiled, then got out of the car. After settling myself in my Lexus and placing the phone in the built-in recharge cradle, I put in a call to Koby's cell.

I got his voice mail.

I left a brief message.

Next I tried the hospital. I was transferred about ten times and finally wound up talking to Marnie, the pixie nurse I had met the first time I had visited Sarah's baby. She knew about the accident and asked me if I was okay. I told her I was.

There was an awkward pause.

"He's in the ICU," she told me. "Been there for a while. Maybe I can help you with something?"

Tension in her voice. It could have come from dealing with the horror of the accident, but the tightness told me it was probably more personal. That I was bugging her because I was bugging Koby.

"No . . . just tell him I called."

"I will, Officer. Good-bye."

She hung up before I could thank her.

I made it home by nine, then called Louise Sanders to cancel our lunch date at the precinct. She wasn't in, but I left a message on her cell. Then after setting the alarm for one-thirty, I went to bed. The buzzer did its magic at the appointed time, and I was showered, dressed, and ready to go by two. There were messages on my answering machine from that morning. Three from my father, one from Hayley, and even one from Scott, his being two words—"Let's talk."

I'd deal with my messages later.

There was nothing from Koby.

I called his cell, but it was still on voice mail.

I called his house. He wasn't home or he wasn't picking up. This time, I left a message. I told him how proud I was of him. I told him I was okay and hoped he was okay as well. I was still shaken but otherwise fine. Then I hung up.

The ball was in his court. Tired and grumpy, I went to work.

▼

It took some dogged determination, but I managed to catch up with Russ MacGregor while I was on break and he was in the squad room, working the phones before he went out on his next field call. The hit-and-run had given me some clout since I had reacted quickly and according to protocol. But Russ was far from generous. I had fifteen minutes to state my case.

Three things were on my mind: Sarah Sanders's rape, locating the missing David, who was possibly the father of Sarah's baby, and now the hit-and-run. I knew my limitations, and so did Russ. Still, I made a stab at it, trying to tie everything together. Russ was dubious.

"What in the world does this hit-and-run have to do with Sarah Sanders and an abandoned baby?"

"Maybe Belinda Syracuse knew something about Sarah's rape. Girls do talk, you know. And maybe Belinda was murdered because of it."

"Number one, Decker, you don't even know if this rape is real or not. Number two, if you think Belinda's death was related to Sarah Sanders's alleged rape, why wait months before bumping Belinda off, and number three, if these cases are connected, why is Belinda dead and Sarah Sanders alive and well?"

I had no answer, so I ignored the questions. "I think we should explore the possibilities."

"Are you deaf? They had nothing to do with one another."

"Freaky coincidence?"

"It happens, Decker. Anything else?"

He was already walking away, the vents of his navy jacket flapping behind him. I said, "Nice suit."

Russ slowed. "Thanks." He stopped, then suddenly eyed me like a man. Then he thought better of it. "Decker, you did a good job. Everyone has taken note. Now leave the hit-and-run investigation to Homicide."

"That's not what I'm interested in."

"Dare I ask what you *are* interested in?"

"Finding the most likely candidate for the father of Sarah Sanders's child. My vote is a boy named David, who also lived at the center."

"The one who was supposedly beaten up."

"Why *supposedly?* Why would Sarah lie?"

"Because she abandoned her baby and is in big trouble. She's facing a reckless-disregard charge."

"Her mental condition is perfect for a mitigating-circumstances plea."

"But maybe she's also aiming for the sympathy plea. You have no idea if this rape and mugging are figments or are real."

"So let me find out."

"Decker, it happened months ago. It's old news."

"And that makes the crime any less horrific?" How could MacGregor respond to that? "It would be nice to find the guy . . . to make sure he's all right."

"When are you planning to do this, Sherlock?"

"I don't start work until three tomorrow."

"So you're doing it on your own time? Why you buggin' me about it?"

"I make it a point not to step on toes."

He shrugged. "Yeah, sure. Drop by the

center, but give it a day or two. I heard from Justice Brill—the Homicide detective in charge of Syracuse's hit-and-run—that the place is pretty much up to their eyeballs right now, dealing with Belinda's death."

"I can identify with that."

MacGregor must have seen something in my weary face. "You need some rest, Decker. Do you a lot more good than chasing down a half-baked memory." He shook his head. "All right. But like I said, wait a day or two. You gotta think about priorities."

"Of course. Thanks, Russ. Really." I cleared my throat. "Sarah Sanders is willing to come in and make a statement about the rape."

He sneered. "Your idea?"

"How about tomorrow around noon? *Please?*"

Again he eyed me. Then he gave me the "smile." I pretended to be looking the other way. When we reestablished eye contact, it was gone. "Yeah, okay."

"You're a peach, Detective."

"You're a pain in the ass, Decker."

"Don't be mad. If I find something out, you'll get all the credit." On that positive note, I gave him a thumbs-up and walked away.

▼

When I got home, there were two new messages—another one from Dad, and another from Hayley. I picked up the phone but thought better of it.

Instead, I turned on my computer and checked my e-mail. I saw his screen name sandwiched between an AOL discount special and LOW-RATE MORTGAGES FROM HOUSE EQUITY FUNDING. I wasn't wild about electronic communication, but I was the one who had started it. I clicked on it.

Dear Cindy,

Doing a double shift. That is good. Better than thinking about the accident. Call you later.

Love, Koby

It was a rather curt e-mail, especially compared to my gushing phone calls. But he was probably dealing with life-and-death issues and didn't have time for the niceties. So I wrote him back, again telling him how impressed I was with his swiftness of action. I wasn't quite as effusive, but I was complimentary.

Maybe it would make him smile.

Maybe it would induce him to call.

22

This time, Decker was late. From down the aisle, he saw her in the corner booth, sipping coffee while reading the paper. From this distance, she looked so young and vulnerable. Maybe he just perceived her that way because she was his daughter. He took a deep breath, his heart skipping in his chest, and slapped a smile on his face. He slid into the booth on the opposite side.

"Sorry. Bad traffic."

Cindy put the paper down and squeezed her father's hand. "It's fine. Just relaxing."

"That's good."

"It's rare these days."

"You've been busy?"

"Always."

"How's Koby?" Decker asked.

"Fine."

Immediately, he heard the catch in her throat. Feeling like an idiot, he quickly changed the subject. "Well, our Tuesday breakfast is turning out to be a ritual."

"One that I like," Cindy stated.

She was somber. That made him feel real low. One of these days, he'd disconnect from his kids. His heart felt heavy. "You doing okay, sweetheart? Must have been pretty traumatic witnessing the accident."

She started to talk, thought better, and answered him with a nod.

"Traffic accidents in general are horrible. One of my most vivid memories in police work is a bad accident from twenty years ago. Just . . ."

Cindy regarded her father's pained expression. "Did you witness it?"

"No . . ." Decker exhaled. "No, just the first unit to arrive at the scene. That was horrible enough. I couldn't even imagine seeing it unfold. I don't understand how you can be working." He held up a finger to the waitress for coffee. "You're much stronger than I am."

"I don't think so, Dad."

"Oh, yes you are. I'd be a basket case."

"Daddy, I have *never* known you once to be a basket case."

"Then I did my job as a parent and hid it well."

That gave Cindy pause. He must have handled hundreds of stressful cases over his career. And yet, except for the last few months, he had always seemed so placid.

"How are *you* doing?" Cindy asked.

"All right."

The waitress came over with the coffee. "Are you ready to order?"

Cindy ordered toast, fruit, and more coffee; Decker made it times two. They sipped weak brew and smiled uncomfortably.

"We're dancing around each other," Cindy told him. "You're not so good and neither am I."

Decker held out his hand to her. "Can I help?"

"No," Cindy answered. "Can I help?"

"Absolutely not." Decker patted her hand, then pulled away. "And even if you could, I'd say no. Parents take care of the kids, not the other way around."

"Will you ever stop thinking of me as your daughter?"

"Probably not. So tell me what's on your mind."

"I have lots on my mind. That's why I have a therapist."

Decker smiled. "I'm glad you're still seeing someone. Rina tells me I need one."

Cindy's shrug was noncommittal.

"What do you think?"

She laughed. "You're asking my opinion?"

"Yes, I am. I value your opinion. How's your experience been with a shrink?"

She didn't know if her father was patronizing her—trying to make her feel better—but she continued on the assumption that he wasn't. "It's good, Dad. You get to unburden yourself without burdening other people. I don't like to spill my emotional guts. We're more alike than you think."

"I'd be honored to be like you."

Cindy's laugh was mirthless. "Man oh man, you must really think I'm bad off to be acting *this* nice."

Decker laughed. "Okay. Now you're sounding familiar. I feel better."

"So, Loo, how do you feel about talking business?"

"It's better than getting all weepy."

"Exactly. So let me tell you what I found out and you tell me if I'm thinking straight or what." Cindy recapped her discussion with Russ MacGregor, mainly her thoughts about the two cases—Belinda Syracuse's hit-and-run, and Sarah Sanders's rape—and how they might be related. By the time she was done, the food had come.

Decker buttered his toast. "As much as I'd like to agree with you, Cin, I think I'm going with MacGregor on this one."

"That they have nothing to do with one another," Cindy stated.

Decker took a bite and nodded. "You don't even know if the hit-and-run was intentional or not. Have they even found the car?"

"I don't think so, no."

"Okay . . ." Decker polished off a piece of toast. He was hungry this morning. "Even if we assume that the hit-and-run was intentional, why would the two cases be related?"

"Maybe Belinda knew something about Sarah Sanders's rape?"

"So why would someone bother to murder her now instead of six months ago?"

"That's just what Russ said."

"I'm not surprised. Care to answer the question?"

Of course, she didn't have an answer. "I haven't thought it all the way through. Don't want to talk prematurely."

Decker spooned fruit into his mouth. He chewed and swallowed. "Good stall tactic. I've used it myself. Find another link, Cin. In the meantime, why don't you wait until the SUV turns up before you continue on? I'm sure you have better things to do with your time."

"Not really."

"Should I ask?"

"Nah, just feeling a bit blue. It'll pass."

Decker didn't dare intrude. She'd just bite his head off. "Get a hobby, Princess. Didn't you once want to make ceramics or something?"

"That was in tenth grade, Daddy."

"See, I listen."

Cindy smiled. "I still intend to go back to the Fordham Communal Center. I want to find out about Sarah Sanders's boyfriend."

"This guy David."

She nodded.

"Who might be dead."

"He might also be alive."

"And MacGregor's okay with that?"

"Yes, Father, he is."

"So let me know what you come up with."

"I will. Any suggestions?"

"Same ones that you used when you were looking for Sarah—shelters, halfway houses, drunk tanks, flophouses, homeless camps. It's not fun work, Cindy. Sure you wouldn't rather throw clay onto a wheel?"

She tossed a small piece of apple at him. "I don't mind going back to the center. At least, Oliver won't be standing over my shoulder this time."

Decker tried to sound casual. "He give you a hard time?"

"Oliver's Oliver. But he let me handle it."

"That's good."

"Actually, it was. He's a jerk but a good detective. No complaints."

But Decker still sensed how unhappy she was. Probably the effects of witnessing something so traumatic. It blunted the senses for a while. For her, it also revived horrid memories from not too long ago. And who knew what it did to Koby, sticking his hands in all that blood and muck? Decker guessed that they were probably not offer-

ing each other too much in the way of mutual support.

Cindy saw the concern on his face. "I
have an appointment with my therapist tomorrow. I'm sending you the bill. So stop
worrying about me, all right?"

"I'm getting the bill?" Decker frowned.
"How much does he charge?"

Cindy rolled her eyes. "First off, it's a she.
Second, I'm kidding. The Department is
paying. It was part of the settlement. 'Go to
anyone, Cin, just so long as you don't sue
our asses off.'"

Decker smiled.

"I'll be fine, Daddy. It just takes time."

Decker took her hand and squeezed it.
"I'm an impatient man when it comes to my
kids. I love you, Princess."

"I love you, too." Her first thought was to
steer the conversation back to work. Then
she realized that's exactly what her father
would have done.

"I'm very proud of you," Decker blurted
out.

Cindy felt a lump in her throat. "Thank
you, Daddy. That means so much to me."

"I'm proud," Decker reiterated, "but I

have a confession to make. I'm very angry with you for joining the police."

"Lordy-Lord, what a shock."

"I know I've said it before. But this is the new part. After I got the news of the accident, my stomach was in an absolute knot. And then it hit me. I was not only angry for what you put me through by joining the academy, I was angry with *myself* for all the aggravation that I put my own family through—including your mother. I've gained a little insight and it isn't pretty. I think I may have actually *wronged* your mom."

"Mom knew that it went with the territory."

"No, Cindy, I blindsided her. She thought I was going to become this nice liberal, upper-class tax lawyer. Going back into police enforcement wasn't on the agenda."

"But you were unhappy as a lawyer."

"I was, but she wasn't. I must have put her through hell on so many different levels. First off, I made much less money. Then I worried her to death. Also, I was never home. I'm getting paid back for my transgressions."

"If you consider doing your job a sin."

"Neglecting her and you was wrong." He

took his daughter's hand. "I want to thank you for not holding it against me."

"You did the best you could, Daddy. That's all that we can ever ask."

"In some ways, Cin, you are so much more mature than I am."

Cindy choked on her words. "You know how to make a girl feel good."

"I'm reckless when it comes to myself, but a worrywart when it comes to my family. It's hypocritical, but I'm too old to change."

"I don't want you to change. I think you're terrific."

"Cindy, I am so honored to be your father!"

"Thank you." Her eyes started to water. Spontaneously, she leaned over the table and kissed his cheek. "Do me a favor, Pops. Hold that thought the next time you get frustrated with me."

23

There was no love lost between Buck the bureaucrat and me, and tragedy did not bring us closer together. He was as obnoxious as ever, wearing a black turtleneck and jeans. His hands fluttered as he growled out the words.

"We're rather busy, Officer. Our secretary is out, and we've had some bad news."

"Do tell."

"Then perhaps you can come back tomorrow with your pesky little questions."

As he started to close the door on me, I pushed my way in. "Please get Mr. Klinghoffner for me, Buck."

Having lost that battle, he sat down at his desk and glared at me. "You'll have to wait! I'm elbow deep in paperwork."

I went over to his desk. In a single sudden motion of my arm, I cleared his desktop. "Well, now you're not. Go get him."

"I could have you reported!" Buck was fuming.

"Last I checked, the phone lines were open. So if you don't have the balls to do it, go get Klinghoffner."

Slowly, slowly, he got up. "Typical heavy-handed cop. What is it, Officer? Are you jealous because most women still prefer me to big, strong you?"

I ignored him and checked my watch. I had only an hour before Sarah Sanders was coming in to make a statement. I set my angry eyes on him and waited. He tried out a glare, but it was more like a sneer. In the end, he picked up the phone and punched in some numbers. He turned his back to me and spoke quietly. After he hung up the receiver, he told me that Klinghoffner would be down in five minutes.

I told him thank you.

His eyes went from my face to the mess on the floor. I bent down to pick up the papers.

"Don't touch anything!" he blurted out. "I . . . Let me handle it. Please."

I stood up. "Sorry."

He squatted down, scanned the mess, then began by picking up a pile of papers. "You're not forgiven."

I surveyed the room. I found what I was looking for—the requisite coffeemaker. "Can I make it up by fetching you a cup of home brew?"

He was still sitting on his haunches. "My mug is the blue one. One packet of creamer, one packet sugar."

I went over to the stand and filled his order with the efficiency of the neighborhood Star$s. "Mind if I help myself?"

"That's why the Styrofoam cups are there."

I poured myself a half cup, then placed his mug on his desk.

Buck said, "You were there when it happened?"

"Yes."

He turned some pages over in his hands, then placed them down on the floor. He began to collate the piles. "It must have been awful."

"Yes."

"What exactly happened?"

"Some other time, Buck."

"Did you at least find the idiot?"

"It's coming," I fibbed.

"That means no."

"No, it means it's coming."

He huffed disdain.

"It's good to see you obnoxious again. I was getting worried."

He started to talk but changed his mind. Instead, he stood up and shuffled the pages.

"Are your papers in order?" I asked him.

"For the most part, yes."

"Want me to mess them up again?"

"I want you to go away. But since that's not going to happen, at least don't talk." He sat back down at his desk, straightened a pile of papers, then sipped coffee.

"Did you know the girl, Buck?"

"I know everyone here." He looked up at me. "Are you going to ask me more questions? Because if it's yes, I won't even start to concentrate."

"Know anyone who'd want to hurt her?"

"Of course not. That would imply that someone *cares* enough about them to kill them." He bit his lip. "These are the discards of humanity. If it weren't for Mr. Klinghoffner's dedication, the city would have closed us down many moons ago."

"Her brother said that someone from the center had called her, offering to take her back to Fordham."

"Who?"

"We're in the process of checking phone records. Any ideas?"

"No. I'm not here on weekends. I have an administrative job. But of course, someone was here. Check with them."

I eyed him. "Where were you Sunday night?"

Buck broke into a savage smile. "Oh my!" He brought his hands to his chest. "Am I under suspicion?"

"Can you answer the question?"

"Let's see." He cleared his throat. "What time are we talking about?"

"Three in the morning. Monday morning."

"At three A.M.? I was sleeping."

"Do you have a roommate?"

"My dog."

"What'd you do last Sunday?"

"Hmmm. I went out to brunch with a good friend . . . Café Romano. That was until . . . hmmm . . . three, three-thirty. Do you want her name?"

Her name. "Girlfriend?"

"On good days." He sneered at me. "Jealous?"

"Green with envy. Go on."

"Hmmm . . . I went home. I read. Watched TV. Played with my computer. . . . Oh, I went to a video store. I rented *In the Bedroom* . . . something light and breezy." He rolled his eyes.

I smiled.

Buck pointed to the stairwell. "Your interviewee awaits."

I looked in the direction of his pointed finger. Klinghoffner was coming down the steps.

"Anything else?" Buck asked me.

I stood up. "Not at the moment."

"Does this mean you're going to pester me again?"

"Maybe."

"Oh goody!" He graced me with a sour smile. "I'm rather enjoying this *bad-boy* image."

"Don't flatter yourself," I whispered as I passed his desk.

▼

We went into a private office, away from Buck's prying eyes and ears, and away from distractions. Klinghoffner was wearing a rumpled brown jacket, a wrinkled white shirt, and creased brown cords. He looked as if he hadn't slept for days. His eyes were sunken and his skin had a sick pallor that usually accompanied bad news. He mirrored my own internal turmoil.

"They're children," he told me. "Little kids, Officer Decker. That's all Belinda was . . . just a little kid." He sank into a chair, motioning for me to sit as well. "I just can't believe the bastard didn't stop!"

"It was terrible."

He regarded me with sympathetic eyes. "Did you get his license plate?"

"There's an ongoing investigation. But actually that's not why I'm here."

"No?" He sounded surprised.

Before I started to explain myself, I said, "Have the police contacted you in regard to Belinda's death?"

"No. Frankly, that's what I thought this call was all about."

I had no business asking about Belinda, no business investigating the hit-and-run. Not only would it have been unprofessional, it might mess something up in the future. And to that, I said to myself: *So what?* I said, "Her brother told me that someone had phoned her, offering to take her back to the center. Know anything about that?"

"No." He thought a moment. "How odd. I have no idea who that could have possibly been. We're on a skeleton staff over the weekend, just a couple of our teachers, sleep-in caretakers, and the janitor."

"We're in the process of checking phone records from her brother's house. We'd like to look over your phone records as well."

"Of course. Anything to find this monster."

"Her brother said that she was boy crazy. Maybe she was on a secret tryst. Could she have been seeing someone without you knowing about it?"

"Like a boyfriend?"

"Yes, Mr. Klinghoffner, like a boyfriend."

"It couldn't have been anyone from here. None of our students have driver's licenses."

"And since when has that ever stopped a determined teenager from getting behind the wheel?"

Klinghoffner said, "It doesn't, but these kids don't have access to a car."

"She was hit about five miles away from here. She could have taken a bus."

He was straining with thought. "I'll look into it."

"Thank you," I told him. "As I said before, I'm also here for another reason."

Klinghoffner waited.

"I'm interested in Sarah Sanders . . . her baby's father, actually. I think he might have been a student here. She mentioned a boy named David. Probably black. Possibly Down's syndrome . . . or maybe mosaic. That's when—"

"I know what mosaic is," Klinghoffner interrupted. "Why do you ask?"

"Am I on the right track?"

"David Tyler . . . twenty-four, black, and yes, he was mosaic. Again, why do you ask?"

"And why do you refer to him in the past tense?"

"Because he dropped out of sight about six months ago. I tried very hard to locate him." He was pained. "Did Sarah tell you something about him?"

"This is her story. They used to meet in a park and fool around. One day, about six months ago, a gang of boys caught them in the bathroom. They raped her, beat him up and dumped him in the trash. Sarah left the bathroom not knowing if David was dead or alive. She's been keeping this inside, too scared to tell anyone. It only came up because we asked about the father when we interviewed her about the baby."

It took him a while to answer. "And you think that this is true?"

"Would she have a reason to lie?"

"Yes, if she was having sex. That's against the rules here. Maybe she felt a rape would get her off the hook."

"But then what happened to David?"

Klinghoffner sat back and sighed heavily. "David never lived here, Officer Decker. He was pretty high functioning, as mosaics often are. He had his own apartment, knew the bus lines, and was able to get from point A to point Z pretty well. He was able to do this because his life was very circumscribed."

"If he was high functioning, what was he doing here?"

"He had a job. We used to have an art therapist, but budget cuts put a stop to that. David could draw and didn't demand much in the way of salary. And being who he was, he worked well with the other residents. He was well liked."

"By Sarah Sanders?"

"By everyone." Klinghoffner's lower lip trembled. "David was independent . . . but he was less than completely responsible. He often missed days . . . one day, two days. When he missed a week, I grew concerned. I went over to his place, knocked on the door, and when he didn't answer, I opened it with the key."

"You had a key."

"I had a key. I insisted David give me a key, just in case. His place . . . food in the refrigerator . . . some things on the shelves. But his closet was empty. It seemed to me he had packed up and left."

"Did you call the police?"

"Yes, of course. We're still talking about a compromised individual. I told them about David's condition. But since he was living on his own, and since it *looked* like he moved out voluntarily, they said their hands were tied." He gave me an accusing eye. "The police threw it back in my lap."

I didn't respond.

Klinghoffner went on. "I made phones calls to some local shelters, also to his conservator. He hadn't heard from David, either. This was worrisome. David got his money from him. David doesn't really have skills to hold down a normal job. Without his money, he can't survive."

"Tell me about the conservator."

"David comes from a well-to-do family. He was an only child and was born when the Tylers were older. Joe was sixty, Betty was forty-six. Down's syndrome, or in his case the variant mosaic, is associated with maternal age."

I nodded.

"Naturally, when they realized he had special needs, they set up a trust fund. When Betty died six years ago, all the money went to David. He's been living off that fund."

"And the conservator pays the expenses."

"Yes," the director replied. "David was high functioning, but he required help balancing a budget."

"And you haven't heard from David in about six months?"

He nodded. "Honestly, I stopped looking in earnest about three, four months ago. But I did make phone calls. And of course, I called up his conservator, asked him to keep me posted if he did hear from David. I wanted to make sure he was okay."

"But you never heard from the conservator?"

"The last time I spoke to Mr. Paxton was about . . . let me think. Around two months ago."

"You suspect the worst?"

Klinghoffner just shook his head. "It has been a terrible year."

I said, "Have you considered a connection between David's disappearance and Belinda's death?"

He gave my question some consideration. "I don't see how. The incidents were months apart. And I'm sure Belinda's death was nothing but a terrible accident."

I didn't think so, but I kept my opinions to myself.

"No, no, no," Klinghoffner insisted. "It's all just a coincidence. A terrible, terrible coincidence."

"Sir, do you know what happens to David's money if he dies?"

"I haven't any idea."

"I take it that this Mr. Paxton is a lawyer?"

"Yes, he is."

"Do you have his business address?"

"Of course." He stood up. "I'll get it for you. Would you like me to call him?"

"No, sir, I'll do that. As a matter of fact, it would be better if you didn't tell him about this discussion. He might not think kindly about your relaying all this information."

"Why not? We all have David's interest at heart."

"You have David's interest at heart. Where the lawyer's interests are remains to be seen."

Klinghoffner smiled. "Hold on. I'll get you the address."

He returned a few minutes later and handed me a slip of paper—Raymond Paxton, with a Century City address for his business. "I understand your suspicion, Officer Decker. But I must say that Mr. Paxton paid faithfully for David's care for six years. I don't see it, but . . ." He threw up his hands.

"Probably he's as concerned as you are. I just want to talk to him."

"I must attend to other matters now, Officer Decker. I must say I'm glad that the police are finally taking David's disappearance seriously. But of course, it's a bit late in the game, isn't it?"

I answered with an enigmatic smile.

"I hope you pay more attention to the hit-and-run. As I said, I'm sure it was an accident, but since the driver didn't stop, he must be apprehended. It's been a very big blow."

"I know. I was there."

Klinghoffner turned red. "Of course . . . I am so sorry—"

"It's fine, sir. I shouldn't have even brought it up."

"It must have been a terrible shock to witness something so terrible."

"Yes."

"I'm sorry, but I do have to go."

"Of course."

"Not that I mean to dismiss you—"

"No, no, I understand."

But it seemed that everyone was dismissing me these days.

24

If there were D.T.'s from too much food, Decker was experiencing the phenomenon. Rina had learned cooking from a pro, but over the years, she had lightened the cuisine. Her sauces weren't as heavy, her side vegetables barely blanched and often served plain except for a little salt. Mama was still in the old country, serving mass quantities of *heavy* food. But that didn't stop Decker from stuffing his face. If he had eaten any more chicken paprikash, his face would have turned red and blotchy. But self-loathing had an upside: His mother-in-law was very pleased with his gustatory enthusiasm.

"It's always a pleasure to serve you," she told him. It came out: *Eets alvays a plea-*

surrrre to serrrrve you. Her Hungarian accent was light and lilting.

Magda Elias was wearing a blue pullover sweater and white jeans. She was still beautiful and trim—a woman who took pride in her appearance. Her dyed black hair was always coiffed and she always wore makeup. Rina was a simpler, younger version of her mother.

They were eating in the formal dining room—a paean to porcelain. Magda's breakfront was filled with her good dinner china, figurines, decorative plates, and vases. There were also a dozen pieces of expensive European silver. The woman could have opened up an antique shop.

"It's always a pleasure to eat your cooking, Magda," Decker parried.

Magda smiled. "You are being very charming tonight."

"I've been practicing."

She hit his shoulder. He and Rina's parents got along well, although it hadn't always been that way. It had taken a dozen years and the production of a granddaughter to get to this level of congeniality. He thought about that as Cindy came to mind. Decker had slipped up with Koby. He was still smoldering from her relationship with Scott Oliver and maybe that was the problem. He was too involved. Black, white, purple, old, young, female, whatever—he should have done better with her date. He made a pledge to mind his manners in the future, regardless of whom she brought home.

Sammy and Jacob pushed away their plates and groaned. Sam said, "Really dynamite, Omah, but I ate too much. No room for dessert."

"Aaah." She dismissed his announcement. "Just a leetle strudel. Mostly fruit."

"Apple?" Sammy asked.

She nodded. "And a little nut cake."

"There are cookies, too," Jacob added. "I saw them in the kitchen."

"For Hannah!" Magda explained.

"Where's Papa?" Rina asked.

Magda pointed to the back room. Without fanfare, Stefan Elias had retired to the den, to his chair and his TV programs. Usually the routine required Decker to join him between dinner and dessert. Rina began helping her mother clear the dishes. Decker picked up a platter. He whispered to his wife, "So when are we going to talk about Hannah's family-tree report?"

"Soon, soon," Rina told him.

"Why don't you just tell her—"

"Shhhh."

Decker rolled his eyes. "Are you going to wash the dishes?"

"No, the boys are going to wash."

"We are?" Jacob said.

"Most definitely."

Magda interjected, "I have a dishwasher." She had a *deeshvasher.*

Rina said, "This is good china."

"I have a delicate cycle, Ginny. You think I live in the nineteenth century?" She turned to her grandsons. "You just rinse and put it in the racks, okay? Then you work up an appetite for dessert."

Sammy said, "Yeah, I hear that dishwashing is the new aerobics, Omah."

Decker smiled and elbowed his son's ribs.

Magda said, "You go join Stefan, Peter? He is expecting you."

"In a few minutes. I wanted to hear you talk about your family with Hannah."

"I don't have much to tell." Magda's face tightened. "It was not a happy childhood."

"I know that." Decker went over to her and kissed her cheek. "If it's too hard, we can skip the childhood and start with after you came to America." Rina gave him dagger eyes. He ignored her. "It's totally up to you."

"That would be better." Magda went back to the dinner table and began gathering dirty dishes.

"The boys will do that," Rina said. "Sit."

"No, I like to move around."

Decker said, "Like mother, like daughter."

They brought a new round of soiled dishes into the kitchen.

"Oh goody," Sammy said. "I was almost through and just hoping for more."

"Stop complaining," Rina told him.

Magda went back out to the dining room. Decker and Rina followed.

"Sit down, Magda," Decker told her. "The boys can get the rest."

The old woman sat.

Rina said, "How come you listen to him and not to me?"

"He eats my food," Magda retorted. "Where is Channaleh?"

"With Opah," Decker answered.

It was interesting how he called Rina's mother Magda but Rina's father was Opah—grandfather. Decker sat on one side of his mother-in-law, Rina on the other. "The two of them are watching Animal Planet. How about we do this, Magda? You go over your childhood really briefly so Hannah will have something to put down. Not more than a couple of minutes. Just things like where you lived in Germany, what you remember about Munich before you moved to Budapest—"

"Not too much," Magda said. "I moved when I was nine."

"What year was that?" Decker asked.

"It was 1928 or maybe 1929. Before '33. We moved because my mother died." She whispered, "You know about her?"

Decker nodded. "I know what happened to her, yes."

She looked around nervously. "I don't want to tell Hannah this."

"I agree," Decker said. "Too much for her."

Magda went on. "Then in Budapest, my father met my stepmother and they get married. They have three children together. So with my sister and me, we are five. Only my sister and I survived. I was at Monowitz, you know. That was the goyish side of Auschwitz. All the rest of the family went to Birkenau. Only my sister Eva made it through. I still see her. She lives in New York. She married very well."

"So did you," Decker said.

"Yes, I did," Magda confirmed. "I married the *best!*"

Rina smiled. It was wonderful how much her parents still loved each other.

"Is Eva a whole sister or half sister?" Decker asked.

"Half sister," Rina said. "The middle of the three girls from Mama's stepmother."

"And Eva only survived because she was transferred back to Dachau—not to the main camp but to one of the smaller camps." Magda's face tightened. "There were many smaller camps—twenty, thirty in southern Bavaria—all of it Dachau. You know?"

Decker shook his head and looked at his wife.

"Satellite camps," Rina said. "The entire complex was referred to as Dachau. It was very ironic. Hitler had succeeded in making Germany *Judenrein*—Jewish free—but then toward the end when things were falling apart, he became desperate for domestic labor. So he brought the Jews back *into* Germany to work in armament factories—slave labor. Most of these smaller camps produced weapons and armaments, but they were also death camps. We don't have to talk about this, Mama. How about happier times, like earlier in your childhood?"

"They were not so happy. . . ."

"Before it happened," Decker said. "What do you remember about your mother?"

"She was very, very beautiful."

"So you must have looked like her."

Magda's smile was radiant at the compliment. "She made beautiful gowns. The most *wunderbar* fabrics."

"Silks?"

"*Ja, ja, seide*—silk. In such beautiful colors."

The woman was Hungarian, but when she spoke of her childhood, rudimentary German came back. Decker said, "Who'd she sew the gowns for? Who were her clientele?"

"The rich people—the aristocrats, the bourgeois."

"You know, Peter and I just came back from Munich," Rina told her.

Magda was quiet.

"We saw a lot of old Jewish Munich. You lived near Gartnerplatz, right?"

She thought long and hard. "*Nein,* not the

Isarvorstadt. That is for the Eastern Jews . . . the poor ones. My father was only a tailor, but my mother made money, enough for us to move. We were middle class. We even had a cleaning lady twice a week—an Austrian girl from Tirol. All the cleaning girls were Austrian."

She searched the recesses of her memory.

"They used to fight—my father and my mother. He did not want her to work. It did not look nice, like my father was a poor man. But my mother loved to sew." Magda furrowed her brow. "I used to go with her to visit the women, to the beautiful villas in Bogenhausen. *Ach,* such splendor, I remember so clear, especially the villas where the Russian aristocracy lived. There were many Russians in Munich . . . those who fled the revolution."

She was quiet.

"My father did not think this was good for a woman to visit by herself to the rich goyim. They fought about it. It was not happy times." She brushed her hand in the air. "I don't want to talk about it."

"I don't blame you," Decker said empathetically.

Rina tried to hide her frustration. "But you don't remember where *you* lived, Mama?"

"I remember the name of the big street. We lived off of Turkenstrasse."

"Schwabing," Rina said.

"*Ja, ja,* Schwabing, of course!" Magda hit her head. "I am an old woman."

"Schwabing was and still is kind of a bohemian area." Rina kissed her mother's cheek. "Very sporty of you, Mama."

"It was probably my mother's idea. She was very sporty. My father was a good German *bürger.* A good man, but very strict." Her eyes started to water. "He would have been so proud of you, Ginny."

Rina held her hand. Magda brought the free one to her chest. "It is so hard to talk."

Decker said, "We can move on, Magda."

She wiped her eyes with her finger and nodded.

Decker said, "Just for the record, do you happen to remember any names of childhood friends? I think that would be neat for Hannah to hear. You know how your granddaughter feels about her buddies."

Magda gave him a tearful smile. "Let me think. There was Briget and Petra." A pause. "Oh . . . there was also Marta. She was

Marta number one. I was Marta number two. Marta was my name before we moved to Hungary."

Rina was surprised. "You changed your name?"

"My father changed my name. So I would fit in better with the Hungarians, yes."

"All these things I never knew."

Magda shrugged.

"Last names?" Decker said.

"Of the girls?"

"Yes. Do you remember their entire names?"

"Not the first two, no. The memory is gone. But Marta, yes, because in the *schule*, I was Marta Gottlieb and she was Marta Lubke. I was the Jew and she was the Protestant, which was not so common in Munich. Bavaria is very Catholic. My sister and I went to a very liberal *schule*—also my mother's idea. My father wasn't happy about that, either." She sighed. "I remember my father with my mother; then I think about my father with my stepmother. The first marriage . . . I don't think it was a happy one. I won't tell Hannah this, either."

"I think Hannah would like to hear about how her grandparents met and got married and came to the United States," Decker said.

"We escaped in '56 when the Communists came. Another story."

Decker patted the old woman's hand. "You're a real old-fashioned hero."

"Bah!" She slapped him on the shoulder and stood up. "I go see what my boys are doing in the kitchen. Do you want a piece of strudel, Peter?"

"Only if you serve it with decaf coffee."

"What you think? Only decaf at this hour. Otherwise I spend the night on the phone with Ginny." She laughed at her joke.

As soon as she was out of earshot, Rina whispered, "You did a good job of drawing her out."

"Thank you."

"But we barely even scratched the surface. We still don't know anything about her mother's life."

"And we're going to leave it at that," Decker whispered emphatically.

"Peter—"

"Rina, listen to me. She's what? In her eighties? It's a painful memory in a woman who has suffered many painful memories.

We're not going to push her any further. End of discussion."

Rina sighed. "In my heart, I know you're right. I just think she . . . she deserves to know what happened."

"She's fine with it. You're the one who's curious." Decker rubbed his temples. "Rina, from what she told us, it could have been her father who murdered her mother—"

"No!" Rina was appalled.

"Yes!" Decker insisted. "By her own recollection, they had a troubled relationship. How would you feel uncovering that?"

She was silent.

"I have a few unsolved cases that still bug me, but I've learned to live with them."

"It's not your grandmother."

"Then talk to her when I'm not here. I'm not going to be party to any more subterfuge."

"All right," Rina conceded. "You're the detective, I'll trust your judgment."

"Thank you." Decker regarded his wife. "Now that we've got that out of the way, I've got an idea. I asked for the full names of her girlfriends for a reason. The memory may be painful for her, but probably not at all painful to Marta Lubke—*if* she's not dead, *if* I can find her, and *if* she remembers anything."

Rina looked at her husband with new-found admiration.

"Yeah . . . I'm good at what I do." He un-buttoned the waistband of his pants and untucked his shirt. "I ate too much."

"I'll make a light supper tomorrow night."

"For the next six nights, please."

"Thank you, Peter, for going beyond the call of duty."

"Yeah, yeah." He gave her a mock frown, then kissed his wife's lips. "You're welcome. I love you."

"I love you, too." Rina kissed him back.

He stood up. "I'm going to join your father and Hannah and watch Animal Planet. Last time I checked, they were watching a special on Vietnamese potbellied pigs. I should feel right at home."

25

Wednesday morning's e-mail simply read:

Still working overtime. Talk to you soon.
Koby

He didn't even bother to address it with my name.

And not even *love* Koby—just plain Koby.

I could take a hint.

I knew a brush-off when it smacked me in the face.

I didn't bother to answer.

Another one bites the dust.

"Fuck him," I whispered as I wiped away the tears.

▼

I was exhausted doing paid patrol-officer work and detecting on my own time, but work was a good substitute for a life. I debated making an appointment with David Tyler's conservator, but decided to show up in the flesh.

Century City is L.A.'s attempt at a business district. The entire area had once belonged to Fox Studios and there still was a mammoth-size location back lot. But most of the neighborhood was dominated by office high-rises with underground parking that charged outrageous rates.

Raymond Paxton's office was on the twenty-second floor, an ear-popping elevator ride that I wouldn't have taken, had I been afflicted with a cold. I got off, turned left, and walked through a door embellished with a brass nameplate that told me Paxton was a legal corporation. The secretary, a twenty-something Asian with her hair tied in a ponytail, greeted me with the typical "Can I help you?"

"I'm here to see Mr. Paxton," I told her. "I don't have an appointment."

"That could be a problem" was her response. "He's booked straight through until one. Then he has a lunch meeting."

This meant he was in the office. Opportunity presented itself. I showed her my badge.

Now she looked worried. She had on a red silk blouse and she fingered the corner of the collar. "What's this in regards to?"

"David Tyler. And it shouldn't take more than a few minutes."

"I'm not sure I know the name," she told me.

"But Mr. Paxton will know it."

She picked up the phone and spoke into the receiver with muted tones. Paxton came out a moment later. He was around five-nine, dressed in a silver suit with a black shirt and tie. He was also black, and when I realized that I had made that immediate distinction, I sort of realized my father's point. I had also identified his secretary as Asian—using race as a descriptive factor. Confession wasn't easy for me.

"You've heard from David?" Paxton's voice was anxious.

"No, I haven't heard from him. Can I talk to you for a few minutes?"

His expression fell. The lawyer frowned and checked his watch. "Five minutes?"

"More than enough time."

I followed him through the interior of his firm, down hushed and carpeted hallways. These places were labyrinths to me, and I always thought that such convoluted pathways were meant to confuse the enemy. Disorientation distracted from the purpose at hand and gave a home-court advantage when doing depositions. Eventually, we came to an open space. It wasn't his office. It was a conference room, and a small one at that. He was kind enough to offer me coffee and I was smart enough to refuse politely. We sat down across from each other.

He said, "Is he all right? David?"

"I don't know. That's why I'm here. I take it you haven't heard from him since Mr. Klinghoffner called you."

"If I had, we wouldn't be having this conversation." He leaned over the table. "Why are you here?"

"I have a story that might interest you. David had a girlfriend at the Fordham Communal Center, where he worked as an art instructor. Her name is Sarah Sanders. They used to go to the park and have sex. One day, a gang of punks walked in on them, raped Sarah, and beat David. They left him in a trash can. I believe that was the last time anyone who knew him has seen or heard from him. Forgive me for encapsulating this in a blunt manner, but you told me to be quick."

His face registered pure shock. "Is . . . is this true?"

"I don't have any reason to doubt it. Sarah Sanders gave a statement to the police just yesterday, although the incident happened about six months ago. This information was just given to me a couple of days ago. Why? you may wonder. Because Sarah Sanders was the girl in the paper who dumped her baby in a trash can. I found the infant and have taken a personal interest in the outcome and in everyone's welfare."

"Wait a minute." He brought a finger to his forehead. "This is all coming way too quickly for me to absorb."

"What would you like me to repeat?"

He stared at me with dark piercing eyes. "You haven't found David?"

"Not yet. But I haven't started looking for him."

"Okay. And you think he was beaten up and . . . then what?"

"Sarah told us—us being the police—that they beat him and stuffed him down a trash can. Being frightened and retarded, she left not knowing what happened to him. She never told anyone because she was just too scared."

"So are you saying that David is dead?"

"No, not at all. I suppose I was hoping you had heard from him."

His expression turned a mite hostile. "I haven't."

"He hasn't called at all?"

"I said no."

"No other kind of communication? A letter perhaps?"

"Are you accusing me of holding back?"

I was taken aback by his vehemence. I said, "Sir, all I'm trying to do is get some information on David Tyler's whereabouts."

"And I'm telling you I haven't heard from him."

"Fine," I said coolly. "We can leave it at that. But there is another point to this little tête-à-tête. The baby that Sarah Sanders gave birth to. I think she's David Tyler's offspring."

That gave Paxton pause.

"I know that there was money in a trust fund for David. Should it be determined that something happened to David, the money should go for the care of the child. The funds are legally hers—"

"Wait a minute! You come in with this fantastic story of crime and then lay a baby on top of it? Who are you?"

"Would you like to see my badge again?"

"What is this to you, Detective . . ."

I didn't correct him. "Decker."

"Detective Decker, where is the proof of this rape story? Where is the corroboration? And then how do you know that this child is David's offspring? What is this to you?"

"Just doing my job. So there's been no request for funds from David?"

"No. I told you I haven't heard from him!" Paxton got up and went over to the coffee table. Out of nerves, he poured himself a cup.

"So his money is still in the trust?"

He spun around and glared at me. "Of course, his money is still in the trust! Are you implying some illegality on my part?"

"Absolutely not. I'm just trying to be brought up to date."

He stared at me. "I did this as a personal favor to the Tylers. All I take out of it are small processing and conservator fees. And I wonder if you'd be grilling me so extensively if I were one of the big shots from Frisby, Mathews, and Young."

"I didn't realize I was grilling you, and truly I don't understand what you're driving at, Mr. Paxton."

"Deny what you will, Officer, but I know intimidation when I see it."

"Intimidation?"

"You know what I mean. I know how you people feel about minorities!"

I jerked my head back in shock. "You people" being the police. He thought I was riding him because he was black. Man, was he off target. I wanted to scream at him. I wanted to shout: *I'm not a racist, you jerk! I'm just trying to do a job! I've dated black guys!*

Actually, it was *a* black guy—in the singular—but that didn't sound as good.

I softened my tone, trying to get him on my side. "You're entitled to be compensated for the paperwork. If you think I'm implying any wrongdoing on your part, you're mistaken."

It mollified him, but not by much.

I pressed on. "What would happen to the money if there isn't any offspring and David doesn't surface?"

"I don't know. I've never thought about it." He sat down again. "If David passes on before I do, the money is supposed to be distributed to various charitable institutions. Of course, if there is a legitimate offspring, that would change everything." He regarded my face. "But I would need proof, Detective—a blood test, a DNA test. I hope you understand this. I can't give away hundreds of thousands of dollars based on some disabled girl's fantasy."

Hundreds of thousands of dollars. Sarah had chosen well. "That's going to be hard to do with David missing."

"I'm sorry, but I don't see what choice I have."

"Maybe if you saw the baby, you'd change your mind. She's half black and the mother's white. She's a mosaic Down's syndrome. I understand David had the same genotype."

He stared at me. "Did you go to college?"

Now who was letting his prejudice show? "Columbia University."

"And you're a cop?"

"Excuse me?" I replied.

I couldn't swear, but I thought I saw him blush.

"You know, it is possible that David's genetic profile has been mapped," I stated. "Maybe at a hospital. Mosaics are rare. Maybe we can determine paternity based on some previous medical results."

"We're getting way ahead of ourselves. At this point, I'd say you're stepping into personal territory. I'm not saying I wouldn't permit it, but this is all too premature."

"Not really. There's an infant out there who could use some money."

"Who has the infant?"

"The mother, but the baby is under the care of Sarah's older sister. Would you like to see her?"

"Perhaps eventually, but not now. Not until we determine other things. If you want David's medical information, you're going to have to come back with a warrant."

"Why?"

"Because I want to make sure that this girl isn't scamming me to get money."

"I don't think she has the mental capabilities to scam."

"You'd be surprised." He checked his watch. "It's been over five minutes."

"Yes, it has been. Thank you." I stood up

and gave him my card. "You will call me if you hear from him?"

"Yes, of course. And I expect the police to call me as well."

"Yes, I will."

He read the card. "It doesn't say here that you're a detective."

"I never said I was. You did."

"Talk about scamming." He gave me a critical look. "Now if you'll excuse me . . ."

Dismissed again.

Getting it from all sides.

▼

In civilian clothes, on my way home from my shift, I saw her rooting through the garbage. I pulled my Lexus to the curb, got out of the car, and called her by name. She looked up with that stunned deer-in-the-headlights look. She was wearing layers on layers, the top stratum being an old gray knitted sweater filled with holes. When she recognized me, she visibly relaxed and went back to her Dumpster. I took out a ten-spot, flicked it with my fingers, and pulled her aside. Her focus glommed on to the money with feral eyes. Her mouth spread into a gap-toothed smile.

"What?"

I crushed the bill in her dirty hands. Her hair was soiled and greasy but not matted. "Nothing. Go buy yourself something decent to eat."

She stared at her good fortune. "And you don't want nothin' for it?"

I held up my hands. "See. There is such a thing as a free lunch."

Alice Anne didn't get the joke.

"I don' like sompin' for nothin'. Makes me nervous."

"I could take it back."

She shook her head and deposited the bill between her pendulous breasts. "Wanna know anythin'?"

"Want to tell me anything?"

This time, she shrugged.

I thought a moment. "Gangs, Alice Anne. Mixed-race gangs. What do you know about gangs who jump their marks in Mac-Ferren Park, specifically in the bathrooms?"

"Lotsa gangs, Officer Cindy."

"I know that, honey." It seemed they changed every week. You cleaned up one gang and then another moved in to take its place. When you cleaned up that group, the original gang moved back to its original turf. "I was just wondering if something came into your head. Mixed races, Alice Anne: white, Hispanics, maybe Asian. One white guy has lots of pimples; another is bald or has a shaved head—"

"Lotsa shaved heads." She wrinkled her nose. "You mean gangs with whites and Mexicans together?"

"Yes." Alice Anne didn't subscribe to political correctness. "I'm looking for two Mexicans who hang around a white bald guy and a white guy with pimples. The bald guy might be the leader. Any ideas?"

"Lotsa ideas."

"Share with me, Alice Anne."

"There're lotsa gangs working MacFerren, sure."

"Do you have any names?"

"They bother me, too, Officer Cindy. Once they took my shopping cart."

"Did you report it?"

Alice Anne smiled. "Aaahhh, now you're jokin'."

I smiled to show her I was. "So now we both got problems with these people. Names?"

"I seen a gang . . . Mexican and white . . . some Orientals, too."

"Blacks?"

"No blacks. They don't live here no more. But there's more than four of 'em . . . mebbe like twelve of them shootin' off guns at night. I stay away."

"Well, these guys that I want, they could be part of that gang. Tell me about it."

"Part of the BBs."

Blood Bullets. I didn't think they operated this far west—a recent development.

Alice Anne said, "I knowed one boy. They call him Hermano."

"*'Hermano'* means brother in Spanish, Alice Anne. That could be like, you know, 'Bro.'"

She stared blankly.

"*'Hermano'* is not necessarily a name."

"Maybe it was Hermando."

Herman in English. In Spanish, it was Germando, the *G* pronounced as a soft guttural *H*. It wasn't much, but it was a start. "Thanks."

"He has this"—she scrunched up her face as she talked—"has this *big* tattoo of a tiger on his neck. Open mouth . . . teeth showing. You can't miss it."

"Okay." I nodded. "That's good, Alice Anne. Anything else?"

Her head bobbed up and down. "I seen him around."

"Where? At MacFerren Park?"

"At the park, yeah, but also at the coffee shop. Late at night. Sometimes twelve, sometimes one. Sometimes even later. I seen him 'cause I check the garbage there. Twenty-four hours, so lots of fresh garbage."

"That makes sense. Which coffee shop?"

"Boss's."

"The place about five blocks down on the corner?"

"That's the one. I seen Germando there. Lots of times. He likes the banana pancakes."

26

Someone was hitting me over the head, just pulverizing my brains to dust. In horror, I could see the tissue flying around, splattering on the ground, but still the pounding wouldn't stop. It took several minutes before I could translate the repulsive nightmare into sound. . . . Someone was knocking on my door. When I opened my eyes, I felt my heart racing, smelled the sharp odor of sweat that was evaporating off my skin. Shaking from cold, I wiped the wetness off with my damp sheets. I knew I had a breakfast appointment with Hayley Marx, and I wondered if I had overslept and it was she. But checking my alarm, I still had a half hour to go. Ordinarily, I would have been angry at being awoken prematurely, but it was a relief to bury the evil specter.

Street dreams, they're called, all too typical for new cops. First-year med students dreamed of a bleed-out from Ebola; first-year lawyers dreamed of arriving in court dressed only in underwear. So far as I knew, only cops dreamed of getting their heads blown off. I got up, my stomach in a knot, and threw on my terry-cloth robe.

Then, on the off chance that it *might* be Koby, I took off the terry robe and put on a silk one. I took a few quick moments to preen in front of the mirror; then I quickly brushed my teeth and rinsed out the bad taste with some no-name brand of electric green mouthwash. I was still mad at him, sure, but I wanted to look decent and smell good.

I checked through my peephole.

It was Oliver.

I was disappointed on so many levels, I couldn't even begin to analyze my feelings.

I opened the door and tried to keep my face neutral. He was wearing a blue suit, white shirt, and gold tie. He had shaved and smelled nice—a fresh scent without the cloying sweetness common in most men's cologne. His silver-streaked black hair was slicked back, but a chip was falling across his forehead. "I'm meeting Hayley Marx for breakfast, Scott."

"It'll only take a minute."

I hesitated, then let him in. He walked past me, so I closed the door. He glanced around my living room as if it were foreign territory to him. It wasn't, of course, but it was a lot barer than when he had last seen it. I had taken away all my personal effects, intending to pack up and bid the place good-bye, but I had never got around to the actual jump. The atmosphere was about as warm as Motel 6.

"You're moving?"

"No."

"A fan of the minimal look?"

"What do you want, Scott?"

"How are you doing, Cin?"

"I'm doing lousy. Why is none of your business."

"I'm sorry."

"Accepted. I have to go—"

"Can you give me a minute?"

"Why should I?"

"Maybe because you owe me?"

"*Excuse* me?"

He stuck his hands in his pockets. "You know, you should have called me, Cin."

I stared at him. *"What?"*

"I *said*"—his eyes bore into mine, but his voice got softer—"you should have *called* me." A pause. "You know, last year after it all happened. I must have left fifty messages. I left those messages because I cared about you. Surely you could have found the time to return just one of them."

We maintained eye contact.

He said, "You don't want a relationship with me, fine. I'm a big boy. No prob. But you could have just been nice about it. You know how that works—asked how I'm doing, how my cases are going, was Daddy giving me a hard time. You know . . . chitty-chatty. You never had trouble talking to me when you wanted to talk."

He dared me to respond. I didn't accept the challenge.

"I was there when you needed me," he said softly. "I was *good* to you. You owed me civility."

"I wasn't uncivil to you, Scott."

"You weren't uncivil, no. You weren't *anything* to me. As far as you were concerned, I was a fucking nonentity."

A good defense was a well-placed offense. "Nothing I did compared to how vile you were to me Sunday night. I was in shock . . . in *severe* shock . . . and your wretched selfishness just about put me over."

He broke eye contact and turned away. "You serious with this guy?"

"Not in the least," I said.

"Then what's the problem? So I'm a racist. I'm not a nice person. But I was nice to you. I never kissed and told, and believe me, I had lots of opportunity for that."

I gave out a sarcastic laugh. "I don't think it would have been good for your career."

"Your father can't do a thing to me so long as I do my job well. And I do my job very well. I could have made you look bad, Cindy. I could have made you look bad and your father look even worse. You know gossiping is a cop's pastime. It would have enhanced my image to brag about nailing the boss's daughter . . . made you both look like clowns. But I didn't because I *cared* about you. So all I'm saying is . . . is . . . I'm saying you could have called."

I started to answer but then checked my psychological armor. When I stopped a moment, I didn't like what I felt. I thought how hurtful Koby's silence had been and I had only known him for a little over a week. I'd known Oliver for a very long time and he had come through for me. He had been there when I needed a shoulder to cry on, when I needed a warm, strong body to get me through some terrible nights. He had tucked me into bed and fixed me breakfast in the morning . . . made sweet love to me.

He was a jerk, but I'd been one, too.

My eyes watered. "You're right. I should have called. My state of mind wasn't too great right after . . . and then . . . I don't know . . . I just didn't bother. I apologize."

He gave me the strength of his eyes. "Rather formal . . . but accepted."

He deserved better. I swallowed dryly. "Scott, I am so very, *very* sorry." Tears streamed down my cheeks. "I really am."

"Hey . . ." He came over to me. "Hey, it's fine." He put his hands on my shoulders, then drew me to him. I sobbed on his white shirt. Everything came crashing down: this dreadful, stark apartment, the shock of the accident, my horrible first year on the force. I clutched his shirt as I wept on his chest. He wasn't the one I should be crying to and

I was very resentful. He threw his arms around me. "Hey, the score's settled, old girl. It's fine." He patted my back. "I mean it. It's fine. Stop that!"

I sniffed. "Thanks for not gossiping about me."

"Thanks for not gossiping about me. I'm certain I had a lot more to lose than you did."

I laughed and so did he.

"Are you all right, Cindy?"

"No." I wiped my tears. "But I'll be okay."

He was still holding me. It felt good, but it wasn't what I wanted or needed. I kissed his cheek and broke it off. "You've been a good friend and I don't have many. I should keep that in mind."

He nodded. "Thanks. That was nice."

"I really do have to meet Hayley."

"Have time for a cup of coffee tomorrow?"

"Scott, that wouldn't be a good idea."

"Maybe not for you. For me, it would be a great idea."

"You're dating one of my good friends."

"I'd take you back in a heartbeat."

"It wouldn't work, Oliver."

"I'm not so sure." He approached me

from behind, slipped his arms around my waist. My robe was loosely bound, and his hands started to touch skin.

Again I pulled away. "You're good, Oliver, but I'm trying to be better."

"That's no fun."

"I'm trying to pull my life together. Please? Please, please, *please?*"

He frowned. "At least, tell me you were aroused."

"I was aroused."

"You fuck him?"

My face got warm. "Stop it."

"Is it true what they say about bla—"

"Oliver, get the hell out of here."

Still, he stalled. "So how are the kids?"

"What kids?"

"Didn't your friend go to the hospital with the kids in the accident? What was the guy's name again?"

Like he didn't know. Oliver, like my father, was an excellent detective. Those kinds of details would never slip his mind. "Yaakov."

"Yeah, but you called him something else at first."

"Koby."

"Like the basketball player? What the hell kind of a name is Koby?"

He was delving for more info. I said, "It's short for Yaakov—Jacob. When he moved to Israel, he started using his Hebrew name, Yaakov, which is also Jacob."

"Why does he have a Hebrew name?"

"Because Koby's Jewish."

Oliver laughed. "You're kidding me."

"No, I'm not."

"Convert?"

"No, he's born Jewish. He's an Ethiopian Jew. Can we switch the subject? Better still, can you leave and then I can get dressed?"

"Don't let me stop you. You never answered my question. Did the kids in the accident pull through?"

"You know, Scott, I don't know. I haven't heard from Koby since the accident."

"Ouch!" Oliver said.

"No big deal. I told you it was nothing."

"Sure you don't want that cup of coffee?" His smile was downright charming. "Talk it over with Uncle Scottie? Hmmm?"

I was down, he looked good, and it was tempting. But the past year had made me just a wee bit smarter. I kissed his cheek. "You were right to call me on my bad behavior. Let's leave it on a high note." Before I could weaken, I stepped out the door, waiting for him to follow. When he did, I closed the door behind me, hoping I didn't lock myself out. "I won't bother to tell Hayley about this."

"What's to tell? Nothing happened." He smiled. "You still have time to change that."

"Oliver, leave me alone or I'll sic the Loo on you."

"Bringing out the heavy artillery, huh?"

I smiled. When in doubt, punt to Dad.

▼

After breakfast and girl talk/therapy with Hayley (no mention of Oliver's visit, of course), I arrived at the station house a few hours before I was due to go on shift. I looked up any kind of information I could on Hermano or Germando. I didn't know his last name because Alice Anne hadn't known it, but there was a section for distinguishing marks and the tiger tattoo qualified under that category. When I typed it in, I was shocked at Alice Anne's accuracy. A lesson well learned: Never discount anyone.

Germando El Paso was now eighteen and a half, with a warrant out for his arrest for unpaid traffic citations, specifically a speeding ticket and three parking violations. In the past, he'd been picked up for two DUIs, and his license was currently suspended, but hey, when did that ever stop bad guys from driving? He had also been arrested for a misdemeanor possession of marijuana, and had a sealed juvenile record. Since he wasn't on probation, he had no probation officer. But there had been a juvenile officer who had worked with him. I took down his name and gave him a call.

I got voice mail, so I left a message.

I went down into the locker room and changed into my uniform. Homicide Detective Justice Brill snagged me right before I entered the roll-call room. Brill was in his mid-thirties, around five-ten, and good-looking in that seamed Steve McQueen/Paul Newman kind of way. They didn't make movie stars like that anymore. Instead, it was all these slender pretty boys that I could probably beat in an arm wrestle. Brill was married but had a penchant for frequenting gentlemen's clubs. I stayed clear of him.

"We think we found the SUV. It was a stolen vehicle with stolen plates, but you did get the last four digits right. Good for you."

"You impound it?"

"No, I put it up on eBay." Brill smiled, his

eyes oozing sincerity. "You did a good job, Decker."

I took the compliment with grace and aplomb, and a gallon of salt.

He said, "Here's the thing. The front bumper of the car was an inkblot of smashed body parts, but the rear bumper was clean."

"She wasn't hit on the rear bumper."

"Very good, Decker, I see gold in your future." He rolled his eyes. "Now since the plates were stolen, the lab dusted it for prints. Guess what?"

"There were none."

"Bingo. But the lab did find a smear of fresh blood on the top right screw, where you screw the license plate onto the bumper."

"Was the smear enough for a partial?"

"There was a partial, but nothing popped up in the system."

So much for that. "Did the blood match the victim's?"

"We don't know for sure because the tests are preliminary. But the lab did run a simple ABO—victim's blood was O, the smear was B. There was nothing else on the plate." He looked at me. "Any ideas?"

He was giving me a hurdle to jump. I thought about it for a moment. "And the lab didn't find the B blood type anywhere else on the SUV?"

"No."

I tapped my foot. "It's on the screw but not on the license plate."

"Right."

Suddenly sparks popped in my brain. "If there were no prints on the license plates, maybe instead of just wiping it down, he wore gloves. Thing is, license plate edges are sharp. Could be the plate cut the latex while he was fiddling with it. Maybe the edge was sharp enough to cut through the latex and exposed part of his fingertip— hence the partial. Maybe it also cut skin. But he didn't notice it because it was only a few droplets. The blood could have leaked out onto the screw as he attached the plate to the bumper."

Brill stared at me.

I shrugged. "You asked what I thought. It's a theory."

The nod came slowly. "Yeah, it's a theory."

That was as much of a concession as I'd get from him.

He gave me a wise-guy smile. "You know what? When I find out more, we'll discuss it over a cup of coffee."

Why was it that every time a guy wanted play, he offered me a lousy cup of coffee? What ever happened to dinner and a movie?

"Thanks for filling me in, Detective."

"We'll keep in touch, Decker," he said. "You're good."

I smiled. I had so wanted things to work out with Koby. I had genuinely liked the man. But even if I hadn't, he would have been worth dating just to keep the others off my back.

27

Germando El Paso's juvenile officer hadn't returned my call, so I figured I might as well spend another fruitless night following up theories that evaporated like steam. I headed for Boss's twenty-four-hour coffeehouse, a place that catered to freaks, chumps, hypes, and other ne'er-do-wells who couldn't hack it in daylight hours. I was hoping to espy "Mr. Tiger Tattoo" himself. Alice Anne had produced a solid hit, so I made a mental note to slip her another ten-spot the next time I saw her.

I was seated by a toothpick of a guy with bad acne who appeared to be coming off a bad jones. Lucky for me, he was the maître d' and not my server. That position was given to a captivating lady with blue

spiked hair who dressed in black vinyl. She
had a pierced upper lip and a pierced nose
and small silver chain connecting the two
metal studs together. I wondered if it hurt
when she sneezed.

She poured me some coffee and left me
the pot. I had brought the morning paper and
was skimming the usual bad news, having
made myself comfortable in a torn Nau-
gahyde booth in the far end of the restaurant
after sweeping bread crumbs off the tabletop
with my hands. I kept a sharp eye out for my
prey, and though I saw a good sideshow,
Germando wasn't part of it. I sipped coffee
and munched on dry lettuce leaves of what
was professed to be a dinner salad. When
my cell phone rang, I jumped. I had forgotten
to turn it off.

"Decker."

"I just got off shift. Are you still in the
neighborhood?"

The voice from the netherworld. I didn't
want to lie, but I definitely did *not* want to
see him. "It's late."

"You could come to my place," Koby
purred. "I'll fix you something to eat . . . give
you a massage. . . ."

As anger played inside my gut, I tried to

keep my voice even. "Sounds like a booty call."

Silence over the line.

"No, Cindy, not at all."

"Then explain it to me."

The seconds ticked.

"Let's try it again." His voice was more somber. "I'm off all day Sunday. I'd love to see you. How about brunch and we go from there?"

That meant spending money on me. A step up, but I still *wasn't* interested. So now I did lie. "I'm working Sunday."

"Actually, I'm off Saturday night through Monday morning. Actually, Friday night through Monday, but Saturday is *Shabbat*. But if Saturday is your only time, I can see you then. Please. Just give me a time."

What in the world was going through that man's head? Nothing for four days, then "Mr. Solicitous." More than likely, he was horny. "Saturday I meet my mother for lunch. It's sacrosanct."

Another pause. "What does that mean . . . the word?"

" 'Sacrosanct'? It means if I miss a weekend with her, she goes ballistic."

"Maybe after lunch, then . . ."

Not missing a beat. Tenacity had probably been a very useful asset for him. I relented, probably because he had asked me what "sacrosanct" meant. For some reason, I found it endearing. Still, I was cautious. "Actually, I'm still in the neighborhood. I've got a couple of odds and ends to pick up. How about I call you in a half hour? If I'm up to it, we'll meet for coffee. All right?"

"Fine . . . anything. Great. Terrific—"

I hung up before he could think of more adjectives.

After forty-five minutes, the phone rang again.

"Are you still working?"

"Yeah, just like you've been doing for the last four days."

Silence.

I felt bad, not because he didn't deserve it, but because it was unbecoming to be rude. I tossed him a bone. "If you come to Boss's within the next half hour, I'll still be here. Do you know where it is?"

"Yes."

"Then I'll see you later." I disconnected the call.

He showed up twenty minutes later. The first things I noticed were his eyes. How could I not notice? Usually luminous, his pupils were polluted brown muck, the formerly white irises were a combination of jaundice yellow and bright red bloodshot. He liked colors. He certainly had them.

I immediately thought of a drug binge. It wouldn't be the first time that a health professional had dipped into the locked cabinet of a hospital. He smiled sheepishly as he sat across from me. I slid my coffee cup over to him and watched him closely. When he picked up the mug, I saw that his hands were as steady as rocks.

"I was supposed to meet someone," I told him. "I think I got stood up." I smiled. "Wouldn't be the first time."

His tired eyes took in mine. "I'm sorry I haven't called you."

"S'right. You've been busy."

"Who were you supposed to meet?"

"A felon."

"I hope I'm better company, even if the margin is small."

Despite myself, I smiled. "You look exhausted."

"I am. I finally told them that if I didn't get some time off, I would collapse."

"You should be home sleeping, not drinking bad coffee that'll probably give you heartburn."

"Yes." He tried eye contact but couldn't pull it off. "I'd like to make up my bad behavior to you. Can we see each other this weekend?"

"What bad behavior? All you did was work." I paused, thinking of Nurse Marnie's possessive voice over the line. Once there had been something. "Unless you have something else to tell me."

He looked up. "I don't know what you mean."

"Busy with someone else?" I was trying to sound casual. "What happened, Koby? Did she flake out on you or something? Call me for backup sex?"

His eyes swung back to mine. "No. It is *nothing* like that. I really have been working—three 12-hour shifts and one 16-hour shift."

I was silent.

"Ask anyone at the hospital," he insisted. "And you can ask many people because I've practically lived there this past week." He rubbed his bloodshot eyes. They watered with irritation. "Cindy, I have cash burning holes in my pockets. Please let me spend it on you."

I studied his face.

"Please?"

I shrugged. "Sure. Let's go out Sunday night."

He blew out air and leaned back in the booth. "Thank you. I will try to redeem myself."

"I'm tired. I'm going home." I stood up, pitched a ten on the table, then walked away.

"I'll walk you to your car."

"I'm fine, Koby. I carry a gun."

"I suppose I should keep that in mind." He caught up with me, held my arm. "I really missed you."

"You have a funny way of showing it."

He held the door open for me. "I know."

"So what was that all about?"

"Some other time, please? I'm so tired."

I took pity on him. "Sure."

As we walked out the door and onto the sidewalk, I saw the tiger tattoo before I saw the face. I broke away from Koby and took a couple of giant steps forward. "Hey!" I shouted. "Police!"

Germando took off.

I tore after him, grateful for my rubber-soled shoes, but I was out of my league. Koby however was a lightning bolt. A dozen long strides and he landed within striking distance. He whacked Germando between the shoulder blades and my traffic felon stumbled forward, falling flat onto his face. When I caught up, I was panting like a dog. Koby hadn't broken a sweat. I leaned my knee between Germando's shoulder blades and whipped his arms around his back.

"I said, 'Police!' That means you *stop!*"

"I no hear—"

"Well, now you hear! I am a police officer, Germando. Hold the *fuck* still or I'll break your *fucking* arms!"

"That's brutality!" He craned his neck to look at Koby. With my knee in position, he was pretty well pinned. "You hear her—"

"You're talking to *air,* my friend," I yelled at him. "There's no one here!" I retrieved the gun from my purse and held it at the base of his head. "Hold still, Germando. I've got bullets about an inch from your brain stem and I don't want any accidents. I am going to cuff you."

Out came the cuffs from my purse. As soon as he was in manacles, I felt my heart rate drop. I looked up . . . Koby staring at me, shocked and wide-eyed. I took out my cell and called for police backup and a transport.

His mouth was still agape. I said, "You can go now. In fact, it would be real good if you went now."

He closed his mouth and turned to walk away.

"Hey," I shouted.

He pivoted around.

"Thanks," I told him. "But don't *ever* do my job for me again, okay?"

He didn't answer. He stared, blinked, then jogged off. I saw his Toyota hook a U, just as I caught the flash of a cruiser's crossbar.

Good thing the occupants of the black-and-white were on a case. Otherwise a cop could have given him a ticket for crossing a double, double yellow line.

28

"Let's go over it again, Decker."

I threw my head back, squirming in the hard seat, and studied the ceiling's fluorescent lighting in the interview room. This wasn't so bad, I rationalized. It gave me empathy with the scumbags that I'd be grilling one day. "What specifically, Detective?"

"You went to Boss's because . . ."

"I went to Boss's because I was looking for Germando El Paso, who often eats the banana pancakes there. I was looking for him because he had outstanding warrants."

"Traffic warrants."

"Warrants just the same."

Brill rubbed his forehead. "And this is

what you do on your off-hours? Hunt for dudes with unpaid tickets?"

"I consider it a civic duty."

His smile was wry. "You need a life."

"I agree," I answered. "But that doesn't change this situation. It was a righteous bust and I did not plant that bag of X on him, no matter what he says."

"You've got no witnesses to back you up."

"Neither does he."

"He claims you were with someone."

"He claims a lot of things." I looked at the one-way mirror. "Who's back there?"

Brill followed the direction of my eyes. He wore a black suit and a white shirt. A badly knotted red tie ringed his neck. He had dressed hurriedly. "Someone from the DA . . . the Loo."

"Detective or uniform?"

"My Loo."

"He can come in and ask his own questions, if he wants."

"Don't be a smart-ass."

"Believe me, Detective, I'm not trying to be snide." I looked at my watch. It was two in the morning. At least, Koby was home sleeping. Thinking about him depressed me. "I'll start from the beginning—again. I'll repeat it as many times as you want me to repeat it."

Brill gave me a hands-up.

I started to talk, then stopped. "Let me start from the *very* beginning. This whole thing has its roots in the abandoned baby I pulled out of the garbage a couple of weeks ago. All right?"

"Go on."

I glanced at the tape recorder in the middle of the Formica table, which was scarred and scratched and held a dirty ashtray. "I found the mother on my own, I'd like to add—"

"Not the time to brag."

"I'm only mentioning this to show the DA on the other side of the mirror that I am obsessive."

"Seems to be a family trait," Brill answered.

"You said it, sir, not I."

He smiled. "You found the baby; you found the mother."

"I pulled out the baby; I found the mother." I readjusted my weight for the millionth time. "So now we're up to date on that. After I found the mother, I wanted to know about the father—"

"Why?"

"I thought this poor little baby from a retarded mother deserved to know her entire genetic history."

"Why?"

"Because I became attached to her. I visited her a couple of times in the hospital—on my own. This whole thing didn't come out of nowhere."

Brill waited.

I said, "So I went to the mother's home to interview her about the baby's father. I did this with Detective Van Horn's permission *and* with Detective MacGregor's permission. I visited her on Sunday. I took my father, Lieutenant Decker, along with me because I knew I needed somebody experienced, and Detective Van Horn had gone on vacation. Detective Russ MacGregor, who had been assigned to the case, was away for the weekend."

"And it was during this discussion that the girl"—Brill flipped through his notes—"Sarah Sanders . . . she mentioned being gang-raped and her boyfriend was beaten up and thrown into a trash can."

"Exactly. But because the case was six months old, Lieutenant Decker suggested that I don't act on my information until I informed Detective MacGregor of this latest development. Which I did."

"And?"

I smiled. "He thought it could be a fantasy. Still, the girl came in and made a statement. On the off chance that her story might be true, I asked MacGregor if I could look into it. He said that if I wanted to find the father on my own time, he wouldn't have a problem with that."

"To find the father, not to solve a six-month-old fantasy crime."

"Look . . . sir. I went after Germando because I had heard that he hangs with punks who harass the homeless and jump people in public bathrooms. I looked Germando up. I knew he had an outstanding warrant. I knew I could pull him in on that. Why would I bother planting a bag of ecstasy on him?"

"To make the bust look more righteous."

"The bag has been nothing but a pain in the neck."

"But you didn't know that at the time."

"I know the Department's attitude toward

rogue cops. Give me a lie detector test if you have doubts."

"What about this guy Germando claims you were with?"

I looked at my hands.

Brill pointed to the mirror. "They don't like it when you're not forthcoming. If you lie about this, no one's going to believe you about the bag."

I pursed my lips. "I sent him home."

"That doesn't look nice."

"Why should he get involved?"

"He's already involved."

"Ask anyone in the restaurant. We weren't together more than ten minutes."

"We did ask people, Decker. And what you said is true. And that in and of itself is suspicious. Ten minutes is more than enough time to buy a baggie."

I stared in disbelief. "You think he was a dealer?"

"You tell me."

"Why?" I snapped. "Because he's black?"

Brill's face remained flat. "You tell me."

"He's a critical-care nurse at Mid-City Peds. We were arranging a date."

"That can be done on the phone."

"He just got off shift. He wanted to see me in person. The poor man had been working for almost four days straight. I took one look at him and sent him home to get some sleep."

"Name?"

I sighed heavily. "Yaakov Kutiel. He was the same guy I was with when I witnessed the hit-and-run."

Brill was silent.

"He was just walking me to my car."

"So he's your boyfriend?"

Not anymore, I thought to myself. "We've dated." I was losing patience. I took a couple of deep breaths. "I didn't plant the pills. End of story."

Again he was silent.

"If I were you," I said, "I'd start thinking about how I could use this boon."

Brill looked at me.

"Like using the pills to get him to talk about Sarah Sanders's rape."

"If it wasn't fiction."

"Can't we at least find out?"

"We?"

It was time to show them I had an ego. "I made the bust. My presence in the room will make him nervous. But you can do all the talking."

"Gee, thanks, Decker."

"If he wasn't the point man in the rape, maybe you can use the pills to get him to flip and tell us who it was."

"What makes you think he wasn't the point man?"

I shrugged. "Sarah described the meanest guy as being a white guy with a shaved head. Let's just put him on the griddle and see how high he jumps."

Brill got a call on his cell. He stood up, spoke a second, then hung up. "Excuse me."

I shrugged.

He left the room. I knew they were conferring on the other side of the mirror. Ten minutes later, Lieutenant Mack Stone from Hollywood Detectives came into the room with Brill. Stone was in his mid-fifties, around six-two, with a thick build, fleshy features, and a head of dark, curly hair. He sat across from me, giving me one of those intense looks.

"How's your arm?"

"My arm?"

"Connor says you have quite an arm."

"Oh." He was referring to my position on the LAPD Hollywood Bowling League—

women's division. We made first last year. "Ready to do it again, sir." After my awful rookie year, I was determined to be ever the good sport.

Stone frowned, the creases on his forehead like wrinkles on a bulldog. Stubby fingers raked through his hair. "Germando El Paso. What do you want with him specifically?"

"I want to see if he was involved in the gang rape."

"Where'd you get your information about his involvement?"

"A street person."

"Who?"

I shrugged. "A bag lady, sir."

"A bag lady?"

"Yes. But before I went after him, I looked him up and made sure I'd have something to hold him on if I caught him. The last thing I wanted was to be hung out to dry. The baggie was a bonus, sir. And it sure as hell explains why he ran from me."

"He looks like a fast little mother. How'd you run him down?"

"I'm very quick, sir."

"I mean, you wouldn't have pulled a gun on him for a traffic warrant."

"I would never point my weapon at a fleeing traffic violator. That is flagrant misuse of a firearm."

"How'd you get him down without your gun?"

"I caught up with him and whacked him on the back. He tripped and fell."

Stone studied my face. "Ever made the list of forty-four?"

I laughed. The list of forty-four was reserved for those officers with the worst civilian complaint records. "Uh, no."

"Charges against you?"

"None." I looked at him. "Why? Is El Paso thinking of throwing a brutality charge at me?"

He smiled. "Not by the time we're done with him."

▼

"You're in deep turd, *mi amigo,*" Brill said. "You're looking at a felony drug conviction: possession with intent to sell. That's a lot of jail time. Then, when you combine it with your traffic warrant and your prior drug conviction, I think a case could be made for three strikes."

El Paso's pitted, thin face lost color, his ashen cheeks in stark contrast to the black shirt he wore. His legs were housed in a pair of baggy, saggy jeans. His nose and forehead were scraped from his fall, adding more markings to his punk visage. He had tattoos on his hands, tattoos on the back of his neck. I'm sure if he took his shirt off, he'd be a gallery of blue ink.

Three strikes meant a mandatory life term in prison. Germando's charges didn't qualify, but he didn't know that.

"She plant them," he shouted out.

"No, she didn't plant them," Brill said. "You know how we know that?"

Germando didn't speak.

"We found a witness who was with her."

"See, I tell you she was with someone. A black man. A dealer—"

"No, he isn't a dealer," Brill explained, "but he is her boyfriend."

"Her boyfriend is a dealer?"

"No, Germando, he's not a dealer. But being as they're close, when we get him on the witness stand, whose side do you think he's going to be on, hmmm?"

Germando grew sullen. "I wan' my lawyer."

"Sure," Brill said. "But before you make the call, I want to tell you a little story. It might help you out if you listen. Might help you out big time."

El Paso raised his brown eyes to my face, then to Brill.

Justice said, "This story goes back maybe six months ago. A rape, *amigo,* and not *just* a rape. This is a gang rape in the men's bathroom at MacFerren Park. And not just any gang rape, it's the gang rape of a retarded girl who was fooling around with her retarded boyfriend. Someone beat the crap out of him, then threw him in the trash can. He was left for dead. Sound familiar?"

His eyes got wide, but he shook his head. "No. I never hurt no one."

"Nothing like that."

"I don't hurt no one."

"I'm not saying you did. Just that you might have been there."

"Nah . . . I no there."

I said, "We put you in a lineup, Germando. We bring the girl in." I pointed to his neck. "That tiger on your throat is a pretty obvious calling card."

"You say she's retarded." El Paso rubbed his watery nose. "No one will believe her."

"I think you're wrong about that," I told him. "I think lots of people will believe her."

I leaned across the table and poured him another glass of water. "The point is . . . are you sure enough to take a chance in front of twelve people who'd love to give a banger twenty to life?"

Brill said, "You want to call your lawyer now?"

Stark silence. We both waited him out.

El Paso said, "Wha' happens when I call my lawyer?"

"Then we stop talking and you're charged with felony drug possession," I told him.

His eyes darted back and forth. "And if I no call him?"

"Then we keep talking," Brill told him.

"We talk about the story Detective Brill just told you," I added.

"I never touch that kind of girl. She no right in the head."

"But you know who we're talking about," I said.

He shrugged. "Maybe."

"Maybe isn't a good answer," Brill told him. "Maybe makes us think you'd say anything to avoid a drug conviction."

"I hear about it," El Paso said. "I hear that they do a re-tard. Me? I no interested in the girl. Too ugly."

"Who did her?" Brill asked.

"Wha' you give me if I remember good?"

"Up to our lawyers," Brill said. "I've got to present the situation to them. But I can't present the situation if I don't know it. That means you have to tell it to me."

"But once I tell, I have nothin'."

"You have to trust us," I said.

El Paso laughed.

"That hurts my feelings," I said.

"Not as much as you' dealer boyfrien' hurt my back."

"Bah humbug!" I lit a cigarette for him. He took it.

Brill said, "Start talking, Germando. I'm tired."

"I know. You look like shit." El Paso gave me a lecherous smile. "Now, you, mama, you look *good*."

I took his cigarette away. "Germando . . . if *I* can take you down like I did, those gorillas inside will have you touching your toes in an eye blink. Now be polite and start talking." I stuck the cigarette back in his mouth, then sat back in my chair and folded my arms across my chest.

Brill's eyes went from my face to El Paso's ugly mug.

"I don' do nothin' to her," he reiterated. "I just wait at the door till they done."

"Who did something to her?"

"Maybe Juice Fedek . . . Pepe Renaldes maybe. I don' remember. Long time ago."

I said, "The boy you beat up—"

"I don' beat up no one," El Paso stated.

"Someone beat him up," I said.

"Not me. Maybe the others."

"Was he alive when you left?"

El Paso shrugged. "I jus' wait at the door."

"Where'd you get the bag from?" Brill asked.

"What?"

"The bag of X," Brill said. "Who'd you buy it from?"

Again El Paso asked for his lawyer. This time, he was adamant. The door to discussion was officially closed and dead-bolted.

29

Juice Fedek was Joseph Nicholas Fedek: twenty-one years of age, a young man with a seasoned record—two breaking-and-entering charges, one assault, two misdemeanor drug possessions, two DUIs with a suspended license for a year. Eight months in county, bumped into early parole due to overcrowding. Then he was picked up on a DUI, served an additional four months, another early release, same reason. Where he parked himself was anyone's guess and Germando claimed he hadn't seen him since his last tour in the cellar.

Pepe Renaldes was gainfully employed by Do-Rite Construction—bonded and licensed. The company's claim to fame was custom-built homes in Brentwood, a liberal, ritzy white area in the West Side of Los Angeles, a neighborhood I knew intimately because my mother and stepfather lived there. They had their book clubs, their wine-and-cheese parties, and their endless discussions on the state of the world. I loved my mother dearly. As my father admitted, she had not been given a fair shake in her first marriage. She was happy now, and that was good. But I could take the intellectualizing only in small doses. Their lifestyle had all the pitfalls of backbiting academia without the college credits.

Since both lads were lacking outstanding warrants, I had no choice but to wait until a game plan was formulated between El Paso's lawyer and the DA. I had wanted to show their mugs to Sarah Sanders, see if she could pick them out of a six-pack, but I was told to hold off. With my hands figuratively bound, I went on my shift and worked a solid eight hours, getting home around twelve, exhausted and depleted.

Lots of phone messages, but none from Koby. No e-mails from him, either.

Why wasn't I surprised?

Saturday was devoted to finding David Tyler. That meant phone calls to homeless shelters, halfway houses, and other community centers for the developmentally disabled. Then there was my "sacrosanct" lunch with Mom. As I traveled around Brentwood, I looked for houses going up and Do-Rite Construction signs, but was out of luck.

There were still no messages from Koby when I got home. That would die unless I got things going again. So on Sunday, I swallowed my pride. I went shopping and bought him an orange shirt—on sale and nonreturnable. Afterward, I wondered why in the hell I did it, because who was this guy to me.

I should have dusted him, except I was lonely. Over the past year, I couldn't find the energy to attend parties or barhop, so where was I going to meet guys except at work and that was O-U-T—out. There had been chemistry between us and I was loath to give that up. Still, I waged an internal debate.

In the meantime, I hopped in my car and went over the canyon to visit Dad, wanting to fill him in on my search for David Tyler— or so I told myself. What I really wanted was some old-fashioned pats on the back for a job well done with Germando El Paso. As I approached my father's house, Koby's gift in hand, I wondered why I was carrying it.

Yeah, right.

I knocked on the door. Rina answered. "Hi, honey. Your dad isn't home. He took Hannah out for one of those painting things. You know, you paint a plate and they charge you fifty bucks for something you're going to put in a drawer and never use."

I smiled. I knew what she was talking about.

"Come in. I'll find the address for you."

"Nah, never mind. Just tell him I stopped by."

Rina studied my face. By the look on hers, I must not have appeared neutral, let alone happy. "Cindy, you drove out all this way. Why don't you wait for him? He'll be back in an hour."

"No thanks. Just tell him I've gone through about a quarter of the possibilities and I'm still looking for David. He'll know what I mean. He can call me later on. Just to discuss a few things."

Rina pulled me inside. "How about some coffee?"

I smiled and shrugged. She hooked a thumb in the direction of the kitchen. I followed obediently. I swept my hand across the kitchen counter.

Rina said, "What's wrong, honey?"

"Nothing." What a stupid response. "I'll get through it, Rina. Thanks."

She didn't push it. "What's in the bag?"

"Oh." I took out my purchase. "It's for Koby."

The shirt was bright orange, more vivid than I had remembered. Rina stared at it.

I said, "I got it on sale. Nonreturnable."

"I can . . . understand that."

I smiled. "Koby likes color."

"Well, then, he'll certainly like that."

"He ruined one of his shirts at the accident, using it to stop some bleeding. I thought I'd replace it."

"That's very thoughtful of you."

"It will be if I give it to him."

Rina waited for more. I didn't offer up anything. She poured two cups. "It's fresh. You take yours with cream, right?"

"Cream and an Equal. Girly coffee."

"Me too."

I drank the coffee. It was good and had cinnamon in it, and that only made me feel worse.

She said, "This, too, shall pass."

"I guess everything passes eventually. You die."

Rina smiled. "Now you're sounding like your father."

"God forbid."

"No, that's a good thing. I love your father."

"That makes two of us." I put the cup down. "I don't know, Rina. This was going to be a peace offering. Now I have doubts if it's even worth it. Maybe I should cut my losses."

"You know best."

"I like him. But men are so damn difficult."

"Get me in the right mood, I'll agree with you," Rina said. "This weekend, your father has been a doll."

"Maybe it's me."

"Want my advice for what it's worth?"

"Sure."

"The shirt's not returnable. It's for a rather specific taste. Give it to Koby. Otherwise it'll go to waste."

▼

The day was spectacular, even if I wasn't. His car was in the driveway, and for a moment, I just wished it would all go away—all the bad feelings that got in the way of life—

so we could hop inside and cruise on an endless highway. I rang the bell, and when he didn't answer, I went by the side and peered over the gate. This time, the back door wasn't open, but I could see motion in the garden. I tried the latch, but it was pad-locked. He wasn't expecting visitors, but I didn't care. I hopped the fence.

"Hello?" I called out.

"In back."

The orange trees were still heavy with blossoms and perfume. I stopped at the entrance to his backyard. He was right. A week later and the garden had turned all color and aroma. He was trimming the rose-bushes, wearing faded jeans, a green tank top, and sneakers without socks. He gave me the courtesy of a glance, then clipped off a stem containing a ruby red bud.

"Wow!" I brushed my black slacks off, dirty from my excursion over the fence. "It's beautiful back here."

"Thank you." He glanced at me, then be-gan to peel thorns off the branch. "But I think I have the better view."

I thanked him. "How's the back-room floor coming?"

He spoke to me, though he was focused

on the flower. "It's not coming. I don't use power tools when I'm upset."

He held out the stem to me.

I took it and sniffed it. *"Très élégant!* And as long as we're in a giving mood . . ." I lifted the bag. "A little more pedestrian, but like someone said, it's the thought that counts."

He regarded my present, wrapped in tissue paper and placed in a shiny gift bag with rope handles. "For me?"

"Unless there's someone behind you, yes."

His eyes, although no longer bloodshot, still lacked sparkle. They went from the gift to my face. "I'm utterly stunned. I don't know what to say."

"'Thank you' is always in fashion."

"Thank you."

"Take it and open it."

He did and pulled out the shirt. His smile was a brilliant crescent of white. "It's perfect!"

"If you wear it with black on Halloween, people will think you're a jack-o'-lantern."

"Especially with my big teeth." He looked at the label. "Right size." He held it up to his chest. "What do you think?"

"It says you."

"Then I think it is in serious trouble." His smile dimmed, and he put the shirt back in the bag. "I would like to wear it tonight for you. Is that a possibility?"

"Maybe."

"How much on a scale from one to ten?"

I couldn't bring myself to smile. "I'm sorry I came down on you. I don't like when other people do my job better than I do."

"I don't do your job."

"I wouldn't have caught him if you hadn't been there."

"I was a competitive runner. No doubt I could outrun anyone in your department."

"But it wasn't *anyone*. It was *me*. And the guy was my responsibility. Koby, what if he had taken out a gun?"

"Then I would have perfect backup."

"C'mon! I'm trying to make a point."

He grew glum. "I hear you."

"I'm . . . I don't know. Sorry, all right?"

"It was more than just my speed," he spoke softly. "You were already mad at me."

I didn't confirm or deny it. Again silence came between us. I said, "I saw the look on your face when I took that guy down. I'm sure I conformed to your image of the heavy-handed LAPD cop."

"I flinched," he admitted. "But I know there are two sides."

I nodded.

"What did he do?"

"Technically, I arrested him because he has an outstanding warrant for unpaid traffic violations. But I wanted him in connection with a gang rape of a retarded woman."

Koby screwed up his face in horror. I thought what my father must have thought dozens of times. Why did I tell him?

He said, "Did arresting him help you out?"

Eventually. After I fielded about a thousand questions. "Yes, it helped quite a bit."

"I'm glad." He tucked the clippers inside his pants pocket and looked at his watch. "How about if I make coffee? You relax here while I shower and get dressed. Then maybe we take a ride to the beach and watch the sunset. Then we have dinner."

It sounded not only wonderful, but like instant therapy. But I was still tense. "Koby, why didn't you call me? I was freaked out after the accident. I know you were busy with life-and-death issues, but a kind word or two on my message machine would have gone a long way. It wouldn't have taken more than . . . two minutes."

He looked away. "I should have."

"So why didn't you?"

He regarded a rosebush and took out the clippers. Again he spoke without looking at me. "I have these moods, Cynthia." He snipped off a dead head. "I was hoping that maybe they wouldn't surface until we were farther along . . . so you could see the good side of me."

I was puzzled. "What do you mean 'moods'?"

"Moods."

"Koby, everyone has moods."

"Mine are very dark."

"Like depression?"

He faced me. "An angry depression, I think. I am not nice to be around. I have found the best way to deal with it is to throw myself into work. So I work until I cannot work . . . until I am in a state of exhaustion. Then I sleep—one day, two days. And then . . . it passes. And it always does pass. Because the world is a good place."

"Have you ever gotten help for it?"

"From a therapist?"

"Yeah, from a therapist. I see a therapist. It helps."

"Why should I bother? It passes."

"You should bother so you know what triggers it."

"I already do know. This time, it was the accident. The little girl loses a leg but she lives. The baby died, Cindy, massive head injuries. That was it."

"Koby, you work with dying babies all the time."

"Yes, but those babies are sick. With those babies, one shoe has already dropped. There is expectation. So you are prepared. When it is a healthy baby . . . and *all* the mother had to do was put her in a car seat . . . it makes me . . . It was the suddenness! One moment, I am elated with you . . . such a wonderful evening. Then . . . *boom!*" He punched one fist into another, the smack so loud it made me jump. "It's like in *Zahal* . . . doing *shomrah*—watch. One moment, you sit around smoking and talking about women with your *chevrah.* Then abruptly, your friend is dead from a sniper's bullet. Or when you're a child and you walk out of your *tukul*—your hut—and the women are weeping. But that is nothing new because death is all around.

Until someone tells you that your mother has just died. It's the unexpected death. It's not like the hospital. In the hospital, the defenses are up. Am I making myself understandable?"

I exhaled. "You've had lots of trauma in your life."

"I told you we all have baggage."

"But some baggage is heavier than others."

He nodded somberly. "Indeed. I don't blame you for walking."

"Did I say I wanted to walk?"

We were silent.

"That man Oliver . . . ," Koby said. "Do you still like him?"

I let out a small laugh. "That, my friend, is so *over.*"

"Not to him."

"Is *that* what it was all about? *Oliver?*"

He shrugged. "Perhaps a small part."

"Small part, huh?"

"Very small."

"Teeny, *teeny,* tiny." I nodded. "Okay."

"Cindy, under normal circumstances, it is nothing. In combination with everything that happened, I just wonder, that's all."

I waited until I caught his eye. "You know,

I never said anything about your friend Marnie. You shouldn't have brought up Oliver."

His gaze shifted, falling somewhere over my shoulder. He was silent.

I said, "I see you're pleading the Fifth. So as long as you opened the door, let me say this. Relationships with people you work with are big mistakes. One that I never intend to repeat."

"We're in agreement."

"So how about this: *I* don't ask . . . and *you* don't ask." I gave him a knowing look. "Besides, I have a feeling the score isn't even *close.*" He actually blushed. I said, "Koby, there is *no one* else in my life at the moment. Put that baby to bed, all right?"

"I'm a fool." He snipped another dead head. "Forgive me."

I took the clippers away from him. "You're not a fool, and as far as I'm concerned, it's yesterday's news. But in the future, you've got to let me know you're interested."

"Believe me, that is not a problem."

"So if you're having a black mood, just say I can't talk, I'm having a black mood. That way, I'll know it isn't me. I come from a divorced home. Trauma is not foreign to me, either. I like order, same as you."

"I can do that."

I gave him back his clippers. "And maybe you want to consider talking to someone."

"I'm talking to you."

"I'm not a therapist."

"No, but your hourly rates are very reasonable." He took in my face, then ran a finger slowly across my cheek. "God gives me a chance at Heaven and I throw it away. I must be psychotic."

I let out a small laugh. "I think you're overstating the case."

"You are *so* gorgeous, Cynthia. It is a thrill just to look at you."

"And a cheap thrill at that."

"Now who's making nervous jokes?"

I didn't answer.

"You are pure heat. . . . Everything about you is fire." His focus was penetrating. "There is this place in Malibu Canyon . . . next to a creek. All around are beautiful mountains and open sky. Lots of vegetarian dishes. The food is very good and the atmosphere is intimate."

I knew the place. It was beautiful and very romantic.

"Shall I shower and put on the shirt?"

His eyes were already in sexual fantasy. But I had things on my mind. "This is the deal, Yaakov Kutiel. You told me your baggage. So now you've got to hear mine."

"I'd be honored."

So I told him. I talked, and talked, and talked, and talked.

We never got to the mountains. He didn't even have a chance to wear the shirt. We never made it out of bed.

30

I was awakened by a kiss on the cheek, my enchanting prince dressed in jeans and a blue T-shirt, with a plastic-wrapped, laundered set of blue scrubs draped over his shoulder. He was holding a cup of coffee.

"Good grief." I sat up and pulled the covers over my breasts. "What time is it?"

"A little after ten." He offered me the mug. "For you."

I took the coffee and sipped. "Good stuff. Ethiopian. I know because a friend of mine bought me a pound."

"There's more where this came from. Plus, toast, juice, and the paper. But alas, you'll have to eat alone. I must go to work."

I rubbed my eyes and noticed Koby's.

Like sparkling Tokay. Finally, the brilliance was back. "Did you sleep well?"

"With you by my side, I slept with the angels. And yourself?"

"Great. I was knocked out." I sipped more coffee, glancing around his tiny bedroom. It had a king-size bed, one nightstand with a phone and a clock, and a small closet with a mirror. No TV, because there was no room. Sunlight was streaming through the sheer curtains, the windows looking out to the rose garden. In actual size, the house was as small as my apartment. But with the homey factor, it wasn't even close. "I'll be leaving shortly."

"Take your time." He pulled something metallic out of his pocket and dropped it on my lap. "Lock up when you leave."

A key. "Should I put it in the mailbox?"

"You can keep it. Use it with or without me. My house is close to your work. If you ever need a quick nap, the place will serve your purpose."

I met his eyes. "I don't know, Koby. This is a little rushed, maybe?"

"If you don't want it, put it in the mailbox." He sat beside me, laying his plastic-wrapped scrubs on the floor. "You say for me to show you I'm interested. Now maybe you believe me."

"I meant responding to my phone calls, not moving—" I stopped myself. Talk about slips of the tongue. Now who needed to take it easy? But my first thoughts had been, If I lived here, where would I put my clothes?

Koby broke into a slow smile. "I think I am *mad* for you, Cynthia." He caressed my arm. "I think it scares me . . . how much I am mad for a woman."

Men and their emotions. I gave him an out. "Don't worry. You barely know me."

"I know how I feel. I knew it when I first saw you. I felt it in the heart. I felt it other places as well."

The bed was still redolent of pheromones. "We do have chemistry."

He kissed my bare shoulder. "We have passionate colors." His hand snaked under the covers. "Black and red, a lethal combination."

I gasped. "I thought you were going to work."

"That's what I am doing." He slipped his fingers between my legs. "I am going to work."

"Work as in a job." I was desperately trying not to be so damn wet under his touch. I was failing miserably. "Salaried work."

"Ah, but this is *so* much better."

I pulled his hand away. "You'll be late."

"You are very cruel," he told me.

Much nicer than saying, *You know you want it bad, bitch.* My eyes went down to his crotch, then up to his expectant face. He raised his eyebrows. He was waiting for a sign.

I smiled.

His clothes were off in thirty seconds. Fifteen minutes after that, he was dressed again. He eyed me in bed and I saw him grow. "I am like a schoolboy." He checked his watch and frowned. "As frustrated as one, too."

"It'll go away as soon as you pull into the hospital parking lot."

"No doubt." He started to sit next to me, then thought better of it. He picked up the scrubs. "Can we see each other tonight?"

"I get off late."

"So we'll sleep in tomorrow."

"I can't," I said. "I have to go to a lecture with my mother at nine in the morning."

"Lecture on what?"

"Art history or something. Mom's doing a master's. She's an eternal student. But I promised I'd go with her. I dare not back out."

"I defer to *Kibud Aim*—honoring one's mother. Tomorrow night?"

I nodded. "That'll work."

"Do I get to meet her? Your mother?"

"Yes . . . when the time's right."

"You said that with hesitancy. She won't approve of me?"

"We'll find out. She professes to be liberal, but you're the first black man I've ever dated."

"Doesn't matter." He kissed my forehead, brushing hair from my eyes. "As long as you approve." He lifted up my chin and brought my lips to his. He kissed me softly. Then again, and again. He sighed, then kissed me again. "Oh my God, I got it *so* bad!"

You and me both, hot stuff. But someone had to be mature. "Go. I'll see you tomorrow night."

Reluctantly, he stood. Wordlessly, he left. I waited until I heard the front door close before I got out of bed. I showered and dressed. Because it was a lovely morning, I put my coffee, juice, toast, and paper on a tray and brought the ensemble out to his rose garden, placing my breakfast on the small, round table, settling into a patio chair. The lot, like all of them in the area, had been cut into the mountains, so I was afforded a view of hillside homes and rooftops. There were houses below me, houses above me, and it was all very charming. I felt as if I were in the artist colony of Montmartre, the Paris neighborhood where the Moulin Rouge still stood. Blue was breaking from the clouds, and in the distance, I caught a glimpse of Silver Lake—truly silver in the muted light.

A good guy, fabulous sex, coffee and the paper while breathing in the aroma of perfumed flowers, *and* a lake view to boot.

I could get used to this.

But alas, I, too, had work to do. When I was finished, I took everything back inside and washed and cleaned up. I knew he kept kosher, so I opened his cabinets and drawers, and sure enough, he had two sets of dishes and two sets of flatware. I placed the ones I had used with their matching set.

I shut the front door and locked it.

I hefted the key several times, then slipped it in my purse.

▼

I owed Scott Oliver in ways he hadn't considered. Since we stopped seeing each other, I had avoided visiting my father at his work out of embarrassment. Now that Scott and I were on speaking terms, I could go see the Loo without fear of running into him. I knew that Oliver was a clotheshorse. While buying Koby a shirt, I had bought Scott a tie. He wasn't in when I came into the Devonshire Detective squad room, so I put the bag on his desk with a thank-you note. Homicide sat in the back of the squad room, its own little fiefdom. I hoped to be a full-fledged member one day, but for now I'd have to be content with vicarious thrills, knowing most of the gold shields here, and knowing that my father was in charge.

I made small talk with a few folks, then left them alone to do their job. I went to pester my father. His door was open. He always kept it open unless he was in conference. Protocol dictated that I knock, so I did. He was on the phone, taking notes, and when he heard the rap, he looked up and gave me five splayed fingers. I mouthed for him to take his time.

"Hold on," the Loo said. To me sotto voce, "Come in and close the door." To his caller, "Yeah, I'm here, go ahead."

I closed the door and sat down across from him, watching him chicken scratch on a yellow notepad. "That's not going to work, Alicia, especially with Malcolm Standish. He's a stickler. Look, rather than bring the case to the grand jury and risk a dismissal, it makes more sense for you to get warrants for the phone calls and bank accounts. Then I'll have one of my people just go through the paperwork and see if we can't get a more direct connection."

More listening.

My father rolled his eyes. He had taken off his suit jacket and loosened a blue tie. He wore a white shirt and gray slacks. His hand made furrows through his hair. "Alicia, I'm telling you this from twenty-five years of experience, if you move too fast, you're going to come away with nothing. We've got a good start. Don't force it, it'll . . . Yes, exactly. Go to Standish and ask for the warrants. He'll appreciate the attention to detail. He's simpatico to these kinds of cases if you cross your *t*'s and dot your *i*'s . . . Yeah, specifically because we're on the border. Yeah . . . yeah . . . okay . . . call me when you get the warrants, and I'll go through the paper. Fine . . . fine . . . bye."

He hung up and exhaled loudly.

"Trouble?"

"Not too bad. At least, she was open to suggestion. I must spend half my time telling young assistant DAs how to do their job."

"You should have been a lawyer."

My dad smiled at the joke. His eyes went to my face. "I want to ask you a question, Cindy."

I leaned back, curious. "Sure."

"I want to know what is the purpose of your having voice mail on your cell phone if you never return messages."

My face went warm. "I'm sorry, Daddy."

"I understand you dropped by yesterday. Rina said you looked upset. That gave me concern. So I called you three times. But you didn't answer. Are you okay?"

"I'm fine, Daddy. Again I'm sorry."

"Were you sleeping off a depression or something?"

At this point, I could have gotten annoyed with him, but that wouldn't have helped at all. "No." I leaned over and kissed his nose.

"No, I was with Koby and it was a rather emotional afternoon and evening, and then the time slipped away. It was wrong. For the third time, I apologize."

"Why are you here, Officer?" he grumped at me.

"To aggravate you."

"You're doing a fine job at that," he groused. "I heard about your bust. Congratulations."

"Thank you. Have you heard good or bad things?"

"Mostly good. A couple of nasty comments about the convenient bag of X."

"Scum is scum."

"Did they hassle you?"

"Yes, but the one good thing about being honest is you have only one story. It's easy to repeat and you don't get mixed up in your lies."

"You want to tell me about it?"

I told him about it. "I looked up the two names El Paso spit out. Joseph 'Juice' Fedek is not living at his last listed address, but Pepe Renaldes is. He works on a construction crew with a posh West Side builder—"

"See why I do my own renovation work?"

"Not all of us can build houses, Dad. Ideally, I'd like to bring Sarah Sanders down to the station and have her look through some six-packs from mug books and see if she picks out El Paso or Fedek or Renaldes. If she does, I'd like to check Renaldes's employment record. I also want to hunt for Fedek. I want to do all those things, but no one's letting me do anything. So I'm here, taking out my frustration on you."

"Why not? Everyone else is. What is the status with the case right now?"

"Russ MacGregor and Justice Brill are waiting to see if there's a drug plea. They tell me that El Paso's willing to roll, but the DA would rather put him away with a sure thing than take a chance on an iffy six-month-old rape case."

"That makes sense, Cin."

"Yes, it does. Unfortunately, if they do it, it means that two very vicious men are out there, able to prey on the public instead of being locked up behind bars."

"If Sarah's story is true."

"That's why I'd like to show her the mug books and see if she could pick them out."

"I'll tell you the same thing I just told the young DA over the phone. Have patience."

"Do you see me going behind anyone's back? In the meantime, just because I'm obsessive and dedicated, I'm still looking for David Tyler. I figure if I find him and if both he and Sarah independently ID Fedek and Renaldes, then the rape/assault case is on much more stable ground." I sat back in my chair. "At first, I thought the bag was good, something we can use to really squeeze El Paso. But I think they're going for the slam-dunk drug conviction. Better for the statistics."

"You're too young to talk that cynically."

"I'm not cynical, I'm practical. And I'm in a fine mood. A good date makes everything seem a little less hopeless."

Dad faced me with unreadable eyes. "If you two are still speaking, you can bring him around again for *Shabbat* dinner. I promise I won't glare at you this time."

I shrugged. "Maybe."

"Have you told your mother?"

"It hasn't come up."

"You haven't brought it up. What are you

worried about? Your mother's much more liberal than I am."

"I'm not worried, Dad. I just want to see how it goes before I even bother." We both knew I was stalling. I checked my watch. "So I guess I'm off to serve and protect and look for David Tyler."

"Any leads at all with him?"

"Goose egg. For all I know, he may be dead. Sarah Sanders did say he wasn't moving when she left the bathroom."

"Yeah, I've been thinking about that. David could be dead, but I doubt if he was dead from the assault. Cindy, the City changes the trash. People do use the john in the park. If there had been a dead body in it, someone would have noticed."

"Unless the boys killed him, then came back to take him away and dump him in a less obvious spot."

"I don't think so, Cindy. It would draw way too much attention. This sounds like an impulsive type of rape. Why hassle with coming back? All it could do is screw them up."

"Because David could identify them."

"He's mentally disabled. How much credibility would he have even if he *could* identify the perps? And that's a big if."

I saw his point.

Dad said, "I know you're working your way through the decidedly unglamorous part of detective work: the shelters, halfway houses, drug rehab, missions, Salvation Army, other areas that have homeless. It's a tedious chore, but it's your best bet right now."

There was a knock on the door and in walked Oliver. He was holding up my tie. It was a nice one—a gold-and-sky-blue Mimi Fong print that I had gotten at deep discount. Furthermore, it went with the navy suit he was wearing.

"What do you think?" I asked him.

"It's beautiful, Cin. Something I would have picked out. What is it? Battle pay?"

"You might say that."

My father's face held a sour look. "You bought him a *tie?*"

"Yes, I bought him a tie when I bought Koby a shirt."

"You bought Oliver a tie and Koby a shirt, but your father gets nothing."

I got up and hugged him around the neck. "Daddy, you'll always be my number one guy."

"You're choking me," Dad grumped.

Oliver said, "So you and the guy are back together?"

"For the time being, and the *guy*—like you, Scott—has a name."

"Yeah, he's got a name. The *black* guy. Or *if* I feel like being politically correct, the African American guy."

"If you want to get technical, then he'd be just the African guy. Or the Asian guy, because I think he's an Israeli citizen. Now if he were an American citizen, then you'd have to call him African Asian American guy. So *that's* why it's much more convenient to call him Yaakov."

"You call him Koby."

"That's reserved for friends, Oliver."

He smiled. Dad drummed his fingers on his desktop. "Anything official you need to talk to me about, Detective?"

"No, not really," Oliver answered.

"Then close the door on your way out."

Oliver laughed and left.

I said, "So it looks like my weekend is booked. On Saturday, I've got my workout at the gym, afternoon is lunch with Mom, and then I've got bowling practice from six to eight in the evening. Then maybe if Koby's off, we'll go out. Sunday morning is brunch with my friend Hayley. I'll look for David in the afternoon, then Sunday evening if Koby and I are still in good standing, we'll go out again."

"I'm getting tired just listening to you. You're hyperactive, Officer Decker."

"Loo, it's better than crying in my beer."

31

Since last week's dinner at Mama's, Rina had made a valiant effort to restrain herself, mentioning her grandmother's case only a couple of times. Peter had played coy, refusing to take the bait. Since subtlety wasn't working, it was time for the direct approach. After the dinner table had been cleared, she sashayed into the kitchen and slid her arms around his waist as he washed dishes. He had rolled up the sleeves of his white shirt but had still managed to get his cuffs wet.

"I'll do that," she said.

"I'm almost done," Decker told her. "But you can keep hugging. It feels good."

"I love a man who knows how to scour a roasting pan."

He smiled. "What's Hannah doing?"

"Her homework. So what's going on?"

"Not much."

Rina broke away. Nervously, she smoothed out her denim skirt and hiked up the sleeves of her pink sweater to her elbows. She picked up a towel and began to dry the dishes. "Just answer me one question. Did you find Marta Lubke?"

"Yes."

Rina was flabbergasted. "You *did?*"

"Yes."

"Is she alive?"

"That's two questions."

She punched his shoulder.

"Yes, she's alive," Decker answered. "Even better, so is her older sister. I was going to tell you after Hannah went to bed. But since we started, what else would you like to know?"

"For starters, how'd you find her?"

"That would be giving away my trade secrets." Decker winked at her. "I logged onto Google and got hits for around a hundred Lubkes . . . probably not the smartest thing to do since the Lubke I was looking for was from Germany. But I thought I'd test the waters here, maybe find a relative. From what I pulled up, I began a process of elimination mostly by age. I found about ten Lubkes who were old enough and sent out e-mails to all of them. I got unbelievably lucky. I received an e-mail response from an Anika Lubke. That, in itself, is pretty good—a woman in her eighties savvy in computers. You wouldn't believe where she lives."

"Los Angeles?"

"No, but almost as good. She lives up in Solvang."

"You're kidding!"

"Right north of Santa Barbara. I told you it was good."

"You're the best. So what did Anika Lubke write back?"

"That she was from Munich. And this is where it gets *really* unbelievably lucky. She has a sister named Marta, whose married name is Wallek. She lives in St. Louis, Missouri, which I understand has a large population of people of German descent."

"The home of Anheuser-Busch. As in Busch Stadium."

"As in Budweiser beer," Decker said.

"There was an expression my friend Ellie in Munich used to use—'*Bierbauch Bayer.*' It means beer-bellied Bavarian. Beer is a cultural icon in Germany, especially Bavaria."

"Well, beer doesn't do too bad in the good old US of A, either. The upshot of this entire thing is that last night I got an e-mail from Marta. Did I do well or what?"

"I can't believe you found out all this information in so short a time."

"Thank the Internet. Both women are widows, by the way." Decker held up a wet roasting pan. "Can you dry a little faster so I have some room for this in the dish rack?"

Rina picked up the dinner plates and stacked them on the counter. "Happy now?"

"I just didn't want to nick the stoneware."

She smiled. "You're wonderful. I love you."

Decker started washing the utensils. "I love you, too. You want to hear the interesting part?"

"There's more?"

"Lots. Guess what Anika's married name is?"

Rina finished with the dinner dishes, then picked up the pan and began to dry it. "Being as there must be about a million German surnames, I give up."

"Even if you went through them all, you wouldn't be close. It's Emerson."

"She married an American."

"She married a Brit."

"That must be a story."

"It must be one hell of a story. But I don't know it because it's not the kind of thing you e-mail to a stranger."

"Are you sure you've got the right Marta Lubke?"

"Yes, I'm positive because she remembers your mother for the same reason your mother remembered her. They were both Marta. And she remembered some of the other girls when I mentioned their names. And both of them remembered your grandmother's murder. How much detail they recall . . . that I don't know."

Rina put her hand over her mouth and froze. Slowly, she let it drop to her side.

Decker said, "Marta Lubke and Anika are well into their eighties. I think your mother has been playing a little loose with the years."

"I'm stunned." Rina swallowed. "Not by Mama cheating on her age, but that you really found someone she knew as a child."

"Marta Lubke Wallek was very excited that Marta Gottlieb Elias is still alive. She would like to contact your mother, Rina, *if* that's okay with your mother. She said she has quite a story as well. We need to tell Mama what's going on."

Rina sighed. "Of course. It won't be easy to tell her about it. Mama will wonder why we were searching for Marta Lubke."

"Just tell her that after she spoke about her childhood, you wanted to find someone from her past."

"All right." Rina was uncertain but was resolved to do the right thing. "We'll forget about my grandmother's murder. I'll tell Mama what's going on. Actually, I'm much more excited about a possible reunion between the two of them. Better than digging up old bones."

"Very noble of you." Decker laid the clean utensils on top of the rack. "However, I think I have a better idea."

Rina waited.

"I don't think we should bring the two of them together until we know more about Marta and Anika Lubke. Remember, your mother is a camp survivor, and we don't want to cause her any more pain. I think we should talk to the women first."

"You want to go to Saint Louis?"

"No need because the fates are with us. Marta Lubke Wallek is coming in to visit her sister. How about we take advantage and make a little vacation out of it? We'll leave Saturday night, right after *Shabbat*, stay overnight in Santa Barbara, then continue on to Solvang on Sunday and come back Sunday night. Surely the boys can watch Hannah for twenty-four hours. They're both over eighteen."

"Sammy works on Sunday."

"Jacob doesn't."

Rina made a face. "I don't know, Peter. What about Cindy?"

"Saturday is her day with Jan. Sometimes they go out at night. That's inviolate. But she can certainly pick up some of the slack on Sunday. I'm sure she won't mind a morning or afternoon shift." Now Decker made a face. "By the way, she's bringing Koby over for *Shabbat* this weekend."

Rina's eyes brightened. "So they're back together?"

"For the time being, yes."

"I like him."

"You like his circumcision," Decker remarked.

"Yes, I like that he's Jewish. I've never

hidden my partisan feelings. So when are we going to visit Solvang?"

"Marta is visiting her sister in three weeks. How does that work?"

"Perfect. No major holidays in the way. And it will give me plenty of time to prepare . . . cook Sunday dinner for the boys and Hannah."

"Rina, they're capable boys. They can cook for themselves."

"I know, but it's not hard for me to cook a little extra."

"Can I give you a cross to nail your hands on, Saint R?"

"I like cooking for my family. So sue me."

"I don't want to sue you." Decker took her in his arms and slapped her to his chest. "I'd rather screw you."

She punched his shoulder. "What got into you?"

"I wish something would get into you." He raised his eyebrows. "If you would examine my motivations, you'd see I have other reasons for wanting you alone for a night away." He kissed her hard on the lips.

"*Eeeuuuu!*"

They both looked toward the door. Hannah scowled at them, turned on her heels, and stomped out. They broke into laughter.

Decker said, "I'll see what she wants."

Rina held him tightly. "She'll survive for a minute."

She gave him a long, slow kiss, the kind that makes body parts move independently.

"My oh my," Decker said. "What got into *you?*"

"Are you complaining?"

"Not at all." He broke away. "I'll go check up on Hannah." He was still stiff. "Maybe you should check up on Hannah, and let me take a cold shower."

"Not too cold."

"Believe me, darlin', there's plenty more where this came from."

32

The secret of optimal performance is to keep the mind focused, but the body completely relaxed. Completely loose." Koby shook out his arms. "You watch basketball, no?"

"Occasionally," I told him.

"You ever see the pros make long shots? The trey—the perfect three-pointer—is usually a swisher, all net with just a flick of the wrist. So loose. Or a slugger at bat, the follow-through on his swing, the whole body moves in one motion. It's very hard to do because the natural thing when you concentrate is to tense up, right?"

"Right."

"It's a mind-set, Cindy, one of the reasons why pro athletes are so arrogant. They have to think they're the best, otherwise they won't relax."

"They're arrogant because they make ten million bucks a year and have thousands of women willing to minister to their genitals."

Koby smiled. "I say it's *one* of the reasons."

I rubbed my arms, bouncing on the heels of my feet. We had already done preliminary stretching, but it was still cold outside and my muscles were starting to tighten. Gray clouds hung in the L.A. skies like wet gym clothes. Even though it was the ungodly hour of seven on a Wednesday morning, there were people on the outdoor track. Koby had waved to a few of them.

"When I ran competitively, I used to think of my joints as very thin rubber bands, that it was no effort at all to stretch them and that they'd always bounce back. It helped me maintain a long stride."

"You have a long stride because you have long legs," I told him.

"Yes, I am African. We are built to outrun lions. Even so, anyone can improve the performance. Are you ready?"

"Sure. Why not?"

"This was your idea, Cindy."

"I just thought it was something we could do together that didn't involve spending money or having sex."

He smiled. "If you like, we can go back to sex."

"Notice you said nothing about spending money."

"First we have sex; then I spend the money." He laughed and took my arm. "Come on."

"Please pretend like we're going at the same pace."

He trotted by my side as I jogged around the oval, keeping up a steady patter of conversation. Mostly, he spoke about work. It was good because it gave him a chance to vent his frustrations and, at the same time, distracted me and made the time go quicker. He did the talking because I needed all my breath for running. I hadn't realized it, but slowly, slowly, he had picked up the pace. After forty-five minutes, I was shot and broke to a fast walk. As I cooled off, I told him to go out and stretch his legs. Within moments, he was burning rubber, pure poetry in motion. By the time we got back to his house, I was feeling very amorous with all the endorphins flowing.

That pleased him immensely. He suggested we take a run every morning. The hot shower shook out the last remaining bits of lethargy. As I walked into his kitchen, I noticed that my cell phone was beeping.

I checked my voice mail.

Koby came in and saw it instantly in my face. I don't know who felt worse.

I checked my watch. It was quarter to ten. I didn't start work until three. "They want me at the station in an hour . . . by eleven."

"What is it?"

"I don't know." I rolled my shoulders. "Last time I spoke to the Loo from our Detectives bureau, he mentioned something about the guy I arrested filing an excessive-force complaint."

"Shit." Koby came over to me, took my shoulders, and looked me square in the eye. "Do you want me to come with you?"

"No, Koby, of course not. I'll be okay." A weak smile. "It's fine."

"You're sure?"

"I couldn't be more positive."

"Whatever it is, Cynthia, I'm here for you. Call me when it's over. Focused mind, loose body. Never let them see you sweat."

▼

Brill closed the door to the interview room. Stone was there, so was the deputy DA—a slight man with an Ivy League haircut and tortoiseshell glasses perched on his nose. He appeared to be around thirty and wore an olive green suit with a yellow shirt and patterned tie, the predominant color in it being red.

This wasn't good.

I sat down at the table, Detective Brill and Lieutenant Stone on either side of me. The DA had elected to stand. He introduced himself: Geoffrey—with a *G*—Adamson.

"We've got a problem," the DA began. "It might be hard to prove that the bust wasn't staged."

I waited for him to continue.

"Not that I think you staged it."

Thanks for the vote of confidence.

I didn't speak until I was sure my voice was clear. Then I said, "I never touched that bag. Officer Bader found it on El Paso when he patted him down. If you can get prints off the plastic—"

"All that means, Officer Decker, is that you wore gloves."

I felt myself go rigid. *Loose.* I made myself slouch.

"And the fact that you sent your friend away makes it look really bad."

I was silent.

"Why did you send him away?" Geoffrey with a *G* persisted.

"At the time, I didn't think I'd need him to vouch for my honesty." I made hard eye contact. "I sent him home because he had been working for four days straight and he was falling off his feet."

Adamson took in my words as if they were profound. He walked as he talked. "So how long between the time you sent him away and the first cruiser arrived?"

"Around thirty seconds. He pulled out of his parking space just as the cruiser came down the street."

"Not a lot of time, but that doesn't really help much."

"So why did you bring it up?" Stone said. "Look, Geoff, you and your people can think what you'd like. I know she didn't plant the bag. She's willing to take a lie detector test—"

"That doesn't impress me."

"Well, it impresses me," Stone insisted.

"We don't want the case to go to trial. And any PD will threaten trial because we've all got Rampart hanging over our heads. Another scandal real or imaginary will make all of us look bad."

"So you're ignoring a bag of X because no one was there to snap my picture when I took him down?" I asked him.

"You weren't in uniform, Officer Decker," Adamson told me.

"I know. I've been doing this on my own time."

"And that makes you look like a hot dog."

At this point, I shut up.

Stone shook his head. "Damn amateur videographers are never there when you need them."

I smiled.

"What's the upshot?" Stone said. "You take the bag away and give him four months in County for the traffic warrant?"

"That's about it."

Brill said, "The thing is, Decker, now El Paso has no motivation for nailing his two compadres for the Sarah Sanders rape."

"Fedek and Renaldes," I said.

"Yes, them," Brill said. "El Paso's not going to flip to avoid a four-month County stint. So unless we have something on Fedek and Renaldes now, like an outstanding warrant, DA's office says they're off-limits."

"El Paso admitted he was at the scene of the rape," I said. "Can't we use that?"

"But before that, he had asked for an attorney and you didn't give him one," Adamson said. "That conversation has to be disregarded."

I held my hands tightly in my lap . . . caught myself tensing and unfurled my hands.

"Can't I have Sarah Sanders look through a six-pack and see if she can pick out El Paso? I got *that* information from someone else."

Stone said, "You got information saying that El Paso was at the rape or just that he was a gang banger?"

I sighed. "The latter."

"Unfortunately, Officer Decker, that won't work."

He was being nice. I didn't want to try his patience. "Sir, would it be okay if I brought Sarah Sanders down and had her look at mug books?"

"Yeah, sure," Stone said. "As long as you

start with the *A*'s and don't do anything to show prejudice."

"This is the developmentally disabled girl?" Adamson said.

"Yes," I answered.

"The one who abandoned her infant baby."

"Yes."

The DA said, "Considering her mental capacity and it's a six-month-old rape case, her testimony isn't going to hold much weight."

"How about if it's independently corroborated?"

"By whom?"

"By the boy she was with. By the boy who was assaulted while she was being gang-raped. His name is David Tyler."

"Decker, the boy is missing," Brill pointed out.

"What if I could find him? Then what if I gave them both mug books and independently they picked out the same people. Would that work?"

Adamson shrugged. "It would make a stronger case. Do you know where the boy is?"

"I'm working on it." *Relax, relax.* "Now maybe I'll work a little harder."

Adamson checked his watch. "Give me a call when you've found him. In the meantime you don't say Germando El Paso and the rape in the same breath—especially not to Sarah Sanders."

"I understand," I told him. "I'm not happy, but I understand."

"Next time, don't send your witnesses home," the DA added.

"I'll try to remember that, sir."

Then the little prick had the nerve to wink at me as he left. I turned to the lieutenant. "That's sexual harassment."

"It's a tic, Decker." Stone laid his hand on my shoulder. "You did a good job. It's a shame that some rotten apples got in the way of a righteous bust. But I understand his position. Now go get some lunch before your shift starts."

I remembered my manners. "Thank you, sir, for your support."

He smiled at me. "You're welcome."

Brill said, "I'm still on the hit-and-run from a couple of weeks ago, Cindy. You okay from that?"

"An occasional street dream. No big deal.

Thanks for asking, Justice." I turned to the lieutenant. "Can I go?"

"Absolutely."

I stood, and before I reached for the doorknob, I gave a nice little feminine wave. As soon as I was alone, I called Koby and had him paged. He picked up the line five minutes later.

I said, "It's okay. I'm okay. A little disappointed, but I'm not in any trouble."

"*Baruch Hashem.*" He sounded genuinely relieved. "What was it?"

"I'm on a cell phone, Koby. We'll talk later. What time do you get off?"

"I'm doing a twelve-hour rotation. More money, and we're off at the same time. Shall we meet at home?"

"*Your* home, you mean?"

"No, Cindy, I mean just plain *home.*"

That was sweet and I told him so. I told him that I'd see him later.

I was sweating. Whether they saw it or not, I don't know.

33

Work came, work went. A routine week and I liked it that way. The following Sunday, Koby and I finally managed that romantic dinner, driving down Pacific Coast Highway just as the sun was sinking over the horizon, the sky bursting with fireworks in a palette of hot pinks, regal purples, and flaming reds. When we turned right onto Malibu Canyon Road, the mountains were bathed in reflected light, turning the surface mossy green and rust orange. The moon could be seen swimming in the pale gray sky of dusk. It was a wonderful moment, an incredibly delicious evening, and I was giddy even before sipping my first glass of wine. We shared food while we cracked wise, the banter eventually turning into a series of racy innuendos. By the time we hit the road, we couldn't wait. So we checked into an old Malibu beach motel—a series of tiny, private cottages with beds the size of coffee tables, foam rubber mattresses, and scratchy sheets. No view of the ocean, but that didn't matter. It was all lightning and thunder, and when it was over, the shower worked.

I felt as if I were finally living those glorified high school days that had eluded me as an adolescent. It was nice to walk on air and *really* nice that the guy involved was incredible in bed. It was too early in the relationship to feel this way and I knew that the carpet could be yanked from under my feet at any moment. Still, I had carried Koby's key and he hadn't asked for it back. In fact, the only thing he had asked for was my key in return.

It was just past midnight when we made it back to the city. I had fallen asleep in the car, but I awoke around Sunset and La Brea, about twenty minutes from Koby's house. I roused myself and rubbed my eyes. "Are you all right?"

"I'm fine. Nice nap?"

"Yes, I'm fine. Need me to drive?"

"No."

"You're not tired?"

"Not tired at all. Too aroused."

"Aroused like in *up* aroused or aroused like in sex—"

"That one."

I was amazed. "How can you be horny?"

"Because I fantasize while you sleep."

"You're an animal."

"No, Cindy, I'm a guy. We are simple: cars, sports, and sex. At this hour, not many cars on the road and no game is on . . . I think about sex."

I gave him the eye. "Was I in your fantasy at least?"

He grinned. "You *were* the fantasy."

I hit his shoulder. "Liar!"

He laughed. "No, no, I prove it to you when we get home. I act it out for you."

Again, I slugged him. "Would you like me to de-arouse you?"

"Not particularly."

Silence.

"What?" Koby asked.

"I told my mother about you," I said.

Koby's hands gripped the wheel, but he didn't answer.

I said, "Did it work?"

"Very much. It has died a sudden and pitiable death. What did she say?"

"She asked if it was serious."

"What did you tell her?"

"I said I've known you only about a month and serious was still a relative concept. I told her I like you very much. She wants to meet you."

He smiled. "You like me very much?"

"No, I think you're a bum."

"I work too hard to be a bum."

"That's true. You must have worked like a dog to afford the down payment on your house."

"No, a dog has a better life." He laughed at his joke. "The house has a story. I have a friend who had a start-up in the late '90s. Usually I am cautious, but I don't know. I gave him a couple of thousand that quickly turned into twenty—eight months maybe. The house came up, I took out my profit. A year later, the company went under. Pure luck."

"The secret was you weren't greedy."

"Whatever it was, I don't question, I just say thank you. When you want, I will meet your mother."

"How about this weekend?"

"Sure."

"You're a sport, Koby." I pulled down the passenger vanity mirror on the sun visor and began to play with my hair. "We usually have lunch on Saturday. I told her that wasn't good for you because of *Shabbat*. I think the fact that you're traditional about *Shabbat* bothers her more than your complexion."

He made a face. "Why?"

I smoothed back a strand of bothersome locks. "My dad's wife is very religious."

"Ah. So I'm identified with the enemy camp."

"More or less . . . although my mother remarried before my father."

"Do you get along with your stepfather?"

"Yeah, Alan's all right." I took out a tube of lipstick and touched up my mouth. "I don't see him a whole lot. I usually meet my mother alone, so I only see him when they have parties. They have quite a few of those—about six a year."

I narrowed my eyes and studied the traffic behind us.

Koby said, "So what day did you pick for us to meet?"

The seconds ticked by.

"Cindy?"

"Next Sunday . . . hold on a moment."

"What's wrong?"

"Hold on!" I glanced in the side mirror. "Don't do anything, Koby. Don't look in the mirror, don't pick up your pace. Just keep driving. I think we're being followed."

He didn't speak. But once again, he gripped the wheel. It must be something he did when he was nervous. He had reason to be.

"Bronze Chevy Nova," I said. "Haven't seen one of those in a while. Primer on the left side. The windows have been darkened. That's illegal, but right now it's beside the point. I can't make out the driver's face this far back. He's just a shape right now."

"Should I slow?"

"No. I told you, just keep driving."

He swallowed. "Is it the guy I whacked in the back?"

"Maybe. Although I thought he was still locked up in County."

"The hit-and-run driver from the accident?"

"Could be. We're driving in the same car. Why *anyone's* following us is up for grabs."

"And you can't see him?"

"No."

Koby was quiet. It suddenly dawned on me that he wasn't a fellow cop. It was up to me to guide us both through this. "I'm a little tense. Sorry if I'm short. It's probably nothing."

"It's fine, Cindy. Just tell me what to do."

I patted his knee. "Just keep driving, all right? It's no big deal. We're on a major boulevard and there's still enough traffic."

"Why don't you call 911?"

"Because I want to make sure I'm right. What I wouldn't give to get his license number. There's no front plate. You know, that's what I'll do. I'll call that in and let some cruiser stop him."

I took out my cell phone.

The battery was dead.

It had been a long evening.

"Does your cell work?" I asked him.

"I don't have it with me. I didn't want intrusions tonight."

"Sweet thought but unfortunate, because we have a big intrusion. Okay. Time for Plan B. How do you feel about driving in this situation?"

"What do you mean?"

"You know . . . sudden turns . . . screeching tires . . ."

"This car doesn't have so much pickup."

"You know, there's a way to pop the clutch and press the gas at the same time. It'll push it to the max."

"Maybe you should drive."

"Then miss the next light and we'll switch places."

He did. It was hard getting over the gearshift without bodily harm, but we succeeded. With the wheel in my hand, I felt better. I adjusted the rearview mirror. I plunked my purse onto his lap. "Ever hold a gun?"

"I was in the army."

"I'm not talking about an Uzi, Yaakov. I mean a handgun."

"Yes, I have shot a handgun."

"Are you a good shot?"

"I was a decent shot, but it's been over ten years. I'm sure I'm rusty."

"I've got a nine-millimeter Beretta semi-automatic standard police issue in my purse. You can take it out."

He retrieved it, studying its features. "Do you have the magazine?"

"It's not loaded?"

"No, Cynthia, it is not loaded."

"Check my purse. If I don't have one in there, we're out of luck."

Rummaging through my purse, he fished out a magazine and shoved it into the chamber. "We're in luck."

"Okay. This is what I'm going to do. I'm going to turn right in two blocks, floor it, pull over, and cut the lights. I'm going to park on the wrong side of the street. The driver's more likely to miss me that way. Then as the Nova passes, I'm going to try to read off the license plate on the back. Stay low in case they decide to shoot."

"Maybe I should read the license plate while you cover me? I have no doubt that you're a better shot. And if you're on the wrong side of the street, I'll be on the correct side to read the numbers."

"Except if they start shooting at us, you'll be closer."

"A comforting thought."

"Koby, I am so sorry!"

"Don't be ridiculous. We'll handle this." He rolled his shoulders. "I'm psyched."

"Ready?"

"Go."

I made a quick right and punched the

accelerator as I jammed the gears. The car bucked backward, then shot forward with surprising speed. I cut the lights, pulled over, switched off the ignition, and ducked. The Nova sped by, but even so, I got most of the plate and what I didn't get, Koby filled in. I turned the car's ignition, did a U-turn without lights, then headed back into traffic.

Apparently not soon enough. The Nova had other ideas. It must have been souped up, because within moments it was kissing the Toyota's rear bumper. I pulled a sharp left into a darkened residential area.

The Nova followed.

Another right, another left. There was no way the Nova could maneuver that easily. Yet there it was, riding my ass.

Getting closer and closer.

I pushed Koby's head down and smoked the gears. A volley of shots made neat little bullet holes in his trunk and blasted through the rear windshield, shattering the glass.

"Shit!" I screamed as I strained the engine forward. I screeched out a two-tire right and tried to accelerate, hearing the engine whine, feeling the knocking of the gears.

"*Kus sa mack!*" Koby rolled down the window, and using the side mirror for a view, he twisted his right arm and fired a round into the Nova's hood. I noticed he shot one-handedly and I noticed he shot like a cop—his palm parallel instead of perpendicular to the ground. He obviously had hit something, because the Nova began to smoke. Before he had a chance to reload, I turned right, and the Nova tore away. I pulled over, turned off the ignition, and caught my breath. *"Oh God!"* I grabbed Koby's hand. *"Oh God, are you okay?"*

He patted his chest with his hands. "No bullet holes. Just a racing heartbeat."

I was huffing and puffing. "All right." Inhale, exhale, inhale, exhale. "Okay. We're about five minutes from the station. Once we file the report, it's going to take a while. There'll be lots of questions. Are you up for it?"

He exhaled hard. "I think, yes."

I waited a few moments, trying to antici-pate what was going to happen. I didn't like the setup I was seeing. I swallowed hard. "Koby, if it goes down that you fired my gun, it'll be bad for both of us, especially if you hit someone."

"It was self-defense."

"Yes, exactly, and once they see the car, it won't be a problem. But there are much stricter regulations about a civilian discharging a weapon than a cop." I looked him in the eye. "There's no way I'm going to let you handle that kind of heat. You drove, I shot. It's your car. It makes more sense anyway."

"But that's not what happened."

"Yes, you're right. It's a lie. They will have me sign an affidavit and I will perjure myself. I want you to do the same thing. If you hit someone fatally, I will take responsibility—"

"I'm not asking you to do that."

"Listen to me!" I held his face. "Please, please *listen* to me! Please don't argue. Okay?"

He didn't give me the satisfaction of an immediate answer. "I don't want you to get in trouble because I was rash."

"Yaakov, you weren't *rash.* You saved our *lives!* Just . . . just trust me on this! Please!"

We were both breathing hard. Finally, he relented. "Whatever you . . . you think."

"That's what I think."

He nodded. "Okay . . . okay. I drove and you shot. Except that I smell of gunpowder and you do not."

Gunshot tattooing. It was unlikely that they'd check my hand, even more unlikely that they'd check his hand, but just in case, I took the gun from him, rolled down the window, and fired off a couple of shots. "When we get into the police station, go to the bathroom. Wash your hands with lots of soap and go clear up to your elbows if no one's watching you."

He nodded. "So I just tell them what happened or . . ."

"Tell them *exactly* what happened, except you were driving and I did the shooting."

"That the car was following us and you wanted the license number?"

"Yes. And I tried to call for backup, for help, but my cell was dead. And you didn't have yours because you didn't want the intrusion. Just stick to the facts."

"Except that I was driving."

"Exactly." I blew out air. "Yaakov, I'm *so* sorry—"

Before I could continue, he grabbed my neck and kissed my mouth—long, slow, and hard. "We're whole, Cynthia. Nothing . . . *nothing* else matters. I say '*meqseft yasferawal*' in Amharic, I say '*Gomel*' in Hebrew at *beit knesset* on Saturday, and in English I say 'thank you, *Hashem,* for saving us from catastrophe.' God has choice of languages. Now let's get out of here."

34

The adrenaline was pumping full force. So intent on the task at hand, Decker almost missed him when he walked into Hollywood. But his peripheral vision took in the figure sitting on one of the blue hard plastic chairs, his face drawn and tired. With effort, Koby got to his feet.

"She's with the detectives, I think."

The desk sergeant looked up from his perch. Decker showed him his shield, exchanged a few words to be polite, then counted to five. He blew out air, then looped his arm around Koby. "How are you?"

"Not so brave as your daughter."

"What happened?"

Briefly, Koby told him what had occurred. Decker took in his words and listened intently, but something was off. Not that Koby wasn't good because he was: straight face, loose posture, and good eye contact. He had probably fooled the detectives to whom he spoke. But Decker knew bullshit when he heard it, specifically because he knew his daughter. He heard *her* words and *her* phrases, not Koby's punctuated speech patterns.

Decker gave him a hard eye. "Let's take a walk."

Koby eyed him back. "Thank you, but I think I shall stay here."

Decker grew testy. "Five minutes."

"I'm fine, sir. I want to wait for Cindy."

"She'll be there for hours." Decker was all business. "Take a walk with me."

"I will wait here, sir," Koby said. "And if necessary, I will wait for hours."

The lad had spoken.

This was just great. Decker was now in a pissing contest with his daughter's boyfriend. And of course, that was the problem. Decker could bully his daughter. He knew all the tricks that parents knew. He knew when to go full force, he knew when to hold back, but eventually he could always make her come around because they had a history together. Koby was not just his daughter's boyfriend. Koby was a thirty-two-year-old man with lots and lots of survivor skills and—Cindy's father or not—he'd be damned before he let *anyone* shove him against a wall.

It was time to go back to the basics. Build some rapport and that meant finding a common denominator. That part was easy. Decker took a step back, giving him some personal space. He kept his voice low and urgent.

"Son, you want what's best for Cindy, I want what's best for Cindy. If she's having a difficult time with those guys in there, you can't help her. But *I* can. Please. I'm asking you for help for Cindy's sake. Come outside and take a walk with me."

Koby looked away. Then abruptly, he picked up his leather jacket. Decker held the door open and they took a few steps away from the station house onto Wilton Place. At this time of night, there was no car or pedestrian traffic. The darkness was gloomy, the air damp and gelid. Decker gave off a shudder from the chill.

"Let's talk in my car. It's warmer."

Koby regarded him suspiciously.

"What?" Decker narrowed his eyes. "You think I'm going to roust you?"

"I don't trust cops."

"You're dating one."

"She is not a cop; she is Cindy."

"And I'm her father."

"Even more reason not to trust you."

Decker glared at him, then shifted his eyes away and broke into laughter. "Okay. Then we'll freeze our asses off and talk out here."

The silence between them matched the silence on the street.

Koby ran his hand over his face. "My God . . . I'm sorry."

"No, no"—Decker threw his hand on his shoulder—"I'm being pushy because I'm anxious. Koby, I'd like to talk in my car because it's more private and it's warmer. But if that's not what you want, I'm fine here."

"Where's your car?"

Decker pointed to his vintage black Porsche 911 Targa parked by the curb. Koby's eyes widened. "That's your *car?*"

"No, that's my *hobby.* I usually drive a '99 Toyota Camry, but I wanted to get here in a hurry and this baby moves." Decker clicked the unlock button on the remote and held out his arm. "After you."

Koby went into the passenger's side. Decker sat behind the wheel. He said, "Son, I am going into the interview room. I'm going to hear what my daughter has to say. Now in order to *help* her, I need to know the truth. Whatever you tell me stays between the two of us."

Staring out the windshield, Koby said, "I told you what happened."

"No, you told me an *approximation* of what happened. Koby, I'd *die* for Cindy. I certainly would have no qualms about *lying* for her. We're on the same side. But to help her as much as I can, I've got to know what really happened—in your words, not Cindy's."

Koby ran his hands down his face, then blew out air. "It was like I told you—"

"No, it wasn't—"

"Let me *finish* . . . please."

"Sorry," Decker said. "Sorry. Go on."

"It was like I told you." Koby spoke softer this time. "We were driving when Cindy noticed a car following us. We pulled over to get the license, and then as we pulled out, the car came after us and opened fire. We fired back. . . ." He regarded Decker. "I fired back. She was driving. I did the shooting."

"With her gun?"

"Yes, of course—a Beretta nine-millimeter semiautomatic. I don't own a gun."

"Go on."

"When it was over, she said it will look bad for her if they find out that I fired her weapon. If there is death or injury in the other car, I would get into bigger trouble than she would. So we switch places in the story. I don't want to do it. I tell her that I will take responsibility. She begged me to listen to her. So I listened."

"She was right."

"No, I don't think so."

"I know how the system works. I'm telling you she was right."

"I don't need her to cover for me."

"Actually, what you both need is to get out of this as cleanly as possible."

"I hide behind her skirt," he whispered. "It's *emasculating!*"

"Fuck that!" Decker told him. "You helped my little girl! To me, you've got a fine set of *baytzim* in your jeans, and right now I'm the only one you have to impress. The rest is *bullshit!*"

Koby looked at him. "You know Hebrew."

"Selected words."

"*I* should be talking to the detectives, not her."

"Koby, she'd *still* be talking to them because she's the *cop*." *Patience,* Decker told himself. "She did the right thing. But even if she was wrong—and she's not—but even if she was, it's too late. So let's move on, okay?"

He rubbed his forehead. "What next?"

"First let me ask you a couple of questions," Decker said. "Why was she driving your car?"

"We switched places after she noticed the tail. She said she knew how to pop the clutch to get maximum pickup if we have to make a quick exit. I think she wanted to drive, so I don't argue." Koby ran a finger across the hammered metal dash. "Over the years, I've found it is not so good to argue with women you like."

"I'll second that."

"I really, really like"—he regarded Decker—"I *love* her, Lieutenant. I cannot tell her no."

Decker smiled. "You're in trouble, guy."

"I know. It is not good to feel so strong about a woman." Koby leaned forward onto the dash and regarded the empty street scene. *"Ye-isat gize.* What can I do? I am weak."

To be in love was to be weak. . . . Cultural differences . . . or maybe not. Decker gave him a pat on the back. "Had you ever fired a handgun before?"

"I was in the army."

"Ah, right. They might paraffin you."

"I washed my hands with soap up to the elbows." He sat back in the seat and stared upward. "Cindy told me to do it."

"She's my daughter, all right." Decker organized his thoughts. "Now that I know what went on, I can help her. You did the right thing."

Koby blew out air. "She will be mad that I told you."

"She'll get over it. You did what was best for her."

"I hope you are right."

"I know I'm right. I don't tell you how to administer CPR, you don't tell me about LAPD." Decker paused. "Actually, I could tell you how to administer CPR. I was a medic in Vietnam."

Koby turned to him. "I was a medic, too."

"How old were you when you went in?"

"Seventeen."

"A youngster. I was nineteen. Two years?"

"In Israel, the service is three years for boys, two for girls. It was bad over there in Vietnam, no?"

"Yes, it was very bad."

"You were in combat?"

"Yes. My tour ended right before the Easter offensive. I wasn't in the front lines, although they usually sent us with the infantry in teams of six to eight men. I did dustoffs—rode the chopper in, then evacuated the wounded after the raids. It could have been worse."

"For me as well. I was in Lebanon toward the end, so the fighting wasn't as fierce. Still, it was right after the Berlin Wall fell and the Soviet Union was still a presence. Between the USSR and Syria and Iran, Hezbollah was very well armed. Lots of border skirmishes. They kept me up north for a while . . . near Ma'alot, where Arafat—*yemach sh'mo*—and his Fatah thugs shot up a busload of schoolchildren on a field trip. So tension was high but not nearly as bad as Gaza. I was there for six months, dodging booby traps from Hamas and the PLO, trying to prevent them from blowing up civilians. It wasn't as bad as today—for some stupid reason, the world thinks it wise to arm the PLO—but it had its moments."

He paused, then gave a half smile to Decker.

"Upon reflection, with all that's going on in the world, this is not so terrible."

"It's all perspective, my man." Decker shook his head. *What crazy times!* "Your car's going to be impounded. I'll make sure a cruiser takes you home. You have any other source of transportation for getting to work?"

"A bike. I'm fine down the hill. Up is not so good."

Decker smiled. "Call a cab and go rent a car tomorrow. I'll make sure you're reimbursed one way or the other. Wait outside. I'll go in and send around a black-and-white for you."

"I'd like to wait for Cindy."

"She really is going to be tied up for hours. I'll take care of her." Decker clenched his jaw. "Believe me, Koby, I'll take *good* care of her—of *both* of you."

Koby eyed him. "You're not a man to cross."

"I'm *very* protective of my children."

"I'm sure that is true, Lieutenant Decker. Still, I wait for Cindy."

Decker regarded the face—the determined eyes, the stubborn mouth. He wasn't going to budge until he saw her. Decker had thought Koby was decent. Seeing how he reacted in a crisis improved the impression considerably.

"How about this? How about if I get her so she can say good-bye to you?"

"I will wait all night for her. But I go when she says okay. How does that sound?"

Decker nodded. "Fair enough. I'm cold. Let's go back inside."

▼

The coffee sat in my stomach like battery acid—a combination of fatigue and neurotransmitters racing through my system. I had gone over the events about a dozen times. By the look on Justice Brill's face, he still wasn't satisfied. Both he and Lieutenant Stone were being gentlemanly, but I had the distinct feeling they were sick of my face.

Brill said, "So it was what? An '80s Nova . . . '90s?"

"Around 1990," I answered. "Bronze paint but peeling. Primer around the driver's door.

Illegally darkened windows. I seem to recall a dented front bumper and grille."

"You shot out the hood?"

"I'm pretty sure I hit it. It was smoking pretty bad when the car finally peeled off."

Stone said, "But you didn't hit the front windshield."

"I don't know, sir." Third time he asked the question. "I might have. The windshield didn't shatter. That much I do know."

"And you didn't call for backup because your phone was dead?" Brill inquired again.

This time, I pulled the cell phone out of my purse. "You get a connection, you win the prize."

Brill depressed the power button. "You know there are lots of new products on the market with longer battery life."

"I'll buy a new one tomorrow . . . today." I rubbed my forehead. "As soon as the stores open."

"And your friend didn't have a cell on him?"

"No."

"He's a nurse, but he doesn't carry a cell?"

"He's a nurse, Detective Brill, not a doctor. He's not on call."

"This is the same guy you sent away at Boss's?"

They were covering the same ground, but I had no choice but to bear with it. "Yes."

"And the same guy was with you at the hit-and-run?"

"Yes."

"You two have run into an amazing spate of bad luck."

"We've had other uneventful dates, Justice." I regarded Lieutenant Stone. "Are you going to send a shooting team?"

"To do what, Decker? We don't have the Nova in our possession and the plates on it were stolen, so we can't get an address on them through the DMV. When and if the Nova's found, then we'll talk."

"Any hospitals report admissions of gunshot-wound victims?"

"Still checking."

The door opened and my father walked in. One part of me was vastly relieved, the other part immediately tensed.

"Mack," he said.

"Pete." Stone stood and they shook hands. He made introductions. "Detective Brill, Detective Lieutenant Decker."

"We've met," Dad answered.

Stone said, "I think you know the other party here."

"Yes, we've met as well."

Daddy placed his hand on my shoulder. I craned my neck up. "The plates were stolen. I'm voting Germando El Paso over the hit-and-run guy, but you never know."

"El Paso's locked up," Brill pointed out.

"His buddies aren't," I countered.

"Koby won't leave until you tell him to do so," Decker informed me. "It's two-thirty in the morning. The guy could use some sleep."

"He's still here? I told him to go home as soon as he was done being interviewed."

"I think he'd like to say good-bye." Decker looked at Stone. "Borrow her for a couple of minutes, Mack?"

"As long as you bring her back."

"Promise."

"Don't know if I believe you, Pete."

"If I could get away with kidnapping her and locking her in a closet, believe me I'd do it." To me, Decker said, "C'mon."

I stood up. "Excuse me."

When they were out of earshot, Daddy took me aside several yards away from the squad room. No one was in the hallway. He spoke softly. "Where's your gun?"

"They took it."

His voice dropped to a whisper. "Did you clear his prints before you gave it in?"

I regarded my father with surprise.

"If you get mad at him, you'll make me look bad. So don't you dare do it! I twisted his arm and he told me out of concern for you."

"The answer to your question is yes," I told him.

"Good. Let's go."

But I didn't move. I whispered, "And you wouldn't have done the same thing?"

"I would have done exactly the same thing."

"Germando must have told his buddies about me. I screwed up and now Koby's paying the price. I can't be content with just doing my job well! I've got to throw a noose around my neck and drag innocent people into my extracurricular affair. I'm such a goddamn jerk—"

"Stop it!" Decker held my shoulders and gave me the fire of his eyes. "Cynthia, if you aren't calm out there, we'll never get Koby to leave. If you like him and want what's best for him, you will go out there and convince him to go home so he can get some sleep!"

My eyes watered. "He was just . . . terrific. I owe him."

"Sweet. Can we go now?"

I cracked. "Do you have to be so *damn* hard?" Tears leaked out. "I'm fine, but surely a *little bit* of sympathy wouldn't mar your hard-nosed reputation!"

My father exhaled forcibly, then grabbed me and hugged me tightly. I was transported back to when I was a little girl and afraid of the dark. He was always so big and strong and invincible. He wasn't around much, but when he was, I always felt safe. I felt safe now. I wondered if he'd ever lose his fairy-tale touch.

"I love you, pumpkin."

"I love you, too, Daddy." I broke away and tried to act adult. "I'm fine." I wiped my eyes. "Really." I gave him a tearful smile. "Just more fodder for my therapist."

"Cynthia, you proved you're tough. Now do us both a favor and quit."

"Not a chance. What would I do?"

"You've got a master's from Columbia in criminal science. Go to law school."

"You, the law school dropout, are telling me to do that with a straight face?"

"I did not drop out, I finished."

"You want some medicated shampoos, Daddy?"

"What?"

"To help you pick out those nits. You may have the degree, but you're still a dropout."

"You know, I'm not the only one who's unhappy about your profession. He doesn't like cops, either."

"Who?"

"Koby. He told me he doesn't like cops."

"Maybe he just doesn't like you."

Dad laughed. "That's possible."

"He's black. He's got some preconceived notions about the police that are sometimes not so preconceived. I love my job, same as you, Dad. I wouldn't trade my badge for anything."

"Even if he asked you to do it?"

"He'd *never* ask that of me. Only you do that."

"It's a father's prerogative."

"Shall we go?"

"Now who's being hard?"

That gave me pause. "I love you, Decker.

Thanks for coming down. Now maybe you should go home and get some sleep."

He smiled enigmatically, making me wonder what was on his mind. But I didn't ask. Instead, I opened the door that led out to the station house's lobby. Koby saw me and stood up. Without thinking, we ran to each other and embraced, his lips brushing the top of my hair. I nestled into his tight body, then reluctantly broke away. "Go home and get some rest, Yaakov. I can take it from here."

He took my hand. "Is everything okay?"

"Yeah, yeah." I kissed his hand, then let it go. "No problem. Go. Do you have cab money?"

"I'll have a cruiser take him home," Dad said to me.

"Right! Thanks."

Koby said, "Are you sure, Cynthia? I shall wait if you want. As a matter of fact, I would like to wait."

"Don't you have to work tomorrow . . . or rather, today?"

"I'll be fine."

"Get some rest, Koby. Your being exhausted won't do either of us any good—

Oh my God! What are you going to do for a car?"

He smiled without showing teeth. It constricted his face instead of opening it up. "I suppose insurance will give me about fifty bucks." He shrugged. "Don't worry. I rent something. Your father said they'll reimburse me."

"Yeah, also about fifty bucks. Take my car."

"No, no. I'll find something."

"This is all my fault. Take my car."

"Not a chance."

"I can loan you something," Dad offered.

Koby's eyes moved to my father's face. "It's all right. I have friends."

"I'm sure you do," Dad said, "but I've got a spare."

"It's a vintage Porsche," I told him.

"No, I don't think so!" Koby smiled.

"No, no, no . . ." Decker smiled back. "Not the Porsche. We still have Rina's old Volvo. The boys use it when they're home."

"But they are home," Koby said.

"Yes, they are. But they don't need their jobs to keep a roof over their heads. They have friends, too. Take the car until you figure something out."

He regarded Decker. "How old is old?"

"Ten years and lots of dents. It's a clunker, Koby. Don't worry about it."

"Thank you." A pause. "Thank you very much, sir." He tried out another smile for my benefit. "Well, I suppose you're in good hands."

"Thanks," Decker answered wryly.

Koby let out a small laugh. To me, he said, "You'll call?"

"Yes, I'm good about that—unlike others in this room."

He answered my wisecrack by sweeping me into his arms and kissing me deep and slow, lacing his long nutmeg fingers into my thick hair. I responded in kind, melting into his body, wrapping both of my arms around his neck.

I saw my father avert his eyes and turn his face.

He didn't want me to see him smiling.

35

Standing in the corner, arms across his chest, all ears and no mouth, Decker stayed in the background while his elder daughter, the first issue of his loins, fielded questions flung from every angle. It was a test of endurance, not only for Cindy, but also for himself. Could he really listen to all this crap for hours and keep his yap shut? Finally, at four-thirty in the morning, both he and Cindy appeared victorious. As Stone and Brill wound down the interview, Decker thanked his Hollywood hosts and excused himself, telling Cindy he'd wait for her outside.

He called Rina. She answered on the third ring.

"I'm still here, but everything's fine," Decker said.

"How's Cindy?"

"She was a pro. Have you been up all this time?"

"No, I've been sleeping . . . restlessly. The kind of sleep where you know you have to wake up and catch an early-morning plane."

"You're going to be wiped out."

"Not too bad. I can always catnap in the afternoon."

"Then maybe I won't feel too guilty asking you this. Can you take Hannah to school for me?"

"You're not coming home?"

"No."

Silence over the line.

"Taking Hannah is no problem," Rina said. "What are you up to?"

"I need to spend time with Cindy. As a matter of fact, I'm going to call in and take the day off."

"Oh my . . . she must be really shaken."

Decker didn't dispel the notion. "I don't want her left alone."

"What about Koby? Isn't he around? Or is he outside the emotional loop?"

"The man is crazy about her. Getting him

to leave Cindy was like peeling Super Glue off the fingertips, but she finally managed to convince him to go home. I'm sure he's not sleeping too well, either, but he'll survive."

"Maybe you should let the two of them comfort each other, Peter. At some point, you need to pull back."

Decker smiled inwardly. "There's no ring on her finger. Right now, I still have seniority. Try to get another hour or two of sleep. I'll see you tonight, all right?"

No one spoke for a moment. Then Rina said, "Why do I think you're up to something?"

"Cindy just came out. Gotta go." Immediately, Decker disconnected the line. Then he turned the phone off.

▼

She gave her father a tired smile. "I'm so sorry to drag you out."

Decker hugged her. "You didn't drag me out. I came of my own accord."

"I can take a cab."

Decker burst into laughter. "Yes, exactly. I'm going to let you take a cab." He tousled her hair. "Stop being ridiculous." He waved to the desk sergeant and opened the door for her. "Let's get out of here."

Together they stepped into the misty predawn morning. Cindy said, "Really . . . thanks for coming. But equally important, thanks for not interfering."

"See, I can behave myself."

They walked to his Porsche. Again he opened the door for her. Cindy smiled at his courtly behavior and Decker smiled back, always the gentleman. After her father slid behind the wheel, she asked if she could borrow his cell phone, wanting to call Koby.

Decker didn't start the motor right away.

"First things first. Are you okay?"

She nodded. "I'm fine, Loo."

"Good."

She waited for her father to fork over the phone. When he didn't, she said, "Uh, can I have your cell now, please?"

"No."

She had asked the question as a formality. "*No?*"

"No. Let him sleep."

"Dad, he's waiting for my phone call."

"I'm sure he is. But if you call him, he'll insist on seeing you. Right now, that's not a good idea."

Cindy waited for an explanation, but none

came. Instead, Decker said, "What's your status right now?"

"I have the day off."

"It wasn't out of charity," Decker said. "They're pulling you off active duty pending an investigation."

"They want me to call in at noon."

"Standard procedure."

"What are they investigating? They don't have the car; the license plates are stolen; no one checked into the hospital with gunshot wounds."

"Not yet."

Cindy was silent.

Decker said, "You were shot at, Cynthia, and you discharged your weapon. Or at least Koby did. Someone's going to be checking out your story. So if you have something to add or subtract, now is the time to tell me."

Leaning over, she kissed her father's stubble-coated cheek. "I told them everything. I was completely straight with them other than the minor modification. So let them check me out."

"You didn't tail the car or try to stop it or—"

"No, no, no." She was adamant. "I pulled

over just to get the Nova's license plate because the car was tailing me. I had planned to go back to the station house and run it through DMV. I didn't try to apprehend anyone. I certainly didn't instigate anything."

"And they fired first?"

"That's insulting, Dad."

"I had to ask, Cynthia."

"Yes, they fired first."

"Then you should be fine." Decker rubbed his neck and rolled his shoulders.

"Are we going?" Cindy asked.

Decker sidestepped the question. "You know, if Koby hadn't fired back, it would have made your life simpler—"

"Dad, you *weren't* there."

"Just hear me out, okay?"

Livid, she sat back in the seat, arms crossed over her chest, immediately defensive and angry. But she kept her mouth shut. Decker knew she was listening with half an ear.

He said, "If he hadn't fired back, it would have made your life simpler. Don't interrupt, even though you're dying to, all right?"

"I'm not interrupting! Go on!"

Decker said, "If he hadn't fired *your* weapon, they wouldn't have pulled *you* off duty. They would have just given you the day off, done a one-two inquiry, and that would have been that. Because no one in the opposing car could have possibly gotten hurt and there wouldn't have been even the remotest possibility of a lawsuit . . . which now there is, of course. If someone got hurt, lots of questions are going to be asked, and guess whose derriere is in the hot seat?"

Cindy spoke through a clenched jaw. "He did the right thing!"

"Stop fuming! Why did he have to shoot?"

"Because we were under attack."

"You couldn't get away?"

"No, Dad, I couldn't get away. That was the *point!*"

"Would you have done the same thing if the positions had been reversed? Would you have shot at the Nova?"

"Yeah." She nodded. "Yeah, I think I would have—"

"You *think?*"

"I *definitely* would have, all right?"

"I hope you mean that. I hope you sincerely feel that that was the right way to fly. Because he bought you lots of hassle—"

"He did the right thing!" She turned to

him, her face red and furious. "You know, maybe I will take a cab—"

"Stop—"

"I just dealt with those morons for four hours and I'm not in the mood for this garbage, okay?"

Decker held her arm. "You want to know what I think?"

"No, actually, I don't want to know. But I'm sure I'm going to find out."

"I *know* that Koby absolutely did the right thing. And I know why." His eyes zoomed in on his daughter's. "The question is . . . do you know why?"

Cindy glared at him. It was then that Decker noticed her eyes were wet. She wiped them and said, "I'm a little tired for a test right now. Get to the point."

Decker shrugged. "If he hadn't shot back, if he hadn't reacted . . . nobody, and I mean *nobody*, would have wanted to work with you. They would have taken one look at his shot-out car and they'd all be thinking, what the *hell* was *she* doing while this was going down? Was she ducking while he was dodging bullets? What if that had been *my ass* behind the wheel? No one wants a partner who freezes."

Cindy's mouth opened. A moment later, she shut it.

Decker said, "He knew the cardinal rule, Cynthia. It's better to be overreactive and alive than rational and dead. Do you know why he knew it?"

She looked away, waiting for him to continue.

"Because for that one brief moment, he was back in combat being hammered by the PLO or Hamas or Hezbollah or whatever terrorist organization they have over there. Your boyfriend understands survival—the mentality that says, *It's either you or me, buddy.* Do *you* understand that mentality, Cindy?"

She took in her father's eyes, but couldn't quite hold them. "Probably not in the same way that you two do. But I think after my experiences last year, I've shown myself to be a good fighter."

"Cynthia, you are as tough as they come. Like I told you, life has thrown you some bad curveballs, and you cope far better than I do. But you're also a good girl. Compassion isn't always the answer."

"You think I'm sheltered."

"Of course, you're sheltered."

"How can you say that after what happened to me?"

"Nobody could have survived what you did. I'm so damn . . ." Decker's eyes turned moist. "Honey, all I'm saying is you need to *recognize* threat. You have to ask yourself, if you had been in Koby's position, would you have ducked in the passenger's seat or would you have taken out your gun and opened fire?"

"I gave him the gun, you know."

"That's not what I asked."

She was quiet, giving the question some honest thought. "The best I can come up with is I'm almost positive I would have done the same thing. Fair enough?"

"Fair enough."

"Now can I have the phone, please?"

"No, you can't." Again he drilled into her eyes. "Koby's bought you a whole lot of goodwill."

"So let me call and thank him."

"No, because right now, I'm going to buy you a set of balls."

Silence. Cindy blinked, staring at her father. "I've done okay for twenty-eight years without them. What on earth do you have in mind?"

Decker answered her question by starting the Porsche. It roared, then purred. He peeled rubber, going south onto Wilton until he hit Olympic. Then he went east toward downtown L.A. "Somebody tried to kill you, Cynthia. Aren't you curious?"

She didn't answer. The question was rhetorical.

Decker said, "Am I correct in assuming that you still have no idea who perpetrated the hit-and-run against Belinda Syracuse?"

"Yes. I don't have a clue."

"It's an open case?"

"So far as I know."

"So let's junk that because we haven't any leads. Now Sarah Sanders's rape is a different story. Tell me about the guy you hauled in."

"Germando El Paso."

"Yeah, him. Do you know where he is at the moment?"

"In County lockup."

"You checked."

"Not me, personally. I think Brill made the call."

"But as you stated so succinctly, El Paso's buddies aren't locked up. Refresh my memory. Tell me about them again."

She rubbed her forehead. "Germando gave us two names—Joseph Fedek and Pepe Renaldes. Fedek's whereabouts are unknown; Renaldes has an address."

"What's the address?"

"I don't remember off the top of my head. I wrote it down in my notes."

"Where are your notes? At home?"

"They're in my locker. Go back to the station house and I'll—"

"No, I don't want you going back there. Do you remember the area he lives in?"

"Oh gosh . . . let me think. I remember he works for Do-Rite Construction."

"No good. We don't want any third party involved."

This time, she gave him the full force of her eyes. "The DA told me that Renaldes is strictly off-limits because El Paso talked without an attorney present. If I talk to Renaldes, I could mess up a future indictment for Sarah Sanders's rape case."

Decker glared at her. "And you give a solitary *shit* what this little *prick* has to say when there's someone out there who's trying to blow your head off?"

Cindy looked at her lap. "Phrased in that manner, I suppose not."

"What area?" Decker repeated.

"Okay . . . okay . . . uh . . . I have this recollection of Exposition Park. If I could just dash in and check my locker, I could—"

"Cindy, you've been temporarily relieved. You don't go near the station until they tell you to come in." Decker spoke through gritted teeth. He hit Western and headed for the freeway on-ramp. "Okay. Exposition Park. Near USC or . . . ?"

She closed her eyes. "Maybe Forty-second Street. Why does that sound familiar?"

"It's a musical, Cynthia."

"Yes!" Cindy lifted a finger in the air. "Yes! Brilliant!" She grinned. "Exactly! It wasn't Forty-second, it was Thirty-second and Broadway, because I remember thinking that his address sounded like a musical!"

"Specific numbers?"

"Can you congratulate me first?"

"Congratulations." He turned left onto 10 East and ripped pavement. The Porsche's engine sang. "Numbers?"

She twirled a strand of hair with an index finger. When she spoke, she had to shout over the roar of the engine. "You know, Renaldes could be listed."

Decker took out his cell phone.

"I'll do it," Cindy told him.

"No, I will."

"Dad, you're going ninety on the freeway!"

Decker ignored her and called up information.

"You're crazy!" Cindy shouted. "I have a maniac for a father."

"I can't hear! Quiet!"

"Oh God!" She slumped in her seat. "I wish I were a Catholic. Then I could cross myself."

Decker hung up the phone and put it back into his pocket. "He wasn't listed. Let's try again. Specific numbers?"

Cindy sighed. "I seem to remember a six or a seven in the beginning."

"So that means three numbers if we're talking around Broadway and Thirty-second."

"Yeah, you're right. It was a three-number address. I think it was an even number."

"That narrows it down. I'm five minutes away. Let's just poke around. See if something jogs your memory or maybe we'll happen to come across a shot-out bronze Nova."

"I will be happy to go along with whatever plans you've devised, including leaning on scumbags like Pepe Renaldes, should we find him. But not until you give me the phone and let me call Koby."

"No."

"Dad—"

"Not a chance!"

"Daddy, he's worried about me. And frankly, I want to talk to him."

"No."

"If you don't give me the phone, I'm going to leave at the next stoplight."

"We're on the freeway."

"Daddy, give me the friggin' phone *now!*"

"Now that's conviction!" Decker smiled at his daughter and handed her the phone. "Finally."

36

Gray skies hovered over the awakening city as the Loo parked the Porsche curb-side. We were in an area of high crime, and the lone sports car sitting on the empty block just cried out, *Jack me! Chop me!* I asked him how comfortable he felt leaving his baby without backup, and he showed me his Beretta. At that point, I gave up. The man was on his own private mission, masquerading as my avenging angel.

It was an immigrant neighborhood, mostly Hispanic, and while the inhabitants weren't steeped in dire poverty, most of them were surely poor. Because the area predated its current population and there had been wealth a time ago, there remained some magnificent old mansions built with the kind of detail that failed replication. But most of those estates had been bought up by the nearby university and were used for graduate-study centers. The rest of the architecture was a mixture of old and older, of fixer-uppers and buildings in serious disrepair. There were several turn-of-the-century Victorian houses replete with gingerbread, scallops, and curlicues, but the dwellings sagged under age, waiting for that expensive face-lift. There were also some Arts and Crafts bungalows with shingled sides and roofs, and spacious front porches. But the majority of the single-family houses were broken stucco boxes with little to offer except protection from the elements. Even those were preferable to the rows of dingbats—lifeless, square apartment buildings without charm that were shedding stucco chunks like a diseased leper molting facial features.

I thought about asking Decker what his game plan was. We couldn't very well start by ringing doorbells. He suggested we take a walk and shake out our legs. While we ambled down the wrong side of the tracks, we poked around exterior mailboxes, read labels on newspaper deliveries, and scanned the directories of apartment buildings. Nothing came close to Renaldes. After an hour of fruitless effort, I told Dad that this was ridiculous.

"Patience." He rubbed his hands together. "Let's just hang for a while."

"Dad, we don't even know if we're on the right block."

"I think we're close."

"You're in denial." It was six-thirty and I was sleep deprived. Thinking had become hard work. "You know, construction crews start pretty early."

My father looked at me.

I said, "In my area, we get loads of Hispanic guys waiting on street corners or by paint stores, hoping to be picked up by the boss man."

"I thought you said this guy had a steady job."

"I said Renaldes had listed Do-Rite Construction as his current employer. I don't know how long ago he might have worked for the company. Or even if he worked for the company at all. I never got a chance to check it out, because my superiors in title told me to back off. But now I'm thinking that if Renaldes listed Do-Rite as his employer, he probably worked construction with other companies, too."

Decker didn't answer me.

"Why don't we drive around—"

"I wanted to get this guy while he was sleeping."

"Daddy, we don't know where he lives!" My father could be incredibly thickheaded sometimes. "I think it would be a better use of our time if we found some crews and asked about Renaldes. You'd have no trouble convincing anyone that you're a West Side contractor looking for hands. You're fluent in Spanish and you're driving a flashy car."

"Contractors drive Porsches?"

"The ones who work in Brentwood certainly do."

"I thought they drove trucks."

"Both."

"I'm in the wrong business."

"Didn't Mom try to tell you that a long time ago?"

Decker flashed me a sour look.

"Contractors and real estate agents: They drive Porsches, Mercedes, Beemers, Jags. . . . It's all part of the image. Can we talk about my idea now?"

"Coming in, I didn't see any work crews."

"We didn't look for any crews. Besides, it's later now. Let's go hit the lumberyards or the paint stores and see if we can't get something going."

My father tapped his toe, unwilling to comment.

"It's a good idea, Decker," I told him. "Much better than anything you have. You know, Daddy, I'm the one who was shot at and was yanked off active duty. Plus, I haven't slept in over twenty hours. If you don't start pulling your weight, I'm going home."

My father slipped his hands into his pockets. "Point well taken."

"Thank you. So do we go or what?"

Decker took out his keys. "I guess we go."

▼

Using the ruse that Pepe Renaldes owed my father, the boss man, a considerable sum of money—something that the men we talked to found very easy to believe—we came away with a half-dozen addresses in the right neighborhood. All it took was two hours of our time and two hundred bucks in twenties. Neither one of us had that much play cash, so Dad withdrew money from his ATM. I asked him if he really thought it was worth the effort, and he retorted by asking me exactly how much did *I* think my life was worth? He was overstating the case, but after his lecture on threat, I felt it best not to challenge.

The first address didn't exist and the second one was a Kinko's. The third was one of those squashed stucco houses. That looked promising, although the occupants' last name was Martez. Inside were a mother and her two sullen teenage daughters, who were polishing their toenails, mixing the smell of acetone with the odor of bacon grease. She insisted that there was no Pepe Renaldes in residence, but since she was less than convincing, Decker searched the house. She let him do it because Decker was big, and Decker was authoritative, and Decker must have said something to her in Spanish that scared the bejesus out of her.

By the time we hit the fourth address—a dingbat apartment building—it was almost ten and the hopes of finding Pepe Renaldes in bed were fading fast. It was a two-story building of brown stucco, fronted by a patch of straggly lawn that had a couple of full-size palm trees dropping premature palm nuts. The little black balls littered the sidewalk and poked into the soles of my shoes. The place had no lobby, but it did have a directory— twelve units with number four looking very promising because the occupants were listed as *R* and nothing else. This little bit of Heaven was toward the back and secured by iron grilles on the front door and windows. As we approached the unit, I could hear ferocious barking in the midrange level coming from inside. I had reservations about dropping in, but Dad had other ideas.

"Okay," he whispered. "You stay out of sight."

"It's got bars and a dog, Dad. How do you propose we get in?"

"You leave that to me."

"You can't push in the door. And even if you did, there's a dog—"

"Just stay back and let me handle this."

"Do you have another gun?"

My father smiled at me. "Aw . . . you care." His face turned grave. "Stand over there, all right?"

"Do you know what you're doing?"

"Very much so." He knocked on the door. The dog went wild. I could picture my father charging in and the dog responding by going for his throat. I was naked without my gun and didn't like that feeling at all.

We waited . . . thirty seconds . . . a minute.

Decker knocked again. He shouted something in Spanish.

The dog had worked itself up into a frenzy. There was yelling from above. Dad yelled back at him.

"You're going to cause a riot," I told my father.

"Nah, he's just screaming for someone to shut the dog up."

"Obviously, no one's home."

"Or sleeping. If he was out last night, Cin, he might be sleeping late." Dad knocked again.

The dog kept up its vocal pyrotechnics.

Dad pounded this time.

"Let it ride—"

"You want to take control of your destiny or leave it to assholes?"

I exhaled. Dad gave the door another thrashing. "Last time," he announced.

The dog was barking itself hoarse.

Ten seconds . . . twenty.

The dog quieted—a bark or two but without real feeling behind it. To my utter shock, I heard movement behind the door. My father pushed me out of the way. *"Yo, Pepe,"* he said. *"Soy Miguel."*

I couldn't understand the rest of his speech. I caught words but nothing else. I thought about Dad with his Spanish and Koby speaking three languages. I could barely cope with my native one.

Muffled Spanish came from behind the door.

Dad responded, *"Un hombre blanco— alto con pelo rojo. El la busca, hombre. El dice que usted le debe dinero. Yo no le dije nada pero el dice que tiene una pistola, amigo. Si me da cincuenta dolares y una cerveza, pienso que yo puedo hacerlo esperar."*

Silence.

I whispered, "What did you say?"

He shut me up with a movement of his hand and put his finger to his lips. A couple of perfunctory yelps from the pooch, then I could hear the clunk of the dead bolt being opened. Dad pushed me against the wall.

The image of a charging pit bull leaping at my father's face became quite vivid.

"Give me your gun," I told him.

"What?"

"Don't argue!" I spat fiercely. "You told me to have convictions—I have them now. Give me your gun now or I'm going to yell police!"

He gave me his gun.

Slowly, the door started to open. Just a crack at first, then it opened a little wider. Immediately, Decker shoved full force with his body and the door flew open.

As expected, the dog sprang upward, but Dad had come prepared. He gave the canine a swift, hard kick in the cranium, sending the midsize pooch across the room and crashing into a table. Pepe was going in one direction, while the dog, a pit bull mix, was shaking itself off, readying itself for round two.

I jumped on Pepe's back, squeezing my legs around his waist and encircling his throat with my left arm. I jammed the bore of the gun into the nape of his neck. "CALL THE DOG OFF!" I shoved the gun deep against his cervical vertebrae. "CALL IT OFF! CALL IT OFF!"

The pit bull started charging. Dad picked up an end table. I screamed and shot at the intractable beast, grazing its head but not deterring it an iota. Dad threw the end table, knocking it again on the head as Renaldes did a rain dance, trying to shake me off his back.

"CALL IT OFF!" I shot a bullet past his temple. "CALL IT OFF!" Another bullet past the other ear.

"Don' shoot!"

"OFF NOW OR THIS TIME IT'S YOUR FUCKING HEAD!"

He finally started making overtures to the beast, calling him by his name, Fuego, cooing at him like a parakeet. Although Fuego was still pissed, he was disoriented from being slammed by flying furniture.

I was still holding on to Renaldes. "Put him in a closet!" I demanded.

"Get off—"

I zinged another shot past his ear. *"EL PERRO* IN THE CLOSET! NOW!"

At last my demand sank in. Pepe bent down, almost falling on his face under the burden of my weight, but somehow he managed to grab Fuego's collar and lead him into a closet. As soon as the pit bull was secured behind the door, I jumped off, and at the same time, my father grabbed Renaldes by the throat. He pushed him down onto a tattered couch and tightened his grip. Renaldes's face started turning a very unhealthy red. With his right hand, Decker motioned for his weapon. I gave it to him and he shoved it into Renaldes's mouth. I do believe Pepe pissed in his pants.

I realized that my own mouth was open and closed it shut. I had never seen this side of my father. I must have looked as shocked as Koby did when I took down El Paso. Behind the closet, Fuego started barking again—loud and angry, ordering a rematch with my father.

Renaldes was struggling under Dad's bulk, but he was clearly outmatched. Pepe had some muscle definition but was on the short side—smaller than I was. He had a shaved head and dark eyes, which were popping out of their sockets. He had been wearing a terry-cloth robe when we barged in. Now it had opened up, revealing a chest inked with tattoos—a devil, a snake, a spider, et cetera, et cetera, yawn, yawn. It was hard to say anything about his complexion because he was bright pink from pressure and fear.

Decker pulled the gun out of Pepe's mouth and placed it on his forehead. He whispered, "You went after the wrong person, *amigo*."

He choked out, "*No se—*"

"Shut up and listen!"

"*Por favor—*"

Decker tightened his grip. Renaldes was literally about to explode. "I said, shut up and *listen!*"

He was on the verge of passing out. I brought my hand over my father's fingers and pried them open, just enough to loosen his grip and give Pepe some air. Decker didn't even realize I was doing it.

Decker spoke low and slow. "Someone shot at a cop last night. Someone in a bronze Nova with stolen plates. Now if you're straight with me, guess what, Pepe? You'll live. If you give me bullshit, you'll die. *Muy fácil. La verdad o la muerte. Comprendes, amigo?*"

The man's head bobbed up and down. The dog was now thumping against the closet door. I looked around the room, then pushed the coffee table in front of Fuego's escape route. I pounded on the door to shut the beast up. It worked for a moment, but then Fuego continued yelping.

"Who did it, Renaldes? *Quien?*"

"*No conozco.* I don't know—"

Again the gun was shoved down Pepe's throat. Decker counted to ten. "Let's try it again. *Quien tiene un carro*—a bronze Nova?"

Renaldes's eyes rolled back. My heart was beating a mile a minute, adrenaline pumping through my system. Fuego was damn near hysterical. "He's losing consciousness!" I called out over the barking. "Ease up!"

My father regarded my face, his eyes as feral as any zoo animal I've ever seen. I think he forgot about me.

"Ease up!" I repeated louder.

Decker lessened his grip and took the gun out of Pepe's mouth.

"Sit him up," I told my father. "I'll get a glass of water." I patted Pepe's red and sweaty face. "I can't control him for too much longer. Don't piss him off."

I went into the kitchenette, banging on the closet door as I walked past it. My chest hurt and I could barely catch my breath. The sink was filthy, filled with crusted dishes from the Jurassic age. Little black ants were crawling on the countertop. I opened a cupboard and searched for a clean glass. I found a couple of blue plastic mugs and filled one with cloudy tap water. I debated taking a drink myself but nixed the opportunity to hydrate myself, fearing unseen microbes. I brought it back to Pepe, again banging on the closet door as I passed it.

I think Fuego started to get the hint. His resumption of barking was slow on the uptake.

Pepe was sitting on the couch next to my father, his bald head down, hands clasped and shaking. My father was standing over him, the gun still in his right hand. I gave the small man the water. He drank greedily and actually thanked me.

"You okay?" I asked Pepe.

Renaldes eyed Decker. "He *es* crazy!"

"Excitable," I corrected.

Decker growled at me. "You want to ask him about the Nova, hotshot?"

"Take it easy," I responded testily.

"My finger's getting itchy."

I rolled my eyes at Pepe. His eyes said thank you. Somehow Decker and I had fallen into "Good cop/bad cop," except it wasn't completely playacting. I sat next to Pepe.

"Sunset and Marchant . . . a little after

twelve o'clock last night. Bronze Nova, tinted windows, primer on the driver's door, dented hood, stolen plates." I gave him the numbers. "They shot out a '92 black Toyota Corolla. There was a cop inside the car. Big trouble, Pepe. You don't want anything to do with it."

"I don't know nothin'."

Decker shoved him against the back of the couch, water splashing all over his bare chest. Renaldes's face went white with fear.

"Will you stop?" I scolded. I got up to get a towel, banging the closet door as I went. I found several napkins purloined from Tasty Taco and gave them to Pepe to wipe off the droplets.

Again I sat next to him. I said, "Renaldes, we have a credibility problem."

He gave me a blank look.

I said, "I don't believe you. *No creo* you."

Decker smiled.

I said, "Look you are in very serious trouble. *Mucho problemos, usted tiene. Comprendes?*" I glanced at my father. "Could you translate this?"

"No need. He understands perfectly."

"You're a big help." I turned to Pepe and

pointed to Decker. "He's crazy." I pointed to myself. "I'm not. Work with me, Pepe."

"I was no drivin' last night. I here."

"Who can alibi you other than Fuego?"

A blank stare.

My eyes went to my father's face. "Please?"

Dad asked the question in Spanish.

Renaldes shrugged, shook his head. "I here," he repeated.

"Alone?" I asked. "*Solo?*"

"*Sí, solo.*"

"Bullshit!" my father spat out. He placed his gun on the top of Renaldes's head.

Gently, I pushed it away and touched my forehead with an index finger. I studied Pepe's face. His complexion had gone from fire to ice; it was now holding a sickly blue pallor. I said, "Renaldes, I believe you. But he doesn't and that's a problem."

Pepe's eyes darted back and forth. "I no there. I don' know!"

Again my father showed him the gun. I chided him with a wag of the finger. To Pepe, I said, "Look, I got an idea. Tell me who owns the car and maybe I can get this guy"—a thumb in Dad's direction—"maybe I can get him off your back."

His eyes went from my face to Decker's. I'm not sure he understood everything, but he sure understood the tone. Dad translated what I had told him. Renaldes turned his attention to me.

"Wha' car?"

"A Chevrolet Nova. Bronze. Primer on the driver's side. Tinted windows. Dented. Old."

Renaldes said, "I don' know de *carro*. I don' know who drive . . . I no there. *Pero si el carro es caliente* . . . if eet's hot, I know de peoples dat . . . de peoples dat chop."

My father and I exchanged glances.

Pepe sensed a reprieve. "I give you de *numeros* . . . de address."

Dad said, "No, you're going to *show* us the address."

Renaldes looked at me. I regarded my father. "We're driving a two-seater."

"So give him a thrill. Sit on his lap."

37

Pepe told Decker that he kept his clothes in a box under his bed. I pulled it out and the Loo selected a couple of items, keeping the gun on Renaldes as he got dressed. I took the opportunity to look around the place, periodically knocking the closet door to keep the dog quiet. I was beginning to feel sorry for the beast, but then I seemed to recall some trivia tidbit stating that a pit bull's jaw could apply around two thousand pounds of pressure. The image of half my face gone kept me honest.

Rifling through his drawers, I found a bag of pills and a pistol—a Colt .32, fully loaded. I showed it to my father while Pepe tied his sneakers.

"*Amigo,*" Decker said.

Pepe looked up.

"You've got a permit for this?"

No response.

"Didn't think so. We're going to borrow it."

Knowing I was more familiar with the standard police issue Beretta, Decker and I exchanged weapons. He said, "You ever fire this thing, Renaldes? Because I'm going to take this into the lab and it could give you problems if it was used in a crime."

"I fin' it," Pepe told him.

"Yeah, like you found these pharmaceuticals?" I held up the bag of pills.

Renaldes regarded me with tired eyes.

"Hey," I said. "You play nice, we place nice."

Decker took one of Renaldes's belts, pulled the small man's hands behind his back, and secured the wrists together. "Don't take it personally." He held one arm, I took the other, and together we spirited him to the door.

"Wha' 'bout my dog?"

"If it doesn't take too long, he should be fine," Decker answered. "Let's go."

The Porsche had a micromini backseat. I squeezed in as best I could lengthwise;

then Dad placed Pepe in the passenger's bucket. We undid Renaldes's hands, then retied them around the seat back. I had a gun, so did Dad. The Loo started the car and we were off.

In frank talk, we were kidnapping Pepe and that didn't sit well with my inner child. It also gave me insight—just how easy it was to justify jumping the line. My father wasn't crooked—I was sure of that—but he seemed to have no problem disregarding due process when it served his purposes.

So where did that leave me?

I stood loyal to my father, and to justify my uneasiness, I convinced myself that I was his imaginary angel sitting on his right shoulder, telling him when to rein it in.

I was holding a gun, prepared to use it if I had to, but the guy wasn't giving us a lick of problems—just the opposite. He was a passive kind of guy who had lived in the same unit for almost three years. I was beginning to doubt that this wimpy guy was really involved in raping Sarah Sanders. I wondered if maybe Germando El Paso had reversed it for his convenience. Maybe Renaldes had been the lookout while Fedek and El Paso did the nasty. I kept that filed in the back of my head, should we ever make progress on the case.

"You getting hungry, Pepe?" I asked him.

"A leetle."

"You be good and I'll buy you some food after it's over."

He nodded, his fingers constantly wiggling against the binds that tied his wrists.

Decker was silent, driving deep into the industrial part of L.A. County, going east on the freeway to the address given to us by Renaldes. We passed a skyline of old buildings, some of them abandoned with shot-out or boarded-up windows. The sky was dull and smoggy and I had to fight to stay awake. I closed my eyes for just a second, then yanked open the lids when I realized I'd fallen asleep. Pepe apparently had the same idea. He was snoring, chin to his chest. I hadn't noticed it before but he had a pencil mustache as well as a little swatch of beard under his lower lip.

As soon as Pepe had entered the picture, I hadn't addressed my father by name or title. He had been equally circumspect with me. Even while Pepe snoozed, we didn't chat; both of us knew people heard things in their sleep. It was a tense ride and I was dreadfully tired and sorely uncomfortable. Another ten minutes went by before Decker took the off-ramp into the heart of L.A. County industrial life. The air was thick with slag, smelt, and pollutants, and it hurt to breathe too deeply. The blocks were long— warehouse after warehouse—all of it monotonous and ugly.

The address Pepe had given us corresponded to a body-and-paint shop, and from what I could tell at first glance, it seemed to be a legitimate one. If it had been a chop shop, it would have been hidden. But it wasn't. Also, there were no large semis, which provided the usual method for transporting stolen wares. But there were stacks of cars in an open lot, many of them in various states of disrepair. Nothing vintage, just worn and cheap. Renaldes jerked his head up and blinked several times.

He spoke to my father in Spanish. Dad nodded and parked across the street in another open lot. We sat for a moment, thinking about a game plan. Pepe had slumped low in his seat. Again he spoke in Spanish. I recognized anxiety in his voice. My father translated.

"He said the owners of this garage are

subcontractors for some used-car sellers. They do the painting and bodywork for the dealers. Sometimes they smuggle the hot cars in with the legit cars. Sometimes the dealers buy them. They don't ask questions."

More Spanish.

The Loo said, "The guys have guns. He told me to be careful."

Renaldes said, *"Habla con Señor Angus o Señor Morton. Yo no puedo entrar. . . .* I no go inside. Dey keel me."

"Let him stay here," I told my father.

"All right," Decker said. "Just keep an eye on him."

"I'm going in with you. They have guns, you need backup."

"I'm not planning on a shooting match."

"Yeah, I wasn't planning on getting shot at, either." I leaned over the passenger's seat and flashed Pepe three 20s from this morning's ATM withdrawal. I tore them in two and put half in Pepe's pocket. "You stay there nice and quiet, you not only get to go home, but you'll be sixty bucks richer." To my father, "Can you translate that?"

"When it comes to money, I'm sure he understands."

I gently thumped the back of my father's seat. "I'm squished. Let's go."

He got out first, then gave me a hand. The parking lot was unpaved and all dust. The Porsche's tires had churned up the dirt and it was still flying in the air as we walked toward the body shop.

"Let me do the talking," I told Decker. "I'm less threatening and you're a better shot if it should come to that."

"What are you going to say?"

"Listen and you'll find out." We walked into the garage. Three cars were up on racks: a ten-year-old red Honda Accord, a six-year-old green Mitsubishi Montero, and a ten-year-old white Suburban, their underbellies serviced by two young Hispanics. One of them was holding a wrench. He saw us and wiped his sweaty face with the back of his arm. I showed him my badge. "I'm looking for Angus or Morton."

He eyed me suspiciously, then shifted his gaze to my father. The sight must have had impact. He jerked a finger over his left shoulder.

"Thanks," I told him.

He had pointed out a tiny office—an all-glass enclosure with two desks, two phones, one computer, and piles of color-coded paper. Only one of the desks was occupied. The guy working was as fat as a barn, with shoulder-length, matted mousy brown hair and an untrimmed goatee. He wore jeans and a white T-shirt that exposed arms inked with tattoos, starting at the wrists. He also had a tattoo on his neck and a tattoo on his forehead, both drawings different renditions of bulls.

Angus . . . bull. Ha, ha, I got it.

I rapped on the glass and held up my badge to the window. The Loo did the same. Angus got up and waddled over to the door. He opened it, his bulk blocking the entryway. He reeked of cigarette smoke; his fingernails were stained amber. "What?"

"You Angus?" I asked him.

"What?" he repeated.

"I'm looking for a car," I said. "Bronze Nova, maybe a '91 or '92, lots of primer on the driver's side. Tinted windows. In real bad condition, man. At least four bullet holes."

"Don't have it."

"So then you don't mind if we walk around to check."

His eyes traveled up and down my body.

His voice remained steely. "Yeah, I do mind. What do you want?"

"The car," I told him. "The Nova's driver had the temerity to shoot at me last night. I took it personally."

Angus didn't talk.

"You don't want to handle something that hot," I said. "He shot at a cop."

"Maybe he didn't know it was a cop."

"But now you do, so that makes you an accessory if you have the car."

Angus said, "I don't see a warrant."

"That's because I don't have one. Otherwise we wouldn't be talking." I smiled. "C'mon, man, let's play like good sports, okay? How much you pay for it?"

Angus was quiet.

"Look, *hombre,*" I tried again. "All I want is the car. I can cause you a lot of grief or you can be a good citizen and report it to your local police. I'll even throw in a reward for your time and effort. What do you say?"

"Five hundred bucks," Angus told me.

"That's ridiculous! You probably didn't pay more than a hundred for it." I rummaged through my wallet. "I got twenty-seven bucks on me."

"Get out of here!"

"No need to get nasty." I turned to my father. "How much do you have?"

Dad checked his wallet. "Sixty."

I turned back to Angus. "I'm going to need some pocket change. I'll give you eighty bucks. Take it or leave it."

He didn't deliberate too long, holding out his hand a moment later.

I gave him the bills. "Where?"

"Not here," Angus said. "But I know where. You don't come back here no more, it'll show up where it's supposed to show up."

I turned to the Loo for advice. Decker said, "Either we flex muscle or we believe him. What do you want to do?"

"How long will it take to show up?" I asked Angus. "I really didn't appreciate being shot at."

"By the end of the day."

"Can you put some speed on it?"

"I could if you give me more incentive."

"I don't have any more cash."

"I got an address."

"How much?" I asked him.

" 'Nother hundred."

It would have been worth ten times that much to streamline the investigation. Still, I knew I had to show grit. "Fifty," I told him. "It's coming out of my pocket."

"Big fuckin-A deal. You'll make it up next time you bust a crack house."

"I'm not in Vice and I'm not on the take. I repeat: fifty bucks because it's coming out of my pocket."

Angus gave the offer some thought. "Seventy-five and I'll say before three o'clock."

Again I turned to the Loo. He turned to Angus. "Which police department and precinct are you going to phone?"

"Don't know. Haven't thought about it."

Decker said, "Do Industry PD, the precinct on Twenty-third and Preston."

"Okay. You got a phone number? I'll call you when it's cleared."

"Not necessary," Decker said. "Just do your job and we'll all be happy."

"Tell me how the car came to your attention?" I asked him.

"Not much to tell, sweetheart. Guy comes in here six-thirty in the morning and tells me he needs to dump a hot mark. All those bullet holes, I'm figuring it was a messy holdup or gang warfare. Either way, I don't want no part of that shit. I tell him where to go for scrap. That's it."

"Who's the guy?" I asked.

"Don't know him."

"You don't know him?" I tossed him a look. "You gave out the address of a chop shop to a guy you don't know?"

"He's the stepbrother of a greaser that used to work for me."

"Okay," I said. "What's the greaser's name?"

He brushed his tongue over his teeth. "We're back up to a hundred."

"Fine," I said. "What's his name . . . the greaser?"

"Germando El Paso."

My father and I exchanged glances. Decker said, "What'd this guy look like?"

"I dunno. Maybe around five-ten."

"Hair color, eye color?"

"I don't pay attention to that kinda crap."

"Think, Angus," I told him. "It's important."

"Real short hair . . . stubble. Look, I got work to do, 'specially if you want me to do what you're asking me to do. So get outta here and let me do it."

"Where's the scrap yard?" I asked.

Angus narrowed his eyes. "You don't got

no warrant. I ain't got nothin' else to say to you." He started to turn his back.

"Thank you," I told him.

He stopped, pivoted around, and stared at me.

"Thank you very much," I said. "I'll get you the money. I promise."

His eyes took in my face. He nodded.

"One more thing?"

He waited.

"You're *sure* you don't know this guy's name? You can understand why I'd want to know that."

He was silent.

I said, "Angus, how about if I say some names. You don't even have to tell me yes or no. I'll just look at your face. And I'll throw in an extra twenty-five."

He didn't move. I took it as an indication for me to continue. I rattled off a few fillers before I got to the meat. "Pepe Renaldes?"

Nothing.

"Juice Fedek?"

Angus was good, but the tic of the eye was involuntary.

"Juice Fedek is Germando El Paso's stepbrother?" When Angus didn't answer, I turned to my father. "Hence the mixed gang."

"Are you leavin' or what?" Angus stepped out into the working area and looked across the street at my father's Porsche. "Is that your wheels?"

Decker said, "You touch it, you're dead."

"Need any parts? I got an '81 nine-one-one engine with twenty thousand original miles."

"As tempting as it is, I think I'll pass."

I said, "When you locate the car, tell the Industry PD to call Hollywood substation. Tell them you heard that the Nova was used in an officer-involved shooting."

"Yeah, yeah, yeah." Angus shook his head and said, "You know, this talk ain't doing wonders for either of our images."

"C'mon," my father told me. When we were across the street, he put his arm around me. "Masterful."

"I learned from the best."

He took in my eyes. "I don't know if you had the best this morning."

"Then it's good that I've seen him work under less emotional conditions."

"Very good for him."

The Loo unlocked the door. Renaldes

was just where we'd left him. I pushed forward the driver's seat and squeezed into my space. I leaned over and tucked the remaining halves of the three torn twenty-dollar bills into his pocket. But I still had severe reservations. This man, however cowed he was at *this* moment, was potentially a willing participant in a gang rape. I kept that in the back of my mind. I patted his shoulder. "You did good, Pepe."

He smiled. "You fin' him?"

"The less you know, the better," I told him. Evasiveness helped keep his anxiety level up. I weighed my words carefully. "You know, if we need you again for something else, you'd better come through."

Dad translated my words into Spanish.

He squirmed. *"Que quiere?"*

"Nothing right now," I told him. "But you never know."

"Well stated," the Loo complimented. He started the engine and we were off. I made Decker stop at a Burger King and bought Pepe a Shaq pack. I placed the bag on the floor of the car. He eyed it ravenously.

"I no can eat with the *faja*."

"'*Faja*' is the belt," Dad told me.

I said, "You'll eat when you get home. In the meantime, you can smell it."

To me, the odor was greasy and nauseating. It was especially sickening because it took us over an hour to make it back to Pepe's apartment. Traffic was in full swing: bumper to bumper, chrome reflecting in the sunlight, exhaust clogging up the air, and it wasn't even afternoon rush hour yet. Finally, by one-thirty in the afternoon, we were back where we started, Renaldes delivered in one piece, a chastened man. I undid the wrist restraints and he picked up the bag of food. He took out some French fries and stuffed them into his mouth before we got to the door of his apartment. As soon as my father inserted Renaldes's key in the lock, the dog went nuts. When he opened the door, I could smell feces and urine. Someone had shown displeasure in a very primal way.

Pepe didn't seem to notice. He was already unwrapping his hamburger. Before he made his escape, I grabbed his arm and glowered at him. "You say anything about this visit, I tell Angus. And don't even think about leaving town. I got eyes in the back of my head. *Comprende?*"

He regarded my face, then looked at my hand around his arm. Slowly, I let it go.

"*Pistola?*" Renaldes said. "*Este es un mundo muy peligroso.*"

That much I could understand. I said, "If it's clean, you'll get it back." I slapped his cheek. "Stay out of trouble."

We walked back to Dad's Porsche. It felt wonderful to sit in a normal seat. I didn't realize how raw and tender my back muscles had become by my contortions in the backseat. I gave my legs a long stretch.

I said, "Think Angus is reliable?"

"No," Dad answered. "But we know where to find him if he isn't. Where's your car?"

"At home."

Decker got back on the freeway. Within minutes, my eyelids closed. By the time we arrived at my apartment, I had napped over forty minutes. I woke up, tired and groggy.

"I'll walk you to the door," Decker told me.

"You don't have to—"

But he was already out of the car. He opened my door, and I leaned on him as we climbed the stairs to my unit. Behind the wall, I could hear my phone ringing. I managed to unlock my door and grab the receiver before the caller hung up. Dad followed me inside.

"Where've you been?" the voice asked me.

Shit! It was Lieutenant Stone. I had forgotten to call in at noon. It was almost three.

"Sleeping." It was the truth. "I'm so sorry, Lieutenant."

"Stone?" my dad mouthed.

I nodded.

"Shit," he mouthed back. "Sorry."

I waved him off. "What's up, sir? Any new gunshot-wound victims show up in any hospital since I left the station house?"

"Not yet."

"Well, that's good."

"Decker, I just got the strangest call. Someone from Industry PD told me about a shot-up Nova about to be junked. They had heard from an anonymous tip that it was used in a cop pop."

"Oh my God!" I didn't have to pretend to be surprised. I *was* surprised. Angus had worked even quicker than promised. I made a mental note to fire off the money in today's mail. "Is it true?"

"Brill's going to Industry to check it out."

A long pause. "How do you think word got around that fast?"

I smiled. "Obviously, someone bragged."

"And where were you all this time?"

"Sleeping."

"Alone?"

"Yes, I was sleeping alone, but I wasn't alone in the house. My father's been with me the entire time. He took the day off because he knew I was rattled. He's here now. Want to talk to him?" I called him to the phone in a loud voice, speaking with enough volume so that Stone could hear over the line. I told Dad that Industry PD had a fix on the car. He clapped his hands, gave me a thumbs-up sign.

He took the phone but held it open so I could hear Stone's responses. Dad said, "You've got a location for the vehicle?"

"A possible location," Stone answered. "You've been with her the entire time?"

"Yes, I have been with her the entire time."

A long pause. "Doing what?"

"Mostly reading while she slept." He glanced at one of my magazines—a subscription to *Earth and Heaven* that I acquired with odd-lot miles from Delta. He read from the cover article. "Did you know that the universe is expanding at roughly twice the rate than previously thought, according to the latest redshift data?"

"Very interesting, Pete," Stone said. "Don't you think the Nova just popping up like this is a big coincidence?"

Decker's smile was slow and wide. "The world runs on coincidences, Mack. So does our business. Would you like to talk to Officer Decker again?"

"No need. Just tell her that if this tip pans out, I'll need her for vehicle identification. Then we'll have to clear her gun with a shooting team. Once we get the okay from them, she can report back for active duty. That'll probably come through day after tomorrow, but when I say to call in at noon, I mean call in at noon."

"Why are you castigating me? I'm not my daughter's keeper."

"I'm not castigating you, Pete; I'm asking you to pass along the message with feeling."

"Got it." Decker winked at me. "Thanks for everything, Mack. I'll remember this."

"Yeah." A weary voice. "Fine. Bye."

Dad hung up the line, then depressed the

flash button. "Someone's beeping in." He handed me the phone.

"You *tell* me this morning you call by nine. That was *six* hours ago. I call you a dozen times. Where have you been?"

"I'm just fine, Koby. Thanks for asking."

A pause. He said, "How are you?"

"Tired and nauseated. I've been out, but if anyone asks you, I've been home sleeping."

Another pause. "Cynthia, what is going *on?*"

"Nothing." I softened my voice. "Really. I'm all right. How are *you?*"

"I'm all right, now I know that you're all right. I don't know where you are. I was crazy with worry."

So now you know what it's like to wait and wonder. Of course, I didn't say that. The poor man had been shot at, his car totaled and impounded. He was tired and grumpy and worried and without a set of wheels. It was not the time to make points. "I'm sorry I didn't call. Honestly, I was preoccupied and forgot."

"You *forgot?*"

"Koby, my father's here. He's about to leave. Could you hold for a minute so I can say good-bye to him?"

Another exasperated sigh, but he said he'd hold. I put the receiver down and got up. I smiled at my father. "What can I say, Decker? Thanks a heap."

"Anytime."

Tears suddenly fell from my eyes and streamed down my cheeks. I hugged my father with profound gratitude that went *way* beyond this incident. "I love you."

He hugged me back with equal enthusiasm. "I love you, too, Princess."

I finally broke away. Or maybe he broke away. He said, "I'll let myself out."

"No, I'll walk you to the door." I whispered, "He can wait."

Dad's smile was immediate and conspiratorial. As soon as I closed the door and locked it, I plopped down on the couch, phone in hand. "I'm back. Where are you now?"

"At work."

"You found a car?"

"Marnie picked me up."

"*Marnie?*"

"Yes, Marnie. When can we see each other?"

"I guess soon, or Marnie will move in on my territory."

"Stop it, Cynthia! I'm in no mood. She's engaged to a very nice doctor and it is you who have the key to my house."

I didn't answer right away, waiting for him to apologize for snapping at me. He didn't. So I said, "I'm sorry. The humor is defensive. I'm still shaken. I'm sure you are as well."

A loud sigh. "I'm sorry, too. I just want to hear your voice, that's all."

"Well, here I am."

"Baruch Hashem!" There was a long silence over the phone. "I *ache* for you. Please. When can we see each other?"

"You tell me."

"Can you come pick me up after work?"

"Of course, Koby. What time?"

"Eleven."

"I'll be there unless I have to do vehicle identification." I apprised him of the situation.

"That's incredible!" His voice turned bright. "That is *so* lucky."

"Yes, it is very lucky," I told him.

I smiled to myself.

Sometimes you make your own luck.

38

The *William Tell Overture* was never my favorite piece to begin with. It was especially obnoxious as a jingle coming from my cell phone. I wanted to pull the covers over my head and keep sleeping, but because my current work situation was tenuous, I reconsidered. I reached down to the floor, rooted through my handbag, and came up with the infernal machine.

Koby shifted onto his stomach, then pulled the covers over his head. "Ignore it."

I depressed the call button. "Hello?"

"It's Brill."

I sat up, my heart reminding me I was alive. "What's going on?"

"Just giving you a heads-up and it's all

good. Shooting team is just about done. You're fine."

Suddenly, I could breathe easily. "Oh my God, that's great! Did Forensics pull anything from the Nova?"

"Lots of prints. We'll run through the electronic file by midafternoon."

"Thanks, Justice. That's a real load off."

"That's why I called."

Koby yanked the covers off and bolted up. My eyes followed his body—upright as well as erect—as he walked to the bathroom.

"Someone will officially call you," Justice told me. "You want to know where the shots landed?"

"Where?"

"All in the hood of the car, nothing through the windshield. Your aim was good. Except you fired six and the team only recovered four."

"I must have shot a couple of wild ones," I lied.

"Yeah, so long as they didn't land in the wrong place. So far, so good."

"Thanks again, Justice. Call me as soon as the prints go through, even if there isn't a hit."

A pause. "Maybe we should have that cup of coffee, Decker."

"Whenever you're ready to talk about the Sarah Sanders rape case—with Russ Mac-Gregor's permission, of course—I'm up for it."

"Yeah, that too. You have the day off. How about a drink when I get off—around six. I should know something about the car's prints by then."

"Can I get back to you? I've got to arrange my schedule with my boyfriend. He's still half-asleep right now."

"Sure, Decker. Call me back."

"Thanks, Justice. Bye."

Koby slithered back into bed. "What schedule are we arranging?"

"Detective Brill wants to talk to me."

"About what?"

"Prints in the Nova. He's running them through this afternoon. He suggested talking over drinks when he gets off from work."

"He asked you *out*?"

"He's married, Koby."

"A ring on the finger is not a ring on the gonads."

"And that's why I mentioned my boyfriend. He's not stupid."

"Are you going?" He sulked.

"I'll call and find out what popped up on National Register. If it's legit, yes, I'm going. I've been in this position before. I know these guys and I know how to steer it to business. Our dating makes it that much easier. Plus, Brill's a superior. I need a jump start on the Sarah Sanders rape case, and if he can help me, great."

"There are sexual-harassment laws in this country, you know."

"He's not harassing me, he's throwing out feelers. Don't worry."

But his face held resentment. He waited a moment; then his long fingers skittered over my nipples.

"Let me brush my teeth," I told him. As soon as I returned to bed, he turned to his side and propped himself up onto an elbow. He took in my nakedness.

"You are so gorgeous."

I stroked his cheek. "So are you. Please don't doubt me."

He brought my hand to his erection. "I don't doubt you, but I know men."

My cell went off again.

"Let it *ring,*" Koby snapped.

"It might be important."

Koby plopped down onto his back, smoldering eyes on the ceiling, and said nothing. This time, it was Rina.

"I just wanted to know when you're going to pick up the old Volvo."

"Oh . . . hold on." I turned to my bedmate. "When do you want to pick up the Volvo?"

He exhaled loudly. "What time is it?"

"Around nine."

"I have to be in at three. Twelve, twelve-thirty?"

"How about twelve-thirty?" I asked Rina.

"That's fine. I'll see you then."

I hung up.

"Turn it off," Koby said. "If it goes again, I will break it."

I turned it off.

He leaned over and kissed me.

Within moments, there was another annoying jingle—*Für Elise* and it was his phone.

"Oh my God!" he snarled.

"You can answer it," I told him. "*I* won't get cranky."

He glared at me and picked up his phone. "Yes? . . . Mikal! . . . Shit!" He sat up. "Sorry, mon, I forgot to call. I can't come down; my car's wrecked. . . . No, no, I'm fine.

Some dude ran a light. . . . No, it's totaled, utterly gone. My woman has another set of wheels. . . . Her old man does. Look, just run without me today. I see you on Thursday, mon. . . . When? Saturday? . . . Maybe. I'll talk to the woman. Okay. Bye."

I stared at him. "When did you become Jamaican?"

"What?"

"Never mind. Talk to me about what?"

"A party Saturday night. Do you want to go?"

"Do you?"

"If you want." He eyed me hungrily. "I think I'd rather be alone with you." He put his phone on his nightstand. No sooner did he lay it down than it rang again. He started to laugh and so did I.

"Go ahead," I told him.

"Yes?" His voice was hard. "What time? . . . I can't. . . . I can't. . . . You're not hearing me, Marnie, I can't. I have no car. I have to pick one up. . . . I'm picking it up at twelve-thirty, so one-thirty at the earliest. Why not call Lisa? . . . When? . . . How long? . . . So call up Pat and insist that she come in or you shall report her. You have to control the people on your shift, Marnie.

I keep telling you this. She's missed more days than all of us together. . . . I know she's a single mother, but I have a life, too. I am sick of covering for her. . . . No, I am not yelling, I am frustrated!"

He rolled his eyes.

"Yes, I know it's not your fault, but certainly it is not my fault. Look, I try to make it by two. That is the best I can do. . . . It's okay. . . . I know. . . . I know you do. . . . No problem, Marnie. . . . Yes, I will. . . . I must go." He clicked the phone off. "Marnie says hello." He lobbed the cell across the room. It didn't break, but the battery fell out.

He stared at me with appetite. "Shall we try once more?"

"Are you sure you want to attempt this?" I asked him.

"If we don't, I shall truly be foul."

"I don't think I want to see that."

"It would not be good."

An hour later, he had done a one-eighty: a completely different man—relaxed and smiling and joking. After we showered, he insisted on preparing us breakfast. He turned on his stereo, zydeco music pumping out of the speakers. Nifty accordion playing. I heard him singing along with the vocals.

By the time I had dressed and walked into his kitchen, he was almost done cooking.

"Coffee's ready."

"You work fast."

He kissed me as he poured eggs into a pan sizzling with chopped peppers, tomatoes, and onions. "I set up outside on the patio. It is a beautiful day."

"That looks good."

"Shakshuka."

"Ethiopian?"

"Israeli. Moroccan, I think. You are depleted. You need protein. We both do."

"I thought it was good to eat carbs when you're depleted."

"No, carbs are for immediate rise in blood sugar. Protein is digested slowly. It does not give you the rush, but you don't crash, either. Take the paper and go outside."

Five minutes later, he brought out food, drink, and my cell phone. He kissed my lips, then sat down. "Ah . . . this is nice." He leaned back in the chair, hands behind his neck. "It is good to breathe."

I poured a refill of coffee. "Very nice." I started in on my plate of eggs. "Delicious. Thank you."

"You're welcome."

It wasn't the first thing he had made for me. He was a good cook—simple dishes but with lots of spice. He favored red chili flakes. My mouth was burning after a few forkfuls. I washed it down with juice, then sipped coffee. I regarded his face. "Sex is really important to you."

He eyed me behind a coffee cup. "Yes . . . I hope it's important to you, too."

"Of course. It just doesn't seem to . . . alter my disposition as much."

"I am very moody. I told you that."

"Yes, you did."

"We are reversed, Cynthia. I work with women; you work with men. It is early in the relationship, so I am not so secure. And with recent circumstances, we've been dealing with a lot."

"I've dragged you into a lot of muck. Sorry."

"If you come with muck, I will take the muck." He took my hand and kissed it. "When it's my turn to drag you into muck, then you will remember this."

"Fair enough." I bit into a piece of rye toast and stared at the rosebushes. "Well, since sex seems to be a very big factor here, for both of us, I guess I could go on the pill. Make it a little more spontaneous."

His smile was wide. "That would be very nice."

"You don't like condoms."

"No man does. But it's your body." He slathered butter onto the bread. "I do what you want."

"I have no problem with the pill, but if we stop using condoms, you've got to be absolutely monogamous."

"I know."

"Like one hundred percent. I can't be worrying about . . . things."

"Disease, you mean. I understand, my love. I am thirty-two, not sixteen."

"I couldn't even imagine you at sixteen."

"It never slept."

I smiled. "So it's not a problem for you?"

His laughter was musical. "I am *mad* for you, Cynthia. I don't even *think* about being with another woman. Is it a problem for *you*?"

"Being with another woman?" I shook my head. "Not at all."

He tossed me a disgusted look.

"No, it's not a problem." I smiled. "I'm fine with it."

"Good. So go see your doctor and give me the prescription. I can probably pick up some free samples for you from one of the drug companies."

"At a *children's* hospital."

"We treat teenagers."

"Ah." I finished my eggs. "So how easy is it to get drugs?"

He looked at me. "Pardon?"

"Like hard drugs. How easy would it be to filch them?"

"With the classified narcotics, everything is kept under lock and we all know who has the keys. It is not simple. I don't do drugs, I've never done drugs, but those at the hospital who do usually suck nitrous oxide because it is very accessible and usually wears off immediately. It is stupid. Every year we have at least one of our own staff unconscious because of improper mix of oxygen and nitrogen. Why do you ask about drugs?"

"Cop's curiosity. You can get the pill so easily. I just wondered."

"I cannot easily get narcotics from lockup, but if I was desperate enough, I would know ways. Almost anything else— antibiotics; cold medicines; antihistamines;

analgesics, both OTC and some low-dose prescription pain medications like Percocet; even Percodan or Vicodin, which have codeine in them. The hospital has closets filled with samples from the drug companies. It's a perk of the job . . . like free coffee for you."

"I don't get free coffee."

"Well, here you do." He picked up part of the paper and handed it to me. "So let's enjoy our time together before reality intrudes."

I scanned the front page of the Arts and Entertainment section—vintage '50s musicals on stage, movie remakes, TV reunion specials. Didn't anyone have an original thought anymore? I looked at Koby's face, his eyes focused on the morning news, his brow furrowed with tension as he read the articles about our troops overseas. He was much more familiar with that region than average Joe American. I wondered how much he identified with our soldiers.

Bad news wasn't good for either of us. We were both highly intense people, and even though I had a *strong* feeling that he often used sex like an opiate, as long as he wasn't pushy and he was faithful, what did it matter? He had been shot at two days ago, his car had been totaled, and still he cooked me breakfast.

This was a wonderful man.

"Kiss me," I told him.

He put down the paper. "That's a nice invitation." He leaned over, took my face in his hands, and brought my mouth to his—a slow and passionate and edible kiss.

"Now that was *so* good," he told me.

I wrapped my arms around his neck and pulled his lips to mine, my fingers massaging the back of his scalp as our tongues did a slow dance.

We became more and more amorous.

A few minutes later, we got up and headed for the bedroom.

▼

I wiped foam from my lips with the back of my hand. The beer was ice cold, in contrast to the hot, smoky room. Seven in the evening and Bellini's was thick with cigarette carcinogens. It was a step up from the usual cop's bar, offering a pretty good selection for dinner—nothing fancy, but good and filling. Hayley and I had often gone there after shift when we still did Day watch. The place was small in size, dimly lit with background jazz: This time, it was Miles Davis doing the honors. Baseball was on the big screen—Dodgers versus the Diamondbacks in Arizona.

Brill found us a booth in the back. By choosing Bellini's, making us visible, he was making some sort of a statement, though I wasn't clear on the message. I did know it wasn't pure altruism. Not with the way he was sipping his beer and eyeing me with those baby blues. I nursed my drink and I let him do it. He looked sharp—shadow pinstripe suit, white shirt, red-and-gold tie. Big gold ring on his left finger. Gold watch on his wrist.

"Are you hungry?"

"No, I'm fine." I added, "I had a big lunch."

"With the boyfriend?"

"Exactly." I could see the TV from where we were sitting. Shawn Green just got a stand-up double. Randy Johnson looked pissed.

"What's his name?" Brill asked.

He knew the answer to the question. He had interviewed Koby for over an hour. "Yaakov Kutiel."

"Seemed like a good guy," Brill said. "Especially considering the circumstances. Does he have insurance for his car?"

"Yes, but you know how that works. Blue book on it isn't going to be much."

"Lucky for him he found a girl with a Lexus."

"You've noticed."

"Only the best for Daddy's little princess."

"Now you're getting nasty."

Brill smiled, signaled over the waitress. "Wanna clarify something for me?"

"If I can."

"You have any idea where that phone call came from?"

"Not a clue."

"For something to go through the grapevine that fast"—he gave me the "cop stare"—"it defies logic."

I didn't deny it. On the TV, the throw to the plate was too late. Green scored on McGriff's perfect, long single. Fred McGriff had advanced to second. One out, Dodgers up by three at the top of the third. A close-up of a disgusted Johnson. The waitress came over. Brill ordered lamb chops with roasted potatoes; I settled for another beer.

"Any ideas?"

I thought long and hard. Anything I'd say could be used against me. "No."

Brill smiled. "All right. Let's leave it at that."

"Let's."

"Prints—we found a lot of those. Stop me when you're interested."

"I'm interested in whatever you have to tell me."

He pulled out his notebook. "Here goes: Bobby Cantrell, Mohammed Nelson, Benny Rodriguez, Tomas Marin, Mabibi Ralson, Joseph Fedek—"

"Stop."

"Yeah, I thought so. Let me finish with the rest: Leonard Chatlin, Mike Robinson, Cristofer Anez, and Ted Bass. Now, Cantrell, Rodriguez, and Anez have been officially logged into our penal system. Tomas Marin lives out of state, but that don't mean he can't travel. Mabibi Ralson is dead. So that leaves Joseph Fedek, Mohammed Nelson, Leonard Chatlin, Robinson, and Bass. The good news is, there are addresses for Mohammed Nelson, Mike Robinson, and Ted Bass. The bad news? None for Chatlin and Fedek. Since a cop discharged her weapon, it's a serious offense. Stone gave the case to me. So I gotta check out all these dudes. I'm not pleased."

Pepe Renaldes hadn't made the list. That made me feel a little better. I said, "What can I help you with, Justice?"

"You're not allowed to help me. Conflict of interest."

McGriff had scored on another double by Brian Jordan. There was action in the Arizona bull pen. I said, "What would it hurt if I made a couple of phone calls?"

"A lot if Stone found out."

"I can be discreet."

"In that case, you can check out *everyone* on the list, including our prison buddies, except for Chatlin and Fedek—especially not Fedek. I'll take the heavy stuff. You just verify the obvious. I repeat, don't you dare go after Fedek."

"I wouldn't even know where to find him."

"Yeah, just like you wouldn't know how to find the car."

"You give me an awful lot of credit."

"I give your father a lot of credit."

My beer came. I thanked the waitress. Brill gave the server a wink and me a wry smile. "You go back on active duty tomorrow. How

long do you think it's going to take you to re-
alistically check out the names?"

There were seven names, including the
cons, but not including the dead guy. "I
could probably do it in a couple of days. But
I want to be careful. How about a week?"

"Sounds good. We'll meet next Tuesday
and you can give me an update."

"What time and where?"

"Somewhere private. How about your
place?"

"What time and where?" I repeated without expression.

Brill frowned. "Are you comfortable
here?"

"Sure. Bellini's opens at twelve," I told
him. "Is that good for you?"

"We'll meet at one."

"Done. Now can we talk about Sarah
Sanders?"

"Why? Do you have anything new?"

"Since Joseph Fedek made the fingerprint list, I'm assuming the attack wasn't
random. Maybe El Paso contacted Fedek
from prison and said something to him
about my investigation of Sarah Sanders.
Maybe Fedek got scared."

"Cindy, how would he know where to find you? You weren't even driving your car."

I thought a moment. "El Paso could have seen Koby's car when he drove away."

"Koby?"

"Yaakov. My boyfriend."

"You call him Koby?"

"He calls himself Koby. It's an Israeli nickname for Yaakov."

"He's *Israeli?*"

Here we go again. "Yes. He's black and he's Jewish. Hollywood's our area, Justice. We both work there, and since we're both night owls, we play there as well. Maybe Fedek was hanging around the streets, just waiting for our paths to cross."

"Could be you're right. But we can't do a damn thing with Sarah Sanders until Fedek's in custody. Right now, that's the big problem."

His food came. He rubbed his hands together. "Looks good." Slowly, his eyes rose from his plate to my face. We regarded each other for a few moments. "Sure I can't *tempt* you?"

He was pointing with his knife to his food, but the implication was obvious. I sipped my second beer. "Justice, I'm really *not* hungry.

But I thank you for the offer." I stood up and left thirty bucks on the table. "My treat."

Brill smiled. "You got class."

"We'll talk later." I started to walk away.

"I hear you applied to Detectives," Brill said.

I turned around. My face got warm. "Yeah, I know it's a little early, but I did well on the exams. I figure, what do I have to lose?"

"Yeah, I was talking to Stone about you. For what it's worth, I told him I think you'd season well."

"That was very nice of you." I smiled as the heat under my cheeks spread across my face. "Really. Thanks a lot."

"Course you'd need the right rabbi."

"Of course." Was Justice setting me up to be his partner? I didn't dare dream that high. Then he winked at me. "Thanks for dinner. Lunch'll be on me."

"Great."

Sharing the tab . . . that was good.

39

As predicted, it took me a week to check out the names on Brill's fingerprint hit list. At the time a bronze Nova was gunning me down, Bobby Cantrell was in Folsom Penitentiary, and Benny Rodriguez and Cristofer Anez were in Lompoc Federal Prison. Tomas Marin had moved to Texas, where he worked construction in Houston, and Mabibi Ralson was indeed dead.

Mike Robinson was thirty-eight years old and employed with an insurance firm. He was the original owner of the Nova and traded it in for a new GM Saturn in 1996. Ted Bass worked as a film editor and had *no idea* how his prints were found in the Nova or even *why* his prints were in the police system. He lived in West Hollywood and was with his lover at a dinner party the night in question.

Mohammed Nelson developed pictures in a MotoPhoto lab in South Central. He was six-four and hostile and claimed he didn't remember where he had been the night that someone tried to take me out—very reasonable because several days had passed since the shooting. I could have prodded him with cop attitude, but since I was on my own, I chose to be a nuisance instead. Guys will do anything to get rid of a nagging woman. He finally figured out that during the time period in question, he had been at a party where black-market pharmaceuticals had been passed freely from person to person. I was able to confirm his presence at the party.

I presented the list to Justice complete with times, dates, and alibis. He was thrilled, suggesting that we should talk about the case one more time, just to nail down all the details. There was no mention of my apartment as the meeting place. It was Bellini's for lunch—safe, appropriate, and in the open.

Since my suspects had checked out clean, our biggest hope lay in snagging

Joseph Fedek and Leonard Chatlin, both with records of misdemeanor possessions and drunk-and-disorderlies. At the time of the mug shots, Fedek had a shaved head and an eyebrow pierce. Leonard Chatlin was clean shaven and very pimply. Sarah had had pretty decent recall for something that had happened so long ago.

The problem lay in LAPD's inability to locate Fedek and Chatlin. But because both were scumbags, and in general, scumbags didn't learn from experience, I knew that there was a very good chance that they'd be picked up again on another offense *if* they still were in L.A.

I also made a call to County Jail. After being transferred from one extension to another, one department to another, I finally was able to confirm, by checking the visitors' list, that Joseph Fedek had paid a call to his stepbrother Germando El Paso a week before my shooting. Nothing but circumstantial evidence, but it told me what I suspected. El Paso had offered me up to Fedek.

Using Justice Brill as the contact name, I put out the word with other LAPD substations and West Hollywood Sheriff. If anything comes in—even something as meager as loitering or a DUI—on Joseph "Juice" Fedek or Leonard Chatlin, *please* don't let him go without contacting Detective Brill or—in an emergency—Officer Cynthia Decker. I figured I'd go round-robin, calling each division about once a week. Any more than that and I'd be considered a pest.

Now it was a waiting game.

A week passed before things finally settled down. Koby and I squeezed in an elegant dinner at one of my favorite spots. Musso & Frank was among the oldest and best restaurants in Hollywood. Built to look like a hunting lodge with high-beamed ceilings and lots of wood, it was one of those places that had a bar scene, without being tacky, and everything imaginable on the menu. The management boasted the best sand dabs in town (the truth) and famous martinis. I was on my second cocktail when Koby casually mentioned that a guy, two tables to my left, kept staring at me.

I didn't turn around. I flicked my hair back and sipped my drink. "What does he look like?"

"Harmless. Middle-aged, graying hair. Jacket and tie. Looks like a lawyer."

"Alone?"

"No. He's with a woman, probably his wife. Also two other couples: They're both white."

"The guy's black?" I asked him.

"Yes. I don't mention that?"

"No."

Koby smiled. "The men are in suits, women in nice dresses. There is nothing wrong except that he keeps looking over here."

I put my napkin down. "I'll make a trip to the bathroom."

With the humidity down pretty low, I was having a very good hair day, my shoulder-length tresses filled with body and none of the frizz. I wore a sleeveless fire engine–red dress that had a loose crossover bodice and plunging neckline. Because Koby was six-one-and-a-half in bare feet, whenever we went someplace nice, I wore heels that put me close to six even. When I stood up, he gawked at me and swallowed hard.

"Maybe he eyes you because you are so beautiful." He exhaled and shook his head. "Sometimes I must pinch myself."

I bent over, giving him a view, then kissed

the top of his head. "I'll do that for you. Excuse me."

I took the opportunity to reapply my makeup. I liked looking good for him. Upon returning, I had a full view of the table—three 50-plus couples, and yes, the men did look like lawyers. In fact, they probably were. I knew for certain that the lone black man was.

Raymond Paxton—David Tyler's conservator.

I had called him three times in the past several weeks and all I ever got was voice mail. The first two times, I just wanted to know if he had heard from David. The third time, I told him I was looking for David in my off-hours. I gave him names of shelters I had been to, explaining that I didn't want him to plow old ground, should he happen to be looking for David as well.

Not even the courtesy of a follow-up call from a secretary. Not that he was required to answer me, but it would have been polite. He saw me heading toward his table and stood up, excusing himself before I could intrude on his party. We met halfway between our tables and found a corner at the busy bar. I sat; he didn't. I expected hostility. Instead, I got an immediate apology.

"I'm sure you've been busy." I kept my face expressionless, although I maintained eye contact. Typical cop stare. I didn't know if we got it from TV or vice versa. Paxton wore khaki pants, white shirt, red tie, and blue blazer. Very preppy. I wondered if he had attended an Ivy.

He said, "It takes two minutes to make a phone call. I didn't call back because I didn't trust you."

My shrug was noncommittal.

"I couldn't figure out what your game plan was," he told me. "I still don't know."

"I'm looking for David Tyler."

"Yes, but why?"

I actually gave the inquiry some thought. "I don't know, Mr. Paxton. I suppose it's because in life I've been given a great deal and he's been given a raw deal."

Paxton looked down. "His trust fund is significant. The first couple of months he was gone, I hired a private detective, you know."

"I didn't know. You never told me."

"The man was a con artist."

"That's too bad."

"My own fault. I didn't do my homework.

Since you seem to be on some sort of mission with David, I could give you money for your time and expenses. But you'll have to make it official. I'll need a written report of your progress."

I held up my hands. "Maybe money for gas . . . wear and tear on the car. Other than that, I'm fine. How about giving some money to the baby instead?"

"I can't do that unless I have medical evidence that the child is David's offspring. Otherwise I could be sued later on. But there are . . . things I could arrange. Why don't you have the mother of this child hire a lawyer? It would be easier if I spoke legalese with him . . . or her."

"All right. I will." I held out my hand. "Thank you."

He waited a moment, then shook it. "I apologize for being rude, Officer Decker. I'm not a big fan of the police."

"Neither is my boyfriend."

"The man you're with is your boyfriend?"
I nodded.

"I thought he might be your partner."

"Not in this getup." I smiled. "Once he was DWB—driving while black—and it put him in the wrong place at the wrong time. He spent a night in jail because of a mix-up in identity with a rapist. After hearing the story and the circumstances, I told him I would have done exactly what the cops did." I shrugged. "He didn't want to hear it."

"I'm sure I could agree with him, having had a similar experience." Paxton pointed to the dining room. "After you."

We went back to our respective tables. By the time I sat back down, the waiter had brought our Caesar salads. "Sorry it took so long."

"Everything all right?" Koby asked me.

"Actually, yes, everything is very all right." Even if I didn't find David, at least his baby might be provided for. Certainly, Louise Sanders could use some monetary help. Things were tough for her. If Paxton came through, then it was well worth his initial snubs.

I picked up my fork. "Wow, this looks good. I'm starved." I took several bites. "Delicious!"

Koby stabbed a crouton and chewed it slowly, a half smile on his lips. "I love it when women eat. It's very sensual."

"You'd get lots of female fans with that statement." I laughed. "Sometimes I wonder if you're for real or is it, you know, like the Ethiopian restaurant. You just have all these great lines and angles to get into women's pants."

"It's only your pants, my love, and I think I don't need a line *or* an angle. You seem always very willing."

A warm flush crawled over my body. "Will you please eat? You're making me nervous, staring at me like that."

"Why?"

"Because I know what you're thinking."

"What are *you* thinking?"

"That you look very handsome."

His smile turned white and luminous. "Thank you."

I stole a glance at his face. "That you look *very* good."

"Thank you again." His eyes had turned hot and hungry. "You know, Cynthia, we could ask the waiter to pack our main dishes."

I put down my fork. "Yaakov, I'd really like to make it through a meal."

"Certainly." He sipped his beer, licking foam off his upper lip with the tip of his tongue. He raised his eyebrows. "Would you like another drink?"

"No . . . I'm okay." I picked up my fork again. "But thanks."

"Anything you want, my love. That is my motto."

"Did you take your charm pills today, Koby?"

"With you, I don't need them. It is all natural feelings."

"That's sweet." I gave him a shy smile. "Really. I mean that, Yaakov. I feel the same way. I think you're wonderful and sexy and brilliant . . . fun . . . just the best."

He grinned. "It is you who takes the charm pills."

"Yeah, I'm the one who needs them." I laughed. "I wish a little of your smoothness would rub off on me."

He took my hand. "You are not slick, Cynthia, but you are always sincere." He kissed my fingers one by one, then gently swiped my nose with his index finger. "Eat."

I speared another leaf of romaine, my eyes sweeping over his face. Again he was studying me, those long, luscious lashes sweeping over those magnificent pale whiskey eyes.

He really looked *fine!*

I nibbled on salad, but suddenly everything was tasteless.

Who was I kidding?

Oh my God, I was sinking again.

I summoned the waiter, requesting our entrées to go, along with the check.

40

The coast of California is God's kissed countryside from San Diego to the Oregon border—blue iridescent seas on one side, towering verdant mountain majesty on the other. Traveling north from Santa Barbara on 101, Decker couldn't have asked for lovelier weather. It was in the low 70s with the sun playing peekaboo behind woolen tufts of crystalline clouds. As he turned east onto 234, going deep into the Santa Ynez Valley, the Porsche began to climb between granite walls of imperial rock and twist seamlessly through the winding canyons. The temperature dropped and a fine mist hovered above.

"Spectacular," Rina whispered.

"Hannah's getting bigger," Decker answered. "We should really do this more often."

"Yes, we should." Rina adjusted the baseball cap on her head, enjoying the wind and sun on her face. "It's nice to feel young."

"Free," Decker said. "We never had much of this."

"I know. Instant family when we married. Poor you."

"Not poor me," Decker told her. "Rich me. I wouldn't trade it for anything. Still, you've got to find a balance. We shouldn't have to use a project as an excuse to get away for a weekend. But since we did come up with a purpose, what is the game plan here?"

"I have a couple of questions about the murder, but if I don't get to ask them, I'll be fine." Rina took in a deep breath and let it out. "It's really all about my mother's childhood. I don't even care about the murder anymore. That was just the catalyst."

"I'm thrilled to hear you say that. Basically, I think we should just let the ladies talk." Decker took in a lung's worth of pine-scented air. A minute later, they were off the freeway, the exit for Solvang putting them onto Mission Avenue, a two-way boulevard lined with imposing cedars, regal in size and wide in girth. For a few miles, they passed farm country and orchards, patches of foot-high baby avocado trees dotting the earth like plugs in a hair transplant. A hundred yards later, they drove by an ostrich ranch. No sign of the big beasts, but coming up from L.A., they had seen a genuine llama ranch, so Decker was sure the flightless birds were somewhere near.

Soon they drove by the official green sign welcoming the visitor to Solvang—population 5,332.

Danish Disneyland.

The little tourist town really had an amusement-park feel to it, down to the street names—Vester, Aarhus, Nykobing, Midten—using Hof and Sted instead of street, avenue, or lane.

Lifted right out of a fairy tale: picture-perfect cottages with mullion-paned windows, dozens of gables, and multipeaked roofs topped with special tiles evoking thatched straw. Cute little bungalows of sparkling white stucco and red brick, over-whelmed with gingerbread, set on lots with meticulously planted flower gardens. Almost all the dwellings had exterior walls deluged with Tudor-style trim—stripes and triangles and squares of brightly painted wood appliqué, light blue being the most common color for the decorative beams. But some of the owners had chosen brown or green or in some cases bright red. There were lots of white picket fences and many second-story balconies ringed with white dowel railings. Two of the motels on Mission Avenue had life-size windmills, another had a clock tower with a weather vane.

Decker had never seen streets so clean, as if they were washed daily.

The business district, also on Mission, was a couple of miles long with architecture that was nearly identical to the residences. The shops and restaurants and *bacaris* were owned by individuals with names like Mortensen, Petersen, and Olsen. And the names weren't just for atmosphere. Both he and Rina agreed that they had never seen so many white-haired, pink-complexioned elderly people in such a small geographical area. When they drove past the local school—across the street from a Lutheran Church—it was all fair skin and light hair, except for a clique of Native American children.

Anika Lubke lived in a bright yellow one-story house, the door surrounded by two bay windows and the sides trimmed with blue wood beams. Set into a pole was a Danish flag guarding the entryway; the hand-painted address numbers were red on blue-and-white delft tiles. The front yard was a pallet of color, a profusion of wildflowers. Someone had plunked a stuffed Nordic seaman, complete with beard and cap, smack in the middle of a daisy bush—the Danes' answer to a scarecrow. Decker parked the Porsche and checked his watch. Ten-forty: They were twenty minutes early.

"What do you think?" he asked Rina.

"I don't think they'd mind. But if you'd feel uncomfortable, we can walk around for a few minutes."

Before they could decide, the door opened. The woman who came out was tall and thin, wearing a housecoat printed with calla lilies. Her white hair was tied into a long ponytail, her complexion fair with rosy cheeks. "You are Lieutenant and Mrs. Decker?"

"Hi," Rina said from the curb. "We're a little early."

"No, no, it's fine." Her accent was light and crisp. "Come in, please."

The pathway to the front was narrow. Decker told Rina to go first. The woman introduced herself as Anika, then stepped aside, allowing them to walk into a compact living room with blond hardwood floors and yellow washed walls. The furniture was simple in design and made by someone with a utilitarian eye. The couch and chairs were straight backed and upholstered in tiny blue checks, holding a couple of rudimentary pillows. The coffee table was a trunk, with hand-painted flowers and swirls, which looked to be genuinely old. The walls were hung with oil still lifes, mostly florals: original paintings but not very good. There were also a couple of sketches and a map of Denmark. No family photos. Maybe she kept them in the bedroom.

The air was heavy with the smell of cabbage.

"Lunch is not ready." Anika flailed birdlike arms. "I do apologize."

Rina smiled. "It's not a problem." Up close, Anika was wrinkled, her face furrowed and drooping with fatless skin. But her blue eyes sparkled, as did her teeth, though Rina suspected they were dentures. "The food smells wonderful, Miss Lubke, but unfortunately we can't eat it. We're kosher—"

"*Ach!* But of course."

"I insist that you eat when it's ready." Rina inhaled deeply. "I'm sure it's my loss. What is it?"

"*Hvidkälsrouletter*—cabbage roll with meat. I can make up some vegetarian."

"No, no, no," Rina said. "Please don't bother. If you want to serve us anything, I wouldn't mind some tea."

"And you, Lieutenant Decker?"

"Tea is fine."

"*Kommt sofort!* Right away." She moved with a sprightly walk. A minute later, she returned from the unseen kitchen. "I put the water up to boil. Marta is in church. We were odd—Lutherans in Bavaria. The state is very Catholic, their churches rococo in style because it is near Italy. Also, there were many Russian aristocrats in Bavaria, so the churches have that onion-dome Russian architecture. Inside, they are filled with marble and gold, with angels and cherubs floating in a sky that is painted on the ceiling. It is not my idea of Heaven."

Her speech had the singsong inflections of those who spoke Nordic languages.

"Anyway, Marta will return soon. Ah, the kettle boils. I'll be back."

After she left, Rina whispered, "How old is she?"

"Eighty-four or -five. Maybe even closer to ninety."

"The woman has energy."

"So does your mother. They must have grown them strong in the Old Country."

Rina tapped her toe. Neither she nor Peter had sat down. Anika came back with a tray. "Sit, sit. Please."

Decker sat. The sofa was as uncomfortable as it looked, with its stiff back and no lumbar support. By using pillows, Rina managed to ease herself into a decent position. Anika poured tea, then perched on the edge of a chair, her spine ramrod straight.

Maybe discomfort was a cultural thing.

Rina sipped tea. "Thank you for seeing us."

"Thank you for contacting us. I must say I was very shocked. Who thinks to hear from seventy-year-old ghosts? That's how long it has been since your mother I've seen."

"I can understand how surprised you must have felt."

"Very." She poured herself a mug of tea

and sipped slowly. "It brought back memories very hidden. I don't remember your grandmother's death individually, but the deaths as a group I remember. I think that they scared my mother. Soon after your mother moves away, we move . . . to Hamburg."

"You told me you married an Englishman," Decker said. "How'd that happen?"

"*Ach,* such a long and *traurig* story."

" '*Traurig*' is sad," Rina said.

Decker said, "I didn't mean to pry."

Anika smiled. "But you didn't. I wrote to you in my e-mail that I married an Englishman." She thought a moment. "The people are all dead. I'll tell it to you. In Hamburg, I met my husband when I was seventeen."

"The Englishman," Rina said.

"No, no, a German man. We got married. It was not happily ever after like the *Bruders* Grimm. Right after the wedding, it is 1933 and Germany elects Hitler, who brings us into war. No excuses, Germany deserved what it got because our parents elected the demagogue."

She shook her head.

"If you asked any German people after World War Two if they voted for Hitler, they all say no. No, no, no, we didn't vote for him. Nobody voted for him! No one knows how he got power!"

She waved her hand disgustedly in the air.

"My husband was drafted and captured as a POW. He was a *staatsbeamte*—a civil servant—but because his title contained the word '*staats*,' the English thought he was some important state official. In a camp, they put him with others that had *staats* in their title. They played cards and talked philosophy the entire time. Meanwhile, from him I don't hear . . . maybe a year. I am young and stupid, and after the British invaded the North, I get younger and stupider and fall for an Englishman because he wears the winning uniform. I blame my parents. If they had not moved, I would have probably fallen in love with an American soldier. I would have been better off."

Rina smiled and nodded, but Decker shrugged confusion.

"Toward the end of the war," Rina explained, "Germany was being blitzed from three fronts: the British in the North, the Russians in the East, and the Americans in the South. That's why the Russians liberated

Auschwitz and the Americans liberated Dachau. So she's saying that if she had stayed in Munich, which is in the South, she would have met an American."

"Ah, I see," Decker said.

Anika sighed. "I get a divorce from my poor German husband, who can't believe that his young wife runs off with the enemy." A sigh. "I hurt Hans very bad. Later, I hear a very nice girl he remarries. They have four children. He is very happy . . . much happier than me. Serves me right. Where was I in the story?"

"You just divorced your German husband," Decker reminded her.

"Ah, yes. I marry Cyril Emerson and moved to a small town in Devonshire. You can think how much the English working class loves a German girl. I was miserable. So then we move back to Hamburg, and he is miserable. Finally, we reach a compromise. Hamburg is not so far from Denmark. So we move to Copenhagen and we're both miserable. Still, we live in Denmark for thirty years. I birth two sons who move to America. So at fifty-six, I divorce Cyril, return to the name Lubke, and off to America I move. To St. Louis because Marta is living there."

"How did Marta wind up in St. Louis?"

"Her husband was an executive in Anheuser-Busch. Marta loves St. Louis. I don't like St. Louis. It is searing hot in the summer and bitter cold in the winter. Snow is nice, but the city has no mountains except the Ozarks . . . very sorry mountains. Ten years ago, I came to Solvang for a visit. After being in Copenhagen so long, it was very familiar for me. I loved the cooler temperature. I love the real mountains. Here, a home I found. Twice a year, I visit Marta. Twice a year, Marta visits me. She gets the good deal."

Rina laughed. "I think so."

"Would you like more tea?"

"I'd love some more tea," Rina said.

Anika picked up the teapot and disappeared into the kitchen.

Rina held in a laugh. "What a character!"

"She has a personality," Decker said.

She came back several minutes later with scalding hot tea. "Ah, the steam, the aroma . . . only thing English do well is tea." She poured three refills. "I try to think back that far, Mrs. Decker, to the time of the deaths. It was a very peculiar time."

"How so?" Rina asked.

"All of Germany was imploding. Munich was no exception. The city was in terrible chaos, and the deaths made even more chaos. München held much militaristic presence, of uniforms and armies and parades. It was the birth home of the Nazis, yes, but they were not the only political party. There were many and every group has its own flag, its own identity. Every party is color coded. Brown for Nazis, the Social Democrats are green, Communists are red or black shirt with red bow ties. Then there are the royalists. The Bavarian monarchs were expelled by the Communists in 1918, but many relatives remained and dressed in old *Bayerischen* royal uniform for every parade on every occasion. There were always demonstrations in Konigsplatz . . . in every public square. I go to a school in Turkenstrasse—"

"My mother's *schule,*" Rina said.

"Yes, your mother's *schule,* too. Next door was the seat of the Nazi newspaper *Volkischer Beobachter.* We used to see the Brown Shirts goose-step. A few times Hitler, too. It was all part of the show. Looking back as an adult, I was very frightened, I think, because these groups used to come to the *schule* and talk. They ask about our parents—what they did, who they knew, what newspapers were at home. The newspapers in Europe are different than newspapers in America. They are political-party papers, so by asking about the newspapers, the groups know the parents' party affiliation. So when the deaths happen, like your grandmother, Mrs. Decker, the talk is that maybe your Omah was on the wrong side politically."

"Do you think her murder was political?"

"After the first one is found, everyone says that yes, it must be political. Everything in Munich was political. There were several other murders of young women that were political, one very famous—a farm girl named Amalie Sandmeyer who was murdered by the *Fememord,* a very secret right-wing group. Everyone is afraid of the *Fememord.*"

"Why was Amalie Sandmeyer murdered?" Decker asked. "Was she a spy?"

"On the contrary. She was a working girl and was too naive to realize what was happening. Weapons at the time were illegal in München. If you find weapons from World War One, to the police you must bring them. But all the groups have secret caches. Amalie found a secret cache of weapons, and like the dumb good girl she was, she reported it to authorities. The problem was she found a Nazi cache and the police had many members in the National Socialist German Workers Party. Everyone knew her murder was political."

Anika drank her tea and appeared to collect her thoughts.

"But then another is found dead. Then it was your grandmother. By then, mothers tell their daughters never to walk the streets alone. That there are madmen other than Hitler."

"I found my grandmother's *mordakte*— her homicide file," Rina said.

"*Mein Gott,* how did you find?"

"It's a long story. But her file was found with those of the two others murdered before her. The cases were all packaged together in one big box apparently. I was sent a copy, not the original."

"What was in your grandmother's file?"

"Not much," Decker said. "A pathology report, interviews, witnesses, crime scene report. Comparison of her murder to those of the two other women—Marlena Durer and Anna Gross. From what I could tell, the police investigation was pretty primitive. Do you remember any other murders?"

"There were two more after your grandmother, Mrs. Decker. Then we move. But the last I remember well because it was a young girl who lived near me in Schwabing. Her name was Johanna, a little older than I was but close enough in age to truly frighten. *Ach,* it was terrible murders in a terrible time that only got more terrible before it got better."

The woman had turned red and was panting hard.

Rina said, "Thank goodness it's in the past, Anika."

"Yes . . ." The old woman took a few moments to steady her breathing. "Yes, it is all in the past and every day I walk past mountains, sky, and beauty." She exhaled loudly. "Your grandfather did a good deed when he moved your mother away. The other families stayed, the motherless children receiving not pity but suspicion: 'What did your mother do to deserve her death?' If you want my opinion, Mrs. Decker, I say your grandmother was murdered by the same hand, even if the women were different.

Thinking about it . . . it was all so much the same."

"Any idea who might have done it?"

"*Ach,* no, sorry. A madman, a political man, a man who was both mad and political. You choose." Anika clenched her jaw. "There was one investigator . . . he talked to us. I remember him well—strong, blue eyes, and black curly hair. He had . . . I don't know . . . a swagger in his step . . . a charisma. He spoke softly but with much intensity. If we see anything, if we hear anything, we must tell him. He was terrifying and appealing at the same time. I don't remember his name."

"Heinreich Messersmit?" Decker tried.

She shrugged.

"Rudolf Kalmer?" Decker paused. "Axel Berg?"

"Maybe that was it. I wonder what happened to him?" She waved a bony hand in the air. "Now he's dead. They're all dead. I should be dead."

"God forbid!" Rina said.

Anika smiled. "I was glad when we moved. Hamburg was different—a free state, a port city, more international, less

Bavarian. And the beer in Hamburg is stronger." She looked at an empty wrist.

Decker said, "It's twelve-ten."

"Marta should be here soon," Anika repeated. "Maybe we take a walk?"

But just then, the door opened.

Marta was definitely Anika's sister, having the same wrinkled face, same long jawline, and white hair, except she had it tied into a bun. She wore a fitted blue suit but had orthopedic shoes on her feet. She met Rina's eyes, then clamped a hand over her mouth. "Oh *mein Gott,* it is Marta Gottlieb!" Tears welled in her blue eyes. "I can't believe . . ."

She started to cry. Anika said, "My sister is emotional."

Rina held out her hand. "I do look like my mother."

But Marta was weeping too hard to respond. Anika hit her shoulder. "Stop!"

"You stop!" Marta choked back. Finally, she took Rina's hand and clasped it. "How is your mother?"

"Mama is fine. Very fine and very well."

Marta exhaled. "We were very good friends once. A lifetime came between us."

"I know."

"She was in Auschwitz?"

"Yes."

"*Ach* . . . terrible, terrible." She brought her hand to her chest. "Such a strong woman. If anyone could survive, it would be Marta. I would have surely died." She wiped her eyes. "It smells good, Anika. I am hungry."

"They can't eat. They are kosher," Anika explained.

"Yes, yes . . . I should have thought of that."

"It's really fine," Rina said. "Peter and I have to start heading back. We still have a young child at home. How long are you staying in town, Mrs. Wallek?"

"Marta, please. This time, I stay through August. A long time. I must see your mother. Please. It would do well for me. I think it would do well for her, too."

Rina nodded. "I'll ask her. But I have one favor—no more talk about the murders. It should be only pleasant recollections."

"Yes, yes, of course," Marta said. "So many bad memories." A sigh. "It is bad to be senile, *ja?* But not so bad to forget some things."

"Selective repression," Rina said.

"Exactly," Marta said. "Our lives now are very short. It is not a time to dwell on the past." She squeezed Rina's hand. "We can come to Los Angeles."

"We can?" Anika said.

"Yes, we can," Marta insisted. "I can drive."

That thought was truly terrifying. Decker said, "How about if I arrange to have you driven down? Arrive in style."

"No, I wouldn't accept!"

"As a present to Rina's mother," Decker insisted. "It would be my pleasure."

"He doesn't want you to drive," Anika told her sister.

"I want you two to be comfortable," Decker said. "Let us talk to Magda—Rina's mother—and I'll e-mail you some dates."

Again Marta brought her hand to her chest. Again, her eyes watered. "That would be wonderful. Thank you so much." She kissed Rina's left cheek, then the right one. The tears came streaming down. "I am so sorry!"

"Please, Marta—"

"All the pain and suffering that we did to your people!"

"Marta, it's a new world." Rina squeezed her hand and sighed. "Hopefully."

"Yes, hopefully." She smiled. "That's all we have . . . hope."

▼

As soon as they hit the freeway, Rina said, "I wonder how Mama will react when we tell her we've found Marta Lubke."

"*We?*"

"I was hoping you'd help me out. Give me a logical reason for why we'd be looking up Marta."

"That's easy. Tell your mother that talking about her past made you curious."

Rina nodded. "I think that will work just fine, you devious devil you."

"I take exception," Decker said. "You're just as devious as I am. I'm just better at it than you."

"More practice."

"That's true enough." Decker stroked her cheek. "Are you really all right with the outcome? Having your grandmother's murder remain an open file?"

"Honestly, yes. Like I said, it wasn't about the murder, it was about my mother's childhood." She felt her eyes mist. "I have only known my mother as a burdened woman. I think I needed to know that once she was a little girl." She put her hand on Peter's knee. "Are *you* okay with not knowing the specifics?"

"Doesn't bother me at all." He let his thoughts go for a moment. "Besides, we both know a little more now than we did going into it."

"You think it was a political thing?"

"Maybe. But it also could have been a serial killer who used politics to mask his murders. We really don't need the gruesome details."

"I agree." Rina felt her eyes closing. "Do you mind if I take a nap?"

"No, of course not. Do you mind if I listen to a CD?"

"No. As a matter of fact, the background noise will help me sleep."

Decker turned on the L.A. Quartet—four guitarists, four virtuosos. A beautiful woman by his side, superb weather, great music . . . soon he was flying at eighty plus, ready to take on the big, bad world.

Eyes still closed, Rina said, "Serial killers have this sameness to them."

"Man, you are right about that. Cut from the same mold."

"Why is that?"

"I don't know," Decker answered. "But I'm sure if the German police ever found this psycho and interviewed his neighbors, they'd say what an ordinary guy he was— although he tended to keep to himself."

41

The days passed to weeks, the weeks melded into the months of summer, an intoxicating time of night-blooming jasmine, warm nights, and fiery lovemaking. Afterward, as we lay in a pile of sweat-soaked sheets, swatting mosquitoes that had squeezed through the screens of the open bedroom windows, my legs draped over Koby's lean and sinewy body, I was thankful for the moment and hopeful for the future. Yaakov and I went from a dating couple to an item. I met his friends; he met mine. Between the two of us, there was always someplace to party, but most of the time we elected to spend our rare free evenings together sharing a bottle of wine in between our physical calisthenics.

When our schedules didn't coincide, I

spent my off-hours hunting—for Joseph Fedek, for Leonard Chatlin, for poor David Tyler, who had dropped out of sight. The good news was Raymond Paxton was true to his word, helping Louise Sanders and me with cash as well as with personal items. I had several good pictures of David. I went through dozens of homeless camps and shelters, and lots of abandoned buildings, flashing David's photo and receiving blank looks for my efforts. I called local municipalities and got addresses. I checked them out. I found nothing.

Sometimes Koby would come with me. One hot day toward the end of August, I specifically *asked* him to come with me. The address I had was southeast in a black area outside of L.A. I thought that maybe David would go there because he was black and might feel safer, less conspicuous among his own.

It was a twenty-minute freeway drive into a district of heat and smog and dirt and concrete. The apartment buildings were run-down, the streets pocked and littered, and the buildings desecrated with graffiti warfare. The area held many more liquor stores than schools and libraries, and not much hope where hope should be. It had a few storefront churches and a lot more thrift shops.

The directions I had were good. Once we were off the freeway, I gave Koby a series of rights and lefts and he found the shelter sandwiched between a fast-food joint and a Laundromat. But there was no parking directly in front of the building, forcing us to pull into a space a half block away. I knew I was out of my element, but Koby appeared comfortable. Maybe more protective than usual, looping his arm squarely around my shoulder. This wasn't our usual Hollywood beat and was probably as foreign to him as it was to me. I was dressed for the heat in knee-length cutoffs and a green tank top, my hair pulled back in a ponytail. Koby wore a red muscle shirt and jeans, his skin now the color of chocolate, made much darker by all of our forays into the California sunshine.

As we headed toward the shelter, a couple of homeys passed by. Big men, both as tall as Koby; the one with a shaved head was at least twice as wide as my boyfriend. But it was his dreadlocked partner with the tattooed arms who spoke up.

"Yo', niggah! Whatchu axin' for yo' ho' bitch?"

Koby's eyes narrowed and I saw him clench his fists. Immediately, I pulled out my badge and flashed it in front of their faces.

"Move along, gentlemen," I told them.

"Dreadlocks" stared and started to speak, but I didn't give him a chance. "I said, move along!" Then making solid eye contact, I added a please.

They paused long enough to give me 'tude and defiance, but then they probably figured I wasn't worth the effort. They ambled on, Dreadlocks spitting a couple of inches from my foot. Koby looked over his shoulder, his eyes fuming. When he started to turn around, I took his hand and pulled him forward.

"Here we are." I opened the boarded door, and still holding Koby's hand, I dragged him inside. We stood in a small anteroom with peeling stucco walls that held a rack filled with flyers and pamphlets of services. Through an archway, I saw a communal dining room. There was a lone desk, the woman behind it around fifty and completely round with clipped kinky hair of gray-and-black knots. She wore a white tank top and was sweating profusely. It was hot inside and the lethargic ceiling fan didn't help much. She eyed us suspiciously. Again, I took out my badge.

She read it, then scowled. "LAPD? Someone should give you driving lessons. You're in the *wrong* district, sister."

I ignored the hostility. "I'm trying to locate a runaway." I took out his picture. "He's twenty-four with Down's syndrome characteristics. Black, obviously. Originally, he's from my district in Hollywood. His retarded girlfriend was gang-raped. He was beaten up and tossed in a trash can like garbage. No one has seen him since and that was around nine months ago."

She listened to me, then turned her eyes to Koby. "I don't see your ID."

"He's not a cop," I told her. "He's my boyfriend."

Instantly, her eyes narrowed as she studied my face. There was disapproval of me, of course, but also an ever so slight softening in her expression. I had seen it in other blacks before—that by dating Koby, I *might* be more trustworthy than an average white cop.

"What do you want?"

"For the last three months, I've been trying to find this kid on my off-hours. I'm going through the lists and this place popped up. I'm just asking if you've seen him. And if you haven't, do you know of other places where I should look?"

She took in the picture. "You already looked in L.A.?"

"Everywhere. I was thinking that because he's black, maybe he perceives himself safer here."

"That'd be a switch." Her laugh was bitter. "Comin' here for safety."

"I'm grasping at straws. What smells so good?"

"The kitchen." She hooked a thumb over her shoulder, indicating the location was through the doorway behind her. "Cookin' up supper." She glanced at Koby, then returned her eyes to me. "What's your business in a nine-month-old crime?"

"It's a long story."

She crossed her arms and waited.

I took a deep breath. "His girlfriend gave birth to a baby girl. She threw the kid away in a Dumpster. I retrieved the baby. I think the kid deserves to know both her parents. Especially since this poor boy was frightened away. He's not indigent. There's a trust fund for him. If I could prove he's the father of this baby, the kid might get some money, too. Lord knows, she deserves it."

"And you're not gettin' any finder's fee?" Cynical eyes.

"I'm not getting a dime," I told her.

She laughed contemptuously. "Just your average nice white do-gooder cop."

I held my ground. "They exist."

She glanced at the picture. Then took it and studied it in earnest. "Lemme show it to Urlene."

I said, "And you are . . ."

She hesitated. "Cerise."

"Cynthia Decker."

I held out my hand. She gave me a limp-fish shake, then regarded Koby. "You don' talk?"

"Just here for the ride," he answered.

"You said it, bro'. 'Cause all yo' be gettin' is a *ride*." She stood up—her lower torso encased in black stretch shorts—and tramped through the archway into the kitchen.

I threw my hands over my face.

"Don't worry about it," Koby whispered flatly.

But his eyes were roiling like storm clouds. He was slipping.

We lived in a liberated and somewhat libertine age and the vast majority of the time our skin tones were as relevant as vestigial tails. So when it happened, it was always like a dash of cold water, this thinly veiled hostility. Koby got the worst of it from white men; I got it from black women.

Your men aren't enough? You've got to steal our men, too?

About a month ago, Koby had taken me to a party hosted by one of his friends. It was 80 percent black, 15 percent Hispanic and Asian, and a few stranded whites. By subconscious design, we Caucasians wound up talking together. We swapped stories and formed a consensus. It was easier to deal with hostile women any day of the week. Women sniped with words, men shot with guns.

Of course, Koby's attraction to me had little to do with my being white and very much to do with my being Jewish. Even more important, I had never been married. Although Koby wasn't Orthodox like Rina, he was well rooted in tradition. He was born into the Jewish priest class—

Kohanim—and I found out from Rina that *Kohanim* cannot marry divorced women without giving up their priesthood. Which didn't translate into much; it was a symbolic thing that most American Jews couldn't care less about. But I knew Koby and I knew he cared—the reason he had asked me soon after we met if there had ever been an ex-husband in the picture. It was obvious he was looking for something more than a casual lay.

Cerise came back a few minutes later. "Yeah. It'd be like I thought. He's been here, but not for at least four months."

I was utterly flabbergasted. "He was *here?*"

"Didn't I just say that?"

"Oh my God, he's alive!" I grabbed Koby's arm and broke into a smile. "I can't believe it!"

"I don't know if he's alive. I haven't seen him in months."

"You made my summer!" I was grinning. I took her hand and pumped it. "Now it's just a matter of finding the right spot. Did you talk to him at all?"

"Girl, we get over a hundred souls walkin' through that door every day of the week."

She pulled her hand away and shook it up and down. "I jus' remember him 'cause he got that Down's face. I'll tell you one thing. He looked a lot older than that picture."

"But you think it was him."

"I knowed it was him. He ate in our kitchen for mebbe two months."

"Did he ever talk to anyone?"

"Now, how would I know that? He never talked to me. Just ate his food and crawled back under the cracks. That's where all these people are from, Miss Cop. The cracks."

"Do you have any idea where he might have gone?"

"Into another crack."

"Any other shelters around here?"

"I thought you said you had a list."

I pulled the slip of paper out of my purse and showed it to her, pointing to a specific address about five miles away. "This was going to be my next stop."

She shrugged. "It's as good as anything I can help you with." She stood up again. "I got business. You can let yourselves out."

As she walked back to the kitchen, I saw her shaking her head. I took Koby's hand

and laced his stiff fingers with mine. "C'mon, big boy. Let's get out of here."

He didn't answer me, and that was always a bad sign. Something ugly was brewing inside his brain, and if it was going to erupt, I felt we should be in a safe environment. I pulled him back to the car—still there and still intact.

"Uh, you have the keys," I told him.

He reached into his pocket and unlocked the doors. We got in and his autopilot took over, turning on the motor, pulling out of the space, finding the freeway on-ramp. I gave him directions to the next shelter. He barely seemed to process the information.

He wasn't kidding when he said he had "dark moods." I'd gone through this before, and as requested, I had left him alone and let him work them away. But today we were together and neither of us had an escape valve.

I said, "It's over, Koby. Let's move on—"

"*Pigs!*" he spat out.

"That's why none of them are worth a second thought."

"They call *me* a nigger?" He pointed to himself. "I am black. They are *niggers!*"

I blew out air. "I know it's okay for you to

use the N-word, but please don't. We whites have a problem with it."

"It is what they are! Ignorant swine!"

"At least, Cerise was helpful."

"If she'd been white, you would have called her a bitch!"

"I'm trying to be charitable."

"Your knee-jerk liberal roots are showing," he growled out.

"Okay. She was a bitch! And the two boys were punks. But punks come in all colors."

"But it has to be my own people to hurl such insults."

"Not at all. Look, Koby, we're spoiled. We hang out in Hollywood, where anything goes. I mean, just yesterday night when we went to the Twenty-four/seven café at two in the morning, at one table there was that bull dyke pouring her heart out to a drag queen. Then there was that Asian girl with blue hair talking to her leather-clad, pincushion white boyfriend with around a zillion pierces. Then there was that Chasidic guy doing a deal with that porno producer—"

"We don't know for sure he was a porno producer."

"C'mon, he was something sleazy. The

point is, we were the most conventional couple in the place. Yaakov, there are places in the good old USA where I wouldn't take you on a bet, and it's not just the Deep South or rural Texas. It's lovely areas with pretty little homes and green lawns and posters in their windows that say, 'The South shall rise again.'"

His jaw was still clenched. "Your bigots do not excuse my people's stupidity!"

"No one's making excuses. It's just that stupidity comes in all colors, including the white liberals in the West Side. God, Koby, you remember the party Mom gave for Alan's birthday? The looks on the guests' faces when they met you. Man, if their smiles had been any more frozen, I could have chipped them off with an ice pick."

"It wasn't *that* bad."

"Yeah, it was especially fun when M Hauser handed you her dirty wineglass asked for another *chilled* Chardonnay, though all the hired waiters were wearing tuxes, and carrying trays."

He waited a beat before he spoke in the memory. His eyes darkene that was uncomfortable."

"Koby, you were *seething*."

"She was very apologetic."

"She was apoplectic!"

He pressed his lips together. "What does that mean?"

"'Apoplectic'? It's an old word for a fit . . . like a seizure. But now it means someone in a snit. And she certainly was in a snit. In fact, she was horrified because the worst thing in *that* world is being 'aware' of color. And of course, they're all *very* aware of color. They think it's great that Jan raised a *liberal* daughter, but they wouldn't want it for their own, believe you me."

"They'd be even more horrified to find out you're not a liberal."

"On social issues I am."

"You're a *cop*, Cynthia. With cop ways of doing things and cop opinions."

"Definitely. I have a big problem with anyone who breaks the law."

"We're in agreement. So that is why I don't make excuses for those jerks."

"I'm not making excuses; I'm just thinking this out. Even my dad, who truly adores you, even he had a reaction when he first met you."

"Your stepmother didn't."

I hesitated for just a moment. "I don't want this to be construed as a criticism of Rina, because I think she's a great person. But to Rina, the world is divided into two categories: Jews and non-Jews. If you're Jewish, you're in; if not, you're not. You're Jewish, ergo you're in. She may be color-blind, but she has her standards. Sammy could bring home the most beautiful, brilliant girl, and if she wasn't Jewish, heads would roll."

I exhaled and shook my head.

"We all do it . . . this us/them thing. With me, it divides between law-abiding citizens and felons. Even in your field, where there isn't supposed to be any bias, I bet biased decisions are made all the time. If a kidney is available, can you honestly say to me that they consider a seventy-year-old in the same way that they consider a twenty-year old?"

"Maybe not." He switched on the stereo, turning up the volume to drown me out. Ska with a booming bass line blasted through the speakers of Rina's Volvo.

I turned off the receiver. "Definitely not," I continued. "Young people get preference, you know that. And why? Why is one life worth more than another life? Now, suppose the seventy-year-old was a major cancer researcher and the twenty-year-old had Down's syndrome. Then who'd get the kidney?"

"Yes, yes, you prove your point, Cindy. You should be a lawyer as well as a cop. That way, you can *legally* defend your self-righteousness. Can we now *stop* talking and listen to some music?" Again he turned on the receiver full volume.

I sat back in my seat and looked at the roof of the car. We rode with the music blaring for about a minute until he abruptly turned it off. The stillness was thick.

"I'm sorry," he said.

I placed my hand on his knee and dropped my voice to a soothing lilt. "Yaakov, those two kids were punks. And you know how I feel about punks. And I didn't particularly like being thought of as your bitch for sale. But there's this side of me that says there's something sad about them. Their self-esteem must be in the toilet, their images of themselves so low that they can't possibly conceive of a healthy, good-looking white woman falling in love with a black man who isn't a pro athlete, a badass rapper, a movie star, or her *pimp.* To them, it's as absurd as a blue sun."

He was silent. But then ever so slowly, a small smile played upon his lips. "You're in love with me?"

I stared at him in amazement. "Um . . . let's think about this. I spend every waking moment of my free time with you, and lots of my nonwaking moments, too." I tapped his temple. "Duh!"

He didn't respond. We tooled down the freeway for a minute without speaking.

At last he said, "Every morning I say *Sha'charit*—prayers to God."

"I know. Those little black boxes with the straps."

"Yes, *tefillin.*" He licked his lips. "In the prayers, there is always *Shemoneh Esrei*—the silent devotion to God. You take three steps backward; then you take three steps forward and start. But before you step forward . . . this is the chance for personal prayer, for personal requests."

A small smile.

"I used to ask God for things—for money,

for a raise, for a better position, for a new car at a price I could afford, to help me win the lottery, to let me meet lots of loose women."

I punched his shoulder lightly. "Did He help you out?"

"Not with the lottery, but very good with the women."

I punched him again, but harder.

"Silly things." He let out a laugh. "But now . . . now I don't ask for things. I just say, 'Thank you, God, for sending me Cynthia.' That is it." A pause. "I don't tell God this at prayer time, but I do also say thank you to Him for giving me the privilege of having sex with you—"

I broke up into peals of laughter. "That's *terrible!*"

"No, it's not!" He glanced at me with serious eyes. "I look at you and I say I can't believe I am having sex with this incredible-looking woman! All my friends are jealous, even if you are a cop. They think you look like a supermodel."

"Oh please—"

"Except you have this big, beautiful, black-girl ass. Tight and round and—"

"You talk about my *ass* with your friends?"

He smiled sheepishly. "It comes up in natural conversation."

I whacked him. "You're awful."

"Not at all." He grew serious. "My friends make fun of me. They say I am moonstruck. They say I am pussy whipped. They say, 'What has happened to you, mon? What is wrong with you . . . that you let a woman bring you to your knees?' But what do they know? They have never brushed their lips against yours. They have never felt your soft touch in the middle of the night. They have never *held* you . . . body and soul united . . . lost in rich ecstasy that lifts even the most ordinary man to a momentary king. They have never had a true union of *Kiddusha*—of holiness between two people who are destined, who are *bashert.*"

His voice had become a whisper.

"God has made this *shiddach* . . . this match. Only God could make such a match. I am . . . *hopelessly* in love with you, Cynthia Rachel Decker."

I absorbed his words, trying not to cry, but I couldn't hold back. My eyes watered up, but I managed to wipe them before tears rolled down my cheeks. Waiting until I could find my voice, and when I finally did speak, I was choked with emotion. "I'm hopelessly in love with you, too, Yaakov Elias David Ben Aaron Hakohen Kutiel." I leaned over and kissed his cheek. "That's quite a mouthful."

"Blame my father." He cleared his throat. "I think we have a long, long future together." He tapped the wheel nervously. "At least, that is what I want."

This time, the tears escaped my eyes. We rode a few minutes in silence, both of us drinking in the moment. For twenty-eight years, it had been just me, myself, and I. But now, in all honesty, I couldn't remember what my life had been without him. Being that dependent on someone was terrifying. Being that dependent on a man was utterly terrifying!

"If you have doubts, I will wait as long as you want," he told me. "I only wish to make you happy."

He had misinterpreted my silence. Still, I held back. "Be careful what you wish for."

He didn't answer. Disappointment crushed

his face, darkening his expression. It was time to take the emotional plunge, a scarier dive than I would have ever imagined. But if I blew it now, I knew I'd regret it for the rest of my life. I took a deep breath and began to stroke his leg. "Yaakov, I have *no* doubts whatsoever. What you want is exactly what I want—a long future together . . . our *entire* future together actually. But I'll tell you this. If you break my heart, I'll kill you."

He glanced at me. "Do you mean it?"

"Mean what? Spending the rest of my life with you or killing you if you hurt me? I mean both."

At last his smile was large and genuine. "Now that sounds like the Cynthia I know and love." He broke into musical laughter. "Now I feel *so* good."

I continued to caress his thigh. "These stupid people . . . it wasn't the first time, and it won't be the last."

He shrugged. Light had returned to his eyes. "So we learn to live with ignorance."

"Exactly. And let's be happy it's now and not fifty years ago. What the heck? Every relationship has sticky points."

"Even relationships with God. Like Avraham Avinu and his ten trials."

"Sorry," I told him. "I don't know what you mean."

"Abraham. His faith in God was tested by ten trials."

"Oh, like Hercules?"

"Who is Hercules?"

"He also had trials."

"He was Jewish?"

"Greek. Anyway, go on. What happened to Abraham?"

"Avraham lived when Nimrod was the leader of the civilized world. A sound ruler, but a cruel man. He did *avodah zarah* . . . idol worship. Avraham believed only in *Hashem.* Nimrod put Avraham through ten trials to test his faith in God. I forget all of them, only each one grew in severity, and the last was trial by fire. Nimrod threw Avraham into a furnace."

He stopped talking.

I said, "And I take it that God saved him."

"Naturally. Otherwise there is no Bible."

I waited for him to continue. But he didn't. I giggled. "Is this a shaggy-dog story?"

"A what?"

"A shaggy-dog story—a story without a punch line."

"No, not at all. I'm saying that if a relationship is strong, it survives anything. I think that is you and me."

My hand was still resting on his knee. "I think so, too." I moved my fingers to between his legs.

He gasped. "If you do that, I will crash the car. Already your father looks for a reason to shoot me. This will be his excuse."

"Stop that! He loves you!"

"Nonsense! I have sex with his daughter: He wants to shoot me."

I smiled, noticing he made no effort to pull my hand away. By now, he was hard: I loved making him hard. Then I retracted my hand and sat back up in my seat.

He groaned. "You are so *cruel.*"

"Koby, do you have any idea where we are?"

"No, it is all unfamiliar. But if we find a motel, I think we should stop."

I smiled. "I think we took a wrong turn."

"In a metaphysical sense, there is no wrong turn."

"Yeah, but we're in a physical world, so how about we retrace our steps."

He smiled, but then his eyes narrowed. I was attuned enough to his nuances to recognize residual resentment. He was still smoldering. He said, "You know, in Israel, there aren't these racial problems."

"Yeah, well, we're not in Israel, we're in America. Welcome to the melting pot!"

42

If a chemist combined 115 degrees Fahrenheit with the accommodations of steerage, the result would be Cochise Penitentiary—a medium-security installation deep in the desert where the sands of the Mojave sank below sea level. The site was as fiery as the bowels of the earth, the surrounding terrain flat, bleak, and tan, broken up by occasional spindly cacti and roadkill. Brill and I had the luxury of doing most of the trip in an air-conditioned Ford Escort, but then the temperature needle started nudging the red zone. Since we weren't on a survival show and there was no million-dollar check waiting, the idea of being marooned in this godforsaken land wasn't at all pleasant. Brill turned off the air-conditioning and opened the windows.

Immediately, we were sandblasted by scorching air and grit. Brill went profane, pounding his fist on the dash. "Asshole couldn't have waited a couple months before he fucked up?"

"Asshole" was Joseph Nicholas Fedek. Like all rotten apples, he eventually made it to the compost pile, picked up on a B-and-E charge in Rampart Division, home of scandal and Dodger Stadium. And Brill had a point. The Inland Valley area in late August was hell.

"Look on the bright side," I said cheerfully. "Germando El Paso would probably give up a nut to get out of Cochise early. That gives us real bargaining power."

"What a dumb shit! All he had to do was stay clean for *six* weeks on a stupid traffic bust. The jerk plays hotshot dealing X from his County cell, then buys himself a year and a half of misery in this inferno."

"How did El Paso get the bag into County?"

"Rumor says his girlfriend sneaked it in way up in dark places."

"Didn't someone pat her down?"

"You take a peek; you don't fist fuck her. I can't believe I gave up my Saturday for *this!*"

"At least you're getting paid."

"Yeah, time-and-a-half along with a bad case of crotch rot."

He adjusted his butt in the seat. He wore a pair of ecru linen pants and a short-sleeved white shirt, both articles of clothing darkened with sweat stains. I had on a white blouse and a dark blue cotton skirt that fell below my knees. My hair was tied back, knotted into a tight braid. I looked like a parochial-school girl.

"That's the turnoff." I pointed to the sign.

Brill took a swig from his water bottle. We had two cases sitting on dry ice in the back. "I see, I see."

It took us another twenty minutes to arrive at the institution—a three-story cinder-block edifice surrounded by six guard towers and a sea of barbed wire. Cochise wasn't very big, and it didn't house the more violent criminals. It had an infirmary but no hospital and it didn't have a psycho ward. Whenever someone freaked, he was immediately transferred out to San Quentin or some other maximum-security facility.

We checked in with the parking-booth guard, who assigned Brill's Escort a space in a sizzling lot of dirt and pebbles. Asphalt in this heat would have been a tar pit.

"Keep the windows down," Brill told me. "Just remind me not to touch the steering wheel when we come back."

It took us about a half hour to go through all the sign-in procedures. We checked our weapons into a gun locker and walked through a double-door sally port into the main facilities. There was some minimal air-conditioning, but inside was still hot and dry and smelled of sweat, piss, and barely controlled fury. The cell doors were open, but the hallways were almost entirely empty. Most of the blue-shirted inmates lazed on their cots, staring at the ceiling, listening to the ball game, or playing a torpid game of solitaire.

Rest time, the guard explained.

He led us into the interview cell—hot and smelly—with a wall clock and a barred window showing a view of heat waves rising off the sand. The area had the requisite metal table and chairs, the furniture bolted into place. We sat and waited and drank tepid water.

Germando came in around ten minutes later, dressed in prison blues—a uniform not a lot different from Koby's blue scrubs, reminding me once again that it was all context. Sweat coated his face, and the tiger tattoo on his neck looked as if it were stalking prey in the humid jungles of Southeast Asia. El Paso's expression was one of contempt. He still had his dinky mustache and a plug of beard under his lower lip. He slouched in one of the metal chairs.

Brill gave him a cup of water.

El Paso didn't drink.

Brill rubbed his eyes. "This is the story. We picked up Juice Fedek, got him on a solid B-and-E, so he's going to do time. We're in the process of getting a warrant for his place. And when we do, we're going to find his gun. And then that means Juice is going to do lots of time and not in Cochise. He's going upstate to San Quentin. Because once we find the gun—and we will find the gun—we're going to connect it to an attempted-murder indictment. He's going away for a long time because the idiot was popping lead at a *cop*. And anyone associated with him is going away for a long time."

El Paso shrugged. "Wha' this have to do with me? I been here for the last two months."

It was my turn. "I was shot at by that bastard because he didn't want me looking into the Sarah Sanders rape. There was only one person who could have told him about my investigation. And that same person told Fedek what car to look out for."

A smile spread across El Paso's lips. "I don' know what you talk about."

"Then I'll make it clear. When I arrested you, you saw my friend drive away in his car. You noted the make and model. You told Fedek, your stepbrother, that I was investigating Sarah Sanders's rape and you told him what car to look for. You set me up!"

A smirk. "You *es* crazy. I thin' the heat is too much for your head."

"This is the thing, Germando." I gave him a venal smile. "Fedek is going to take you down. You know how I know this? Because I'm going to offer him a deal: immunity in the Sarah Sanders rape case to testify against you. That means, Germando, you're not going to serve your five to seven here in Cochise, which is primarily for drug dealers. You're going to the big-time ass-hole reamers."

"This is what *she* wants," Brill said. "I got other ideas. You interested in hearing about them?"

El Paso was silent. But his jumpy eyes told the story.

"Guess not," Brill said.

We both got up at the same time.

El Paso didn't move or speak.

We waited. Finally, I called out for the guard.

Still nothing.

The guard came.

Germando waited until the key was actually in the lock, the guard about to let us out, before he caved in. He said, "Wait a min . . . I listen."

My voice dripped contempt. "You had your chance, Germando. You blew it!"

"Wait, wait, wait!" He bolted up. "I listen now!"

"Sit down!" Brill ordered.

El Paso sat. "I listen now," he repeated. Chastened to the core.

Brill blew out air and looked at me. "What do you think?"

"I think we should leave! I didn't want to come here in the first place."

"Well, we're here," Brill said. "Might as well talk to him." He looked at the guard. "Sorry to bother you."

"No problem." The khaki-uniformed guard walked away.

We took up our seats at the table, all of us sipping what tasted like slag water. Brill turned to me. "Go."

"Me?"

"Yeah, you."

"Okay," I said, "there was once this retarded girl—"

"I don' do nothin'."

"You gonna let me finish?"

He was silent.

"There was once this retarded girl," I told him. "She was gang-raped and her retarded boyfriend was beaten up and left in a garbage can for trash collection." I leaned over. "If the DA offers Fedek a chance to drop a charge of attempted murder on a cop in exchange for a single count of rape and testimony about the others who were there, guess what Fedek's going to do?"

"I no touch her!"

"So this is what I want you to do," I said. "I want you to tell us about the rape."

"What do I get?"

"First we have to hear your story," Brill said. "But before we hear you, we've got to let you know that you can have an attorney present because we will use whatever we want to use from your statement. But once you get your attorney, the control factor moves from us to your lawyer. Then things start slipping away because that means we've got to bring in our lawyers. Then it's the lawyers talking to lawyers instead of us talking to you."

"I don' need no lawyer. Look what happen when I have a lawyer."

"A very good point," I told him. "You're here and he isn't."

Brill said, "So if you talk to us, you've got to sign this paper saying that we told you about your rights in English and you read your rights in English and Spanish and agree to waive them."

"Wha' paper?"

"This paper." Brill showed him the card. "You've got to sign it right here. That says you agree to talk to us without an attorney.

And you also understand that what you tell us could be used against you in court."

"And it also says that if you want an attorney, you can ask for one at any time," I said. "But like Detective Brill told you, once you've asked for an attorney, it's out of our hands."

"I don' need no lawyer," El Paso said.

Brill took out a pen. "Sign here."

El Paso signed the waiver card.

"Germando, I need the pen back."

El Paso returned the pen, unhappy because he'd lost a potential weapon. Brill pocketed the card. "What happened with Sarah Sanders?"

"The retard *muchacha.*"

"Yes," I said. "What'd you do to her?"

"I don' touch dat *muchacha.* Juice do her, I no do her."

"Who else?" Brill said.

"Leo."

"Leo who?"

"Leo dat's Juice's friend."

"Last name?" I asked.

El Paso shrugged.

"Do better," I told him.

"Leo Shithead . . . I call him dat."

Leo's last name was Chatlin. I let it go. "Who else?"

"Pepe Renaldes."

"I don't think so. Try again."

"Wha'?" El Paso said. "Wha' you mean?"

Brill looked at me with confusion. I raised my eyebrows, feeling my heart take off. I had met El Paso and I had met Pepe Renaldes and I knew in my gut who was the rapist and who was the lookout. I was taking a tremendous chance, because I hadn't cleared any of this with Brill for obvious reasons. I couldn't tell him that I'd met with Renaldes behind his back. I said, "One more time. Who raped her?"

"Dat's wha' I say," El Paso replied. "Joey Fedek, Leo Shithead, and Pepe Renald—"

"No, no, no," I said louder. "If you're going to give me bullshit, El Paso, I'm going to walk from this."

"I don' know wha' you want!" El Paso yelled. "I tell you the truth!"

"Let's start from the beginning," I tried again.

Brill said, "A word with you, Decker?"

"In a minute," I told him. My heart was pumping out of my throat. Abruptly, I pounded the table. "You think I'm *dumb,*

Germando? You think I don't do my home-work? You think I don't talk to other people including *you-know-who* to get their side of the story before I come up here to this hell-hole?" I was trying to avoid Brill's burning eyes. "One more time, El Paso, and this time I want the truth. It's going to come down to that if you want a deal. I want to know who *raped* Sarah Sanders."

I locked the man in eye-to-eye combat. He finally got the point. He rubbed his forehead and sat back in his chair. "I don' say nothin'."

I said, "Then you'll go down for rape, bud."

His head sprang up. "And if I say things?"

"We talk to the DA," I told him. "Maybe we can swing a lesser charge of sexual molestation, maybe add another twelve months here in Cochise. That's a lot better than five-plus in San Quentin."

Germando stroked his chin, eyes moving between Justice and me. I think he misinter-preted Justice's fury—directed at me—as be-ing meant for him. "Hokay. It was Juice, Leo, and me dat did her. Pepe was lookout."

"Much better." I didn't dare so much as

glance at Brill. I couldn't face him. "Tell us the story."

"Nothin' to tell. First Leo and me hold the boy, an' Juice does her. Then we get tired of him because he screams. So Juice beat the shit outta him and dump him in de trash. Then I do the girl. Then Leo do the girl. Then we leave." He shrugged. "Dat's it."

I finally screwed up the nerve to turn to Brill. "A word."

Brill was livid. If I had had any hopes of his recommending me for the Detectives squad, they were squashed by now. We asked for the guard.

"Wha' you doing?" El Paso bolted up.

"We'll be back," I told him.

The guard let us out. We spoke in a private interview room as hot as a sauna because it had walls instead of bars. Brill wiped sweat off his face with a towel, trying to find the right words. "What did you just pull?"

I said, "I think I can get Pepe Renaldes to corroborate the story."

"Yeah, I figured that out, Decker. You went and talked to Renaldes without telling me—"

"I never mentioned Sarah Sanders to him."

"I told you *not* to talk to him. Stone told you *not* to talk to him. The DA told you *not* to talk to him."

"Actually, it was just *implied* that I shouldn't talk to him."

Brill almost spat at me. "I just drove down here for nothing because *you* just fucked up the case."

"I didn't want Renaldes to go down for a rape he didn't commit."

"You fucked up *everything!*" His eyes tore into mine. "Do you have a single brain cell in your head, Decker?"

I crossed my arms, my eyes slicing into Justice's orbs. My voice was low and menacing. "Someone shot at me, Brill. You think I'm going to wait around and let some dickhead DA call the moves when it's my life on the line? So yeah, I went and talked to Renaldes. I wanted to know who was using me for target practice. And if he couldn't tell me that, at least maybe he'd lead me to the Nova. Which he did."

"You're an idiot!"

"You say idiot, I say survivor. The tag line here is I'm pretty sure I can get Renaldes to roll against Fedek and Chatlin. If we get Renaldes and El Paso telling the same story, we can probably lock up Fedek and Chatlin for a very long time with charges of rape and attempted murder of a police officer, and that's what *I* want because one or both of those assholes tried to kill me!"

I was covered in ripe sweat. Brill was still glaring at me, but the intensity was gone. He said, "So what do we do with the DA?"

"We tell him that we got El Paso to confess and name names. Then we tell him that we're going to visit Renaldes and bring him on board. We know he'll cooperate because he didn't participate in the rape. So that means we've got El Paso's and Renaldes's testimonies against Fedek and Chatlin. And we can tell the DA that we found out about Renaldes because El Paso gave him up. That's it! Done! Okay?"

"No. Not okay. If you ever, ever, ever pull shit like this again, you're going to be writing traffic tickets for a very long time."

"I am duly warned—"

"I mean it, Decker!"

I lowered my eyes, then returned them to Justice's face. "I know you do. Thank you for going with me on this."

"Who said I'm going with you?" The rage had returned to his eyes. "If I back you up, you'll owe me big time."

I spoke softly and with deference. "I know and I will return the favor. I am nothing if not loyal."

"Maybe sooner than you think." His eyes moved up and down my body.

"No, no, no," I said. "That is out of the question."

A smile came across his lips. "What on earth are you talking about, Decker?"

I wasn't amused. "Sorry. My head's a little scrambled."

"I think so." He rubbed his forehead. "If shit falls, I'm not getting dirty."

"I'll take the crap."

"For a two-year vet, you've got steel. I'm surprised." Brill's eyes tore into my face. "You know what I think? I think you had help with Renaldes. And I think you know what kind of help I'm talking about. Or should I say *who* I'm talking about."

"And I think you should ask El Paso about Fedek and Belinda Syracuse."

A blank look.

"The hit-and-run I witnessed?"

"Oh, that." He was taken aback. "Why

would Fedek have anything to do with Belinda Syracuse?"

"Both Belinda and Sarah Sanders lived at Fordham Community Center. Maybe Sarah told Belinda about the rape. Maybe Belinda was about to go to the cops."

"You have nothing to back that up. The hit-and-run was a different vehicle and a different MO. Why would a shit like Fedek take out Belinda with a car instead of a gun?"

"You're probably right, Justice, but it's still a remote possibility. Just throw it at El Paso and Renaldes and let them deny it."

"You're full of good ideas today." His expression was sour. "Why the *fuck* am I putting up with you?"

"Maybe because you want me for your partner instead of that piece of dead meat you've been riding with for the last eighteen months."

"Henry's not dead meat."

"Henry is two months from retirement. When was the last time he put himself on the line?"

Justice frowned. "I don't want you. You're too damn impetuous. You need to slow down."

"So be my rabbi, Justice." I sighed. "Forget it. We'd better get back to El Paso."

"Yeah, we've been gone so long, he probably thinks we're doing it." He smiled. "There's still time."

I held in a scream. "Brill, stop trying to get play. I've got a very serious boyfriend; you've got a wife; let's both be constructive, all right?"

He continued to stare at me.

"You want me to partner with you. I'm dying to do it. But if I have to worry about this kind of garbage, I'm going to ask for a transfer. And then they'll ask why."

He thought about it and shrugged. "You still owe me."

"I know, I know. . . ." I patted his shoulder. "Patience, Brill. The time will come. It always does. Shall we get a move on?"

He pointed to the door. "Ladies first."

I went first.

It was nice to know that chivalry wasn't dead. It just had been redefined.

43

As summer waned, bleeding out the last bits of extended daylight, I found that time took on an urgency of purpose, all the pressure self-imposed, of course, because no one was rushing me to the next step. But there I was on the threshold, one foot in the air, ready to cross the line. When I pulled up at my father's house that radiant Sunday morning, I still had reservations. Someone, please tell me what important decisions were ever made easily?

He answered the door, a surprised look on his face. "Hi, baby. Did you tell me you were coming?"

"Nope. This is a pop-in, one of those times I get to catch you in dirty clothes and in need of a shave."

He stroked his chin. "The shave, yes; the clothes are clean. Come in, honey."

Dad was in a white T-shirt and jeans. I wore white cotton pants and a deep green blouse—the type of outfit that could be for business or pleasure. I continued to stand outside. "How are you doing?"

"I'm fine." He was perplexed. "Any reason you're still at the door?"

"How about we take a walk?"

My father's expression turned more quizzical. "If you want privacy, I'm the only one home."

"In that case . . ." I came into the living room—quiet and peaceful. "Where is everyone?"

"Rina and the kids went to an Israel rally in town."

"And you?"

"What can I say? My Zionistic fervor can't compete with Sunday baseball." He smiled. "Sometimes I just need to do something mindless. Let someone else handle the strategy while I criticize."

"Boy, do I know that feeling. You work hard, Dad, you're entitled."

The Loo studied my face. "Cindy, you look bothered. Is everything all right?"

"Great. I haven't had a street dream in two months. Pretty good, no?"

Decker frowned. "Very good, except I didn't know you were having them."

"Well, they're gone, so why worry you?" I smiled. "No feedback yet on my application to Detectives. But at this point, I'll assume that no news is good news."

"It's early, and by that I mean early in your career. If it comes, great. If not, don't be the least discouraged, especially not after what you did with those punks Chatlin and Fedek."

"It was Brill's bust."

"It was your legwork. Even Brill's not denying it."

"Yeah, Brill's been okay."

"Sit down."

"You know, I'd rather stand. I'm a little antsy."

My father studied me. "If it isn't work, it must be personal. Is everything all right with Koby?"

"Great." I didn't make eye contact with him. "We're planning some vacation time together. We're going away."

"Fabulous. Where?"

"Israel."

"What?" Dad was horrified. "*Now?*"

"Yes, now." I took in Decker's worried eyes. "Koby wants me to meet his family. *I* want to meet his family."

Decker was stunned. "And this can't wait until calmer times?"

"No, because who knows the future? Besides, I've survived bullets and maniacs before."

"And that's supposed to calm me down?"

I took my father's hand. "I *need* to do this." My smile was plaintive. "Daddy, I think he's the one." I took in a breath and let it out. "I mean, I *know* he's the one."

"Oh my, my." The Loo's eyes abruptly moistened. "Are you sure?"

"I can't picture my future without him. So I guess that's that."

Decker covered his mouth with his fist. Then he dropped his hand and managed a wistful smile. "He's a great guy, Cindy. A great guy and a good man. You chose well." His hug was brief but with feeling. "I love you, Princess."

"I love you, too, Daddy. Nobody will ever replace you in my heart. Lots of guys out there in life, but a girl only has one father."

"You deserve the best." His voice was

choked. "You tell him that if he ever, *ever* gives you a hard time, I carry a gun and know how to use it."

"Daddy, *I* carry a gun."

My father laughed and so did I. Then he turned serious. "When are you leaving?"

"We'll be in Israel for Rosh Hashanah—that's the main reason we're going right now—but we'll be back before Yom Kippur." I shook my head. "Listen to me, planning my schedule around Jewish holidays. I'm beginning to sound like you."

"There are parallels in our lives," my father noted.

I considered his words. "Yes, you're right. Except Koby's more flexible than Rina. He may not go out to a restaurant or a movie on *Shabbat,* but he does drive and turn on lights . . . watch TV if there's a play-off game. He'll even work if the hospital's short staffed."

"He's still a far cry from what you were raised with."

"That's true. So I suppose some of your current lifestyle has rubbed off. Keeping kosher doesn't seem as daunting as it once did. Of course, people often revert to what they grew up with when they have children.

So we'll see what Koby's like when the occasion arises."

"You have *plenty* of time for that."

I bit my lower lip to keep from smiling. I had hit a sore spot. The Loo wasn't ready for the role of grandpa. I said, "Can we talk business for a moment?"

Dad turned all cop. "Of course. What's wrong?"

"Something's really bothering me. I figured I'd bug you about it."

"Go on."

"I've got these loose ends, an unsolved crime that at first I thought was connected to Sarah Sanders's rape. I thought it might have been the work of Joseph Fedek or one of his cohorts. But after talking to them, grilling them extensively, I don't think Fedek was involved."

"What crime are you talking about?"

"Belinda Syracuse. The hit-and-run that Koby and I witnessed."

"Yeah, yeah. How's that going?"

"It isn't. It's dead in the water."

"They've got the car, don't they?"

"They hauled it in a long time ago. They've even got some DNA from a blood smear on the license plate. But they don't have a suspect, so there's nothing to match."

Decker held out his hands and shrugged.

"I went to Fordham Communal Center the other day. I saw a picture of her—Belinda Syracuse. Weird to see what she looked like with her face whole."

My father nodded.

"I went there to check in with Mr. Klinghoffner, to see if by any chance David Tyler had contacted him. He hadn't, of course."

"Still looking for him?"

"Off and on. Anyway, Klinghoffner had pictures of both Belinda and David Tyler posted on his wall. Like a memorial."

He waited. "And?"

"I suddenly remembered seeing her before, when she was alive. The first time I went to Fordham to find the information that led to Sarah Sanders's discovery, Belinda Syracuse was working in the backyard garden."

"She lived there, Cindy."

"I know. But it was something else. The way she looked when I saw her. She had this longing in her eyes . . . like a girl in the throes of heartbreak. I can't get that expression out of my mind."

I looked around the living room, shoving my hands in my pants pockets.

"I have this gnawing in my gut about it. Like I'm on top of it, but I have no evidence. Just this vibration . . . like she's talking to me."

"Tell me about it."

"Okay. Here goes. There's this real obnoxious guy who works at Fordham. His name is Buck. The first time I went there, we started talking—Buck and me—and I saw Belinda Syracuse staring at us through the window, holding a hoe, her nose pressed against the pane of glass. With this hurt look in her eyes . . ."

I was seeing the memory as I spoke.

"This man Buck, he turned around and smiled when he saw her. Then he got up to talk to her. It was completely out of character."

"I don't understand."

"He's an *asshole.* Why was he being so nice to her?"

"Maybe he's not as big an asshole as you think."

"Or maybe he can be charming when he wants to be . . . when there's something in it for him."

"And your point is . . ."

He knew what my point was, but he wanted me to tell him. "Let me see if I can formulate some theories." I collected my thoughts. "When we last talked to Sarah Sanders, she was embarrassed when talking about sex."

"Yes."

"And we thought she was sitting on something else."

"Yes."

"Do you think that she and David . . . Do you think that they would have sex with each other without having had it before?"

"Absolutely. It's a natural thing. Being mentally disabled doesn't mean your plumbing doesn't work."

I didn't say anything.

"Did you need someone showing you how to do it? I didn't."

"Daddy, we knew about sex way before the actual feelings came about. We knew about it because we're of normal intelligence and we had information about it that we could comprehend."

"They have sex education in the center. You told me that yourself."

"Very clinical stuff, Dad, not the same peer-to-peer giggling and gossiping and bragging that most of us go through. I was just thinking that maybe . . . maybe Sarah Sanders had had experience before David."

"That the gang rape wasn't her first *forced* sexual experience."

"Why not?" I exclaimed. "Maybe that's what Sarah Sanders was sitting on. That someone in the center had been molesting her. It wouldn't be the first time a retarded girl has been taken advantage of sexually. And it could be that it was more of a seduction than a forced sexual encounter because that would make Sarah reluctant to give him up. Because she might have felt that she had some complicity in it."

Decker said, "And you like this obnoxious guy for the molester?"

"Yes, because he truly is odious."

"Molesters are often charming, Cindy."

"That's exactly what I'm saying! He's a jerk, but he was nice to Belinda. Why?"

"Okay. Even if he was molesting Sarah, what does that have to do with the hit-and-run?"

"Now, this is where it's getting a bit . . . speculative. Maybe Buck was also molesting Belinda."

"Because he got up and talked to her?"

"Just hear me out, okay?"

"Go on."

"Buck knew we were talking to Sarah. And he knew we were investigating a gang rape. If Buck was molesting her, maybe he thought his molestation would come out in the course of our investigation. And if it did, then the other girl, Belinda, maybe she'd also have a story to tell. Now could be he figures he can handle Sarah Sanders, especially since at that time she wasn't regarded in a positive light. She had abandoned her baby. You know, his word against hers. Sarah wasn't much of a threat. But if there had been others . . ."

Decker didn't speak.

"Okay, it's loony. Forget it."

"It's not loony; it's a . . . theory."

"Dad, I have a good relationship with Louise Sanders now. I set her up with David Tyler's conservator, and she's getting a little money for Ella—that's the baby's name. Actually, it's Cinderella. Louise let Sarah name her daughter. Anyway, David's lawyer gave her enough money to hire a nanny, so I'm definitely on Louise's good side. Plus, Koby and I have visited them several times. Sarah *adores* Koby. I think he reminds her of David. So there's a lot more trust than when we first interviewed her."

"Perfect," Decker said. "Go for it."

I exhaled. "I'm still inexperienced in these kinds of things. I'd like a little help."

"No problem, pumpkin. I have time. Let's go check it out."

"I know I'm bordering on fiction here. Still, aren't you the one who always said trust your gut?"

"Especially in this crazy world. Let me change and I'll leave a note for Rina. Then we'll be off."

"Great." I smiled. "Thanks so much."

"For what?"

"For coming with me. But mostly for listening to me."

"Are you kidding?" He tousled my hair. "Give me a minute."

"Take your time." I smiled and really meant it, because Dad had this expression, this absolutely *glorious* expression, of respect in his eyes—a look that said more than a million words.

▼

I got a hug from Louise. "Come in, come in. It's always nice when you drop by."

"You remember my father, don't you, Louise?"

"Yes, of course. Please come in. . . . Is it Sergeant Decker?"

"Lieutenant," I corrected. We walked inside.

Over the past months, Louise Sanders's living room had been taken over by baby paraphernalia. Plush toys had replaced the throw pillows on the brown leather couch. The coffee table was crowded with plastic squeaky animals and baby books. A mesh playpen stood next to the piano, milk bottles all over the place. Still, the space was pleasant, brimming over with light and mid-morning summer heat. The windows were open, but there was no discernible breeze.

Louise had highlighted her gray hair with some blond streaks. She'd also dropped a couple of pounds. She was taking care of herself and that was good. Maybe I was flattering myself, but I liked to think that I played a small part in that piece of theater.

Today, Louise wore denim shorts and a boat-neck white shirt, sandals on her feet.

"Can I get either of you anything to drink?"

Before I could answer, Sarah walked in. Her blond hair had been cut short for the summer, so now she was all cheeks and face, all round and pink. She wore a loose blue cotton dress; her fingernails and toenails were painted silver. Her eyes narrowed as she looked at me, then around the room. "Where's"—she struggled to get the words out—"Where's . . . Ko-by?"

"Sarah, say hello first," Louise told her.

"Hello."

"Hello, Sarah," I answered. "Koby is out running this morning."

"Where's he running to?"

I smiled. "He's running a race."

"Did he win?"

"It's not that kind of race. You run it to see how fast you can run. Today, he's running a twenty K. That means he's running for twelve miles."

Her mouth opened. "That's a lot of miles."

"Yes, it is."

"You didn't go with him?" Dad asked me.

"They started at seven to beat the heat.

Thanks, but I'll pass." To Sarah, I said, "Is Ella sleeping?"

Sarah nodded.

Louise said, "I just put her down—"

"*I* put her down," Sarah piped in.

"Right." Louise gave a half smile. "She won't be up for a couple of hours."

"That's okay, Louise. We actually wanted to talk to Sarah . . . if that's all right."

The older woman frowned. "What about?"

I glanced at my father. He had changed from a T-shirt to a polo shirt, but he still wore jeans. I thought that gave him a casual touch. He said, "Just to clear up a couple of things."

"Maybe we should all sit down," I said.

Louise started tossing the plush toys into the playpen to clear up room on the couch. "Have a seat."

"You sit, too, Louise," Decker said. "This could concern you as well."

"What's this all about?" Louise sat.

"I'm not sure," I told her. "But I need you to trust me. 'Cause this was all my idea."

"What is going on?" She put her hand to her heart. "Something *else?*"

My father shrugged. I said, "It may take a little time, so please be patient. Because I want to do this right."

Louise looked at me, unhappy, but then she ultimately nodded for me to go ahead.

My father smiled at Sarah. "So you like Koby?"

Sarah nodded.

"I like him, too."

Sarah nodded.

"Why do you like him?"

Sarah giggled. "'Cause he's . . . cute."

Decker smiled. "I'll tell you why I like him. I like him because he's nice."

Sarah nodded.

"Do you ever play games with him?"

Sarah thought a moment. "Sometimes."

"What kind of games?"

"Ball."

"What kind of ball?"

"Handball."

"On the garage door?"

She hugged herself and smiled. "I always win."

"So you must be really good at handball."

Sarah giggled.

"What other games do you do with Koby?"

She thought a long time. "Once, he took me to the high school to play basketball. We brang my handball. I made one basket. He had to pick me up. I was too short."

Decker nodded. "How'd you get to the high school?"

Sarah seemed confused.

"Did you drive in a car or walk or take a bus?"

"We walked."

"You walked."

"Yes."

"Did you have to cross streets to get there?"

"Yes."

"Did Koby hold your hand when you crossed the street?"

Sarah thought a moment, then nodded.

"That's good. What other games did Koby play with you?"

Sarah thought about the question. "Sometimes we drew squiggles."

"Squiggles are fun. Do you like to draw?"

"Sometimes."

"Me too. What else did you do with Koby?"

Sarah shrugged. "I don't know . . . just stuff."

"Did he ever play . . . like tag with you? Or maybe a tickling game?"

I shot a glance at my father. He ignored me.

Abruptly, the girl grew melancholy, very silent. Louise and I exchanged glances. I shrugged. An unexpected sweat came over my body.

Dad said, "You know, tickle your ribs or something like that?"

Sarah waited for what seemed like an eternity, then shook her head. "I . . ." She fell silent.

"What, Sarah?" Dad asked.

"He sometimes tickled Ella's foot. I wanted him to tickle *me.* So I asked him to stop tickling Ella and tickle *me.*"

"And what did Koby say when you asked him to tickle you?"

She squeezed her eyes shut. "He said that big boys don't tickle big girls unless they're boyfriend and girlfriend." Sarah opened her eyes and glanced at me. Then she rubbed her arms. "I asked him to be *my boyfriend,* but he said he was already *Cindy's boyfriend.*" Her eyes watered. "So he didn't tickle me."

Decker nodded. "That makes sense."

She turned her head away. Obviously, it didn't make sense to her.

Decker said, "What about David? Did he ever tickle you?"

Her voice grew quiet. "Sometimes."

"But David was your boyfriend, right?"

She nodded.

"Did you like it when he tickled you?"

Again she nodded.

"So it was okay with you that David tickled you."

"Yes."

"Did any other big boy ever tickle you?"

She eyed Decker with suspicion and didn't answer.

"You know . . ." Dad smiled. "Tickle you to make you laugh?"

She maintained silence. She wasn't as slow as her tested intelligence indicated.

Dad said, "Let's talk about David some more. David used to tickle you, right?"

She nodded.

"And that was okay . . . when David touched you."

"Sometimes I liked it. Sometimes I didn't."

"When didn't you like it?"

"You know"—her face got very red—
"when he did sex."

Louise was about to talk, but she managed to control herself. I put my hand on her
knee and patted it. She eyed me for a moment; then she tried a stiff smile that died.

Decker said, "That's right, Sarah. You told
me that you didn't like the sex at all."

She nodded.

"I want you to think very hard, Sarah. Can
you do that for me?"

She didn't answer.

"I want you to think about the times you
had sex with David. Did you ever tell him not
to have the sex with you?"

Her eyes were downcast. "No."

"That's okay, that you didn't tell him no.
But I am curious. If you didn't like it, why did
you do it . . . the sex?"

Sarah didn't speak for a long time. I was
waiting for my father to repeat the question,
but he didn't. Finally, she said, "Because he
was my boyfriend."

"Ah . . . so it's okay to have sex with your
boyfriend?"

"You have to do sex with your boyfriend.
If you don't, he isn't your boyfriend."

"Ah. *Now* I understand. Did David tell you that?"

She didn't answer. I eyed Louise sitting as stiff as steel, kneading hands that should have been resting in her lap.

"Someone else?"

She was silent.

From the other room, Ella let go with a few halfhearted cries. Maybe we were talking too loudly.

Louise got up quickly. "Excuse me."

Sarah started to stand, but her sister told her to stay put.

"But it's *my* baby," Sarah protested.

"I'll bring her in if she's up, all right? Just sit, okay?"

Sarah didn't argue, but she remained sulky. Decker waited until Louise was gone. Then he smiled and said, "You know, a beautiful girl like you, I bet you had . . . a hundred boyfriends."

Sarah's face softened. "No."

"Fifty?"

"No."

"Twenty-five?"

She attempted to hold back a smile. "No."

"But more than one. I'm sure of it."

She gave a half smile. "Maybe."

"And your other boyfriends . . . did they tickle you?"

The smile widened. "Maybe."

"Maybe, huh?" Dad made a mock skeptical face. In a singsong voice, he said, "I bet they did."

Sarah giggled.

"Did they also do sex with you?"

Instantly, the merriment died.

"Sarah," Decker said. "Remember we talked before. And I told you how it's okay to tell secrets if they're bad secrets."

She didn't speak.

"If you had sex with a man, it's okay to tell me. Even if he told you not to tell."

She turned her head away.

"Please, Sarah. You've got to trust me. You can tell me."

"But he was my boyfriend." Tears were in her eyes. "Then he said he didn't want to be my boyfriend anymore." Wet streaks rolled down her cheeks.

"Who, Sarah?" Decker asked. "Who didn't want to be your boyfriend anymore?"

Sarah shook her head. "I don't want to tell you."

"Sarah, you don't have to keep a bad secret."

"I don't have to, but I *want* to."

Decker glanced at me and shook his head. "Okay, Sarah. If you don't want to talk, you don't have to. But if you ever change your mind, I'll be happy to listen to you."

She nodded, and for a minute, I thought she might actually relent. Instead, she got up. "I want to see Ella."

My father's words rolled through my brain: Molesters are usually *charming.* They often inspire an unbelievable amount of loyalty, enough trust to get a retarded girl to follow the molester into Hollywood and walk alone in the middle of the night. I still retained my last image of Belinda, crossing the street with her head down, her demeanor so forlorn. A disconsolate figure mowed down by some evil force. Someone had to bury this child properly!

"Sarah," I called out.

She turned around.

"How about this?" I suggested. "How about if you tell Louise?"

Sarah fixed her eyes on me. She remained stubborn and silent.

My last-ditch effort. "Well, how about if you tell Koby?"

Slowly, she began to smile. Then she began to giggle. "Well . . . *maybe* Koby."

44

By midmorning, the sky had turned sooty gray, the sun blazing down on the top of my head. It was only one-and-a-half blocks to the Strip, but in the heat it felt like a mile in the Sahara. There was a small café at the intersection of Sunset and Willem. Dad and I settled in at a back table, which was serviced by a red-haired waitress with a crew cut, droopy eyes, and an open mouth. She got the order wrong: a pretty slick trick because all we had asked for were coffee variations. Then she realized she was bringing the wrong java to the wrong table. A minute later, she fixed her mistake.

"Who gets the latte?"

"Me," I told her.

She served me the latte. "Who gets the black coffee?"

My father was the only other one at the table. He looked at me and winked. "Right here, please."

"Six bucks."

"I pay now?" Dad said.

"Now or later."

Decker frowned, then took out a ten. "It's all yours. Just give us some privacy."

She stared at the bill. "Okay. Are you a cop or something?"

The Loo took out his badge. "Yes."

"Wow! Neat!"

"Privacy?" Decker repeated.

"Yeah. Sure."

"That means you leave."

"Oh. Right."

Eventually, she left. Dad turned to me. "I'm reluctant to get Koby involved."

"Why?" I said. "He'll do it—"

"I know he'll do it. That's not the problem. He's a nurse; that's the problem. As a health-care professional, once she tells him about any kind of molestation, he's obligated to report it, just like we would be as cops. The difference is, if he reports it, the case jumps into the system and it's out of our hands. Yeah, we could get involved, but it would be messy. Someone would probably call in DSS. Then some social worker starts talking to Sarah and before long the whole thing about Sarah abandoning the baby comes up. Didn't you tell me that Louise went through hurdles to get legal custody of Ella?"

"Yes."

"Who knows? This might jeopardize the custody decision. Once it's out, we open a big can of worms, Cindy."

I hadn't thought of that.

"Furthermore," Dad continued, "a good lawyer can claim that Koby is biased against Buck or whoever it is, and he'd have a point. It would look like a setup. And in a way it would be a setup because we dragged Koby into it. I'm not saying we won't use him. But if we do it without considering the consequences, the perp could slip away."

"But if we don't jump soon, Daddy, Sarah could change her mind about talking to Koby. Then we're back to square one. Aren't you the one who told me to just go for it?"

"Cindy, this isn't someone who's pointing

a gun at you. This is a crime that happened maybe a year ago—"

· "Belinda Syracuse happened only a few months ago."

"And that's another thing. Even if Sarah was being molested, you have nothing to tie that to Belinda Syracuse's hit-and-run."

"We have DNA on the car. If Buck molested Sarah, we could arrest him and demand a DNA sample."

"Why would the DA bother with a DNA sample? Sarah's molestation isn't a recent rape where there's evidence. It's he says, she says. We have to show a link to connect the molester to the hit-and-run, if there even is a molester. The only thing we do know is that if Sarah tells Koby about any kind of impropriety, it's all over. So we've got to map out the contingencies before Sarah makes the confession."

"But Sarah is the case," I said.

Decker said, "No, Sarah *isn't* the case, Cindy. The DNA from the blood smear on the license plate is the case. Our first priority is to see if we can get a matchup. *If* we do get a match and *if* it is Buck, then we have Buck associated with the car. Now that *still* doesn't place him at the crime. But it will be enough to get us a search warrant for his house and start a file on him. From there, we can probably get his phone records, go through his papers, start asking around town for witnesses who may have seen Buck and Belinda together the night of the murder. *That's* our best bet. And even if people did see them together, Buck can always say that he was just trying to be a nice guy to Belinda, much in the way Koby was just being nice to Sarah."

"Yeah, I was wondering where you were going with that line of questioning."

"I know I made you nervous. I brought up Koby for a couple of reasons. One, to get rapport with Sarah. She obviously likes Koby and I knew I could build on that. But also, I wanted to show you how easy it is to screw up a molestation case, how easy it is to get the facts wrong if you don't know what you're doing. You start saying things like he took her away from home to get her alone. Then he lifted her up to the basketball hoop ostensibly to make a shot, but really he wanted to touch her or look up her dress. Then he held her hand—"

"He was helping her across the *street,* for God's sake!"

Decker said, "Cynthia, I'm aware that Koby's not a child molester. And the mere fact that I can get you rattled so easily shows how simple it is to throw out false allegations. Koby knew exactly what he was doing with Sarah. Why? Because he's a male who works almost exclusively with kids and women, and has probably been trained in how to respond to sexual overtures. His answer to Sarah's request to get tickled was a good one. He refused to engage in any kind of dubious physical contact with her, even if it meant hurting Sarah's feelings. When you question witnesses, you've got to go in without a bias. Which is why I don't want Sarah talking to him. We've got a bias."

I was frustrated. "So what do we do?"

Decker furrowed his brow. "You really hate this guy Buck, don't you?"

"Dad, I don't know him well enough to truly hate him." I sipped my latte. "But I would like to remind you that there were other deaths that resulted from the hit-and-run, including a baby. Whoever killed Belinda is responsible for multiple deaths."

"You've exchanged angry words with him?"

"Yeah, I kind of browbeat him, but then I apologized."

Dad's eyes widened. "Really?"

"Actually, yes. Afterward, we began to talk. He knows I'm suspicious of him."

"Why's that?"

"Because I asked him where he was the night Belinda was murdered. It was a throw-away comment at the time. I wish I had taken him more seriously."

"Where was he?"

"Home with his dog, watching a movie." I shrugged. "He actually seemed to be enjoying the questions. I think they made him feel like a big shot instead of the bug that he is."

"Interesting." Decker smoothed his mustache. "So this is what you do, Cindy. You call him up and ask him out for coffee to go over the night again with him."

I was confused. "Warn him that we still consider him a suspect?"

"Then be smart about it. Be casual. Whose case is the hit-and-run?"

"Brill's."

"Great. I'll talk to him and we'll get the details nailed down. But it'll go like this. You ask him to meet you anywhere they serve coffee exclusively in paper cups. Run a few questions by him. Generic questions. Keep it light. Even flirt a little. Then when you're done, offer to throw away his cup for him. Don't wait for an answer, just pick it up and head for the garbage. Brill will arrange to have a team near the trash with a hidden video camera on you as backup so no one can say that you planted evidence. You throw *your* cup away, but drop his cup in an evidence bag that'll be placed right near the garbage can. If the cup's still partially full, make sure it doesn't spill over the rim. And whatever you do, don't get your cups mixed up."

I sat up. "His saliva will be on the cup. We get his DNA."

"Depends on the residue . . . how much he drools when he drinks. Wouldn't hurt if you wore something sexy."

"Like fishnets?"

"A little more subtle for professionalism."

"You really think you can get his DNA from a coffee cup?"

"It's worth a shot." Decker sat back in his chair. "Let me have a minute to clear my thoughts."

"Take your time."

He did. A few minutes later, he straightened. "Okay. This is the approach. We have two independent investigations going on. One is Sarah Sanders and her dark secret. We suspect molestation, but we don't know for sure and we don't know who's involved. She won't talk to us, but she'll talk to Koby. When the timing's right, you or Brill will talk to Koby and explain that we suspect something's amiss and would he mind talking to Sarah about it. You don't mention, hint at, or imply that this has anything to do with Belinda Syracuse, okay? Because as of right now, it doesn't."

"Got it."

"In the meantime," Decker said, "you, Cindy, have not forgotten about poor Belinda. You witnessed the accident, and it still haunts you."

"Actually, that's the truth."

"Then you don't have to fake anything to convince Brill of your sincerity. You know you have DNA and a partial print as evidence but no one to connect it to. You remember Belinda's brother saying that someone from the center was supposed to pick up Belinda and give her a ride back. Now, you checked out the center's phone records, but of course nothing popped, nothing fit. And you know you can't check personal phone records because that's trampling on Fifth Amendment rights. But you're slowly going down the list of people who might have had contact with her, starting with Klinghoffner."

"Are you serious?"

"I know you don't think it's him, but start with him. Do the exact thing with Klinghoffner that you're going to do with Buck."

"Take him out for coffee."

"Exactly. That way, you don't show prejudice. Then do Buck; then do anyone else who works there—start from the top dog, down to the lowly maintenance man, and you include the women because you haven't any idea if this is a molestation or not. You can collect paper cups and use them as evidence without asking permission from the suspects because they gave you permission to throw them away, ceding the right of private ownership. The cups are now public property."

"Is the Department going to pay for all this DNA testing?"

"A very valid question. The hit-and-run was gruesome and a baby died, so maybe."

Decker held up a finger. "The main thing is we have to set it up without bias. This way, Koby doesn't know what you're doing, and you don't know what Sarah Sanders told him. It's all timing—like an orchestra. Strings can't come in too early, oboes can't miss the beat, or you have a mess instead of music. They don't call it conducting an investigation for nothing."

"You're a genius."

"Be thankful that brains are inherited."

▼

They had decided on an afternoon tea because tea was more casual than dinner.

This was the menu.

Tray one: assorted finger sandwiches— egg salad, lox, tuna, cucumber with toma- toes, and cheese.

Tray two: finger food, including dainty bite-size potato knishes, miniature spinach quiches, vegetarian egg rolls, and fried pot stickers. Accompanying these edibles would be a soy sauce, a sweet-and-sour sauce, and ketchup.

Trays three and four: assorted breads, including but not limited to croissants, brioches, seed rolls, minibagels, olive and basil bread, and a caraway-seed rye. There was also butter, margarine, clotted cream, and strawberry jam for sides.

Trays five and six: the baked goods. Mini pecan pies, assorted mini fruit tarts, éclairs, petits fours, napoleons, cookies, muffins, scones, and cupcakes.

Tray seven: fresh fruit dipped in white and dark chocolate.

Tray eight was just plain fresh fruit.

Somewhere in Magda's dining room, there was also tea, coffee, and mineral water.

Rina's father was taking a nap, and the women were puttering around trying not to get on each other's nerves. Decker had made himself comfortable in an armchair in the living room. He had dressed in a blue button-down shirt and tan slacks—no jacket—and loafers without socks. It was hot even in the city. He said, "I thought this was supposed to be informal."

"Just a little something." Magda paced. "I don't know why you do this to me, Ginny."

"Do what?" Rina asked.

"Dig up bones."

"I got inspired after hearing you talk about your childhood."

"You talk about your childhood. I don't invite your old friends to your house."

"Mama, I asked you first. You could have said no."

"Then *I* look bad." Magda stopped pacing and focused her flaming blue eyes on her daughter. "It's my life, Ginny! Before you talked to Marta, you should have come to me first!"

"I should have, but I didn't," Rina answered calmly. "Again I apologize."

"It is too late for that, *nu?* Now I am stuck! All week I bake and bake and bake—"

"I *said* I would do it for you, Mama."

"And let them think I can't take care of a simple afternoon tea?" Magda glared at Rina. "I'm old, but I have pride."

"I know, Mama. And it's good you baked. You're a much better baker than I am."

"*Ach* . . . nonsense!" She waved her hand in the air. "You are an excellent baker!"

"Yes, I am, but I'm still not as good as you."

Decker smiled inwardly. His wife was saying all the right things. He decided to help her out. "I really like what you're wearing, Magda."

She looked at Decker and brushed her hand over a St. John Knits blue suit with white trim. "This old thing?"

"It's very complimentary to your figure," Decker told her. "Plus, the color enhances your eyes. You should take your daughter shopping."

That got a smile.

"You wouldn't say that if you saw the price tag," Rina told him.

"You look lovely as well," Decker said. "I like you in red."

Rina laughed. "Aren't you full of lightness and cheer. Thank you, darling, I'm glad you like the way I look."

"The dress is too long on you, Ginny."

"Don't start, Mama."

"Let her start," Decker piped in. "Bugging you is taking her mind off her anxiety."

Both women laughed.

"I'll get you some tea, Akiva?"

It was a good sign when Magda used his Hebrew name. Decker answered, "That would be great."

"And a little sandwich, too?"

"No, I'd rather not mess up your artistic presentation."

"I have extra in the kitchen."

"That I'll take. I have a quick question for you."

"What?" Magda asked.

"You are playing host to two women in their eighties, two very skinny women. What in the world are you going to do with all the leftover food?"

"A little they'll take home, some you take home. The boys will eat it all in one sitting."

That was true.

Magda fussed with her clothes. "I get you tea and sandwiches. What kind?"

"Egg is fine."

"Maybe a little tuna? I give you a little of this and that."

"Perfect, Magda."

She went into the kitchen.

Rina said, "Since when did you become the charmer?"

"She's right. We should have gone to her first. We did put her in a bind."

"She could have said no."

"No, not really. It would have made her seem bitter or unfriendly or scared. You know your mother. Image is all." Decker smiled. "I do like the red dress. I was being honest."

"Thank you." She ran her hands down the sides. "You think it's too long?"

"I didn't say it in front of her. But as long as you asked, you could easily take it up a couple of inches and still be fine."

Rina crossed her arms over her chest. "Fine. I'll take it up."

"I'm not saying you *have* to take it up—"

"Why are we having this inane conversation?"

"Because you're nervous? To pass the time until the ladies get here? To fill in dead space?"

"Very funny."

"Rina, this whole thing was your idea. Don't drag me into an argument."

"I did it for my mother."

Decker didn't answer.

"I really did," she said with emphasis.

"I'm not arguing with you."

"I just wanted some . . . some piece of her childhood that wasn't marred by tragedy and death! Some *closure* for her."

"I know that your heart was in the right

place. But you know what they say about the road to hell."

"I really don't need to hear this! I think I'll wait outside."

"Rina—"

"No, I really think I need to wait outside!"

"Fine. See you later."

In a huff, Rina left and Decker sat in a room devoid of female chatter. He loved women, but sometimes he needed to hear voices in the baritone range.

Or better still, no voices at all.

Magda returned, carrying a dessert plate that had a special indentation to hold a teacup. She served him the dish along with a cloth napkin. "Where is Ginny?"

"Outside."

"They're *here*?"

"No, I think she's just—"

"Why does she wait outside? It makes me look like I'm too anxious."

"I think she's a little anxious, too."

Magda made a face. "What does she have to be anxious about? It isn't her life."

"No, that's true," Decker said. "But you are her mother and she wants it to go right for you."

Magda exhaled. "Then she should have come to me first!"

"You're right."

Again the old woman exhaled. "I am still her mother. She is still my daughter. I go out and calm her down."

"You're a good woman," Decker said.

"If you say that after this tea, then I believe you."

Magda went outside.

Again Decker reveled in silence. He felt his eyes close, his mind turning slow and fuzzy. He had almost drifted off to sleep when a slamming car door made him snap to. Still sleepy, he almost stood up, nearly knocking his sandwich plate off his lap. But he remembered at the last moment and recovered the food before it became abstract art on Magda's Aubusson rug. He placed the plate on one of the end tables and peeked out the window.

The driver was opening the door.

Anika came out first, dressed in a white blouse and green linen A-line skirt. Marta followed wearing a yellow cotton suit. Both of the women had donned jaunty little summer hats over their gray locks. Decker couldn't hear words, but he certainly heard the screams.

Magda and Marta fell into an unplanned, unrehearsed embrace, both of them falling on one another's shoulders and sobbing their little eighty-plus-year-old hearts out. In a speck of time, a lifetime of intervening memories flew out the window as two little schoolgirls hugged and laughed and cried and strolled arm in arm up the walkway to the house. Rina had placed her arm around Anika, who looked a bit uncomfortable with her sister's display of emotion.

They came through the door like chirping magpies.

"*Ach,* this is beautiful, Marta," Marta Wallek told Magda. "*Sehr schön!*"

Rina said, "Ladies, you remember my husband, Lieutenant Decker?"

"*Bestimmt . . .* certainly. It is a pleasure to see you once again." Marta smiled, still holding Magda's arm. "Oh, this is so lovely! You were always such the *künstlerin . . .* the artist."

"*Me?*"

"Don't you remember how you draw pictures for everyone in the *schule? 'Die mod-*

edesignerin.'" Marta turned to Rina. "We call her 'the Dress Designer.' In art time, she draws amazing dresses."

"Oh, that!" Magda waved her hand. "That is because of my mother. She designed *beautiful* dresses."

"And you draw them all!" Marta said, laughing.

Magda beamed. "Come. You must be hungry."

"I wouldn't mind," Anika piped in. "It was a long ride."

"Not so long," Marta argued.

"Not so bad until the freeway. Then it was very long."

"Rush-hour traffic," Rina said.

"*Ach,*" Magda exclaimed. "I should have thought of that."

"It was nothing," Marta answered. "We rode in an air-conditioned car." To her sister: "You were sleeping."

"Just thinking with my closed eyes."

"You were sleeping. I hear you snore."

Decker interjected, "You know, I'm flagging a bit. Let's eat."

"This way," Magda said. She glanced over her shoulder and caught Ginny's joyous face, an expression that bespoke gratitude that things were going well for her mother. Despite her misgivings, Magda knew that Ginny had accomplished something extraordinary, giving Magda a tiny bit of solace from a time when fear and evil had been her constant companions. With wet eyes, she smiled at her daughter and mouthed the words "Thank you."

45

There was ample technology out there for an affordable videophone, but we humans with our frailties and our fears and our bad hair days just weren't ready for it. Case in point was my phone chat with Buck. The conversation went surprisingly well, mainly because he couldn't see my pacing and my sweating and my clammy hands. He only heard my deadpan ripostes to his sarcastic comments, making me appear witty and in control. He suggested a café; I mentioned Star$s; we settled on Coffee Bean and Tea Leaf, on the Strip in West Hollywood.

As per my father's request I had had a run-through using Klinghoffner and a few others as my guinea pigs, and we discovered that a multitude of things could go

wrong. Since the meeting with Buck wasn't
until Sunday at eleven, there was time to
fine-tune. Still, as the hour approached, I
felt butterflies in my stomach. The last time
I felt this nervous was when I was in tenth
grade about to make my entrance onstage
in *Guys and Dolls* as a stand-in Adelaide for
Helen Karp, who had come down with the
flu. I had pulled *that* off. There was no reason I couldn't pull this off as well.

I was early, but he was earlier. The place
was decent in size for the typical coffee bar,
and the table he had chosen was not the
best for our purposes. But since it wasn't
that bad, I decided it was more prudent to
stay put than to explain why I wanted to
move. Buck was as thin as ever, but his
complexion had improved from judicious sunbathing. There were still some rem-
nants of acne, but his cheeks were much
smoother. His dark hair was almost shorn,
his brown eyes feigning indifference when
he saw me. He wore jeans and a black muscle shirt, showing off thin arms with some
sinewy muscles. He was reading the *Sunday Times* and had ordered an Ice-Blended,
his cheeks hollowed as he sucked on a
straw, wrapping his thick lips around the

plastic, pressing down with force. It was so wonderful when I thought about all that glorious DNA.

I sat next to him. "You're here early."

He didn't bother to put down the paper. "Am I?" A careless look at his watch. "I suppose I am. I'm hungry. You can get me a bagel."

"You can also get one yourself."

He gave me a bored look. "You asked me. That means you pay. Besides, you're not going to pay. LAPD is going to pay. So let's stop the pretense and just get on with it."

I let out a chuckle. "Plain or cinnamon?"

"I get a choice?"

"I'm full service, guy."

For the first time, I saw that he was actually registering my presence, his eyes skimming up and down my body. I was wearing a sleeveless sundress that showed some cleavage and lots of leg. His cheeks took on a rosy glow. He hid his face with the front page of the newspaper.

"Plain's fine. Two cream cheese." He finished his Ice-Blended. "And something else to drink." He held up the empty cup. "I'm dehydrated from my workout."

I couldn't believe my luck. "What else?"

"Oh . . . I don't know. How about a decaf soy latte?"

"How about it?" I stood, looped my purse around my shoulder, and picked up his cup. "I'll take care of this for you. Be back in a sec."

I went to the trash can, opened the swing door, but placed his cup in the evidence bag that was hanging off the back of Justice Brill's chair, hiding the drop with my body. I had been practicing this step with Brill and had become smooth at the hidden maneuver. In this case, I didn't have to bother. Buck was intentionally ignoring me.

I went up to the counter and ordered. Ten minutes later, I was carrying a paper tray with two bagels, four cream cheeses, a soy latte for him, and a regular latte for me. He made no effort to help me, still buried in the paper. I sat back down and distributed the food. He picked up his latte and continued to read as he sipped coffee. "Cream cheese my bagel for me, will you?"

"No way," I told him.

He peered out over the top. "That was rude."

"So is asking me to cream cheese your bagel." I sipped my own latte. "Anything I cream cheese, I eat myself."

Lazily, he turned the paper. "How about you cream cheese the bagel and I'll give you a bite?"

I knocked the paper out of his hands. "How about if you cream cheese your own bagel and look at me when I talk to you?"

Buck folded the paper. "Now I remember you, the one with the nasty temper."

"Well, Buck, people don't change that much in three months."

"Has it been that long? I wish it were six."

"You know, you could have said no when I asked you to meet me."

"And miss out on the wit and wisdom of LAPD's finest? Tell me, Officer, just what little ditties do our public servants in blue have up their sleeves?"

"Meaning?"

"You didn't ask me out for my charming company. So what gives?"

"Ah, Buck, you cut me to the quick." I smeared cream cheese on my bagel and took a bite. "Good stuff."

Buck lavished on the topping, took a big bite, swallowed, then drank coffee. "We can play games, Officer. I don't mind looking at you while you eat."

"Oh my!" I smiled. "Was that a compliment?"

Again he reddened. "Statement of fact."

This was the time for the sincere smile. "Thank you."

Buck took another bite and stared at me.

I stared back. "Okay, I confess. I do have a motive."

He waited.

"We were cleaning out some open files, trying to breathe some life into the dead cases. Belinda Syracuse came up. I was asked to run through the sprinklers one more time."

"What specifically?"

"Nothing too heavy. Just to reinterview anyone who knew her, who saw her on a regular basis. I started with Klinghoffner, then went on to the secretary, Jamie Hostetter, then Myra Manigan. You're next in line."

"Why are you wasting time with people from Fordham?" Buck said. "She was killed on a weekend pass."

"Apparently, her brother said something about a phone call, that someone from

Fordham had offered to pick Belinda up from her brother's and take her back to the center."

Buck shrugged.

"Did you ever take her anywhere?"

"Me?" He acted as if he were taken aback by the absurdity. "I write papers, I file papers, and I organize papers. I have basically nothing to do with the students."

"Never take them out for coffee or . . ."

"Occasionally, I bring in doughnuts. Does that count?"

"I don't mean to annoy you, Buck, just trying to give the girl some justice."

Our eyes met. Buck broke the contact. He finished one bagel half and started on the other. "I believe we covered this ground before. I don't know who would want to harm Belinda or any of the kids."

An interesting answer, especially since I hadn't asked the question.

"None of them ever confide in you?" I asked.

"I don't have a relationship with them. My job is strictly administrative."

"But you're around. Surely they talk to you."

"Not really . . ." He shrugged and finished

his bagel. "Not beyond an occasional 'Hello' or 'No, it's not time for lunch,' or 'Who stole my stapler?' The kids really don't notice me. I'm more or less a fixture like the corner coffeepot."

That wasn't what I saw. I said, "I think you sell yourself short."

"Ah, a weak stab at charm."

But he was unnerved by the comment.

I laughed. "Remind me again—what were you doing on the night Belinda was hit?"

"Frankly, I forget."

"Before you mentioned a girlfriend to me. You took her out to brunch that day? At Café Romano."

"If you say so."

"The name of the girlfriend?"

"Back then it would have been Erica Tross. The comely lass has moved back to New York."

"When?"

"A month ago." He smiled. "But don't get your hopes up, Officer. I'm currently dating someone else. Are you going to eat that bagel?"

I slid the plate over to him. "You said that day that you had rented a movie, *In the Bedroom*?"

He devoured half of my bagel. "Why are you asking me all these questions?"

"Leaving no stone unturned. Can you play along?"

He glanced at his watch. "For another minute or so. Then I have another obligation."

"Where do you rent movies from?"

"I probably rented *In the Bedroom* from Crystal Video, but that went out of business a few months back. Now it's just plain Blockbuster."

"Your girlfriend moves back to New York; your video store goes out of business. . . ."

"I have the Midas touch." He stood and gathered up his Sunday paper. "Thank you. It's been charming, but I have to go." As he walked away, he said, "You can clean up after me."

I watched him walk away. Then I stood and carefully gathered up his discards.

Help you clean up?

Gladly, Buck. *Gladly.*

▼

Buck was Bradley Durvain.
His DNA was not a match.
So much for my gut.

But since I was the one who had instigated this interviewing charade, I dutifully went through every working member associated with the Fordham Communal Center for the Developmentally Disabled. When it came to gathering genetic information from José, the center's janitor for two years, I interviewed him at Fordham, talking to him during a smoke-and-coffee break. Afterward, I picked up the Styrofoam cup and the two cigarette butts and placed them into two separate evidence bags.

It was only after the DNA match came through that I recalled Sarah's words and kicked myself mentally. She had given me the information when we first found out about the gang rape, but I hadn't been paying attention. Dad and I had asked her to describe her assailants. She had said they were Mexicans . . . like the school's janitor, José.

But he's a nice Mexican. Sometimes he gives us candy and treats.

His real name was actually Hasan Fazul Al-Liby and he was from Iraq, not Mexico. But he called himself José because in the present political climate, being Hispanic rather than Arabic increased his prospects of employment. His being a scumbag did nothing to improve the standing of his people.

Hasan not only gave the girls candy and treats, he took them to the movies. Afterward, he'd take them to his apartment in downtown Los Angeles and have sex with them in front of a video camera. A search warrant produced a cache of snacks and six tapes with compromised women—two mentally disabled girls, including Belinda (the other wasn't from Fordham) and what looked like four homeless women. At least, they weren't little children. With the tapes entered as evidence, Brill brought the DA enough for the case without Sarah Sanders having to make a confession, saving wear and tear on the poor girl's psyche. My father, ever deliberate and methodical, had once again called the correct shots.

When the news of Hasan's "detainment" reached Fordham, another girl—his current "girlfriend"—came out of the woodwork, much to Klinghoffner's dismay. The case began to grow exponentially. It took on a life worthy of newspaper coverage. Brill, along with the assistant DA, began to appear in front of television cameras. I had managed to avoid any kind of association, other than being the first officer at the scene of the hit-and-run. Fine with me: Let Brill take the credit. I figured I had paid off my debt to him and then some. By the time I left for Israel, Hasan was on remand. Denied bail, he was being held at County jail pending trial and was being investigated by both the FBI and CIA for terrorist links. My opinion, for what it's worth, was that Hasan was just your ordinary rotten scumbag with no political affiliations.

He had lured Belinda out only to mow her down because Belinda was going to report his bad behavior after he had stopped "being her boyfriend." I had the correct reasoning, but the wrong suspect.

And I was so damn sure.

It gave me pause, how fortunate it was that the law required evidence to back up hunches and intuition. One day—hopefully sooner rather than later—I'll get a gold shield. Hasan's arrest was one of those seminal events, one of life's lessons that I'd carry with me long after I got used to being called detective.

▼

A week later, Koby and I were scrunched into two coach seats on El Al Airlines headed for the Holy Land. Nervously, I rehearsed my imaginary conversations with his family. In the end, it didn't matter. I was with Koby; I was automatically fine with them. I truly *adored* his kinfolk, but there were just so *many* of them, something I wasn't used to having grown up as an only child. The minute we walked into his parents' apartment, my brain went into overload.

The scene could have been a fraternity prank for rush: Exactly how many people could you cram into a tiny speck of an apartment? It was two parents, nine siblings—including twin teenage sisters who kept asking me about all the stars I see working in Hollywood—spouses, assorted cousins, and dozens upon dozens of children of all races and ethnicities. One stepbrother had married a Russian woman, another a French Moroccan, and a third had hooked up with an American dentist. His two brothers had Ethiopian wives, but his sister had married a Yemenite Jew whose father was a policeman. It was a living, breathing United Nations, but the good part was they all spoke some English.

Still, their sheer number was simply over-whelming.

There wasn't much time to sightsee, only a quick overnight in Jerusalem because everybody said I had to see Jerusalem. It was ancient and exotic and in parts very labyrinthine, but also filled with traffic and it was nearly impossible to find a parking space in city central. It wasn't at all a war zone, not nearly as dangerous as I thought it would be. There were people on the streets, but we were reminded constantly not to drive certain roads at night; the cou-ple of times we did, we carried a gun.

Mostly, it was hopping from one relative to another, one meal after another, everyone ending the repast with the accusing words "So when will you be coming back?" Meeting the family gave me fresh insight into my beloved. Doted on by his parents, cosseted by his five older brothers, worshiped by his four younger sisters, Koby was the favorite, the designated "pet," and when the conver-sation wasn't centered around politics—which was most of the time—it was a swap of Koby stories. The oldest brother of all ten, Yaphet, summed it up succinctly one day at the dinner table. Yaphet bore a resemblance to Koby, but was two inches shorter and twice as wide. His voice was low and gravelly, and he spoke English haltingly.

But he got the point across.

"Yaakov," he growled out. "He got the looks. . . . He got the brains. . . . He got the physical . . . *gevurah*. . . ."

"Strength," Koby whispered.

"I think he is adopted," Yaphet snarled out. "Or my mother decides to play *tricks!*"

Immediately, the table broke into raucous laughter . . . led by Koby's *father.* It was then that Koby turned to me and whispered, "It is time to go back."

▼

We were both thrilled when we touched down at smoggy old LAX. After a day of recuperation, Koby returned to work. I, on impulse, went downtown during the midafternoon heat to check out skid-row denizens. I walked from block to block taking in sad, discarded faces, trying not to bleed for the world. I had almost given up when fate tapped my shoulder.

I knew him instantly. He was sitting on the stoop of a condemned building in an industrial block of warehouses, eating food from a can. His kinky hair had grown bushy and wild, but somehow he had managed to remain clean shaven, a lucky break for me because a beard would have covered his recognizable Down's-like face. He had open sores on his hands and his face was dirty, just caked with grime. His body was swathed in layers of clothes, even though it was fiery hot.

My heart was pounding when I approached him. He looked up and hooked an arm over his meal, a gesture of protecting his food. I extended my hand to him, but he didn't respond.

"C'mon, David," I told him. "Let's go home."

He regarded me with yellow eyes but didn't move.

"People are waiting for you, David. Lots of people."

No response.

"Sarah . . . Mr. Klinghoffner, Mr. Paxton . . . You remember Mr. Paxton, don't you?"

He growled out, "I'm not stupid."

"I'm sorry if I offended you," I said. "Sarah had a baby. She had a little girl. That means you have a daughter. She named her Cinderella. We call her Ella. I think"—I studied his face—"I think she has Sarah's eyes, but your mouth."

He continued to eat.

I said again, "C'mon, David, let's get out of here."

"Don't got nowhere to go. Don't got a home."

"You could have a home if you wanted one."

"Well, I don't got one now."

"You may not have an apartment at this moment, but we can get you one."

"I want to see Sarah."

"I'm sure that can be arranged."

"No. Her sister won't let me."

"Have you ever asked Sarah's sister?"

David didn't answer.

"Things might be different with the baby. It's worth a try."

Again I extended my hand. This time, he took it and I hoisted him to his feet. His smell was strong, even in the open air. He was short and appeared squat, but that could have been the layers of clothes. Immediately, he began to scratch his hands, arms, and head. I got itchy just looking at him. "Those cuts and sores . . . do they hurt?"

"Sometimes."

"They look like bites."

"Could be. Lots of bugs and rats around when I sleep."

"We need to get you looked at and cleaned up. I have a friend who works in a hospital. Mind if we go there?"

"What hospital?"

"Mid-City Pediatric."

"That's for kids."

"They have adults. And they have lots of good doctors."

"All right."

"So should we go now?"

"All right."

I looked at the piles of clothing on the ground. "Anything you want to take with you?"

He thought a moment, then shook his head. "It's all garbage."

"You deserve better than garbage."

He didn't answer me. He concentrated as he walked. I could tell his feet were tender. Slowly, we made it back to my car and I settled him inside. In closed quarters, his stench was foul, not just a dirty smell but reeking of infections. I rolled down the windows, started the engine, and pulled away from the curb.

"When can I see Sarah?" he asked me.

"First we have to clean you up."

"How long will that take?"

"I don't know. We just have to make sure you're not sick before you see Sarah—because of the baby."

"How is the baby?"

"She's wonderful. Very, very cute."

"Good."

"Are you hungry?"

"Yes."

"There's a McDonald's at the hospital. If the doctor says it's okay, I'll buy you a meal."

"Thank you."

As I drove to Mid-City, I called up Koby on my cell. It was wonderful to know someone in the medical field; it just streamlined everything. By the time I pulled up to the main entrance, Koby, dressed in scrubs, masked, gloved, and wearing a hair cap, was outside with a wheelchair. I helped David out of the car and into the wheelchair.

"This is David."

"Hey, David," Koby said. "I'm going to put a cap on your hair, all right?"

"Okay."

"Maybe we take it off later."

"Okay."

"Maybe we give you a short haircut like in the army."

"Okay."

Koby picked up the boy's hands and I saw his eyebrows go up. "I take you to see a doctor, David. But I tell you now, I'm sure we admit you overnight."

"David, I'm going to call Mr. Paxton," I told him. "He can help you with all this."

"Okay."

"Your daughter was brought here after she was born," Koby said. "I took care of her."

David looked up at Koby, and for the first time, I saw him smile. It opened his face and clogged in my throat.

Koby said, "I take it from here, Cindy."

"He's hungry, Yaakov."

"We take good care of him. I shall talk to the attending. I make sure he gets fed. I see you when I get off . . . around eleven."

"I'll be waiting." I went around to the driver's side of the car.

"Cindy?" Koby said.

I turned around.

"He has infestation of lice. Go to the pharmacy and buy a special shampoo—Nix or Rid. You can buy them over the counter. Take a hot shower when you get home and use it as directed. Also, they make a special spray for upholstery. You need to disinfect your car."

I looked at my beautiful, recently washed-and-waxed Lexus. I frowned. What could I do? The drawbacks of altruism, but on balance, the positives greatly outweighed the negatives.

46

To T. S. Eliot, April was the cruelest month, but for Angelinos September was the hottest. And if you asked Rina, the hottest day of the year always fell on Yom Kippur, when religious Jews refrained from food and drink for over twenty-six hours. It wasn't Yom Kippur today, but the afternoon had been a scorcher, not all that unusual even at this late date in the ninth month.

Even now, as the hour approached six in the evening, the temperatures in the West Valley were still in the high 80s. Koby's newest set of wheels, a ten-year-old black BMW 323, had workable air-conditioning, but the temperature gauge had been steadily rising as we tooled down the freeway. So as soon as we hit local streets, he turned it off and we opened the windows. When we got to my father's house, the sun was an orange ball of fire sinking in the sky. I checked my watch. We had made good time.

We both had dressed for the heat—comfortably but appropriate for *Shabbat*. Koby had on an off-white linen suit over a white T-shirt. No tie, obviously, calling it Israeli style, but he satisfied his color fix by wearing a gigantic red-green-and-yellow-striped yarmulke, the colors of Ethiopia. This evening, he was my chieftain prince— tall, lean, aristocratic, and incredibly handsome—real eye candy. My heart did a little tap dance every time I looked at him. I had on an ice blue sleeveless dress, but I carried a white cotton blazer to cover my bare arms in case I decided to go to synagogue.

I paused before I knocked on the door. I regarded Koby's eyes made gold by the strong light of sunset. "Will you sing '*Eshet Chayil*' for me tonight?"

He grinned. "Of course. In my heart, I sing it for you every night."

"But tonight is different."

"Indeed. If you want, I will sing it for you a hundred times."

I leaned my head against his arm. "Once with meaning will suffice." I exhaled and smiled. "Here we go."

I knocked and my father opened the door. First his eyes went to Koby's face, then to mine. He gave me a stern look. "What brings you here on my off-hours, Detective?"

"Well, Lieutenant," I answered, "Yaakov and I were trying to figure out how to celebrate my promotion. We ran through some ideas. One of them was *Shabbat* dinner with you and the family."

Dad broke into a smile exuding pride. "I'll see if Rina has any champagne."

Koby lifted a bottle of Kedem bubbly. "I'm one step ahead of you, sir."

"Hmm . . ." Dad sneered at my date. "And just what have you *personally* done to celebrate my little girl's promotion?"

Koby lifted up my left hand. "I'm one step ahead of you, sir."

My father's eyes widened. They went from my hand to my face to Koby's and back to my hand.

Koby said, "I brought a magnifying glass if it would help."

"It's not *that* small. It's not small at all. What is it? A carat?"

"One point four, actually."

"Shiny little bugger, isn't it?"

"It is a very good stone—E flawless. I could have gotten bigger, but your daughter wanted quality. I have good friends in the diamond bursa in Israel."

"I've been there, so don't even try to pull rank." He stared at Koby, his expression sour. "Does this mean you're going to be a fixture here?"

"I'm afraid so."

Dad broke into a grin.

Then he hugged Koby.

Not me. Koby.

I tapped my father on the shoulder. "Uh, remember me? Your daughter?"

"Yeah, yeah." He broke away from Koby, hugged me hard, gripping me with his fingers. As soon as his eyes moistened, he averted his gaze. "Come on in." To me: "Did you tell your mother?"

"We just came from there. We told her first."

"Smart girl. Set a date?"

"Mom's working on it," I answered. "She's

thinking about squeezing us in somewhere between her trip to the Far East and the Food Is Life banquet." I laughed. "I'm being mean. She offered to cancel her trip to the Far East, but I told her to work around it. We're flexible."

Koby said, "Actually, I wanted to marry in Israel, save you time and money, but Cindy said Jan would kill her."

"She would have," Decker concurred.

"So now you are stuck with my family coming out here. With all of my siblings and step-siblings and cousins and their families, it will be between thirty and sixty people."

Decker opened and closed his mouth. "Okay."

"His father and stepmother are real, real, *real* religious, Daddy," I said.

My father looked ill. "More than Rina?"

Koby thought about it. "Not more religious, but Rina is more . . . sophisticated. My stepmother is Canadian, but my father is very, very old-fashioned. He doesn't speak English all that well."

"He doesn't speak it at all," I corrected. "But he understands. He's very cute. He's really, really skinny. And his stepmother's a doll. When they come out, can they stay here? Rina not only knows the religious etiquette, but she also knows Hebrew. If they stay with Mom, it'll be a disaster. She won't know what to do with them."

"Uh . . . of course." Decker smiled weakly. "But only if it's okay with your mother, Cindy."

"I thought I'd set her up with some of Koby's English-speaking, less religious siblings. Maybe a few could stay with Grandpa."

"Your mother's father?"

"Yes, Dad. I wasn't thinking of your dad in Florida."

"You're going to sic Jack Cohen on Koby's relatives?"

"Stop that!" I scolded. "I love Grandpa."

"I love Jack, too," Dad answered. "He was the best part about your mother. But he's different." He shook his head. "Have you really thought about this?"

I noticed my father turning a slight shade of green. "Maybe we should discuss this later and just celebrate my promotion tonight?"

"Good idea." My father looked as if a headache were coming on. Just then

Sammy walked in. "Dad, could you— Oh, hi, guys." He homed in on my fiancé. "Koby, we need to talk. I've got this emergency situation. A basketball game on Sunday."

"I'm *working,* Shmuel."

"What time do you start?" Sammy asked.

"Three."

"No problem. The game's at ten."

"Sammy, that's enough,"' Decker said.

"Our star forward's grandmother died. I promise you'll be out by one because we're all going to the funeral at two."

"Sammy, you are truly sick," I told him.

My stepbrother ignored me. "Koby, we really *need* you. Otherwise it's going to be embarrassing."

"Surely there are other token blacks in this area."

"Not this late in the series. They've already been snapped up. C'mon. I'm going back to New York next week. *Please?*"

"I have to help Cindy pack."

"I'll help her pack after the funeral." Sammy looked at me. "Where are you going?"

"I'm moving," I told him.

"Oh. Where?"

Koby raised his eyebrows.

"Oh." Sammy looked at Daddy, trying not to smile. "Okay. I'll help you pack, Cin. I promise."

"I can manage. I don't own that much." I regarded Koby. "You can play." I elbowed my stepbrother in the ribs. "Anything to shut him up."

Koby rubbed his forehead. "You are a nag, Shmuel."

"Persistent."

"Just this one last time."

"Thank you, thank you."

"Don't expect miracles."

"Koby, it's all a matter of image! Skill doesn't hurt, either."

Decker wagged a finger at him. "You're overstepping your bounds, young man. I'm only permitting it because he's now family. Say hello to your brother-in-law."

I showed Sammy my ring.

"Really? Cool!" He kissed my cheek. "I gotta go call Yossi before *Shabbat.* He's gonna freak when I tell him. Thanks, Koby."

"And *mazel tov?*" Koby prompted.

"Oh sure. *Mazel tov,* although it wasn't exactly unexpected. But it's still neat."

He left.

"Well, he was certainly excited," I commented.

My father laughed. "Sammy was born politically incorrect, God bless him."

Rina came into the living room. "I thought I heard voices." She wiped her hands on her apron. "Dressed like that, I'm assuming you're staying?"

"If it's okay with you."

"Of course." She kissed my cheek. "*Shabbat Shalom.*"

Without a word, Koby showed her my finger. My stepmother's eyes lit up. "Oh my goodness, it's *beautiful!*" She hugged me hard. "Did you tell your mother?"

"Yes, she was the first one we told."

"Perfect!" Rina hugged Koby and kissed his cheek. "*Mazel tov, mazel tov!* This is so incredibly exciting!"

"All this and a gold shield, too," I said.

"Oh, that's right! We *definitely* need champagne!"

Koby lifted the bottle.

Rina said, "I'll go chill it." Her face was suffused with pure happiness, unlike the happy but wistful expression that my father wore. "Have you set a date?"

"We were just talking about this," I said. "I

asked Dad if you could put up Koby's parents because they're—"

"Of course!" Rina said. "We'll put up anyone you want."

"He has between thirty and sixty relatives, dear," my father remarked.

"Okay. As soon as you set the date, let me know so I can call the caterer for *Shabbat* dinner and lunch on the day of the *aufruf*." She spoke to Koby. "You'll have it in our shul, I take it. Unless you want to do it in your shul."

"Your *beit knesset* is fine."

Rina was beaming. "This is so exciting. I can't wait to meet your family. And don't worry, Koby. We'll put them all up. It's not a problem."

My dad was massaging a wrinkled forehead. Koby put his arm around his shoulder. "Now you see why I left."

Sammy came back in and kissed his mother. "Eema, Eema, you've gained a son and I've gained a forward!" He scrutinized Koby's face. "I guess you can call her Eema although she's only what, ten years older than you?"

"No, she's ten years older than I am," I said. "She's only six—"

"Can we move on?" Dad interjected.

"It's irrelevant because *mother* is a state of mind," Rina pronounced. "Besides, Cindy's mother would be *eema.*"

"No, my mother will be *mom,*" I told her. "Definitely not *eema.*"

"My stepmother is Eema," Koby said. "To me, you are Rina because that's what Cindy calls you. Besides, Rina fits your face."

"Whatever you want, Yaakov."

He focused his eyes on Daddy's face. "My question is . . . what do I call you, sir?"

"What do you call me?"

"Yes."

Decker rubbed his hands and thought a moment. "Lieutenant is fine."

"Peter!" Rina chastised.

"It's my title."

"Maybe a *little* less formal, Daddy?"

"No problem." He threw his arm around my fiancé's shoulder. "Koby, my man . . . you can call me Loo."